D1071290

MORDECAI

THE RIVEN GATES
VOLUME ONE

BY

MICHAEL G. MANNING

Cover by Amalia Chitulescu
Map Artwork by Maxime Plasse
Editing by Grace Bryan Butler and Keri Karandrakis
© 2018 by Michael G. Manning
All rights reserved.
Printed in the United States of America

ISBN: 978-1-943481-13-2

For more information about the Mageborn series check out the author's
Facebook page:

https://www.facebook.com/MagebornAuthor

or visit the website:

http://www.magebornbooks.com/

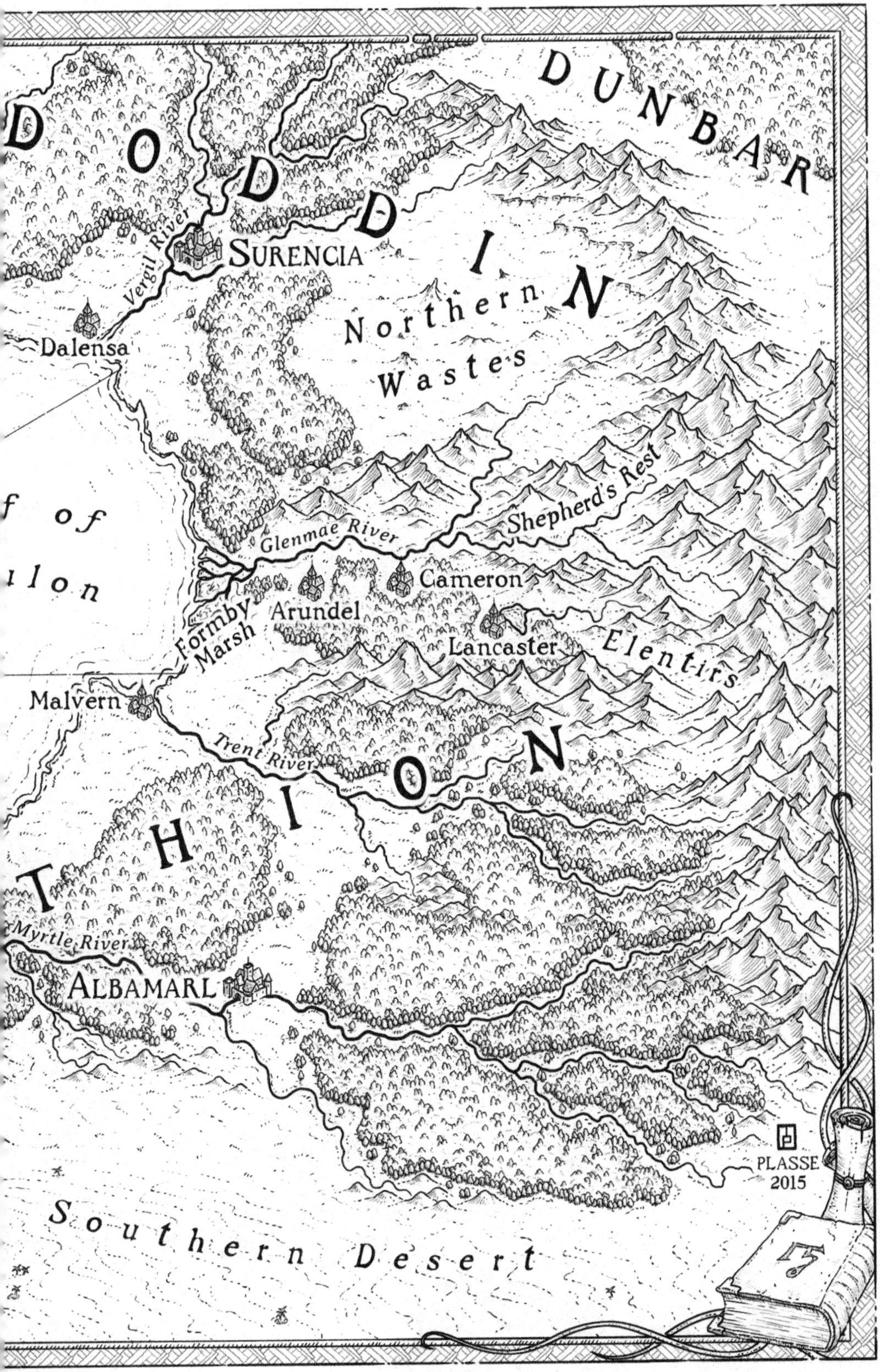

DUNBAR

DODDIN

SURENCIA

Vergil River

Dalensa

Northern

Wastes

f of

lon

Shepherd's Rest

Glenmae River

Cameron

Arundel

Formby
Marsh

Lancaster

Elentirs

Malvern

Trent River

THION

Myrtle River

ALBAMARL

PLASSE
2015

Southern Desert

CHAPTER 1

It was mid-afternoon by the time I walked into Camlin. It was a small village in my mind, but by most standards it was perfectly average. A communal well occupied the center space, between the dwellings of its citizens. More people lived outside of course, in the surrounding area, farmers and herders mostly. The village proper was mainly composed of the small portion of the population that made their living through trade and craft. There was a cooper, a chandler, a weaver, and a carpenter.

The village wasn't quite large enough to support a smithy, which made it perfect for Tom the Tinker, I thought. Without a smith, people would be wanting their scissors and knives sharpened, their pots mended, and perhaps a bit of glue. Glue was always popular in small villages.

I had other small sundries for trade as well, salt, a few spices, several balls of twine, and a small roll of linen cloth. A tinker does well when he can anticipate the needs of those he visits. That was probably the main reason that tinkers were often associated with good luck.

A tinker appears at random, always an unexpected guest, and carries with him small goods that people frequently need but are often out of. For that we are usually welcomed with a smile. The fact that we also carry gossip and news from other places makes us almost as popular as a traveling minstrel—almost.

Again, I wished I had learned to play an instrument, but I had never had the opportunity. It might have made things even easier.

Glancing down, I gave myself a once over before I approached the woman I had spotted by the well. Appearances were important. I didn't want to give the wrong impression.

My beard was of medium length, well-kept but not overly neat. My clothes were worn and patched, but relatively clean, other than the understandable road dust. The cloth pack slung over my shoulder was in good condition and visibly bulging with hidden treasures and unexpected surprises.

I put on a friendly smile as I approached, stopping a respectful distance away, "Excuse me madam, but is there a place hereabouts where a hungry man could get a meal? I can pay." I shook a modestly small purse, making the coins jingle to prove my words.

The woman was of middling age, her features weather-worn and her hands rough from honest labor. She gave me wary look, which was perfectly reasonable, since I was a stranger. Setting down her water jar she answered, "Harold runs the pub, such as it is." She jerked a thumb toward a modestly sized building behind her. Then her eyes lit on my pack, "Are you a tinker?"

I grinned and nodded, "Yes ma'am, I have that honor. Folks call me Tom—Tom the tinker. Do you have aught that needs mending?"

"I do," she replied. "My best pot has lost its handle, but I doubt you can fix it with what tools you might have carried."

"I might surprise you," I said with a chuckle. "Ol' Tom is known for his cleverness at fixin' things. Let me take a look, and maybe there something I can do for you."

The pot in question was a moderately large stew kettle made of iron. It was sturdily built, but age and metal fatigue had not been kind to the handle on one side. The metal had snapped loose where a weld had rusted over the intervening years since it had been made. It wasn't something a tinker's hammer could fix, and glue was definitely not going to do the trick. By all rights, it would need a smith with a forge and proper tools to fix.

"I think I can remedy this," I told her. "If you let me have it this evening, I can give it back to you tomorrow."

Her eyes narrowed, "You'd steal a woman's only good pot?"

"No ma'am, I can fix it. Just trust me with it for a little while."

Suspicious, she returned, "I don' think you can fix it with what you got. If you're still in town tomorrow, I might let you. I'll wait to see if you rob someone else first."

I sighed, "All right. I'll visit Harold's then." I didn't plan on staying that long, and she was clearly too wary to let a stranger have her prized pot. "How's his food?"

"Terrible," she said, spitting on the ground. "His ale's good, but I wouldn't touch the stuff he calls 'meat'."

Touching my hat and giving her a nod, I thanked her, "I appreciate the advice." Then I made my way over to Harold's pub.

Unlike most taverns, it had no sign. The village wasn't quite prosperous enough for such niceties. I had been considering whether I should knock first or simply enter, since there was no outward clue that it was a public building, but I was saved from the decision by the fact that there was no door. The entrance was filled only by a short length of dirty wool. Pushing it aside, I looked in.

Two men, who were probably farmers, sat to one side of a common room that probably wouldn't hold more than six or seven people at most. There was no bar, merely another table and a doorway that led to another room. This doorway was fortunate enough to have an actual door hanging in it.

I nodded a greeting at the two men, "Evenin'."

They nodded back but said nothing. As I took a seat at the other table one of them barked, "Hey, Harold! You got another customer."

I gave the farmer a thankful look, since I hadn't known the proper etiquette for the establishment. After a moment a large man with a balding pate peeked through the doorway. He grinned when he saw me, displaying a wide mouth that was missing several teeth. "Hello! What can I get ya?"

Following the woman's advice, I answered, "Just a cup of ale, and maybe a place to rest for the night."

"Ale, I can do," he said, "but I don't have beds for travelers. This is just a simple tavern, not an inn."

"Just ale then."

Harold left, and a moment later came back with a large clay cup filled to the brim. He placed it in front of me and then helped himself to a chair. "What news from the road?" he asked.

I took a sip and found that the woman's advice was sound. The ale was solid. When traveling, you never knew what you'd find. I wondered at the contrast, though, good ale but bad food, at least if the rest of her counsel was to be believed. Was it simply that Harold cared more about drink than cooking? From the size of his belly, it was hard to believe.

"They're opening a magical road in Halam," I told him.

"No!" exclaimed Harold. "Are you sure?"

"They were breaking ground on the foundation when I passed through," I replied. It was simple truth, and I had indeed seen it with my own eyes.

"That never would have happened if Darogen was still king," Harold expounded in a sage voice.

The two farmers were leaning over, listening carefully to our words. News was a highly valued commodity, and in some cases you could even trade it for food. I might have traded it for the ale, but since I didn't mind paying, I hadn't bothered.

"The new king seems to favor a more open relationship with Lothion," I observed.

"They named one already?" Harold's eyes were wide.

I took another sip and nodded, "Mm hmm. Just last week. The lords met and proclaimed Gerold, the Baron of Ingerhold to be the new king."

Harold frowned, "A baron?" He wasn't familiar with the name, but it seemed strange to him that a mere baron had been named.

"Duke Anselm had the best claim," I clarified, "but he renounced his claim in favor of Ingerhold. Apparently, the baron was a great hero in the battle and made a great name for himself with the people. The lords declared for him unanimously. I'm surprised you hadn't heard about it already."

One of the farmers piped up, "We haven't seen any travelers in weeks."

Harold was more interested in the magic road, though, so he returned to the topic, "I'm not so sure this road thing is a good idea for Dunbar."

I raised my brows, "How so? Everyone stands to profit from the increased trade."

"Trade is well and all, but I don't sees how it will do us folk much good. The lords will take most of the harvest and they'll make a tidy profit from it, but won't be much of it going into our pockets," said Harold.

"You run a tavern," I countered. "More trade ought to mean more people coming to buy ale. Especially since it's a good brew." I took a long swallow to show my appreciation.

He grunted, "I am proud of the ale, but my customers are all farmers, like Tad and Lumley there." He jerked his head in the direction of the other two men, who smiled back at us vaguely. "They ain't going to see much profit from it, so I won't neither. Other men get rich, but common folk like us don't see much of it from down here at the bottom of the barrel."

Sadly, I couldn't fault his logic, but I made a mental note of it. A word in the right ear might do them some good.

The conversation went on for an hour or more and then I offered to sharpen his knives. Harold accepted and paid me with another two cups of ale. Afterward he offered me a suggestion, "As I said before I don't offer beds, but if you need a place to sleep, Widow Timmley has extra room, and I'm sure she needs the coin. She might even have something that needs attention."

The tone in his voice made it clear that he was suggesting I might be able to share the widow's bed instead of sleeping alone. It was a crude remark, and would have earned scorn in more polite company, but behind his words I could sense something else. Was it concern? It gave me the impression that perhaps he genuinely hoped I would hit it off with the woman.

If she was indeed a widow, then she might be in need of help. A woman living alone faced many challenges, of which financial support was only one, and not necessarily the most important.

"In any case, it sounds better than sleeping on the ground, or in someone's shed," I agreed.

He gave me directions to her home, which was easy to find, since it was just outside the center of the tiny village. I gathered up my pack and made my way.

Of course, I had no intention of trying to inveigle the woman into sharing her charms with me. I was married, but Harold hadn't known that. It was rare for a traveling tinker to have a family, after all.

I considered not bothering her, since I didn't really need a place to sleep, but something made me call out anyway, "Hello? Mrs. Timmley? Harold at the tavern said I should ask if you might have a bed I could use. I don't mind paying."

It was a small house, so I had no doubt she would be able to hear me, and I already knew she was inside. After a moment she looked out the door at me. She said nothing for a long minute while she sized me up. For a woman living alone, a strange man, or any man was a risk to bring into her home.

In higher circles, it was unheard of, but here, among the peasants of Dunbar the practicalities of survival were more important. Being a widow, and with no prospects for a new husband, she had little to fear from developing a reputation as a 'loose woman.' She had much more to gain from my coin.

I was surprised by her age. She was awfully young to be a widow. At a guess I would have placed her age in the late twenties or early thirties. Dark brown hair peeked out from the edges of the cloth covering her head, and her looks were marred only by a bend in her nose. It had probably been broken at one time and had healed poorly.

Finally, she answered, "Come in." Stepping back, she let the door swing wide.

Something about the plain response bothered me. She should have been more suspicious, asked a few questions, or given me a warning. Assuming she was only hoping to sell me a place to sleep for the night, that is. Her response didn't make sense if she were actually a wanton woman, either. She would have put on some false charm if that were the case. No, this was the empty response of a woman who simply didn't care anymore.

"Thank you, ma'am," I replied, entering the house. "How much will you take for the bed?"

"What can you pay?" she said, returning the question.

"Is two pennies enough?" I asked. I honestly wasn't certain, but I guessed it was an appropriate amount.

She shrugged, "That's fine."

The room was small, and while it wasn't quite nice enough to call cozy, snug would do for a description. It appeared well kept, for a villager of small means. A pot hung over the fire and a chair was drawn up before it. The smell coming from it was tempting, far better than the odors in Harold's tavern.

"The bed's in there," she said, pointing to the only other door leading from the room, which meant it was probably her bedroom.

"Oh, I couldn't take your bed, ma'am," I told her, removing my hat and assuming an humble expression. "The floor in here will do me just as well."

At last her features shifted slightly, showing mild surprise as she arched one brow, "You paid for a bed. I can sit by the fire tonight."

The words brought me a sense of mild relief, she was definitely not offering herself for the evening. "No, ma'am. I'm not used to a bed. The fire's enough and my pack will make a fine pillow." Both statements were pure lies. I hadn't slept on the ground in years, and I was pretty sure the pack I carried would leave me with a cramped neck if I tried to use it in such a manner.

"Suit yourself," she said, her features regaining their former blandness. "I was about to have supper. Did Harold feed you?"

Now this was a quandary, I hadn't intended on eating, but it was perhaps a chance to talk to her for a while. I decided I could deal with the consequences later. I gave her a broad grin, "A lady by the well warned me about his food, so I'm still a bit peckish." That was an understatement, I hadn't eaten since breakfast.

She went to a well-made cupboard and opened it, taking out two wooden bowls. Whoever had furnished her home had been good with his hands. She ladled each of them full and handed one to me, then went to fetch a couple of wooden spoons.

There was only one chair, so I crossed my legs and sat on the floor before she could offer it to me. My nose had already decided the stew would be worth eating.

Looking down on me, she frowned. "I was going to offer you the chair."

"That's all right, ma'am." I punctuated the answer by shoveling in the first bite and promptly burned my tongue.

As I huffed and blew, trying to cool my mouth, a faint smile crossed her lips, then she sat down. She blew on her first bite carefully before depositing it in her mouth.

"You have a nice home," I said while waiting for my next spoonful to cool down. "I can see some care went into it."

She stared into her bowl, "That was Dan, he didn't do anything by halves. Took his time."

"It's more than that," I suggested. "I can see your hand in it too."

"Maybe," was all she said.

We ate in silence for a while then, but when I was almost finished I put in, "The stew was wonderful. Best meal I've had in ages." That was a half-truth. The stew was excellent, but I was no stranger to good food.

"Better'n what Harold serves up, that's for sure," she said with a snort. "It would be better still, but I'm running short on salt and other things. I've had to be more frugal since…" Her words ran dry.

It was cruel, but I wanted to know more, so I finished the sentence for her, "Since you lost your husband?"

"Yeah."

"If you don't mind my asking. What happened?"

"Halam," was her response.

Understanding struck me then. He must have been in the capital when the recent 'civil war' had taken place. Not that it had really been such, but it was the best description anyone had found for it. "He worked in the city?"

She shook her head, "No, he was just making a delivery. Rotten luck was all it was, bein' there on the wrong day."

I didn't say anything for a while after that, until after she had taken up the bowls and cleaned them. She put them away carefully and then made her way toward the bedroom door. She started to bid me goodnight when I interrupted her on impulse, "What's your name?"

She gave me a severe look, "I'm not looking for a new husband." Asking her first name was an unwelcome attempt to cross into more familiar terms.

I held up my hands, "I didn't mean anything by that. You just seemed like a nice lady. Thought I'd ask."

Her shoulders relaxed and then she opened the door and stepped inside. Before it closed I caught her reply, "Suzanne."

"Goodnight, Suzanne," I said, unsure if she would hear me through the door.

I waited half an hour before I checked on her. I wanted to be sure she was in her bed before I did anything, but by the same token I didn't want to accidentally observe her undressing. It was a matter of respect, though she would never have known if I had watched her preparing for sleep.

Could have been the world's greatest peeping tom, I thought to myself, then chuckled at the irony, since I had assumed the name Tom the tinker.

She appeared to be sleeping in the bed, but I wanted to be sure, so I softly whispered a word, *"Shibal."* The spell would ensure that whether she had been asleep initially or not, she wouldn't wake up for at least an hour. Then I released my illusion with a sigh of relief.

My worn clothes vanished, replaced by supple black hunting leathers. The simple knife at my waist was now a masterful dagger, produced by one of the finest smiths in Albamarl and adorned with the emblem of my family, a gold hawk set in maroon enamel, with a gold border around it. The enchantment on it was of my own devising, of course. The edge was sharper than any razor, and it never dulled.

Opening the door to Suzanne's bedroom, I went in and sat down beside her. With my spell upon her she never stirred.

"You're a good woman, Suzanne," I told her. "And I'm sorry for what happened to your husband. It's a shame that such things happen in this world."

She couldn't hear me, of course, but I felt the need to say it anyway. After all, what had happened to her husband was partly my family's fault. I repeated the sleeping spell, sending her into a deeper unconsciousness, and then I pulled back the blankets that covered her.

She had worn a gown to bed, so she wasn't naked, but I could feel the heat radiating from her body. Perhaps 'heat' wasn't the right word, it was her life force, her aythar, the living energy that everyone possessed. As always, it called to me, tempting me, and I felt the old hunger once again.

It was something I had never told anyone about, my deepest shame. I had once merged my soul with the shiggreth and become the void itself. I had overcome it, and regained my humanity, but it had left its mark on me, and I could still hear it singing to me when my attention wavered. Sometimes I awoke at night, having dreamed I was one of them again, and even after waking I could feel its cold chill, not from some external source, but from within.

I always felt it near the dying, but sometimes, like now, it was the supple health of the living that reminded me. The woman beneath my gaze had awoken the hunger in me this time.

Pushing my dark thoughts aside I reached down and slid my hand over her hip. Sending my magesight inward, I searched, until I found what I had spotted earlier. Suzanne had possessed a slight limp when she walked, the product of some accident in her past. How she had broken her hip was not my business, but it had healed improperly.

Reaching behind her head I numbed the nerves that reported the sensations of her body to her brain, and then I used my power to carefully break her hip again in two places. With that done I realigned the bones and fused them back together. She would have some soreness from it tomorrow, but that would pass, and when it had she would find her limp gone.

Next, I numbed the nerves that led to her nose, and then I corrected it as well. Years earlier I had learned by painful trial and error that those nerves didn't travel through the spine like almost all the others did. It wasn't the sort of mistake one makes twice.

After I finished I gave her an appraising look. She had been a lovely woman before, but without the crooked nose she would be a real beauty. Not that she wasn't already, but perhaps life would be kinder to her now. I couldn't control the future, though. There was no telling what the future might bring her, whether fortune or more sorrow. I hoped it would be the former.

I imagined that her face would swell while it healed, and I wondered what curses she might wish upon me when she awoke. She probably wouldn't realize the extent of what I had done until her nose returned to its normal size again.

Replacing the bed linens, I tucked her in carefully, as I might have done for one of my own children. Then I left and closed the door quietly behind me. Back in the main room, I collected my pack and left a selection of coins on the table. It was far more than the two pennies I had promised her, but not so much as to cause her trouble.

The walk back into town was a short one, and once there I visited the home of the woman I had met at the well. I put her and the rest of her family to sleep before I entered. Inside, I took a moment to find the broken pot, and using a spell, I welded the handle firmly back on. It was a silly gesture perhaps, but I felt better for doing it.

Her home was not as nice as Suzanne's had been, so I left a few coins in the pot and placed it on the table in the front room, being careful not to step on any of her sleeping children who were bedded down around it.

Then I left and made my way into the forest, traveling without light. A wizard rarely needed light to find his way. Once I had gotten far enough I drew a piece of cloth out of my pack and rolled it out onto the bare ground. It had the design for a teleportation circle painted on it.

Using another spell, I copied the design onto the earth below. When I lifted the cloth again to pack it away there was a circle made purely of light superimposed on the ground. It was an idea I had had only recently, but it made creating new circles a much quicker task. I only needed to add the keys to it, and it would be ready for use. I did that using a silver stylus plucked from the pouch at my waist.

The main disadvantage was that the circle would only last a matter of minutes. It would fade shortly after I had left, but that was perfect for my purpose. I preferred not to leave any evidence of my passing behind me.

Stepping into the circle I prepared to teleport myself home, then paused for a second. What was I going to tell Penny? I was returning later than I had promised, and even worse, I had already eaten. I patted my belly. It was a little larger than it had been in my younger days. "There's probably room in there for seconds," I announced to the trees.

If I ate enough, perhaps she wouldn't realize I had committed culinary infidelity.

CHAPTER 2

She was waiting for me when I got home. Not right inside the door, but with my magesight I saw her head turn when I stepped inside. The dragon-bond gave my wife exceptional hearing, among other things.

Penelope Illeniel was sitting in the family room, a cup of tea beside her, and a book in her hand. She wasn't one for staying up late, as I was, so I knew she was waiting for me.

Tossing my hat on the hall tree I hung up my coat and proceeded in to greet her.

"You're late," she said, not looking up from her book.

"Sorry about that," I apologized.

She kept her eyes on the page, "I cooked too."

I winced. I had expected that, but it still made me feel bad. Being the Countess di' Cameron meant that my wife didn't often get the chance to cook at home as most women did. What for them was a daily chore, was for her a lucky chance, especially since all our children were home again.

"I'm still hungry," I lied.

She glanced up at me. "It's cold now."

"Cold or hot, I love everything you make," I answered.

"Liar," she replied. "You don't like my mince pies."

I shrugged, "Well, fair enough, but I don't like *anyone's* mince pies, so I don't count them."

She started to rise, "I'll make you a plate."

Motioning for her to stay seated I headed for the kitchen. "I'll get it, dear. You stay there, and I'll join you."

"Bring me another cup of tea, then," she told me. "There's a kettle on the stove already."

It took me several minutes to assemble a respectable plate of food that I thought I could finish. The tea steeped while I did that, and before I brought it all back into the family room I crammed my mouth full of ham. Hopefully she would think I had been eating while in the kitchen, which would help explain why my plate wasn't as full as usual.

I returned, juggling my plate and two cups of tea, hers and mine. "Here you are, sweetheart," I said, trying to talk around the food in my mouth.

"Thank you, Mort," she said, taking the cup from me. "You don't have to pretend you're starving, though. I already know you ate somewhere."

I gave her a blank look, "What makes you say that?"

She tapped her nose.

The goddamned dragon-bond, I should have known. It didn't just improve her hearing, but all her senses, as well as granting her extraordinary strength and speed. The Countess di' Cameron was one of the deadliest warriors in Castle Cameron, though she was disarmingly beautiful.

"I smelled the stew as soon as you walked in," she explained. "What was it, lamb?"

I had thought it was rabbit, but she was probably right. "I'm not certain," I admitted. "I didn't want to eat it, but I needed an excuse to keep the cook talking."

She laughed, "I highly doubt that. You've rarely met a dish you didn't want to devour."

"Well, it smelled good, but I had a good idea you'd be cooking tonight and nothing holds a candle to one of your meals," I replied. That wasn't strictly true, either. Penny was an exceptional cook, but Castle Cameron boasted an exceptional staff, including its cooks. While I honestly did prefer her food, in the main, I couldn't claim that she was always superior to the professionals who fed everyone.

"You are a wicked man, Mordecai Illeniel," she replied with a twinkle in her eye. "Every time you speak you try to butter me up with that silver tongue."

I answered while chewing a large piece of bread that would probably have been much better two hours earlier, "That's how I got four children."

Penny raised one brow, "I only gave you three. How did your tongue manage the fourth?"

My oldest daughter, Moira, was adopted. We had raised her as a twin to our son, who was biologically of an identical age. "I talked Moira Centyr into entrusting me with her daughter didn't I?"

"I suppose you're right," said Penny. "What did your glib tongue earn you tonight, besides a bowl of lamb stew?"

It might have been a jealous inquiry, if it had come from another woman. My wife wasn't the jealous sort, though. She had her faults, but jealousy wasn't among them. Penny's biggest flaw was her constant fear for the safety of her family. In the last year she had become even more overprotective.

I couldn't say it was paranoia, though. She had every reason to fear. Over the past few months I had been kidnapped, and both of her oldest children had gone missing while trying to find me. All of us had been marked by the experiences as well. Our daughter Moira was dealing with a wound that had left a darkness in her soul, while our son, Matthew, had lost his left hand.

To top it all off, those events had happened shortly after our youngest daughter had been kidnapped and one of our closest servants murdered.

We had also been through some extreme events in our younger days, but while our children were growing up we had managed to create a relatively safe and secure environment for them. Our home had been a closely guarded secret, located deep in the Elentir mountains and accessible only through and enchanted portal in Castle Cameron.

Since Irene's kidnapping, that security was in doubt. A lot more people knew where we lived. No, I couldn't blame my wife for her anxiety. She had every reason to worry.

"Not much," I answered, "other than a few cups of ale. So far I haven't found any sign of ANSIS in the villages closest to Halam."

"How long are you going to keep searching?" she asked. "We've already done a lot for Dunbar. It shouldn't be your responsibility to keep everyone in the world safe."

"There's no one else to do it," I replied. "From what Matthew and Moira learned, if those things take hold somewhere and no one notices, it could be too late by the time they get to us. It's not just their safety, it's everyone's."

Penny sighed.

"What?"

"It's always the same, isn't it?"

"What is?"

She waved her hand, "First it was the Shiggreth, and Gododdin, and the Dark Gods, now it's this ANSIS thing. When will it end?"

"At least it's just one enemy this time."

"Sure it is," she replied. "You know better than that. We have more enemies than most nations ever manage to earn. Most of the nobility of Lothion secretly despise us. The only reason they haven't done anything is because they're scared to death of you. Even the Queen, *your cousin,* doesn't trust us."

"That's not fair," I told her. "Ariadne loves me, and I'm sure she trusts you."

"Clever, Mort. You skirt the truth with facts. Yes, she loves you. In fact, she almost sees you as a brother, since you and Marc were so close, but she doesn't *trust* you. And maybe she does trust me, but it's only in the sense that she hopes I can keep you under control."

"I can live with that."

"You have to," said Penny. "Back to the topic at hand, since you didn't find our elusive enemy, what did you do all day in the hinterlands of Dunbar?"

I smiled, "Well, I was disguised as Tom the tinker, so I mended a few things. I made a wonderful repair of an iron pot. It's better than new I think."

"And in trade the lady gave you some of her stew?" asked Penny.

"The stew came from a different lady," I said. "And what makes you assume it was a woman?"

Penny smirked, "You'd have mentioned the cook before now if it had been a man. Was she pretty?"

"Not half so lovely as you," I returned immediately.

Her eyes widened, "Oh! So she was gorgeous!"

"She would have to be, to be *half* as lovely as you, that's a given," I replied. "Besides, her nose was all bent and crooked."

Penny's intuition was once again too good. "You didn't!"

"Now you're jumping to conclusions," I said.

"No, I'm not," insisted Penny. "That's why you're late. I know you only have to walk through a town to tell if the people have those things in them. You stayed to fix that woman's nose."

I let my shoulders droop in defeat, "And I mended a pot. Also, she had a limp."

Her frown was all for me. "We've talked about this."

"I felt bad. She lost her family in Halam. We're partly to blame for that."

"We didn't bring those monsters to Halam. We got rid of them. Whatever happened, they can't lay it at our feet. You can't fix everyone, Mort. Why do you do this to yourself?" said Penny. She took my plate from my hands and drew me to my feet. Then she wrapped her arms around me. "It's not all your fault. None of this is, but you still act like it's your job to fix everything."

"I know that," I said irritably. Her hair smelled nice, so I laid my head on her shoulder.

"What's going to happen if someone finds out you've been sneaking around healing people?" asked Penny.

"It's not a crime," I protested. "Some would say it's a nice thing to do."

"Yes, it's nice, but that's not the point. People know you're a wizard, and the people of Washbrook know you can heal some things. With just that little bit, we've constantly got people coming to the door, seeking your aid. If they find out just how much you can do, we'll never have any peace. Right now, it's just a broken bone or minor wounds, but if people know you can fix bent noses, or straighten a lame leg—you see where that would lead. Don't you? People will be coming from everywhere, wanting you to heal all manner of sickness and infirmities."

"There's a lot of things I can't fix," I corrected her.

"They won't know that," argued Penny. "And when you tell them they'll blame you for withholding your gift. You've been blamed for too many things that weren't your fault already. Don't let them add this burden to your shoulders."

I nodded, "You make a lot of sense. That's why I always keep myself disguised."

She nipped my ear. "Stupid never dies."

"Now you're using my own words against me."

"Am I wrong?" she said with a smile. Then she pulled away. "Let's go to bed. It's late."

I followed her, giving her derriere a firm squeeze as we went.

"Don't get any ideas," she told me. "I'm not in the mood tonight."

"Dammit."

***

As always, the world slowly began to intrude upon me the next morning, but I was warm and the bed was comfortable, so I ignored it. Mornings were simultaneously my favorite and most loathed time of day.

I suppose it depended on the circumstances that surrounded any given morning, but one thing was certain, it was all or nothing. The good mornings involved me slowly waking up, usually with Penny close by. Those mornings were soft and fuzzy, full of the appreciation one has for a warm bed and nothing pressing to do. They were filled with the scent of my lovely wife's hair, the warmth of her back close against me, and—if I was really lucky, an adventuresome frolic before we faced the rest of the world.

Other mornings were not so kind. No, that was an understatement. The other kind of morning was a misery that deserved to die a cold death. They were composed of a rapid start, urgent events, cold floors and bare feet, or given my uncertain life, sometimes danger.

If anything, my greatest goal in life was maximizing the number of good mornings I encountered, and minimizing the other kind.

Today I was hoping for the good kind. I had every reason to expect one. I had gone to bed at a not-too-late hour, with my best friend beside me, and nothing dangerous on the horizon. Those were all good indicators. However, there were other variables that were always uncertain. Primarily, what sort of wakening did my wife have.

Some days she woke up and attacked the day with a ferocity that I had no desire to share. Those days fell firmly in my to-be-avoided-at-all-cost category, for they usually involved her trying to force me up at some ungodly hour, often using tactics that were cruel and uncalled for.

My magesight wasn't functioning yet. I slept with my mind closed, since it was safer. It wasn't a guarantee that my archmage abilities wouldn't get me into trouble, but it seemed to minimize the risk. Rather than open my arcane senses, I decided to discover the morning more slowly. Reaching across the bed I found Penny's thigh close by, warm and soft.

That's a good sign, I thought, inching a little closer to her.

Something whimpered.

That set me back. Whimpering was not on my list of expected morning events. I cracked one lid open slightly just in time to catch something warm and wet, which made my face scrunch up as my eye closed firmly. "What the hell?"

I reopened my magesight while simultaneously wiping my face and looking through my fingers. A small furry animal was lying between me and Penny.

"Isn't he cute?" Penny cooed. Obviously, she had been waiting for me to wake up.

It was a puppy. Its short tail curled over its back as it wiggled and tried to lick my face again. Valiantly, I defended myself while trying to sit up. If there was to be any frolicking this morning, it would be of an entirely different sort than I had hoped. "Where did this come from?" I asked.

She smiled, "It was a gift from the new king of Dunbar. Isn't he adorable?"

"He's something all right," I agreed.

"Pick him up. He wants you to love on him," she commanded.

And yes, it was a command. Don't ever let women fool you. When they tell you to pet or snuggle with something it's very much an order. To not do so would see you labeled a 'grump' or something similarly unsavory.

Feigning weak enthusiasm, I lifted the puppy to my chest and stroked his head, all the while considering what sort of punishment I could visit on Gerold Ingerhold of Dunbar. He had obviously done this with some malign intent to disrupt my quiet household. I was rewarded with more licking and a warm sensation spreading across my chest.

"Oh my!" giggled Penny. "He peed on you!"

I gave her my best long-suffering look. "Well that's what babies do, isn't it? Why don't you give me a hug?" I leaned toward her with a wicked gleam in my eye.

Penny was too quick. She was up and out of the bed before I could complete the gesture. "Maybe after you change your shirt."

Sighing, I gave the puppy a serious look, "You don't want me to change my shirt do you?"

"His name is Humphrey," said Penny.

Life was perfect. I had only recently been lamenting that my kids were all too old to pee on people anymore. Now we had a dog. "That's the best name you could come up with?" I asked.

"Moira liked it," explained my wife. "I know you weren't expecting this, but she does love animals. I'm hoping he'll help her."

"She can make magic dogs with just a thought," I argued. "Dogs that can talk, and don't pee on anyone."

"It isn't the same thing at all," said Penny.

She was probably right. Setting little Humphrey on the floor, I removed my nightshirt and used my power and some water from the washbasin to rinse my chest.

Humphrey watched without comment.

That done, I headed for the door. "Come on Humphrey, let's go get some breakfast." The puppy waddled a few feet and then sat down, emitting a yip of mild distress. Apparently, he wasn't up to speed on the art of following someone yet. I went back and picked him up. "Obviously, you've got some things to learn," I told him. "And if you're smart, you'll pay attention to me. The women around here will teach you all sorts of bad habits."

"Too bad," said Penny. "You're supposed to inspect the progress on the gatehouse in Halam today. Humphrey will have to stay here and learn tricks from the girls."

I hadn't wanted to remember that.

CHAPTER 3

Getting to Dunbar wasn't that difficult anymore, thanks to the World-Road. After my daughter had started a rebellion and gotten their machine-possessed king killed, the new king had been of a different mind when it came to opening up to the world. Of course, she had almost single-handedly gotten him made king, so perhaps he felt he owed her a few favors.

In any case, Dunbar had agreed to allow me to open one of the gateways from the World-Road near their capital city of Halam. It was a good deal all around. The gateways made it easy for farmers and traders to sell their wares across widely scattered locations around Lothion, Gododdin, and now Dunbar. Prosperity was an inevitable result.

There were precautions of course. One of the big selling points of my design was security. Most of the World-Road itself was underground, near Lothion, and guarded by a massive fortification. From a central location within the structure any of the twenty-three gates (not all of them were in use yet) could be closed at a moment's notice. If the command was given, a massive monolith of stone driven by one of my enchantments would slide down, sealing the entrance.

Those stones were designed to be unstoppable, and as far as I knew, they were. One of them had killed my best friend, Dorian Thornbear. It was something I tried hard not to think about every time I stepped onto the underground road.

Not only were the gates able to be sealed, but the road itself was a circle, and it could be divided into sections, each able to be sealed should an invader manage to make it past one of the gateways. Once closed, the road could be flooded, via an enchanted gate that led to a portal I had placed in the ocean. If that wasn't sufficient, my last fail-safe was even more severe. Another ring gate led to an underground magma reservoir. If that one were used the World-Road would reach the end of its functional lifespan.

After a life filled with danger, I had become a cautious man.

Of course, as I had later learned, too much caution can be a trap as well. My design, my fail-safes, all had been used to in an attempt to kill my family, and only the sacrifice made by my best friend had saved them.

"Dammit," I swore, wiping at my cheeks. "I wasn't going to think about that."

It happened every time I walked the World-Road. Being underground one might expect it to be dark, but it wasn't. It was brightly lit, almost cheerful. I had included enchanted ceiling lights in the design.

I passed several wagons on the road as I walked, nodding to the drivers. They had no idea who I was, of course. As a matter of course, I always traveled incognito, and illusion was a handy tool for that. Today I was a grey-bearded farmer, or perhaps a craftsman. I would remove the illusion once I arrived at my destination, becoming once again the handsome and well-dressed Count di' Cameron.

I would only need the disguise for perhaps a quarter of an hour. The transfer house in Castle Cameron had a circle that led directly to the main tower situated within the World-Road. Once there I had only to descend a multitude of stairs and then walk a quarter mile or so of the road itself, until I reached the new gate that led to Halam.

At some point in the past, Penny had argued with me about traveling without guards, but I had prevailed upon her that I was safer disguised and alone. I didn't really even need the disguise; I just disliked all the bowing and formalities that inevitably ensued when people recognized me.

I paused as I passed the gate that led to Lancaster. Dorian's Gate, as it was called now. I hadn't had to issue an official decree, people had just started calling it that. *And well they should,* I thought sadly. As always, I looked up, staring at the triangular edge that composed the bottom of the monolith that had crushed my friend.

It was unmarked. Its integrity unquestioned. Even my best friend's diamond body hadn't been able to scratch it. There had been some white dust there once, remnants of his body after the gate had crushed it, but even that was gone now.

Legends had grown up about the event. Sometimes they called him the 'Diamond-Knight', but mostly they just called him Dorian the Adamant. Ballads and epic sagas had been composed in his honor. He had held the gate up for several minutes, while his wife, children, and my family, had escaped through it. Until it had crushed him into diamond-dust and gravel.

That he had done so still made me marvel. The stone that comprised the gate weighed thousands of tons, and it had behind it the force of an enchantment powered by the God-Stone. He shouldn't have been able to hold it that long.

But he did.

"Fuck me." I should have gone the other way around. It was a longer walk, but I never went that direction. I came this way to remember, or perhaps to punish myself. He had been there when I should have been.

Stupid never dies, I thought. But Dorian certainly had. He lived on in the hearts and minds of people across the kingdom, in songs and stories. He had become a legend.

Well, in all honestly, so had I, but mine was a much darker sort of legend. In some parts of the world I was called the 'Blood Lord.' Mostly because of what had happened in the Duchy of Tremont. Thousands had died there, their souls devoured and their bodies left to rot.

The bodies were long gone but men still feared to live there, though the land was fertile and vacant.

I hadn't actually been the one who sent the shiggreth there, that had been my spell-twin, but I had his memories. I *remembered* ordering it. I felt the guilt.

And all I had gotten for it was a brief flogging. I had also paid a fortune in gold to the families of those that were murdered. It still felt like an empty gesture to me.

In places with kinder words for me, I was called the 'God-slayer,' but that was the most complimentary thing anyone ever managed to say. There was still fear in the eyes of anyone who realized who I was. The only exceptions were my family members, and most of the people who lived in Washbrook or the castle-proper.

And Penny wondered why I preferred to travel disguised.

I wasn't afraid of being attacked. I was afraid of being recognized. I couldn't bear the sight of fear, loathing, and disgust that I saw in the faces of those around me.

Penny saw it differently, and she was firmly convinced that if people knew the truth, they would see it the same way. But I knew the truth, and if Penny knew it, she would have been afraid of me too.

I had seen the void, touched it, and returned. And some part of it still existed inside of me.

Archmages were special. We could hear the voices of things that no one else could, the earth, the wind, the sea, anything really. We could listen, become, and direct those things, in a way that was wholly different from normal wizardry. But those things left an impression on us.

I was the only one who had ever heard the voice of the void, and I still heard it. It whispered to me in the dark at night. It haunted my dreams when I slept. It called to me from the lips of the elderly and the dying. Sometimes I could even feel it in small children.

The best times were at home with my family. I could forget, in the midst of my children's chaos, or when Penny smiled, amidst the laughter, and the smell of dinner; at those times I felt whole again.

Shaking off the dark thoughts I kept walking and soon the gateway to Halam loomed ahead to my left. It hadn't been hard to activate. The World-Road was built with twenty-three gates. I had only had to construct the other side and link it to this one. What was taking more time was completing the security construction for Dunbar's side.

In order to allay the fears of the nations and cities that had accepted one of the gates, each was built with fortifications on both sides. This allowed each city to close their side if they felt the need. Every gate had a gatehouse at its destination, though in truth, some of them were closer to full-blown fortresses.

I stepped through into brilliant sunshine, dropping my illusion and squinting to shield my eyes as I emerged from the more modest lighting of the World-Road. Workmen were everywhere around me. Most of them were stone masons, but carpenters and blacksmiths were present as well. Not to mention a multitude of apprentices and unskilled laborers.

With my illusion gone my black leather garb was on full display. It was an outfit that I had had made when I faced trial for my crimes after the war with the shiggreth and the gods, dark and shining. The leather was soft and supple, tooled with runes for protection, but what made it so fearsome was the design and the colors; black and red, with no allowance for the maroon and gold of House Cameron. The coat had an aggressive cut, trimmed with a red meant to remind the viewer of fresh blood.

If men wanted to call me the Blood Lord, I had determined to look the part.

I never wore it at home, or in Washbrook. My people still loved me, in the main, but for the rest of the world the outfit was a symbol that said, "Go to hell."

Being an amiable man, people had underestimated me for most of my life. These days, my reputation made that unlikely, but sometimes my smile and easy words made them forget. The clothes were a reminder.

Since we were at peace, and I was no longer a criminal, Penny generally disapproved of my choice in attire.

But here I was, wearing it anyway. Did I mention that I'm stubborn?

Angus McElroy spotted me and came over. He was my man, a master mason by trade. He had been with me a long time and now made his home in Washbrook. In short, he wasn't afraid of me, like most of those around me were.

"Milord," he said, dipping his head almost casually. "I see you wore your finest again."

He was in charge of the building efforts and his men watched him, wondering if he would be punished for his familiar attitude. I stared at them until they noticed my eyes on them and looked away, afraid of meeting my gaze.

We walked a short distance away, and he gave me an exasperated look, "Do you have to do that every time?"

"Do what?"

"Frighten them. They'll be tellin' stories to scare each other tonight," he answered.

My walk down memory lane had left me feeling cranky, and a lot of thoughts passed through my mind. I had overthrown a tyrant, made a good man king, defeated an army of the dead, fought every god known, and helped resurrect a dead race. And after it all, the world had turned its back on me. Actually, it had turned my back on it, and put a set of bloody stripes across my shoulders. I still bore the scars as a reminder.

If I had had my way, the County Cameron would be an isolated nation, and the world could go hang, but it was forever drawing me back.

None of that was Dunbar's fault, of course. In truth, it was no one's fault. But I was cranky, and in no mood to be reasonable. "History has painted me as a devil, Angus, I only do my best to live up to the part."

He sighed.

"How goes the work?" I asked.

"It's a lot easier than that dam you and your Dad had me build," he said with a chuckle.

Another bad memory, though Angus probably thought it would make me laugh. My father was dead, and while remembering him no longer hurt, what I had done with the dam was another stain on my soul. I had used it to drown an army of thirty thousand.

People like Angus didn't see it that way. To them, it had been an act of heroism, but then, they didn't have the blood of a generation on their hands. I gave him a faint smile anyway. It wouldn't do any good to tell him any of that. Angus was a decent man, and he was doing excellent work, as always.

"Do you need anything?" I asked him, cutting to the heart of the matter.

"Well..."

Of course, he did. That was the nature of major construction projects. I trusted Angus to get things done properly and without waste, either of time or materials. He trusted me to ensure he got what he needed to do the job.

As he talked I made mental notes. I didn't need paper, my freakishly perfect memory did the trick. Later I would send orders to Albamarl to have what he needed shipped to him through the World-Road. It made so many things easier these days.

Angus looked nothing like my father, but something about him reminded me of him. Something about every craftsman I met reminded me of my father in some way. The pragmatism, concrete thinking, and no-nonsense attitude that had been so central to Royce Eldridge was present to some degree in almost every man who worked with his hands for a living. As always, I wished I had been more like him.

My father's birthday had been just six days ago and something at the back of my mind niggled at me about that. Something I should remember.

That was the problem with memory, perfect or otherwise. I could recall anything, once I knew what I was trying to recall, but sometimes you just didn't know what you needed to remember.

I pushed it aside. Whatever it was would come to me later. Probably while I was moving my bowels. Most important things popped into my head then.

Angus was still talking. I returned my attention to him. He was waiting for a reply. Mentally I reviewed what he had said, since I hadn't been listening fully. His last question had been, "Is something wrong? You seem distracted."

Nodding I answered, "I was just thinking that I may have eaten too much for breakfast."

He grinned, "The latrines are over there if you need 'em." He pointed in the direction of the makeshift wooden building they had built for the purpose.

"I'm not quite ready yet," I told him. "Maybe after I get to Albamarl and order what you need."

"That road you built is changing the world," he said. "I can work here for ten hours and then take a crap in any of a dozen cities at the end of the day, if I want to." Angus laughed to punctuate his joke.

The thought of walking past Dorian's Gate again wasn't pleasant. "I think I'll fly today," I told him.

The mason frowned, "Even flying, it's hundreds of miles from here to the capital."

Shaping my aythar I slowly lifted myself from the ground, "When I put my mind to it, Angus, I can fly so fast that even falcons weep to see me leave them behind."

He said something I couldn't hear; he was too far below and the wind was already rushing around me. It might have been 'suit yourself' or something along those lines, but I hardly cared. Flying was just the thing to lift the shadows from my soul.

It was my perfect pleasure, the counterpoint of my existence that stood in opposition to the voice of the void. Flying was a talent that any wizard was technically capable of, but none tried to do it the way I did. Gareth Gaelyn would shapechange, others would use a protective construct, but no wizard who wanted to keep living would fly using only their raw ability to shape aythar.

The reason was simple. It was dangerous. Over the past two thousand years, most wizards who attempted it wound up killing themselves, or at the very minimum acquired injuries that made them rethink their choices.

It wasn't hard, but it took practice. Since most learning requires mistakes, and these mistakes were usually fatal, I was the only living wizard who flew this way. I had been unfortunate enough to be trapped in an undead body for a year, and during my time as an immortal I had taken the opportunity to learn. Crashing into a mountain wasn't so bad when you felt no pain and your body would reform on its own.

I shot through the air like an arrow launched from a bow, gaining altitude and speed as I went. When the rushing wind became too powerful, I created a long tapering shield around myself, pointed at both ends. I continued adding speed to my flight.

The ground shrank beneath me, and the tops of the trees began to blur. I was already traveling at a velocity that would be fatal if I hit anything, no matter how strong my shield was. I had once discovered that even if you could create a shield that wouldn't break, your body could still be reduced to jelly from the shock.

It had taken weeks to fill and level the crater that I had produced in the yard of Castle Cameron while learning that.

It was almost a shame I wasn't immortal anymore. That had been my most memorable landing. Exerting my will, I flew faster still.

The sun was devastatingly bright this high up, with few clouds to mitigate its rays. It bathed me in warmth and seemed to thaw my heart. The world below was a rapidly changing vista of trees, rocks, rivers, and mountains. I kept pressing, accelerating even as I added a sonic shield to protect my ears. I knew what was coming.

Without my hearing, I only experienced the shockwave as a powerful shiver that passed through my body. I had broken what my son's friend Gary called the 'sound barrier'. According to him, that meant I was moving at somewhere around seven hundred and forty miles an hour, the usual speed of sound in air. It didn't mean I couldn't go even faster, though.

The force of the air against my shield was powerful and intense, creating heat that I was forced to compensate for. It was exhilarating. Even a tiny defect in my shield would rip me apart. Death was close and friendly, patting me on the back as my stomach fluttered with excitement. I pushed harder, my focus absolute, my will harder than steel. For a short time I was a god—again.

It felt magnificent, and I reveled in the power and majesty of the sky as I tore through the firmament. I kept the blistering speed up for almost an hour before I let my pace slacken. Even with my reserves, using that much power to fly was exhausting. Not to mention a little foolish. Dropping down to a speed that was probably still several times faster than anything ever managed by one of Mother Nature's creations, I cruised over the world.

Having flown many times, I was familiar with the landscape, so I recognized immediately when I was nearing Albamarl. I slowed even more, and used the last part of my journey to relax myself; spinning and diving, twisting and flying in loops, enjoying my mastery of the air.

Briefly I toyed with the idea of increasing my speed again before flying over the capital. A sonic boom would probably scare the citizens half to death. Being a grown up (ostensibly), I dropped the notion as childish. *They're lucky I'm so mature,* I told myself. Then I imagined what Penny's response would have been to that statement. Good thing she hadn't heard my thought.

My first stop was at the office of David Summerfield. It was located across the street from my home in Albamarl. I had only recently acquired the building he was in, so I could install my factor there with some semblance of dignity. David was a solid man, but he had suffered a tragedy in the past year. He had been betrothed to Lilly Tucker, my children's nanny and one of our household servants. She had died trying to stop the kidnapping of my youngest daughter, and while David had managed to forgive one of the culprits, Alyssa, he couldn't bear to live near her.

Alyssa was serving as one of my current servants, under a sort of house-arrest, and she was pledged to marry Gram Thornbear. It wasn't likely she'd be leaving any time soon. So instead, David had begged me to place him elsewhere.

His new job as my factor was something of a step-up, but it made a lot of things easier for me. In the past I had borrowed the use of Lady Rose Hightower's factor when I needed business conducted in the city. It had probably been well past time when I should have hired my own factor to manage such things. Since I was a grown-up nobleman now, after all.

I drifted down slowly, like the leaves on an autumn day, and stepped lightly onto the cobblestones in front of his office. The people on the street looked at me with some amazement and then recognized me, by my clothing as much as my face. They hurried on, keeping their faces pointed firmly at their feet.

I rapped on the door once, just to be polite, then let myself in. It was my building. David stood just inside, standing very close to a young woman who didn't look much like a trading partner. In fact, he had had his arms around her only a moment before, but he had withdrawn them at my sudden knock. Magesight was a wicked thing sometimes.

It had only been a little over a half a year since Lilly's death, but he was a relatively young man, with an important job, living alone in the most populous city in Lothion. I shouldn't have been surprised. Everyone deals with grief differently, and I promised myself I wouldn't judge.

Barely a half a year and he's already moved on, I thought. Yeah, I was judging, but I was determined not to let it show. "Hello, David," I said brightly.

"My Lord," he exclaimed with only a hint of nervousness. "I didn't expect you today."

"I felt like getting some fresh air today, and Angus needs more materials for the new work in Halam," I told him. "I figured it wouldn't hurt to run my own errands for a change. Introduce me to the young lady."

He took her hand immediately, stepping back and giving a half bow as he presented her. "My Lord Cameron, this is Sarah Beckins, who I have only recently had the benefit of meeting. Sarah, this is Mordecai Illeniel, the Count di' Cameron." He had probably added that 'recently' part for my benefit.

I took her hand and brushed my lips across her fingers, barely making contact, as was the custom. "A pleasure to meet you, Sarah."

She blushed and curtseyed, "The pleasure is mine, milord."

It was clear she was not a noblewoman, but she was definitely well mannered. I released her hand and glanced around the room. Making a quick assessment, I asked her, "Do you work at the flower shop down the street?"

Her flush became much deeper and I knew I had hit on the truth. For a moment I felt like Lady Rose herself with my inductive leap. "Y—yes, milord," she answered, stammering slightly. "I am surprised you know of it."

I smiled, hoping to make her more comfortable. I had scared her, scared both of them, and I felt a little guilty for it. Still, I didn't want to waste a good leap of logic. "My house is just across the street," I said casually. "Though I don't stay there often, I try to keep abreast of what goes on in the neighborhood." I let my eyes rest on David. He would be wondering how I had known where she worked, whether I was watching him somehow.

He was too rattled to consider the fact that there were flowers set in several locations around his office, in vases and pots. I had known a small bit about him during his time courting Lilly Tucker, and never had I noted any particular love of flowers. Oh, he had brought her flowers on occasion, but these flowers were in his office.

And they hadn't been there two weeks ago. So obviously, he had taken to stopping at a flower shop regularly. The easy answer for why, was Sarah.

The young lady made her excuses and left. Once she was gone I gave David a friendly look, "I like her."

"I don't know too many people in the capital, yet," he responded, somewhat nervously. "She's just a friend."

That was a patent lie, based on what I had seen before I knocked, but I didn't mind. It did bother me that he might have found love again so soon after tragedy, but it wasn't my business. I had never been in his position, so I did my best to rein in my opinion.

I rattled off the list of things Angus required and left him to recover from the shock I had given him. As I stepped into the street I pondered visiting the Queen, Ariadne.

Just a few years back, it would have been unthinkable for a nobleman of my rank to visit the capital without making his presence known to the sovereign. It hadn't quite been a law, but not presenting yourself before the crown would have been an almost unforgivable social faux pas.

The rule hadn't applied to peer who lived within the capital, but for one as far removed as I was, it applied. That was before the World-Road had been built. Travel to and from the far corners of the kingdom was now commonplace, a matter of hours.

Because of that, the old social rule no longer made sense. The new rule was predicated more on time and frequency of visits. If you came often, it would be pointless to seek an audience with the monarch for no real reason. I hadn't seen my royal cousin in years, so a visit was technically required. I wanted to see her for my own reasons, though. Not out of any desire for socializing, though, but as a precaution. For the same reason I had been exploring the small towns and villages of Dunbar: ANSIS.

We didn't know for sure, but it was likely that the enemy was still out there. The last thing I needed was to discover it had infiltrated the government of Lothion and taken control of the queen, or her functionaries.

There were only a small number of wizards in the world, and we had yet to find an easy way to spot ANSIS, other than direct inspection with magesight. The little mechanical monsters could be hiding in anyone. I had even begun considering sending the few wizards we had to visit far-flung cities at random.

Was I paranoid? Maybe. But then again, it isn't paranoia if there really is someone, or something, out to get you.

Calling the wind, I rose once more into the sky. *Why walk when you can do this?* I thought to myself.

CHAPTER 4

The royal palace had undergone a lot of renovations since the first time I had been there, a few decades ago. Perhaps renovation wasn't the right word, large portions of it had had to be completely rebuilt. But then, you have to expect that sort of thing when you have a battle between an insane god, an archmage, and an ancient dragon.

They had used the same rose granite that was a defining feature for most of Albamarl, but the architectural style had been changed somewhat, probably due to Ariadne's good taste. Her father, James, had been the first monarch to sit on the throne after the timely demise of King Edward, but Ariadne had already been old enough at that time to make her opinions known when the reconstruction started.

As a result, the palace was less a fortress and more suited to serve as a diplomatic bastion for visiting dignitaries. The gardens had been expanded, more fountains and artistic sculptures added, and the windows were broader and more welcoming. It was far less defensible should an invader breach the walls of the city.

The Queen hadn't been entirely impractical, though. Her actual residence was in the old keep that had survived. It had been reinforced and made stronger, but it was hidden by the newer buildings around it. An invader would have a hard time getting to her if they did get into the city, but the larger portion of the palace would probably have to be given up as a lost cause rather than defended.

I passed over the outer gate and landed in one of the private gardens before marching in to the section that Ariadne reserved for her public business. Given the time of day, I doubted she was in the keep. I passed through the wide hallways of the guest quarters and into the areas where the minor functionaries held sway. A multitude of offices were there, each with its own door and a pretentious sign proclaiming the name and title of whichever lordling or scribe worked within.

Walking briskly, I didn't bother with any of them. By flying over the walls, I had bypassed a host of self-important men and useless protocols. I went past a number of courtiers and their ilk as I stalked the corridors, but since I looked as though I knew where I was going and had a determined look on my face, they didn't bother stopping me to ask questions.

My original plan had simply been to walk and use my magesight to spot the Queen, so I could approach her with a minimum of fuss, but I had forgotten the privacy shields installed by Gareth Gaelyn. A large number of rooms and important places within the palace were protected from prying eyes and ears, and that included magesight.

Glancing around, I decided to interrogate one of the servants. By luck, I knew one of the men who was walking down the hall, his back to me. Picking up my pace, I closed the distance and caught the man by the arm, "Where's the Queen today?"

Being grabbed suddenly, from behind, was not ordinary palace behavior, as was evidenced by the man's startled expression and accelerating heart-beat. He gaped at me for a half a second before his normal bland expression returned. He recognized me of course, for it was Benchley, the former valet of the Duke of Lancaster.

Recovering from his surprise he gave me a short bow, then spoke, "Your Excellency, I don't believe you were expected today." His tone was dry, with a hint of superiority, but unlike the days of my youth, there was a bit of humor in his eyes. "The Queen is visiting with someone of *importance* at present."

His implication of course, was that I wasn't that important.

It was a game we had been playing for years. When I had first met him, I had been a commoner, a playmate of the Duke's son perhaps, but a commoner nonetheless. During my early adventures, he and I had had our moments of contention, mainly over my refusal to play by the rules required of my social standing.

Since then, I had become one of the most important men in the kingdom. By some reckonings, I might be *the* most important man in the kingdom, regardless of my rank. After all, it had been me who had put James Lancaster on the throne. That had resulted in another of my less well-known names, *Kingmaker*.

Benchley knew all this, naturally, but it was a mark of our friendship that he still pretended I was a minor nobody. Well, I think it was anyway. He would never break character long enough to admit it to me.

In mock umbrage, I replied, "Who could be more important than *I am*?"

He answered with his best droll tone, "Any number of gentlemen and ladies I would imagine, milord. Shall I consult the heralds to draw up a list for you?" In the strictest sense, his remark was true, but it was also cheeky enough that if he had used that line with some peers of the realm, he might have been whipped. That's how I knew he liked me. He knew I had a sense of humor.

Probably that was it. Either that, or he was well enough protected as one of the Queen's most trusted servants that he knew most noblemen wouldn't dare try to call him out on such a minor insult.

No, I told myself, *he definitely likes me.* It had to be that.

"I'll pass on the list," I told him with a grin, but before I could ask my next question a roar shook the palace.

Benchley gave me a disapproving stare, "You didn't come through the gate, did you, milord?"

"Well…" A second roar from outside confirmed my suspicion, the Queen's dragon, Carwyn was sounding the alarm.

The only mage who spent a significant amount of time in the palace was probably Gareth Gaelyn, but I believed he kept his residence elsewhere. However, while dragons couldn't personally use the power they contained, they did have magesight. That meant Carwyn served a special purpose as a guardian at the palace, and my arrival had alerted him. A powerful mage shines like a beacon to others with magesight.

Even though he was just doing his job, I thought the roaring was a little excessive. I was Carwyn's creator after all. Surely, he would realize I didn't represent a threat to his royal mistress? A third roar dispelled that notion.

Guards were appearing in the halls and everyone there on honest business disappeared into their offices or lined up against the walls to make it easy for the soldiers to pass and verify who was who.

I gave Benchley a sheepish look, "Perhaps I should go…"

The traitor raised his hand and pointed at me, signaling to the nearest group of guards, "He's over here!"

"Benchley, that wasn't very nice," I admonished him. "After all the years we've known each other!"

He merely shrugged and moved to stand by the wall, the bastard. Within seconds I was surrounded by men in armor, all of them waving sharp pointy things at me. Some of them were yelling orders, but they all spoke at once, so it was difficult to know what they wanted.

"Do you want my hands up or do you want me to lie on the floor?" I asked. "I can't do both."

Another was shouting for me to identify myself, which I thought was pretty silly, since it was obvious by the mutters of a few of them that they already knew I was the 'Blood Lord'. I extended my shield out for several feet in every direction to keep them from getting too close.

"Has anyone seen Sir Harold?" I inquired. "He will vouch for me."

Since I wouldn't let them arrest me, or even approach, they just kept me surrounded until Harold arrived.

Harold had been one of my knights originally, until the Queen had poached him from me. Dorian had trained him into one of the deadliest knights in the kingdom, and I was rather proud of my small part in that. These days he was the captain of the Queen's Guard.

He looked surprised when he pushed his way through the crowd and saw me. Then he shook his head in disbelief. "I should have known," he said.

"Hi, Harold!" I waved at him. "Do you think you could call off your men?"

They stepped aside as he approached. "Did you ever think of just using the gate like a normal person?" he asked.

"I just wanted to make it a quick visit," I told him. "You know, avoid all the commotion of pomp and circumstance."

Harold looked around and waved his hands at all the men surrounding me. "This is your idea of a quiet visit?"

"Well, my plan sort of backfired," I admitted.

Harold sighed, then he gave the order to the guardsmen, "Back to your posts, I'll escort the good Count di' Cameron."

Some of them relaxed, but several were not so easily convinced. One spoke up, "Are you certain, Sir Harold? He looks dangerous, and he's already committed a crime by climbing the walls."

I protested, "I didn't climb anything! I flew."

Harold looked down his nose at the guard, "Ned, do you really think you could stop him with a spear? If he wanted, this man could have buried you all up to your necks in the stone floor with little more than a glance."

Ned stared at his feet somewhat sheepishly, but Harold wasn't done. "If he were really angry, he could easily roast the flesh from your bones, or just rip your spines out of your backs with a thought, and none of that armor you're wearing would hinder him in the slightest. In fact, during the war with the shiggreth I watched him…"

The men's faces went white as the blood drained from them. Hastily, I interrupted, "Harold! There's no need to talk like that." I held my hands out in a gesture of peace as I addressed the guards, "I would never do something like that. Trust me."

Harold gave me a look of mock sincerity, "I speak only the truth, milord." Turning to his men he added, "Back to your posts. I'll regale you with tales of the Count's bloody deeds later."

They left, needing no further encouragement.

"That was a dirty trick," I grumbled to Harold.

"If you dislike my tales, feel free to prove my point by roasting me alive here and now." He gave me a bow that was probably one of the least respectful acts of courtesy I had ever witnessed.

"I used to like you, Harold."

The burly knight grinned, "If you didn't want to inspire fear, why'd you show up wearing those clothes?"

Everyone was a fashion critic. "If you must know, I had to visit Dunbar today," I told him. "This visit was a spur of the moment idea, one I now regret."

"Don't be so glum," said Harold amiably. I had lowered my outer shield, so he moved closer and smacked me between the shoulder blades in what was probably meant to be a friendly manner. "Let's go to my office."

"I just came to see Ariadne," I responded.

He waggled his finger at me, "Ah, ah, ah, you're under arrest, milord. Come have an ale with me. Benchley can let the queen know you've been put in irons."

The Queen's manservant was still standing by patiently, about six feet away. I called to him, "Did you hear that, Benchley? I've been arrested. I hope you're happy. Please let the Queen know her cousin has been locked up and would love to see her at her earliest convenience."

I could almost have sworn I saw a faint smile flicker across his still features, but it was probably my imagination. "Certainly, milord," he answered, and then he left. I followed Sir Harold.

The knight led me back to the small room that served as his office and rummaged around in a cabinet until he found two small wooden cups of questionable cleanliness. Then he filled them both with ale from a pitcher on a side table. The ale tasted as though it had once been quite good, but now it was lamentably flat and stale. Pulling up a chair I sat down and decided not to complain.

"That bit about roasting them alive was not necessary," I grumped.

Harold laughed, "I'll get a lot of good service from the story."

"How so?"

"Soldiers are a bit like children," he explained. "It helps to have a monster under the bed to keep them in line."

I frowned, "That makes no sense."

"Sure it does," he replied. "They'll respect me more, since I was the one brave enough to take you away, and later, if any of them cause trouble, I can always threaten them with messenger duty to Castle Cameron."

"I've been ill-used," I groaned.

He took another deep swallow from his cup before setting it down. "Haven't we all?"

Nodding, I finished mine and poured another for myself. It was good to see Harold again, despite his poor choice in jokes, it was a reminder of days gone by. They hadn't all been bad.

"Perhaps I should visit the barracks and regale your men with tales of your valor," I suggested. "I could tell them about your first valiant charge against the shiggreth in that cave near Lancaster."

His eyes went wide, "You wouldn't!"

Smug, I reiterated my threat, "I just might. It would do them good to hear it I think." Back when Harold had been a newly minted Knight of Stone, he had not yet grown accustomed to his strength when I asked him to charge a ballista controlled by a group of undead monsters. Nervous and pumped full of adrenaline, he had done so, but his first leap from cover had sent him headlong into the overhanging stone ceiling. He had nearly knocked himself senseless.

He stared at me for a moment, then made the offer, "Truce?"

"As long as you promise not to tell them evil-wizard bedtime stories."

"Deal then!" He reached for the pitcher of ale but found it empty. It had been only partially full to begin with, since we had only had a cup and a half each. "Let me get some more."

"Should you be drinking on duty?" I asked.

"Never!" he responded. "I wasn't on duty. But you caused such a ruckus I came running anyway."

That seemed a reasonable statement, so I let him go. After a few minutes he returned with a full pitcher, and this one was noticeably better. It had been freshly drawn from the keg. I took an appreciative sip from my cup. "That's more like it."

Harold smiled, "When I first met you, I wasn't even old enough to drink. They'd only let me have small beer, and then only at supper."

Small beer was a very weak beer served at most meals, even children drank it, since it was often safer than water. I laughed. "When I first saw you, you didn't even have your first chin hairs yet, just this fuzzy down that you refused to shave because you thought it made you look manlier. I thought Dorian was crazy when he told me he thought you'd make a good knight."

He raised his cup, "To Dorian!"

"To Dorian!" I agreed readily. My mood had improved greatly, whether from the flying or the three cups of ale, it was hard to tell. We swapped stories and reminiscences for the better part of an hour, finishing the pitcher and starting on another, when a rapping came at the door.

"Come in!" yelled Harold.

It was Benchley. He entered and gave us both disapproving looks. "The Queen sent me to inform you that she will see you now, Your Excellency."

It wasn't until I stood that I realized I had had too much. The world swam around me, swaying, or perhaps that was me. Harold stood as well and braced me with his shoulder, before nearly falling over himself. "Ooo!" he grunted. "Benchy, give us a hand if you would."

Benchley didn't comment on the abuse of his name, but he did help steady us. After that he escorted me through the palace, his hand firmly on my arm in case I swayed a little too far to one side or the other. Since Harold wasn't called for, he stayed behind. He offered to come, but I told him to rest. No sense in him getting in trouble as well.

Rather than the throne room, or one of the larger council rooms where dignitaries met, Benchley led me in the direction of the old keep. Once inside we went to the royal apartments, stopping at the door to a small sitting room. "Are you ready, milord?" he asked me in what I thought might be a solicitous tone. Perhaps he cared after all.

"I think so, Benchley," I told him. "Thank you. Sorry about earlier." I was still unsteady, but I was able to walk a mostly straight line now.

"Think nothing of it, milord," he replied.

"You're a good man, Benchley, no matter what I used to think," I blurted out.

His face grew puzzled, "Milord?"

"I was a teenager then, Benchley, but I've come to respect you greatly since," I said, unsure whether I was making my remark better or worse.

"Those were interesting times, milord," he agreed in a neutral tone. "Best not to keep Her Majesty waiting." He motioned toward the door.

"Too right." I opened the door and plunged in.

Ariadne, Queen of Lothion, sat across the room in a comfortable chair. Gone was her formal raiment, replaced by a more comfortable and simple gown of soft linen with fur trim. Her hair was loose, and she was in the process of brushing it out.

"Your Majesty," I greeted her. My bow was less than graceful, though, as I quickly discovered that balancing while bending forward was completely different than balancing while standing straight up. Somehow, I managed to get myself back upright with only a small wobble.

"No need for formality, Mort," she said, "not here." Her eyes studied me as she spoke. "Have a seat," she added, waving her hand toward a comfortable looking padded divan.

"Happily, I will," I answered, and then I plopped heavily onto the designated piece of furniture.

"I didn't mean to leave you waiting so long," she continued, "but after finishing my business for the day I really wanted to get out of those clothes."

Being allowed into the Queen's presence while she unwound, wearing simple attire, and being entirely unattended was not something that would have been conscionable, if I had been almost anyone else, but I was family. Technically, we were first cousins once removed, though I hadn't known that for the first fifteen or sixteen years of my life. What made the difference was that I had grown up best friends with her brother, and consequently we had also been friends since childhood.

Not that some distance hadn't grown between us in the intervening years since she had become queen, most particularly after my public flogging, but most of that was on my part. It had taken me a while to overcome my wounded pride. Things were better now, but we weren't as close as we had once been.

"You wouldn't believe how that crown makes my head itch," she said, brushing her head once again. "Though I shouldn't blame the crown I suppose. It's having my hair braided and coiffed all day that does it."

As a count I had a circlet that I wore on formal occasions, but since my hair was short I couldn't really know what it was like for her, so I didn't comment. Instead I went for the more exciting news, "Did you hear? I was arrested today."

A faint smile passed over her features, "Yes I did, though you seem to have survived the experience unscathed."

"Your dungeon was very comfortable, and the jailor was quite accommodating," I responded with a smile of my own.

She put down her brush and then scratched her scalp directly with her nails in a most unladylike fashion. "I hadn't realized my dungeon offered beer to its residents."

"A most civilized custom," I commented. "I'm thinking of building a dungeon of my own, just to entertain friends."

She laughed, covering her mouth with one hand. Even relaxed, some habits had been drilled into her since childhood. "How much did you have? I thought you might fall over when you entered."

"More than I thought," I told her. "Harold and I got to reminiscing, and I let my guard down."

"If you would come in through the gate, you wouldn't be harassed and arrested," she advised.

"I didn't think anyone would notice," I replied. "I forgot about Carwyn."

"He's very protective," agreed Ariadne. "In case you didn't know, I instructed the doormen and the gatekeeper to let you in with a minimum of fuss. They wouldn't have put you through all the pomp and circumstance that most people have to deal with."

In fact, I had not known that. "I am educated by your wisdom, My Queen," I remarked with mock formality. Then a thought struck me, I hadn't visited in years. After my trial I had avoided the capital for months, only returning to speak for Dorian at the memorial. At the time Ariadne had complained of her isolation, but my pain had still been too fresh for me to respond with much empathy.

It had been almost ten years since then, and I had only come to the capital twice, and then only for important occasions of state. Neither time had I spoken to her in private. She had made plenty of opportunities, but I had avoided them. I had avoided *her*.

And yet, she had given special instructions to the men at the gate to admit me without question, for what? It certainly wasn't for practicality. My gut told me the answer, it had been a hopeful gesture.

"Would you get that decanter for me, Mort?" she asked, pointing to a glass container on a sideboard near the wall.

Rather than risk standing, I used my power, levitating it and sending it to her hand with only a slight wobble. "What is that?"

"A spirit made in Gododdin," she answered. "I believe Nicholas told me it is called 'gin'. They make it with juniper berries. I've grown rather fond of it." Removing the stopper, she poured some into a glass. Her face contorted as she took a sip.

The 'Nicholas' she had mentioned so casually was the monarch of Lothion's neighbor, Gododdin. "Should you be drinking that?" I wondered openly.

"Why should you have all the fun?" Ariadne quipped. After watching my face a moment, she added, "Don't get worried. I almost never drink. There's no one to drink with when you're the queen. This is a special occasion." She choked on her second sip.

"You'll make yourself sick," I warned. "Most people mix that with other things, like fruit juices or wine."

Once she had finished gasping for air she replied, "Nonsense, Nicholas told me it was invented as a medicine."

A medicine meant to cure sobriety, I thought to myself. My next words came as a surprise even to me. "I'm sorry."

The Queen's brows went up, then she forced another swallow past her lips. After the inevitable coughing she asked, "What for?"

"For not being here," I said simply.

Her cheeks had gained some color, though whether from my apology or from the drink, I couldn't be sure. She stared at me for a long moment before responding, "Don't. We're having fun. This is your first personal visit—ever. Don't spoil it."

"That's exactly why I'm apologizing," I explained. "When I came, forever ago, for the memorial service, you told me how isolated you were. But I was too angry to listen. Not angry at you, though. I was angry with Lothion, with the people, but since you were the queen, it wound up being you that I punished. I abandoned you. That's why I'm sorry."

Ariadne frowned at me, then she stood and drained her glass. She didn't choke or sputter this time. She placed it on the side table with a loud thud. "I'm not a little girl anymore, Mort. I'm not Marcus' little sister anymore, following you around the castle. I'm a queen, and I'm perfectly capable of taking care of myself, so save your pity. I've done pretty well over the years, without your help.

Agitated, she carried the decanter back to the sideboard, then picked it up again and went back to her seat to refill her glass. "Am I supposed to get sad over all the empty years, with no one to turn to for advice? I don't think so!" She took another brisk swig from her glass.

I winced at her words. She had become queen the same day she had been orphaned, and yet she had never complained. How could she? There had been no one to complain to. Her younger brother, Roland, stayed in Lancaster, both her parents were gone, and I had treated her as though she carried the plague.

She had married, though. A handsome young nobleman from Gododdin, Leomund was his name. That had been something of a relief to me at the time, for it assuaged my guilt at avoiding her. There had been no children, however, and she was in her late thirties. I wondered if I should even mention her husband.

Ariadne's eyes narrowed as though she had read my mind. "And don't even mention my husband."

I held up my hands, "I hear he's a likeable fellow."

She dropped back into her cushioned chair, "Do you know *why* I married him?"

I was definitely in dangerous territory now, possibly almost as perilous as conversations with Penny that started out with a simple, 'we need to talk'. Struggling for an answer I could only manage, "He's handsome?"

She drained her glass and set it down again, "He's a useless peacock of a man. I married him because he wasn't from Lothion."

Twenty years ago, I wouldn't have understood, but I had been embroiled in politics long enough to catch her meaning. She was the first reigning queen in Lothion. If she had chosen a nobleman from her own country the question of whether he should be king might have become a serious problem. None of Lothion's nobility wanted a foreigner ruling them, though, so Leomund had been made a 'prince consort'.

My friend's little sister was crafty. She had neatly navigated around the most dangerous obstacle of her sovereignty. I was impressed. "I never realized," I told her, "but that's brilliant."

"Thank you," she said, bowing her head slightly and waving her hand as though she was accepting applause. "It's still awful, though. I can't stand the man. That's why I keep him at a distance most of the year."

Prince Leomund had become well known as an avid hunter, and he spent most of his time away from the capital, but I had always thought that was by his own choice. "Is that why there has been no—issue?" I asked, referring to the fact that she had produced no heirs.

Now it was her turn to wince. That was one question no nobleman in Lothion would have dared to ask, but it was on all of their minds. The Queen was nearing forty, and the question of succession was beginning to loom. "No," she admitted at last. "I did my duty, but nothing ever came of it." Then she said the words that would never have been possible in public, "I'm barren."

Leaning forward I made a suggestion, "Are you sure it's you? It could be Leomund."

Ariadne snickered in a most unqueenly fashion, "It's me. I've had several dalliances over the years."

Now I was truly shocked. "Just to test the theory?"

Sad eyes hovered above lifeless lips. "Because I was lonely, but it served that purpose too, I suppose."

A dozen different thoughts ran through my head, but the first to reach my lips was, "And Leomund, does he…?"

She nodded, "Probably, not that it matters. We haven't been intimate in years, and when we were it was mostly just a functional duty. He manages his own needs while he's at his lodge."

I just sat there for a moment, dumbfounded, and—sad. My own experience with marriage was miles apart from hers. Penny and I weren't perfect, but we were partners, friends, and yes, in love, despite all the challenges of raising children and ruling over a small piece of the realm. Looking at Ariadne, I saw a mature, self-controlled, disciplined, and powerful monarch; but in my mind's eye I still saw the young girl who had chased us around Lancaster Castle. She had been a wild sprite back then, and somehow, I had always thought she would find more happiness in life.

"Ari…," I began, falling back on her old nickname, "I don't know what to say. I should have been there for you."

"Stop it, Mort." Her eyes were red. "This was supposed to be a happy reunion. Why are we talking about this?"

Because I felt guilty, that's why. "You're right," I said suddenly. "The past is already ruined, but tomorrow, that's another thing. Come stay with my family. You can sleep there anytime you like."

"What?"

"I'll make a portal for you," I explained. "You can be queen all day, and in the evening, if you want some noise, you can step through it and sleep in our guest bedroom. Penny would love it." In point of fact, Penny would probably take some convincing. She wasn't nearly as close to the Queen as I was—or had been. She might even be a little angry with me.

For some reason, while none of my previous remarks had caused her to lose her composure, that suggestion was too much. Tears overflowed the banks and began trickling silently down her cheeks. "I couldn't possibly—what about the guards?"

"Don't tell them," I said. "Or just tell Harold."

"Carwyn will know," she said, bringing up her dragon. "Will he fit through this portal?"

Only if I made it significantly larger than I had intended. Portals required a much greater investment of aythar, and the amount went up exponentially as the size of the portal increased, which was why I had had to use the God-Stone to power the World Road. I shook my head negatively, "No. He'll have to use the World Road or fly, which would also give away your subterfuge. Just explain it to him. It would only be in the evenings, and only when you wanted to get away. He'll understand."

Ariadne was looking around the room, as though she might find some logical reason in her surroundings to say no. "I don't know. I don't think your wife would like it. How could she relax with *me* in her home?"

Women. Why did they have to be so complicated, and perceptive? "She will be fine with it," I assured her. "Trust me."

She shook her head, "No. It's a bad idea."

"Too bad," I told her. "I don't give a damn."

Ariadne stood, straightening her back and looking down at me, "I am your queen. You have to do as I command."

She was more like an estranged younger sister to me, especially since I had counted Marcus as my brother, rather than a mere friend or cousin. "You're family, and I don't care what you *command*. I'll do as I please. If you don't like it, you can try to lock me up, but I wouldn't give you good odds on succeeding."

Without warning, I found myself being hugged. Ariadne squeezed me with surprising strength, burying her face against the leather of my jerkin. Carefully, I wrapped my arms around her and let her have her moment without saying a word. Being queen, she probably hadn't had the luxury of crying in front of another human being in almost a decade. I couldn't imagine the strain such a thing would impose on a person. Penny had always been there for me, and she had seen my tears on a multitude of occasions. So had the rest of my family, for that matter.

After a while she pushed me back and pretended her face wasn't red and her nose snotty. A queen was above admitting such things. "Fine. Have your way. For now, you'd better get home. It's already getting dark."

"Huh?" I had lost track of the time. A quick glance at the window informed me that dusk was well underway. *I promised I'd be home early today.*

Dammit. "You're right!"

She tapped me on the shoulder before I could make my exit. "Say hi to Marcus and Dorian for me."

That surprised me, "What do you mean?"

"When I see you, I think of them. It's as though they're still here. You three were so close, I like to think they're still alive, inside of you," she confessed. "It feels like, if I tell you something, maybe they can still hear it. Tell them I miss them."

I gave her a brave smile and nodded, but I was fighting back my own tears as I left.

CHAPTER 5

Using my handy stencil, I made another temporary circle and teleported back to the transfer house in Castle Cameron. I expected that I wouldn't have to answer any questions from Penny until I got home, but that was not the case.

As soon as I entered the main keep I knew something was wrong.

Not wrong in the usual sense. There was no mortal danger looming, but the castle was bustling with activity. It was always bustling at that time of day, mind you since everyone had to be fed, but there was an air of added excitement. Was there a feast planned?

Impossible, I thought. *The next feast isn't until...* "Oh shit." It had been niggling at me, just below conscious awareness since that morning when I had made note of my father's recent birthday, six days ago. He had been born six days before my mother. This was her eightieth year, and Penny had planned to honor her with...

"Mort!"

My beautiful wife stood before me, dressed in all the ostentatious finery that she normally eschewed. "Yes, my love?" I improvised. How she had found me so quickly amidst all the hustle and bustle of people coming and going, I had no idea. She had a certain skill in that regard.

Penny looked me up and down, obviously finding my attire wanting. "You said you'd be home early today. It's almost time!"

"Well, of course!" I agreed. "I didn't mean to cut it so close." I walked forward with purpose, as though to head straight to the great hall.

"Not so fast," she said, stopping me. "You need to change. You still have a few minutes. You don't want to celebrate your mother's special day looking like an executioner, do you?" *My clothes were good enough for the Queen,* I thought sullenly.

"Good point." I turned to head for the door to our apartments.

A smirk stole across her face. "You forgot, didn't you?"

I could only be grateful she was in a good humor. "Well..."

"Hurry up," was her only response.

I passed my children coming down the stairs. Moira gave me a disapproving glance, and Matthew merely made a sarcastic, "Tsk, tsk, tsk," as I passed them. Irene shook her head.

As they went out of sight I heard Conall exclaim, "Told you so," to his siblings. The brat.

Passing through the portal that led to our true home in the mountains, I found that someone (Penny) had thoughtfully laid my clothes out on the bed. It was a blue doublet with matching woolen leggings and a pair of artfully made short leather boots. Blue was my mother's favorite color. She doesn't miss a trick, not my Penny.

Dressing in short order, I returned the way I came. The halls were now mostly empty, except for a few servers. Everyone had gone in, and they were probably waiting for me to enter so they could be seated. Lady Rose waited at the door, my mother's hand on her arm.

"At last," said Rose, giving me a narrow stare.

"I hope I didn't make you wait," I apologized, directing my words to my mother.

She merely smiled, her blue eyes wrinkling with mirth. Rose was another matter, though.

"What have you done?" she declared, before turning me sideways to examine the laces on my doublet.

"Uh…"

Meredith Eldridge chuckled, looking up at me, "He'll never change."

With a sigh Rose began rapidly unlacing and re-lacing my doublet. I couldn't see any practical difference in her work, other than that it looked neat and a bit tidier than my own. "This is why you shouldn't try to dress yourself," advised Rose.

I couldn't help but admire the speed and dexterity in her fingers. Lady Rose Thornbear was a noblewoman through and through, raised in the science of politics, the art of etiquette, and the most proper skills of making lace and all manner of other things I knew nothing about. "I couldn't find my valet," I said, fabricating an excuse.

"Because you don't have one, you dreadful liar," remarked Rose without looking up from her work. "I keep telling you to get one."

"I meant Penny," I sighed. No one ever got my jokes.

"She's inside, keeping everyone occupied until your mother's grand entrance," Rose informed me. After a moment she added, "And yes, I knew who you meant. It wasn't funny." Finishing up, she leaned in and kissed me chastely on the cheek, while whispering, "You nitwit." Then she stepped back and turned me to face my mother, "Lady Eldridge, may I present to you, your son."

My mother had been enjoying the entire exchange quietly, but she just smiled, "Doesn't he look nice!"

I offered her my arm while Rose went in ahead of us. We had to wait a minute, so our entrance would be sufficiently separated, and as we waited, my mother turned to me, "Have I told you how proud I am of you?"

Too many times to count, I thought. "Mom, this is your day. Let's celebrate you for a change."

"You are my celebration," she replied. "Every day, I hear people talking about you. Every day I see what you've done. I never accomplished much in my life—except for you, and you've never let me down."

I smiled patiently. One thing I had been forced to learn, was how to take a compliment, and she had certainly given me plenty of practice at it. Stepping forward I pressed against the doors and we went in. The hall was full, packed with the entire castle staff, and apparently a goodly portion of the population of Washbrook.

Extending my arm, I stepped as far away as I dared while maintaining a grip on her hand. Her balance wasn't the best these days and I worried constantly about falls. Then I addressed the crowd, "May I present our lady of honor, Lady Meredith Eldridge!"

That was met with a loud cheer and a lot of raised cups. My mother attempted, and succeeded at, a short curtsey, with only a slight wobble. I led her, slowly and carefully, to her seat at the table, and once I was sure she was firmly in place, I took my own. Then everyone could relax and begin to enjoy their food.

This was not her first time in the great hall, of course. My mother had eaten there many times, she was well known, but as the years had passed, she had appeared less frequently. Preferring to dine in the peace and quiet of her own home. While Penny and I made it a rule to be present at least twice a week, she only came once a month at best, these days.

As it was her day, the musicians took their cues from her, and Meredith selected a number of rowdy tavern songs. She had lived most of her life as a commoner, and while she had grown to enjoy the more courtly music, she had retained her taste for bawdy ballads. Her choices seemed to please everyone there.

At some point, Penny leaned over to talk into my ear, "You did well with the lacing on your doublet—was it Rose?"

I gave her a haughty look, "I have gotten better."

"Definitely Rose then."

"Well, my valet wasn't there to help," I told her with a wink.

She pinched me under the table, gently. Her fingers were strong enough to bend steel, so she generally erred on the side of caution. As a result, I hardly felt her rebuke. "Someone had to organize all this, you do realize that?"

Leaning over, I kissed her cheek. "I am grateful for that, and for everything else you do. I couldn't manage a fraction of this on my own."

"You might," she returned, "if you weren't so busy healing strangers and pretending to be a tinker."

Meredith coughed, choking on her wine, which drew my eyes immediately. The wine was watered, as she couldn't take it full strength anymore, but she still had trouble swallowing these days. I studied her worriedly, as she cleared her throat and wiped her mouth with a hand towel. Whenever I looked at her she seemed more frail than the last time.

My mother waved a hand at me, to let me know not to worry, but I was watching her with more than my eyes. With my magesight I watched her heart beating, and beyond that I could see how dim her aythar had become. It waned steadily with the passing of the seasons, like a fire gradually burning down to ash. There was nothing I could do about it, which made me feel guilty for some reason.

It was yet another reason I spent so much time wandering in disguise. So many people had problems I *could* fix, it kept my mind off the ones that I was utterly helpless to solve.

As I watched her, my focus slipped, and the world blurred slightly. The voices were still there, they were always there, but once again I felt the chill touch of the void. It was in the hall with us, hovering inside everyone, but it was strongest in my mother. Her death was closer than ever.

Penny squeezed my hand, "Mort? Are you alright?"

Blinking, I nodded. "Sorry, I need to find the privies." Excusing myself I stood and left quickly. In truth, I did need to relieve myself. Harold's ale was still making itself known to my bladder, but mainly I needed a moment to clear my head.

A figure stood in the corridor, a man by the shape of it, but it lacked the aythar that defined a living being. I recognized it immediately. "What are you doing out here?" I asked.

"I avoid the hall during meals," said Gary, his head swiveling to meet my eyes. "Though I can blend in, I have no sense of taste. I feel…"

"Feel?"

He nodded. "Yes, I have feelings, or at least I think that's what they are. There's no way for us to compare our experience and be certain," he replied. "In any case, watching everyone eat makes me feel lonely. It's a vivid reminder of the difference that lies between me and everyone else."

The android's presence helped calm my nerves. Perhaps it was because he wasn't truly alive, and thus, he wasn't dying. Without vital aythar in him, there was also a complete lack of the void. His remark sparked my imagination, though. "You're all the more human for that," I told him.

"How so?"

"Everyone feels alone to some degree, at different times. Being in a crowd often makes it worse," I explained. "Do you miss Karen?" Karen was his daughter. Not his flesh and blood kin, of course, but the daughter of the man who had created him, the man whose memories he carried.

"I do," he admitted.

"Yet another human trait. We all miss our children when they are away," I observed.

The android smiled, "True. Shouldn't you be at the celebration?"

I shrugged, "I had to relieve myself."

"Another difference between us," said the machine.

My mood was already much improved. "At least you don't have to see this one."

***

Later, as Penny and I lay in bed, enjoying the pleasant quiet before sleep, she asked me a question. "What was wrong earlier, when you left the table?"

I dissembled, "I had some ale with Harold when I visited the palace today. Actually, I had too much. I was getting a headache, and had to relieve myself."

She was quiet for a minute, waiting for me to continue. When I didn't volunteer, she prodded me, "What *else* was wrong?"

"What makes you think…"

"Mort," she interrupted with a tone of disapproval.

I sighed. I knew better than to try and fool her. The damn woman knew me too well. "It was my mother. I can see her growing weaker by the day."

"See in the usual sense, or something more?"

"Both. Ever since my time as a shiggreth, I've had this extra sense," I explained.

"But *you* weren't the shiggreth," said Penny. "That was a twin of you. You only received his memories later, when you destroyed Mal'goroth. That's what you told me."

"That's true," I agreed, "but it isn't the whole truth. While Brexus thought he was me, I was still present. I thought it was me making the decisions and it wasn't until later that I figured out we were two separate beings. I still experienced it all, right there beside him."

Penny rolled over onto her side facing me, her head propped up on her arm. "So what is this sense like?"

"I've told you how being an archmage lets me hear things, voices, such as the earth, or the wind."

"Mm hmm. But you said it wasn't really like hearing."

"It isn't. It's just the closest thing I can come to describe it. Well, this is an extension of that. While I was inside the shiggreth, I developed an awareness of something else. I think of it as the 'void' or 'death' or perhaps 'entropy'. It's the force that lies alongside life, the opposite of creation. I guess it's part of the balance of the world, but I experience it as a sort of shadow. It hangs over everything. It's weakest in the young, but in the sick, or the aging, it becomes stronger," I explained.

"And you saw this around your mother?" she asked.

I nodded. "I see it around everyone. Not all the time, just when I relax my mind or when I use my abilities as an archmage without focusing properly."

"It upset you to see your mother dying," stated Penny.

Once again, I nodded, keeping my lips pressed firmly together.

"Do you see it around me?"

As soon as the question left her lips the void returned to my senses, and in the dim light of the candles I saw it hiding beneath the skin of her face, the slow rot of time, eating away at her vitality. Firmly closing my eyes, I struggled to close my mind, to blot out all my perceptions.

Her arms went around me. "You should have told me sooner. This has been bothering you for years now, hasn't it?"

"Nobody wants to hear that you are watching them die," I said, letting my breath out in a long exhalation. "Most of the time I can block it out or distract myself from it. The kids help, and all the hustle and bustle around here. It's just that every now and then, it gets the better of me." *That, and sometimes I dream about sucking the life out of people,* I thought. I couldn't say that part, though. That was too much. After the horrors Penny had endured at the hands of the shiggreth I didn't think she could handle thinking that I might still have that seed of evil within me.

She kissed my forehead. "You big idiot. You're supposed to tell me these things."

"There's not much anyone can do about it," I mumbled.

Penny squeezed me harder, "You really think that? Perhaps I should teach you a lesson."

I had a good idea what that might be. *Yes, please, teach me a lesson.* I kissed her neck, "I might be willing to learn."

She laughed and pushed me back, "Now you've given away your hand! Was all this to trick me into your wicked embrace?"

I shrugged and gave her my best boyish grin.

"Stupid never dies," she said, repeating my old motto back to me.

"But sometimes it gets lucky," I added. The look in her eyes told me that this was definitely going to be a good night. Then there came a gods-be-damned knocking on our door. *Sonofabitch!* I thought.

"Who is it?!" I asked in a loud voice, making no attempt to disguise my irritation. Since I kept a privacy ward around the bedroom my magesight couldn't tell me.

"Dad," said Matthew's voice through the door. "I have an idea."

"Tomorrow," I yelled.

There was a pause, and then he said, "But you're awake."

"Go away!"

I waited, but there was nothing further said. After a minute I got up and looked out the door to be sure he had gone. The hall was empty. Grumbling, I went back to bed. It took a while to recapture the mood, but I am a stubborn man. Eventually, I succeeded.

CHAPTER 6

Matthew found me again the following morning. He tended to sleep late, so it was a surprise when he showed up for breakfast.

"Dad," he said immediately.

"Ysh hmph?" I replied eloquently around a mouthful of sausage and eggs.

"I've been thinking about our problem."

Swallowing, I paused long enough to say something else, "Our problem?"

"With ANSIS," he clarified.

That was the last thing I wanted to think about, much less brain storm about. I was still groggy. "It's really early..."

"Try this," he said, handing me the mug he had in front of him.

I sniffed it. The aroma was earthy and dark, much like the color of the stygian brew within. It looked something like tea, if it had been concentrated until it was impossible to see through, but the smell was entirely different.

He saw my hesitation. "It isn't poison. I'm not ready to be count yet."

"Ha, if it was, I might drink it just to be done with the job," I grumbled. I took a sip and immediately grimaced at the hot bitter flavor. "Why would you drink this?"

"It's coffee," he told me. "It has a kick to it. It will wake you up."

I drank a little more, but the bitterness set my teeth on edge. "You like this?"

He grinned, "Karen liked it with milk and sugar, but I prefer it plain. I like the bite."

We didn't have plain sugar. It tended to run out quickly, but we did have honey. I added some and mixed in some milk. To my surprise the resulting flavor was rich and mellow. Properly doctored, I could see the drink's appeal. "You got this from the other world?" My son was able to traverse the planes, in fact, he was the only one able to do so.

Matthew nodded, "I don't have much left. I'm hoping I can locate the same plant here, otherwise I'll have to make another crossing."

That made me gulp, and consequently I choked. "Back to Karen's world? They almost killed you."

"Not to hers specifically, to another analog; someplace safer."

"I'm not sure how I feel about that," I mumbled, though with each sip I began to understand better why he might feel it necessary.

Moira walked in then, rubbing her eyes and looking generally disheveled. Seeing the two of us, she spoke to her brother first, "Did you tell him?"

I put the mug down. "Just what are you two plotting?"

"Relax Dad," said my daughter. "We're on your side."

"Side of what?"

"The war," Matthew informed me.

"Is there a war on?" I asked.

"Now you're just being obtuse," said Moira. "He means the war between us and ANSIS. We know you don't think it's over."

I closed my eyes. It was too early for this, and I could see the direction the conversation was heading. It would only end in trouble for me. Whatever they were planning would likely involve some danger, danger I was not inclined to involve them in. Danger that my wife would be even less inclined to involve them in. And no matter who won the argument, I would catch the blame for it. Force them to give it up and I'd have to worry about subversion or rebellion from my kids, allow them to do whatever it was, and I'd be on Penny's bad side.

"It isn't dangerous," added my daughter.

Was she reading my mind? Moira had developed some unfortunate talents during her trip to Dunbar. While fighting the first battle against our new foe she had explored her special gift for manipulating the minds of her fellow humans. As a result, she was now extremely dangerous, to herself, and to others. She could also, with some effort, get around the mental shields of other wizards. I gave her a suspicious glare.

"I wasn't reading your thoughts," she answered, as if to my unspoken fear. "You'd feel it if I tried to intrude, but your block does little to hide your moods and emotions. Our idea won't be dangerous, and it won't upset Mom."

With a sigh, I spoke, "What's this about?"

"We know you're trying to discover if there are any more of them lingering, so you can avoid another situation like the civil war in Dunbar," explained Matthew. "But wandering around the world hoping to catch a glimpse of them is a fool's game. You're just one man."

'Civil war' was what we called the fight with ANSIS in Dunbar. The ancient enemy of the She'Har was an artificially intelligent machine entity, one created by mankind on another world. It had come to our world and begun reproducing itself, and more problematic, it had started out by enslaving King Darogen of the neighboring nation of Dunbar. My daughter had responded by counter-enslaving part of the population, and the fight that resulted had been ugly and bloody.

She had won, at great cost to herself, and succeeded in rescuing me from my imprisonment. Then I had cleaned up what remained of the mess using lava to melt and fill in the hidden area beneath the city that ANSIS had been operating from.

Unfortunately, ANSIS was rather like a disease. It only took a small part of it to survive and start a new colony, or infection, or whatever one preferred to call it. If it had survived, it would be difficult to spot. So far as I knew, only a wizard could discern the difference between a normal person and one that had been forced to play host to one of the parasitic machines; hence my frequent traveling.

"I hope you aren't asking me to let the two of you start patrolling," I replied.

"That's one idea," said my son, "but it doesn't really solve the problem. Even if we all patrol, that's just a handful of people, you, me, Moira, the Prathions, Gareth Gaelyn, Karen—it's a small group—the world is too big."

Moira nodded, "But there are more options than just wizards. The dragons also have magesight."

I held up a hand, "Only a few dragons have been bonded, mainly to wizards. The only ones not bonded to wizards are your mother's and the Queen's. You aren't suggesting we ask Her Majesty to fly around looking for them?"

"No, that was just an example," answered Moira. "The point, is that any spellbeast has magesight, and with a sufficiently complex mind they can spot an ANSIS controlled human as well as we can."

This had actually occurred to me, but I hadn't been in a hurry to press forward with the idea. There were several limitations, but the main one was that we only had one Centyr mage who could produce such spellbeasts, Moira herself. She could only make so many complex spell-minds in a given day, and they required aythar to survive. Each would slowly fade over time, putting a hard limit on how many she could maintain.

Even so, several dozen such creatures would be much more effective than what I had been doing.

"You really want to tie up all your time doing this every day?" I asked her.

"Actually," put in Matthew, "she can do more than you might realize."

Arching one brow, I looked at him curiously. "You know something."

My daughter stood up, and before my eyes she split into two identical people. Both possessed her unique aythar, but while one had a body of flesh and blood, the other was composed entirely of magical energy. "Dad, I'd like you to meet Myra," said the one that was solid.

Remaining still, I worked through the facts in front of me. One of the forbidden techniques my daughter had used in Dunbar had been spell-twinning. It wasn't as inherently evil as possession and mind control, but it had a host of ethical and moral problems. A spell-twin was an easy way to produce a complex spell-mind, rather than creating something unique, the Centyr mage simply copies herself. The biggest problem is that both remain linked to the same aystrylin, the soul-seat, or wellspring of life. They draw on the same life, and eventually, unless they remain in perfect harmony, one takes control and destroys the other.

In Dunbar she had done this not once, but hundreds of times. She had told me that. Even worse, some of her spell-twins had seized control of the aystrylin in the host bodies they had possessed, effectively murdering and stealing the life of those they controlled. By doing that, they could remain alive indefinitely, but by some miracle all her twins had retained enough morality to return to their creator when the battle was over. Then they had fought within her, to decide which would survive.

Moira herself wasn't completely certain if she was the original, or simply the final survivor of her creations.

All of this, as well as a corruption of her personality, was the reason the shade of her original mother, born over a thousand years ago, had insisted she must die. I had vetoed that option. But the cold shock of what I was seeing now made me doubt my resolve for a moment. "What have you done?!"

"Dad," said Moira calmly. "It isn't what you think. Myra isn't new. She's been with me since Dunbar. We're friends. She helped me survive at the end. I just couldn't do away with her."

Softly, I spoke, "She's attached to you?" Briefly, I considered an extreme response. Forcibly removing the doppelganger while she was separated from my child and destroying it before she could respond.

Of course, my daughter read my intentions despite my calm outer demeanor. She raised a shield to protect herself and her twin. "That won't work," said Moira. "Let me explain."

"Myra isn't bad," said Matthew. "She's been with her for over a month now."

I glared at him, "You knew about this?"

He shrugged. "She's the one who healed me after I came back from Karen's world. Moira was worried she would be tempted to alter my mind. Myra is more like she used to be, before all the stuff she did in Halam."

"She can help us," insisted Moira. "The hardest part of producing spell-minds is mental. She can double what I can do."

Myra stepped forward. "Take down the shield," she told her twin.

Worried, Moira did as her spell-twin asked.

The spell-twin looked at me and said, "If you really think it would be best for me to disappear, I will do so—Dad." Her features were determined, but sad.

Matthew and Moira both immediately protested, but I was taken by what she had said. "Dad?" Ignoring them, I addressed Myra, "She created you, not me."

Myra shook her head, "I have no memory of that. From my perspective, I'm your daughter. I remember everything; the day you taught me to dance, the way you laugh, even bad things—like when we were both poisoned.

"I use the name 'Myra', because it saves confusion, because I *know* that in reality I'm only a recent addition to this world, but it still feels weird. You're the only father I'll ever know, and if you don't want me, then I don't want to exist anymore," she finished.

"What in the world?!"

Penny was standing in the doorway, Irene and Conall following behind her. Moira and Myra turned to face her at the same time, and almost in unison said, "Mom."

Looking at Matthew I rubbed at my temples. *It's way too early for this.* "Go tell Peter to cancel whatever is on my schedule for this morning. Then make me some more of this—what did you call it?"

"Coffee."

"That's it," I agreed. "More coffee."

The next two hours were mainly chaos and confusion. Probably Moira should have made her revelation to both of us at the same time, but apparently, she hadn't really intended to do so initially. Either way, a lot of explaining had to be done, and even though I had few minutes head start on the facts, I had not even come close to knowing how I felt about those facts.

Discovering one has a previously unsuspected daughter, who is also identical to the daughter you raised, is a disconcerting feeling. In truth, I was pretty sure they didn't even have a name for the feeling yet. That's how uncommon the experience is.

Penny took longer to understand the situation, but once she did, she seemed to resolve her feelings on the matter much quicker. Myra was her daughter too, and that was that. The two were embracing and crying while I was still staring at my feet, trying to decide what was the right thing to do.

Matthew spoke to me, his words coming at a steady pace, even as the rest of the family struggled with the news. "So, with two of them, we can produce a lot more spellbeasts to search for ANSIS. But I think we can do more. If we use a variation of the immortality enchantment on them they will last longer."

Numb, I reacted, "We already agreed we wouldn't use that enchantment anymore."

"Not the original one," insisted my son. "A variant of the one you made for the dragons. We can modify the conditions so that it has a time limit. That way they won't last long enough to develop problems, but Moira and Myra won't have to spend every minute of every day creating and maintaining them."

In the background I heard Irene crying as well, and then Conall made a joke. The others were laughing and crying simultaneously. There was also some hugging.

"If we use flying forms," continued Matthew, "they can cover a lot of area. You won't have to keep going out on pointless hunts. Instead, we can plan for what we'll do when we do find them."

I focused on my son's face, "Doesn't it bother you in the least, suddenly having two of her?"

He grinned, "It worried me at first, but the new one is nicer."

"Oh," I mumbled. Then I looked at my wife, some marital sixth sense warned me that she had come to a conclusion and was hoping to catch my eye. I could see a question on her face. She was waiting for an answer.

"We already have a dog," I responded. "How bad could an incorporeal daughter be?"

Penny smiled.

Standing up, I located Humphrey. He had been running around during the discussion, excited by whatever was going on, though he didn't understand it. I couldn't help but feel that despite my supposedly superior intellect, Humphrey and I were in the same boat. Gathering him up, I took him outside. We needed a walk.

CHAPTER 7

It was during my walk that I remembered that I hadn't told Penny anything about my conversation with the Queen. I wasn't entirely sure I wanted to bring it up now, but waiting would do no good. I had been married long enough to have learned that lesson, even if I didn't always heed it.

When I returned to the house I found my wife waiting for me. Everyone else had left to pursue their own day. Penny gave me a wry look as I came in, "Done hiding with Humphrey?"

I did my best to look shocked. "We needed some time to bond."

She looked down at Humphrey, who was wagging his little tail and gazing up at us with hopeful enthusiasm. "At least you have a good excuse now," she opined.

"Excuse for what?"

"For your quiet time. You always do that. Whenever you get overwhelmed you run off to think—always alone," she replied.

It was true, I couldn't argue that. "As opposed to you—you talk it out with everyone in the room. I don't know how you manage it. I can't think straight with everyone talking around me."

"And what great insight did you come up with while you were walking Humphrey?" she asked.

"The same one you already came to, before I even left," I said. "We have an extra daughter now."

"No getting around it," she agreed. "It's still weird, though."

I kissed her cheek. "That's what you get for marrying a wizard."

"I was tricked!" she complained with a twinkle in her eye.

"Bespelled and enchanted, my dear," I corrected, then my tone turned serious. "There's something else I need to talk to you about."

Penny put her hands on her hips, "Same here. I hope your news isn't serious. I don't think I can handle many more shocks today."

"Maybe you should go first," I suggested.

"What's yours about?" she asked.

I shrugged. "The Queen, how about you?"

"Lynaralla," she replied, "but I think Ariadne might be more important. You go first."

"I invited her to live with us," I blurted out.

Penelope Illeniel's eyes went wide. "What?!"

"Just some of the time," I clarified. "It's not as bad as it sounds."

She spluttered, "How? Why? Are you insane?"

"Most likely," I answered. Then I told her about my visit with the Queen of Lothion, describing Ariadne's isolation and depression, as well as my proposed solution. The look on her face told me that my wife had some serious reservations, though.

"How is this going to work?" she asked. "She'll just pop in whenever she feels like it? How will we ever be able to relax when the Queen of Lothion could just show up at any moment, day or night?"

"It's Ariadne," I told her. "She needs to get away from being the 'queen.' That's the point of it. She's family."

"*Your* family," said Penny pointedly.

"You grew up with her too," I mentioned.

Penny closed her eyes, "No, Mort, I didn't. I grew up with you, and sometimes when I was lucky, I played with Dorian and Marc too. Ariadne and I were never close. Her first memories of me are probably as one of the castle maids at Lancaster, and she terrified me back then."

"Terrified? That's hard to imagine," I said.

"You were never a servant."

I frowned. "I thought the Lancasters treated their staff well. You never mentioned anything bad happening."

She sighed. "They did, and no, nothing bad happened, but I was poor, and desperate. I wasn't a child anymore and I needed that income to support my father. I lived in constant fear of losing my position. I kept my distance from Ariadne back then because I was afraid she would remember my friendship with Marcus. I thought they would send me away if they knew."

"They wouldn't have done something like that," I protested.

Penny nodded. "I know that now, but I was young, and I was common."

"I was common too," I reminded her.

"You had parents who could support you. I didn't. And as it turns out, you were never common, even if you thought you were. The Lancasters always knew, your parents knew, and they treated you differently."

I didn't think that was particularly fair, but she had a point. I had never been in fear of missing a meal, or watching my father starve. Closing my mouth, I simply nodded.

Penny went on, "I still feel like a fraud as the Countess di' Cameron. Deep down I'm always thinking that one of these days someone will stand up and call me out as a fake."

"You're absolutely brilliant as Countess," I told her. "If you think you're acting, let me tell you, no one else does."

She smiled, then leaned down to pet Humphrey who had grown anxious as our conversation turned serious. Looking up she said, "Thank you. I try, but it isn't always easy. I was so grateful when you built us this house. Secreted away here, in our mountain home, with no eyes on us, I can relax. No matter how hard the day is, when we come back here, I can just be myself. But now—how can I do that with the Queen showing up whenever she feels like it?"

"I know this isn't what you want to hear, but think about Ariadne. She lost her parents, her brother, and she took the throne without anyone to support her. She wasn't raised a commoner, but she was still young, and alone. She's been alone all these years, and she's had nowhere to hide or relax. She wants the same thing you do. Can't we share a little of it with her?"

"Well, we have to now, don't we?" answered Penny. "You've already made the offer. I'll look like a monster if I turn her away."

I shrugged, "I could make up an excuse…"

"No," she said firmly. "I'll deal with it. I just wanted you to know how I feel, and maybe next time, you'll think before you do something like this."

Something in her voice told me she wasn't fine, but it was too late now. I figured I'd be paying for it down the line. The thought made me uncomfortable, so I leaned down as well. Petting Humphrey made us both feel better. Dogs don't judge. "Tell me about Lynaralla," I said after a moment. "I haven't seen her in a while. Isn't she supposed to be back soon?"

Lynaralla was our foster child. Technically, she wasn't human, she was the first Illeniel She'Har produced by Tyrion and Lyralliantha. Physically she appeared to be the same age as Matthew and Moira, which was unusual in and of itself. Normally the She'Har children emerged as fully adult-seeming humans, though with their characteristic pointed ears and the Illeniel's silver hair. Tyrion and Lyralliantha had decided to experiment, producing their firstborn as an apparent teenager, then sending her to us to experience an abbreviated childhood.

In every other way, she had been like most newly grown She'Har, with an analytical mind and a maturity only rivalled by her complete naivete when it came to the most basic aspects of the human heart. Over the past few years that had changed a little, which was perhaps why she had been sent to us. Two weeks ago, she had gone home to visit her 'parents.'

Tyrion and Lyralliantha were trees, or 'elders' as the She'Har called them. So calling them parents lost a lot in translation.

"She was," agreed Penny, "but we received a message yesterday. They have decided not to send her back to us. They want her to stay."

That made no sense to me. While Lynaralla was entirely adult in some ways, she was still a child in many others. I had grown attached to the strange girl, as though she were my own. I knew she wasn't ready for whatever they expected of her. She needed more time. "That's not right," I argued. "Did you tell them we don't think she's ready?"

Penny looked deflated. "What could I say? She isn't ours. She never was."

My wife was no helpless damsel, and the look of defeat on her face made me angry. Reaching out, I lifted her chin, forcing her to meet my eyes. "She's more ours than theirs," I said.

"You can't say that. She's their child."

"The She'Har don't have children," I told her. "Not really." I knew them in a way that Penny didn't. I had lived their memories, worse, I had lived Tyrion's memories. "And her father has never deserved the name. He was a cruel and brutal man. I don't know what he's like as a tree, but she would be much better off with us, at least until she's old enough to understand the world better."

"What would you do then?" asked my wife. The look in her eyes was one I cherished, it spoke of hope, it spoke of her belief in me. Clearly, she thought the situation was hopeless, but she believed in me anyway. How or when I had earned such faith from her, I didn't know, and I sincerely doubted I deserved it, but I would do anything to protect it. More than once in my life I had been saved from giving up on the tortured path I walked, merely because I couldn't bear to disappoint her.

Standing back up, I dusted off my knees and offered her my hand. Being stronger than an entire regiment of men, she didn't need my aid to rise, she could have leapt straight up from the ground and soared completely over my head as easily as some people could breathe. She took my hand anyway. "I'll go talk to Tyrion," I told her once she was on her feet.

"You think he'll listen?"

"I'll be persuasive," I answered.

Penny pursed her lips. "We can't afford to lose them as an ally."

I nodded. "I know."

"It's a long trip. There's no teleport circle there."

"I'll take the World Road to Turlington. I can fly from there. Five or six hours to get there and I can teleport myself back. I can probably be home in time for dinner if things go well," I reassured her.

She gave me a doubtful look. Apparently, her faith only went so far. I couldn't blame her, though. My first trip to the island had resulted in me being forced to fight a host of krytek, the She'Har equivalent of soldiers. It had ended with me threatening to turn the entire island into an active volcano before I was granted an audience with Tyrion, my ancestor and now the elder of the new She'Har. Our relations were considerably better these days.

I hoped.

"I'll come with you," said Penny.

"I fly faster when I'm alone," I argued.

"I'll come with you," she repeated, adding extra emphasis.

"There's no need…," I began, but she cut me off with a kiss.

When her lips withdrew she explained, "I want to make sure we keep them as allies."

I cocked one brow in disbelief. "Me?! I'm more worried about you! If they piss you off, how will I stop you from running around chopping down trees like some madwoman?"

She smiled. "If I did something like that, you can bet I would have a damn good reason."

I wanted to tell her no, but I couldn't do it. She had been through too much, when first I, and then our children had disappeared over the course of the past few months. As a result, she had developed a bit of separation anxiety. If going made her feel better, then who was I to tell her no? It wouldn't cost me anything more than some extra effort while flying.

"Fine," I replied. "We'll both go."

CHAPTER 8

We started out bright and early the next morning. By bright and early, I really mean stupidly miserable. Mornings are not my favorite thing.

It wasn't that I had anything specifically against mornings, per se, really it was the people inhabiting them that annoyed me. Contrary to my family's belief, I didn't actually despise morning, it was more that in the morning I tended to despise them—my family.

The main reason for this is that they insisted on talking, often to *me*, which is obviously unacceptable. Over the years I had often been required to rise early and function in the wee hours of the morning, and this was fine, so long as I was alone. Because of this, if I did have to do something at that time, I would often try to rise before everyone else and be gone and about my business before anyone else could wake up and attempt to communicate with me.

Today that wasn't an option. Penny and I would be traveling together. On days like this I adopted a different strategy. Rather than waking early and leaving silently, I tried to keep my head under the covers as long as possible, so as to avoid the eventual need to face other humans.

Penny wasn't having it, of course. She plied me with tea and her lively chipper personality, which only made me hate the world even more.

Long ago I had determined that I had a descending list of preference for my various family members in the morning. The one I found least offensive was my son, Matthew, mainly because he didn't talk much under the best of circumstances, and mornings were a time of silent truce between us. My other children were variously bothersome, but the nice thing about children is that since you have seniority you can ignore them without serious consequence.

My wife, definitely not, which made her my least favorite morning person. Not only could I not ignore her, but she was positively glowing with vitality and good cheer. For some reason I could never fathom, she actually enjoyed my company, even in the morning, which is how I had long ago determined that she was really a sadist. No matter how dour I was in the early hours, it merely gave her a better target to torment.

"How's the tea?" she cruelly asked, her smile brighter than the sun.

"Fine."

"It's new," she informed me. "You can really tell the difference in the flavor. Old tea loses something. That's why I try to get it in small lots and replace it frequently."

"Mm hmm." I hoped she would have mercy and stop there, or that she might have run out of things to say. I was wrong.

"Of course," she continued, "At certain times of year you can't get it at all, so I have to order enough to last us. That's why it isn't as good in late winter or early spring."

It went on for an interminable amount of time, until I could no longer stand it. Swallowing the last of my tea in one gulp, I sat up and surprised her by pulling her to her feet and kissing her. It was the only way to silence her.

She pushed away after a second. "Trying to shut me up, eh?"

I didn't answer, choosing instead to look innocently into the air above and behind her.

With a sigh she went on, "You need to get dressed. What are you going to wear?"

Contentiously I responded, "What are *you* going to wear?"

She hooked a thumb toward the armor rack on the other side of the room. It wasn't really a rack. It had a human-like shape with a head and shoulders to allow her enchanted mail to drape naturally over it. I wasn't sure why she used it, it was as though she thought chain could wrinkle. Since it was enchanted it wouldn't even rust, much less wrinkle. Mine was stored in one of my magical pouches, in a neat pile at the bottom. Even folding it seemed pointless.

"You're planning to wear armor on a diplomatic mission?" I needled.

She scowled at me, "The She'Har don't have any of our human traditions regarding clothing. It won't matter to them. I'd rather be ready in case this does turn out to be dangerous. What are you wearing?"

I gestured at my night shirt and bare legs. "I thought I'd pair this with boots and a bad personality. They match." Actually, I had planned on wearing a simple grey tunic, my Cameron surcoat, and a pair of neat woolen hose, easy, comfortable, and almost stylish.

She winked at me, "You're planning to wear that on a diplomatic mission?"

"The She'Har don't have any of our human traditions regarding clothing. It won't matter to them. I'd rather be comfortable," I replied, giving her answer back to her.

"And if it's dangerous?" she asked.

I grinned, "I have the indomitable Penelope Illeniel, warrior-countess and wrangler of wizardly children to protect my noble person. What danger could threaten me?" Dammit, her general good mood was infectious.

Having had my mood forcibly improved, we moved on to a quick breakfast and then we were out of the house. We took my private teleportation circle to the World-Road and from there we walked to the Turlington gate. Once there, the fun part of the journey began.

Penny looked hesitant as I stretched out my hand toward her. She took it, but the look in her eyes told me she was having second thoughts.

"What's wrong?" I asked.

"Are you sure it's safe?"

Well, no actually, flying was never completely safe, and my sort of flying was the most dangerous type. That was the main reason I was the only living wizard to fly that way. No one else had had the balls to try it, and I definitely wouldn't consider teaching even my own children to fly this way.

There was an opposing side to that coin, however. I was a master of the art. There were no other wizards to compare myself to, true, but I knew my skill. "This isn't the first time you've flown with me, remember?" I answered, diverting her question with one of my own.

"There was so much going on at the time...," she began. "And so much danger, the flying was the least of our worries then. We haven't done it in years."

Correction, *she* hadn't. I had flown many times. "You've flown on your dragon quite a few times," I observed.

"That's different," she replied. "I'm not really comfortable with that either, but at least there's a lot of dragon underneath me."

"But we're already flying, didn't you notice?"

Jerking her eyes downward, she saw that we were already a couple of feet off the ground. I was actually lying. We weren't flying at all. I had merely created a flat plane of force beneath our feet and gently lifted the two of us. We were simply standing on a raised platform, but the idea was to get her feet wet, mentally speaking.

"Oh!" she shouted. "What happened?" She took my hand immediately, and I was more than happy to pull her into an embrace as she clung to me for safety.

I expanded my shield to enclose both of us and shaped it broadly beneath, us so that it would be easy for the wind to lift us. *Now* we were flying. We rose slowly through the air, and Penny's arms gripped me with a strength that came close to breaking my ribs. I had removed my personal shield, as I always did when we were close together.

Note to self, don't scare her too badly, or she might break me in two accidentally, I thought.

I kept the shield above us open, so we could experience the rush of wind as I slowly increased our speed. "You're alright," I told Penny. "I've got you. Even if you let go of me, you wouldn't fall." Her head was buried against my chest.

"There's no chance of that!" she cried into my tunic.

Honestly, I was surprised at her anxiety. I had to remind myself that in some ways, there were two different Pennys. One was the warrior who had fought with me over the years, facing dangers and monsters beyond belief, and the other was the perfectly normal girl I had originally known and fallen in love with. My wife could do almost anything if it was necessary, if her family were in danger, whether it was me or our children. She would leap into the jaws of a lion if she thought she had to, to protect one of us.

Because of that strength, she had done many remarkably brave things over the years. Not because she wanted to, and not because she had no fear, but rather because she was too strong to let her fear get in the way of standing up for her family. While it had all been happening, she had been so fierce that it was easy to think she hadn't been afraid.

The truth was, she had been terrified through most of it.

Today we were flying, but it wasn't to escape an enemy or save a child. It was just more convenient. That meant that bravery and necessity didn't really enter the equation, and as a result she was letting her perfectly normal fear have its way with her mind.

None of that was what I wanted. I wanted to share my joy with her. So I took it slow and kept our flight gentle and smooth, giving her time to adjust. After we had been flying for ten minutes or so I made a suggestion, "It's alright to look around. You won't fall."

It took a while, but eventually she pulled her face back, keeping her eyes on my face.

"See, it isn't so bad, is it?" I asked.

Her expression was so serious it almost made me laugh, but I suppressed the urge since I knew it wouldn't help. "This is entirely different than flying on a dragon," she argued. "There's nothing under us." As she said the words her eyes darted downward and then came back to mine in a rush.

"The wind is under us," I returned. "Hold onto me and look forward, to the horizon. We're picking up speed, so I'm closing the shield." As our velocity increased keeping the shield open was impractical, not only did the wind blast us so hard it was difficult to breathe, but it really screwed up the aerodynamics.

Penny bravely did as I asked, taking some small comfort in the feeling of weight on her feet that the acceleration brought. My shield was formed around us in tight spear-like shape, broader in the middle than at either end. Since we didn't want to take all day getting there, and possibly because I wanted to show off, I pressed us to ever higher speeds. We cut through the air like an arrow while the wind screamed by just beyond the shield. The ocean was just beginning to pass beneath us, glittering in the sun as we left the coast behind.

One thing about fear, intense fear anyway, is that it can't last. The body simply can't sustain the adrenaline required for true panic for long periods of time. Abstract, or emotional terrors, are different, but the heart in your throat, fight or flight kind of fear, has a limit. Eventually the adrenal gland become exhausted and it fades.

My wife slowly adjusted, her breathing returning to normal and her mind relaxing as it became steadily apparent we weren't about to die, at least not just yet. After a quarter of an hour she showed signs of enjoying it even.

I watched her through it all. This was nothing new for me, so it was more interesting to watch her reactions. Eventually her eyes returned to mine. "Shouldn't you be watching where we're going?"

"You're prettier than the scenery," I observed.

"Only you," she remarked, "only you would say something like that while zooming around at—how fast are we going?"

I shrugged. "I have no idea. If I had to guess, I'd say fast, maybe even very fast, but still less than the speed of sound."

We had discussed the concept before, so she didn't have to ask what I meant by that. Instead she just gulped. "We aren't going to go that fast, are we?"

I gave her my best thoughtful look, "It would be difficult. I can manage it when I'm by myself, but with two of us—I'm not sure. Do you want me to try?"

Her arms tightened painfully around my waist again. "No. This is fine."

The hours passed in mostly silent reverie. I always enjoyed flying, but doing it with Penny added a new dimension of pleasure for me. It was more fun watching her experience it than I would have had on my own. Eventually the island appeared on the horizon, and sooner than I might have wished we were over the shoreline.

I slowed us gently and brought us down in a drifting spiral, like two autumn leaves that refused to be separated. When our feet finally touched the sand, Penny kissed me unexpectedly.

"Thank you," she said.

I smiled. "That should be my line."

The island had no name, or at least none that I knew of. I figured that if anyone should name it, it should be the new inhabitants, the reborn Illeniel She'Har. Given their strange culture, they probably hadn't seen the need yet. If they called it anything, it was probably just 'The Illeniel Grove' to them. Maybe I would make the suggestion to them, if things went well.

The beach was narrow, a thin strip of sand that separated the ocean from the rocks that rose rapidly from it. In most places the island shore was bounded by cliffs, which was why I chose this area to land. Here the ground rose at an almost gentle rate, and shortly beyond the first rocks the trees began.

They were normal trees, palms at first, giving way to pine and cypress as one went further inland. Probably many of them would be replaced by the She'Har eventually, but that would be sometime in the future. For now, I was pretty sure there were still only two actual She'Har elders on the island, my ancestor Tyrion, and his mate, Lyralliantha.

We had only gone a hundred yards inland, before I sensed the presence of a welcoming party, or perhaps a better term would be 'guards.' It depended on your perspective. They were scattered through the forest around us, and they weren't humanoids, as would be expected of the She'Har 'children'. No, these bore a wide variety of inhuman shapes, for they were krytek, the short-lived soldiers of the She'Har.

Penny stopped moving when she felt my hand on her shoulder, then she tensed. Doubtless her extraordinary hearing had alerted her to the approaching forms. Technically these were our friends, but it's hard to stay relaxed when a spider-like monstrosity the size of a warhorse steps out of the woods. Its friends weren't quite as frightening, but the collection of strange looking beasts covered in spikes, claws, and sporting long fangs wasn't reassuring.

And these were probably the least dangerous of the krytek.

The ones that bothered me, or rather 'would' have bothered me, if we weren't allies, were the ones created with magical abilities. Most of those were much smaller and less fearsome in appearance. There were only one or two of those sort in attendance, which told me this was more of a welcoming party than an attempt to intimidate. At least from the She'Har perspective.

For Penny, who had no way of knowing whether they had significant magical abilities or not, these looked pretty damn threatening.

A small man-cat walking on two legs stepped forward to address us. He looked cute and stood only three-foot-high, but he was one of the dangerous ones. Appearances were always deceiving when it came to the She'Har, but at least he put Penny at ease. The look on her face was screaming 'cute' to me, and I guessed she was probably imagining giving the thing a cuddle.

"You were not expected," said the diminutive krytek in Erollith, a language I understood, though it was foreign to Penny.

"We have come on a diplomatic visit," I answered in the same language, "and to check on the well-being of our ward, Lynaralla." My pronunciation was terrible, but he understood me.

The krytek twisted its head to the side in a remarkably dog-like expression of curiosity, "She is of the Illeniel Grove. Her health is not your concern."

Good thing Penny didn't understand him. His words would have irritated her and triggered a classic 'momma-bear' reaction. To be frank, they annoyed me as well, but I had a much more intimate knowledge of how the She'Har operated, and I knew on a rational level that the creature was just responding according to its best understanding, not with any intent to insult or offend.

Taking a deep breath, I spoke again, "Nonetheless, we are here. May we enter the Grove?"

The krytek nodded. "Of course. The elders have already been informed of your presence. Lyralliantha has given orders to escort you to them."

'Enter the grove' was probably an overstatement, since it consisted of only two She'Har elders, but the phrase was built into the language from long tradition. The small catlike manling led us through the trees and up a slight incline as we went farther inland. As we went I noticed the krytek was leading us in a north-western direction, rather than the more northerly course that would have led us to where the elder trees were.

"Where are we going?" I asked my guide. "This is not the way to the elders."

"You will see," he answered.

Nothing sinister about that, I thought. Sometimes I use sarcasm with myself. Call me weird, but it keeps me sane.

"What's wrong?" Penny asked, sensing something from the tone of our exchange.

Since I was fairly certain the krytek were just as well versed in our language as their own, I kept my reply neutral. "I'm not sure," I told her. "He's taking us somewhere other than where the elder trees are."

"Why?"

I started to tell her I had no idea, but just then I felt a surge of aythar in the distance. It was ahead, in the direction we were heading. It was followed by several more flashes. Someone, or possibly several someones were using power, and they weren't being subtle about it. Then I heard a grunt and a sound that could only be someone crying out in pain. A woman's voice.

Penny stopped, "What was that?"

"Tyrion," said our guide. "He is ahead."

I looked at my wife, and then she said, "That was Lynaralla. Something's wrong."

Before I could reply, she took off—like an arrow she darted ahead—her legs driving her at a speed I couldn't hope to match. Running after her, we left the guide behind, and seconds later, Penny left me behind. We weren't too far from whatever the commotion was, so I resisted the urge to fly. It would allow me to catch up, but it would also cost me the element of surprise if something really was going on. Every mage in the area would sense my use of aythar.

As I ran I heard a man's voice, "You stop when I say you can stop." It was followed by a loud thump and another cry of pain. "You still have strength in you. You fight until you are dead or dying. Nothing else matters."

"Father, please…" Even I could recognize Lynaralla's voice at this range.

"Get up, or I'll kill you myself," came the man's stern command.

"Leave her be!" That was Penny. Her warning was followed by the man's laughter.

Dammit. The trees opened up before me and I could see a wide clearing, more than a hundred yards across. Lynaralla was on her knees, her head bowed and her posture one of dejection. A man stood in front of her, looking in my direction, but not at me. He stared at my wife, who was running toward him.

She had a good lead on me, fifty yards or more, and she looked furious, or I assumed she did. I couldn't see her face from behind, but I knew my wife. She hadn't drawn her sword, *yet.* Perhaps she wasn't ready to abandon diplomacy.

Then the man reached out and grabbed Lynaralla's hair, pulling her to her feet. "We have guests," he intoned mockingly.

Penny's sword flicked out, leaving her sheath so quickly it seemed like silver light in her hand.

The dark-haired man was lean, muscular, and naked from head to toe. He smiled as Penny bore down on him. That was when I recognized him. His face was in my memories, scattered moments when he had looked into still water, or rarer still, when he had been in front of an actual mirror. It was Tyrion.

"Penny! No!" I shouted, but it was too late. Releasing Lynaralla, Tyrion activated his tattoos and met Penny's descending blade with his forearm. A shower of sparks resulted, but neither her blade, nor his arm was damaged.

Strangely, in that frozen moment, it was Lynaralla's expression that stood out in my mind. She looked up, with a look of recognition, horror, and shame as she saw Penny coming to her aid. Her cheek was red and swollen, and blood ran from her lower lip.

My own heart was pounding, but my anger at the sight of the girl's face wiped away any fear or doubts I might have had. The man was an animal. He deserved whatever he got.

I didn't let my outrage overbalance me, though. This wasn't my first time in the fire. Lynaralla needed to be protected first, and I couldn't deal with Tyrion directly until my wife was away from him. With no better choices I decided to leave him to her for the moment while I lent aid to our semi-adopted child.

Penny's movements were a blur, and Tyrion retreated slowly from her advance, blocking some strikes with his arms and dancing back to dodge others. He laughed the entire time, delight written in his eyes. He moved without hesitation, using his power to augment his speed, but still he was not quick enough to avoid her sword entirely.

The ancient archmage wasn't using his enchanted shield tattoos, those would probably have stopped her attacks cold, instead he defended only with his armblades, and when her sword got through, blood ran from the shallow cuts it delivered. Nor did he attack her directly with his power, which would have cut the fight short.

No, he was enjoying this.

"Head toward the beach," I told the girl. "You don't need to see this."

"I cannot," said Lynaralla. "He wants me here—to learn."

My heart clenched. I had an excellent idea what sort of lessons the brutal bastard wanted to teach her. Two thousand years hadn't changed him. He still believed in training his children with trials of pain and suffering. He planned to abuse her until she was just as cruel and hard-hearted as he was.

"At least move back," I said. "Off the field. I don't want you hurt if this escalates."

She nodded and moved in the direction we had come from.

Returning my focus to the fight, I saw that it had shifted. Bleeding from a half-dozen small cuts, Tyrion was no longer retreating. His movements were faster, surer now, and he was pushing Penny back. The look of anger on her face was slowly dying, replaced with desperation as she worked harder to keep his armblades from reaching her.

There was blood running down her cheek.

"Enough!" I shouted, drawing in my will and preparing to attack.

Tyrion reached out, wrapping my wife in a fist of pure aythar, trapping her arms, and lifting her feet from the ground. He was also careful to keep her body between us, though it was her eyes that held his gaze. "You heard your master, enough," he ordered her, smiling as he said it.

"Put her down," I said, a warning in my voice.

Instead, he walked past her, directly toward me. He still hadn't bothered to shield himself. "You come here, to *my* land, and think to give me orders? You attack me, insult me, and now you think you can tell me what to do?" His voice never rose, but the madness in his eyes sent chills down my spine.

Still, I hadn't survived as long as I had by backing down every time I met a megalomaniacal lunatic invested with power. "I came, to talk. I never expected to find you abusing children. Do you expect me to ignore that?"

Tyrion examined me from head to foot before he responded, "You have some spine, grandson, more than I believed. Perhaps it wasn't such a waste of time sending her to you for a while. Even so, she is my property. I will do with her as I will."

"Perhaps you haven't heard the news," I told him, "in this age, children are no longer property. The law protects them much the same as it does everyone else."

He laughed, long and hard. "The only law here, *is mine.* This is not Lothion, or any of the other young nations. This is my island, and I am sovereign here. I will do as I please, with her, with your wife, or even with you. Do you think you can contest my power?"

My blood was pounding in my ears, and I felt both rage and fear. Tyrion didn't sound any different than the gods I had faced in the past, and that meant trouble. He had Penny in his grasp, and I already knew his strength was at least equal to my own. Worse, I could sense a host of presences around us, hidden in the trees around the clearing. Krytek.

We were surrounded. Outnumbered and vulnerable, there would be no winning this confrontation. The only question was how much I was willing to lose.

But I had faced this sort of madness before. It had been in the eyes of Karenth the Just, in the face of Doron the Iron God. I had seen it in the casual indifference of Millicenth, the Lady of the Dawn, and in the cruel smirk of Mal'Goroth's lips. There was no reasoning with such evil. There was only strength and weakness.

"Release her," I began, my tongue thick with anger, "or we will find out. Disadvantage or no, I will do my best to rip this island apart if you hurt me or mine."

Something approaching mirth shone in his lunatic eyes. "Well said." Relaxing his will, Penny dropped to the ground behind him, gasping and rubbing at her arms to restore the circulation. "But I still sense weakness in you, grandson. What did you come here for?"

"Lynaralla," I answered. "We want her back."

CHAPTER 9

Tyrion's eyes widened.

"She's still young," I added. "She hasn't learned enough yet. She should have more time. She's only just beginning to learn what it means to be human."

"I brought her back because I doubted she would learn much from you," returned Tyrion. "I don't want her to grow up soft. When I said I wanted her to learn about humanity, I didn't intend for you to treat her like a doll. She must learn to fight."

"Is that what you thought you were doing just now?" I asked him, venom in my voice.

He glared back at me, "That's exactly what I was doing, but she needs more. Battle is only part of it. Humans lie, humans steal, they are full of duplicity. The She'Har do not understand this at all. *That's* what I expected her to learn with you. Instead she came back talking about family, relationships, and love. Her time with you was worse than useless. That's why I was forced to assume this human form once more." He waved his hands at his naked body as if to illustrate the point.

"You wanted me to teach her treachery and hate," I mumbled, somewhat stunned.

"This is a new world, one ruled by men. If my new children are to survive, they must learn how to navigate it," stated the ancient archmage.

"She won't learn that here," I told him. "Beating her senseless will teach her nothing. If you truly want her to learn these things, then she must learn love first. Don't you remember how you first learned? True suffering only comes from love. If you give her nothing, she will never have anything to lose, or anything to fight for."

Tyrion turned away, staring at his daughter who was now talking with Penny at the edge of the clearing. When he looked back at me he had an evil gleam in his eye. "Very well. If you think love is the answer, show me. Fight for her."

That set me back on my heels. *What?* Just to be sure I had heard him right, I asked, "What do you mean?"

He flashed pearly canines at me, "Exactly what I said. Fight me—for her. You think you're some sort of father to her. Show me what your love can do. If you're as weak as I think, I will keep her here. If you win, I'll let you have her, for—say five years? What do you think? Is that fair enough for you? Or are you too scared to risk it?"

My mind felt blank as I stared back at him, and then I heard my own voice responding, "Until she's ready to return, not five years." *Why did I say that?! I don't want to fight him.* I had often thought my mouth had a different agenda than my mind, and now I was sure it was trying to get me killed.

"That could be a long time," Tyrion said, rubbing his chin thoughtfully. "I'll need more than that if you want to change my offer. Then his eyes lit on Penny. Maybe a night with your woman?"

"What?!" I stared at him in horror.

"This body has passions I had forgotten about," said my ancestor. "There are no women here. Are you worried about losing?"

I shook my head, "I would never agree to something like that."

"Fine," he responded. "You don't have to agree. But after I beat you into a senseless pulp, I'll take what I want anyway." Then he leered at Penny.

"No." I started to turn away.

"You have no choice, boy," said Tyrion menacingly. "Try to leave, and I'll kill you. Your only option is to fight me."

"We're supposed to be allies," I protested.

"That ended the moment your woman marked me with her blade," said Tyrion. "The taste of blood has awakened my old passions." As he said the words his fingers brought some of the blood from his chest to his lips.

Angry and scared simultaneously, I spat on the ground, "You're sick. I'm not agreeing to this."

Tyrion looked more excited than ever. "Don't worry. I won't kill you, even if you lose. You can have what's left of her after I'm done."

The world was vibrating around me. My skin felt as though it was about to catch fire. A voice in the back of my mind was whispering to me, *kill him. Quickly, before he is ready.*

"We'll need some rules, I suppose," continued Tyrion, talking aloud. "No metamagic, and no fire. Let's stick to simple force attacks."

"Metamagic?"

"That's what I call our special ability. The thing that makes us archmages, a magic that rewrites reality, that can change magic itself—metamagic," explained my ancestor.

For a primitive savage I had to admit he had come up with a sensible term for the power that archmages wield. That worried me almost as much as the primal animalistic nature that Tyrion so perfectly exhibited. Despite all appearances, the man wasn't just a beast, he was also fiendishly clever. Could I beat him? We were evenly matched in power, but somehow, I had always assumed I was smarter. Now I doubted that assumption.

"I'm not playing this game," I told him.

"Try to walk away from here, and you will face not just me, but the krytek as well." He moved closer, until we were almost nose to nose, and I could smell the sweat and dirt from his previous exertions. "You don't want that fight. Even the man who bested the gods couldn't win against those odds. This is your only chance. Show me your spirit, godslayer. Fight me."

Kill him now! The voice in my head was insistent. *He's unshielded, only inches away. Drive a force-lance through his heart before he can react, and this will be over.* That would be the smart move, but I was angry. I wanted to beat this animal at his own game. My power shifted subtly as I mentally prepared to fight.

Tyrion's aythar flared around him and he took a step back. "That's it. I can see it in your eyes!"

Could he read me so easily? I pushed my doubts aside and asked him a question, "What about enchantments?"

Tyrion glanced down at his arms, at the tattoos that covered them along with the rest of his skin. "I guess that wouldn't be fair, would it?" he replied.

"For you," I shot back, tapping the pouch at my waist. "I have enough surprises in here to more than make up for whatever advantage you think that ugly scribbling all over your body gives you."

"Very well," he said, nodding. "No enchantments. We will use only what we can conjure in the moment, and no fire."

"Mort..."

That was Penny. Calling to me with fear written on her face. "It will be alright," I told her.

"Father, please! Don't do this." That came from Lynaralla, showing more emotion on her face in that moment than I think I had ever seen her exhibit. She looked positively torn.

Were those tears in her eyes? I was fairly certain I had never seen the She'Har girl cry before. Perhaps her time with us hadn't been a waste. Penny met my eyes, and for a second I could read her thoughts. Not through magic, but simply because we knew each other so well. There was confidence in her, and she was telling me it would be alright. No matter what happened, we would manage.

She took Lynaralla by the arm and led the girl away, her maternal instinct having taken the lead once more. "Don't cry. Mort will be alright. He's never let us down."

The silver haired girl looked up at her with swollen eyes, "It's already too late. I've seen it."

I didn't hear her reply to my wife. My focus was firmly on the man in front of me. "How do we decide the winner?"

"The first one who can't fight or begs to surrender loses," he answered, his voice low and throaty. Then he glanced around, studying the edge of the clearing. "Or the first to leave the battlefield. The tree line can serve as our boundary."

"When do we start?"

Tyrion grinned, "Whenever you want."

He hadn't shielded himself yet, which struck me as odd. *Is he that confident, or is it part of some strategy?* I stared at him silently. As opponents went he was unlike anyone, or *anything* I had ever fought before. Most of the mages I knew were significantly weaker, other than my own children. Worse, most of my battles had been against foes who weren't human at all, who had outclassed me in terms of power by several orders of magnitude. In those fights I had only won through either trickery, preparation, or the use of what Tyrion had named 'metamagic'.

The man in front of me was blazing with aythar, like some strange star shining with hatred and malice. I had seen worse, he wasn't one of the gods after all, but in this case my options were limited. *Just force, eh? Very well, how about this?* I sent a small probing strike toward him to see how he intended to react.

Tyrion didn't move, and my force lance tore a small hole through the skin in his side. I hadn't been aiming to kill, and I was surprised he hadn't at least attempted to shield himself or avoid the blow. Blood trickled from the wound.

"Aren't you going to defend yourself?" I asked.

He sneered, "When you decide to start attacking. I'm running out of patience. You remind me of Gabriel. Do you want to die?"

The mention of the name surprised me. Gabriel had been one of his sons, two thousand years ago, one of the first to die. Gabriel's death had come at the hands of his sister, when he refused to fight her. He was the only one of Tyrion's children to die without ever compromising his principles. He had died for his kindness, refusing to accept the cruelty the world had tried to force upon him.

"I would rather be compared to him than you," I said finally.

"Except you aren't like him, not really," continued Tyrion. "You've done things, evil things that he would never have managed. How do you live with the contradiction?" He began walking toward me.

I didn't want him getting too close. I knew that for certain. At a distance I could deal with him, up close—I wasn't sure. I attacked again, this time sending a sledgehammer of force at his midsection. He had to defend himself from this one, otherwise he'd find himself flat on his back with a chest full of shattered ribs.

One hand rose, flicking my attack away, deflecting it to one side. It almost looked as though he did it barehanded, but I detected his use of aythar. For the barest of seconds, he had shielded his hand and used his aythar like a buckler to turn my attack aside. "Better," he announced, then he stepped into me and punched into my shield with his fist.

The attack came so quickly and from so close I couldn't avoid it. It struck my shield and sent me flying backward. Tumbling, I reached out to the air and steadied myself, landing gracefully ten feet away. My head was pounding, he had almost cracked my shield.

A broken shield would mean feedback, and that would be a definite defeat. Tyrion's refusal to protect himself was starting to make sense. Against a weaker opponent a shield meant safety, and against the gods they had been necessary just to keep my ability to move. In this situation, it was a weakness.

Dammit, I know how he thinks, how he fights. I lived his memories! And yet the knowledge didn't seem to help. Tyrion was a killer, through and through. There was no room for anything else in him. But what was I? *A father, a husband, a protector of the weak.* I had never fought by choice, only when it was forced on me.

Two more attacks came at me, one high and one low. Pulling at the air, I slipped to one side and returned the favor, sending a powerful blow back at him. Somehow it caught him off-guard, and I had put almost everything into it that I could. Unable to dodge, Tyrion crossed his arms and channeled his aythar to stop the attack. It smashed into him and sent him twenty feet backward. The man attempted to roll with it, but he wound up sprawled in the dirt.

Had I done it? It couldn't be that easy.

I started to approach him, but he sprang up from the ground almost too quickly for my eyes to follow. He was channeling his power through his muscles, lending himself enhanced strength and speed, the same trick he had used to match Penny's power earlier. Moving like a jungle cat infused with lightning, he darted to one side and then leapt toward me, his fists tucked in close to his body, ready to strike.

Theoretically what he was doing was something any mage was capable of, but in practice it was not so simple. People like Cyhan, Dorian, or my wife, spent days to weeks learning to cope with their enhanced strength. It was entirely possible to kill or damage oneself if the power wasn't managed properly. As a wizard I had never felt the need to do such a thing, other than to boost my endurance or stamina on occasion. If something needed to be lifted, I used my power directly. If speed was required, I flew. If something needed to be destroyed it was far easier to do it at a distance.

Obviously, Tyrion had different opinions on the matter.

But then, I also had talents that no sane mage would consider learning. Touching the air again, I lifted myself and spun over his head, dropping some twenty feet behind him before he managed to turn himself around. Unleashing a wide scythe-like wave of force at his midsection, I struck again, hard.

Snarling like an animal, he blocked the attack, but I could tell it had cost him. Even so, he looked at me with wild eyes.

He's enjoying this, I realized.

Tyrion raced toward me, attacking as he came, and the world began to blur as I responded in kind, meeting each lance of power as it came. At a distance I could match him, attacking and defending in turn, all at a speed I had never considered before. Conscious thought wasn't possible any longer, I gave myself over to the more primitive side of my brain. Whenever Tyrion closed, I took to the air, deftly avoiding him and putting more distance between us.

I felt his power reach out, stirring the air and tearing at the soil. He was attempting to create a whirlwind, to fill the air with a confusing blend of roaring wind and painful grit. I countered his attempt, stopping him cold while continuing my onslaught. Obscuring the field would only play to his attempts to get close and finish me off. At range I was more than his match. His body was fast, but it couldn't compare with my mobility when I took to the air.

For an observer without magesight our battle was largely invisible. From Penny's perspective we probably appeared to be motionless much of the time, even as we exchanged rapid-fire attacks and counterattacks, punctuated by occasional movement as we shifted locations, constantly seeking an advantage.

The ground vanished as my opponent tried to surprise me by ripping the ground apart beneath me, but I didn't fall. Hovering, I seized the earth as it came free and redirected the loose chunks of dirt and rock. His surprise became my assault as a half-ton of sand and gravel tore through the air at him. Leaping to the side, Tyrion avoided the barrage, only to land in another pit I created even as he had started to move.

Tyrion shot skyward, launching himself on powerful legs the moment his feet touched the bottom—only to meet my earthen attack as it swung back around. Rock and sand blasted his unshielded body, leaving a hundred bloody wounds on him and scouring the skin completely away in a few spots.

Stunned, he fell back, rolling before springing to his feet once more, but I gave him no chance to recover. His counterattack was poorly aimed which made it easy to sidestep as I slammed a dozen hammer-like blows of force into his torso and legs.

I had him now, but how far did I have to go to win? His defense was ragged. I had struck him so many times his body had to be screaming with pain. He continued to block some of my attacks, but my focus was perfect, while he was struggling after taking so many hits. Would I have to break his bones?

My attention was so firmly upon him that I almost missed the tree sweeping toward me from behind. Somehow, he had ripped it free from the edge of the clearing without me noticing. Using the air, I slipped up and to the right, narrowly avoiding what would have probably been a lethal hit. *Is he trying to kill me?*

I pummeled him with my power. He blocked most of the strikes, but a few got through. There was no way he could continue to withstand so much abuse.

The fight went on, and I could feel myself tiring, but it was worse for him. Desperate to put an end to it, I struck harder, and then harder still. *Why won't he just stay down?!* And then I made a mistake. In my fatigue I dodged one blow only to put myself solidly in front of another, a hammer-blow that sent me reeling.

Pain and fear shot through me. Initiative and momentum were everything. Lose those and the fight would be over. My ancestor would show no reserve or mercy if he got the upper hand. Panicked, I let my rage boil over. The counter-stroke I sent back at him had too much power behind it. If it hit it would shatter him, there was enough power in it to destroy a castle gate.

Tyrion saw it coming, but rather than dodge or defend himself, he stood still, his face lighting up with a bloody smile. Everything happened in less than a second. Realizing he was about to die, I tried to stop my own attack. In practice it was similar to what one might feel if you swung a sledge at a rock and tried to pull it back in mid-swing.

With a sledge you'd probably pull the muscles in your back, but with aythar—the result was feedback. Tired from our long fight, it felt as though my mind was torn apart; agony, cold and black, ripped through me, consuming everything. And it was all of my own doing.

I had been flying a couple of feet in the air when it happened, but the pain was so intense I didn't even feel my body hit the ground. I must've lost consciousness for a second, for when I opened my eyes he was there. The world went red as his fist met my face.

More blows followed. Tyrion wasn't using his power anymore, but then he didn't need to. I was completely helpless. It would take a week or more to recover from what I had done to myself. I felt a crack as the bones in my cheek collapsed under his fist. Mercifully he shifted to my body then.

Or perhaps not so mercifully I realized, as my ribs began to break. He had to be using his power now, no fist could survive a punch hard enough to shatter ribs. I heard screaming, but I was pretty sure it wasn't me—I couldn't breathe.

"Broken bones hurt, don't they?" said Tyrion crooned in my ear.

He was pressing something sharp into my belly. Was that a knife? *No, it's a blade of pure aythar. He's going to kill me.*

"The problem with feedback," he continued, "is that you can't heal those broken bones. Mine are already fixed. And all those cuts you gave me, they're closed as well. But you can't fix anything. You're helpless. You might as well be dead." The blade sliced through my skin, cutting through flesh and muscle. I would have screamed if I could.

"Right now, you're probably wondering if I'm going to kill you, and trust me, I want to. But I won't. Family is important to me." Tyrion stopped then, laughing harshly as though he had told a joke. "No, today is a lesson. You fought like a fool. I want you to remember this, remember the pain, the fear.

"There at the end, you seemed like you had finally learned, but then, when you had won, you fucked yourself. Next time, start there and don't hold back." He stood and spat out a bloody ball of phlegm on the ground beside me. "Assuming you recover enough for there to ever be a next time. Now, if you'll excuse me, I have a prize to collect." His eyes traveled sideways to light on Penny. "When I'm done with her, your wife will thank you for losing."

And then he walked away.

For a second, relief washed over me, and then his words registered through the agony clouding my thoughts. I was beginning to pull in short painful breaths, but air was no longer my main concern. Turning my head, I tried to yell after him, but my voice was gone. One eye was swollen shut, but the other was still able to focus on his retreating form.

Penny stood at the edge of the clearing, sword in her hand and thunder in her eyes. It was an expression I wish I could say I had never seen before, but she and I had been through some pretty extreme events over the years. Still, I had never wanted to see her suffer like that. She glared at the bare skinned monster approaching her as though she hoped to kill him with the daggers in her eyes.

When Tyrion was almost to her she leapt forward, gripping his shoulder with one hand and pressing the tip of her sword against his chest. "Heal him!" she hissed through gritted teeth. Blood seeped slowly from where the point touched him. "Heal him now, or I'll push this blade through your damned heart!"

"Go ahead," he replied, meeting her gaze evenly. "Death is the closest thing to me. Press that enchanted steel through! Let me taste your fury." For a moment, time seemed to stand still.

And then he began to move, pressing himself forward. Penny's sword cut deeper until it began to cut against his ribs. Her arm was shaking, not from weakness, but fear.

Quick as a snake he struck the point of the blade aside, cutting a bloody groove across his chest, then he caught her by the back of the head, his fingers clenching into her hair. "That's right," he said softly. "You can't do it. Is it because you fear he will die without my aid, or because you desire what is to come?"

She struggled in his grasp, but he wrenched her head back around to face him. The sword was still in her hand, but it hung limp now. Dragging her close, he caught her ear in his teeth and bit down until the pain made her cry out. When he pulled away there was blood on his lips, though whether it was from a prior wound or from the bite, I couldn't tell.

"The pain lets you know you're alive. It makes your heart race—and ignites your lust," he said, leering.

There were tears in her eyes, but her cheeks were flushed. Something about her expression, the way her lips had parted, the way her breathing came in short gasps now. It sent shivers down my spine. *Is she reacting to him?*

"I'll kill you for this," she growled.

"No time like the present," he replied. "You still have your sword. I won't stop you. Use it!" Seconds ticked past, until at last he covered her mouth with his own.

Penny's sword, the one I had enchanted for her years ago, slipped from her fingers and fell to the ground. She struggled, but the strength had gone out of her arms. When he drew back again he looked at her with smoldering eyes, "You seem to have lost your blade. Use mine, it's almost ready for you."

I was beyond rage now, so far beyond that I tried to touch my power, but the effort only resulted in a swelling of pain that almost sent me into unconsciousness. I tried to move, but my legs were weak, and my left arm wasn't responding at all. Somehow, I lifted myself onto my knees and my one good arm. I doubted I could crawl far enough to reach them, but then my eyes spied a fist sized rock that had been dredged up from the ground during our fight. Wrapping my right hand around it, I lifted and threw it with everything I had left in me.

Tyrion felt it coming, since his magesight was still working perfectly. In the blink of an eye he pushed Penny away and leapt back, clearing ten feet in a powerful bound. He landed among the bushes and small trees at the edge of the clearing.

In a flash, Penny ran toward me. Tyrion started to emerge from the trees, but Lynaralla stepped in front of him.

"No," she said in a firm voice. "You lost."

Tyrion looked bewildered for a moment, but then he realized he had passed beyond the edge of the field. He shrugged and laughed ruefully. "It looks like you're right. I left the field and clearly, *he's* still trying to fight.

"You win, Count di' Cameron!" he called in a loud voice, then he gave a mock bow. "I acknowledge your victory. Take your spoils and go—Lynaralla is your daughter now."

"Go fuck yourself," I said, or I would have if my face hadn't been so badly smashed. My jaw wasn't working properly, and I couldn't get enough air in to speak above a whisper anyway. Hopefully my expression conveyed my feelings.

Penny spoke for both of us, "If I ever see you again, it will be too soon. The next time you lay a hand on me I *will* drive a sword through your chest." The venom in her voice was withering, but it sounded like false bravado in my ears.

"Dear Penelope," answered Tyrion, "try not to profess your love too loudly." Then he laughed at his own joke. "Since I doubt your husband will be flying for a while I'll have one of the dormon take you back to the mainland." With that he left.

The dormon were a specialized type of krytek, massive flying beasts that seemed to be more plant than animal. When it finally arrived, Penny climbed easily aboard and waited while Lynaralla gently levitated my broken body up to her. Within minutes we were airborne. Penny cradled my head with one arm and used the other to keep my body secure during the flight.

She watched me carefully during the hours that followed. The dormon didn't fly nearly as fast as I had, so the trip took nearly eight hours. I kept my one good eye squeezed shut. I couldn't bear to see the pity in her face, a constant reminder of my failure, my shame. Alone with my thoughts I replayed that scene over and over in my head, watching the sword fall from her hand as he kissed her.

The pain of my body was almost a welcome distraction from my thoughts.

CHAPTER 10

The trip after we reached Turlington was worse. Penny carried me through the World-Road. It would have been easier if Lynaralla had levitated me, but my wife wouldn't listen, and I was in no shape to argue. Thankfully, I passed out before we reached Lancaster.

When I awoke we were leaving the transfer house in the yard of Castle Cameron. Lynaralla had used the circle in Lancaster to teleport us there, which was a relief. I'm not sure I could have handled a long ride, and I certainly couldn't teleport us myself.

Barely able to speak, I whispered to Penny, knowing her sharp ears would hear me, "Don't let them see me."

Nodding she removed her cloak and draped it over me. If the guards outside the transfer house had any questions, they dropped them when they saw the look on her face. Soon I was back in my bed.

Lynaralla ran interference when we entered the house. Conall and Irene were both excited to see her, though I'm sure they were curious about the large burden their mother was carrying. Minutes later I was in my bed, staining the sheets with dirt and dried blood.

Of our older children, only Moira was home. Despite my objections Penny brought her in immediately after I was settled. With feedback sickness I couldn't heal myself, and Penny seemed to feel that was important. Personally, I only wanted a dark hole to climb into.

Moira and her spell-twin, Myra, worked in tandem to fix my broken bones and seal my various wounds. I only had one serious cut, a slowly seeping stab wound in my side. I couldn't inspect it myself, but it must have been simple since it didn't take them long to finish dealing with it. If anything serious had been cut, I'd discover it in a few days. Dying from a gut wound was a horrible way to go.

There was a lot they couldn't fix, the feedback sickness, the swelling and bruises, not to mention my broken pride. If experience was any guide, I'd be in bed for at least a week if not longer.

A lot of talking went on, but I ignored it all until eventually they left. Penny stayed the longest, but eventually she decided to let me rest. The door closed, and I was alone, the room lit by a single candle.

In the dim light I lay staring at the ceiling, hating myself for my weakness. Hating what had happened. I hadn't felt such shame since the day I had been publicly flogged in Albamarl. That had faded with time, so it was hard to say for certain, but this felt worse.

Exhausted, I closed my eyes and despite my pain I quickly fell asleep. My dreams were anything but pleasant.

Once again, I watched the sword fall from her hand...

***

"Mort, wake up."

I wasn't sure how long I had slept, and in fact I hadn't really been asleep. I just hadn't wanted to open my eyes. There was nothing good on the horizon for today, just more pain and guilt.

Soft lips brushed my forehead. "Dammit, I know you're awake. Look at me."

None of it was her fault. I knew that. The blame rested squarely on the shoulders of one man, a man who should have died several thousand years ago when his own daughter put a blade through his back. But that wasn't how it felt. My heart wanted to claim responsibility. I had never been one to blame others, no matter the circumstances.

It had been my failure, my weakness, my shame. But that wasn't the worst of it. I had failed before. The worst was seeing her go slack in his arms.

None of it was rational. I had explained that to myself over and over, each time I had awoken from my nightmares. Taking a deep breath, I opened my eyes. I couldn't punish her for this, no matter how screwed up my head was. I had to be strong.

"Hi," I said, my voice hoarse. I forced a weak smile onto my lips, which hurt. Any movement of my facial muscles hurt, the bones were whole, but the tissue damage remained.

Liquid brown eyes stared down at me, framed by a face that could only belong to an angel. Penny. Dark circles made it abundantly clear that she probably hadn't slept. Had she spent the night torturing herself? I didn't have a monopoly on self-doubt and recrimination.

"I missed you," she said. "You slept a long time."

"How many times have we done this?" I asked.

"Too many, and every time feels worse than the last," she answered.

She was right. I had nearly died too many times to remember, and every time it had been her smile waiting for me when I returned. She wasn't much better, though. I had been the one to wait by the sickbed beside her on quite a few occasions. It was almost a ritual for us now.

"I'll be right as rain in a day or two."

Penny's head was bowed, her face hidden. "Elise says there will probably be permanent damage, unless there's something more you can do."

Elise Thornbear was a mundane healer and the mother of my late-friend, Dorian. She knew more about healing and medicines than anyone I had ever met. If she had said it, it was probably true. "Once I get over the feedback sickness I can fix the rest," I reassured her.

One of the great benefits of being an archmage, was that injuries to the self were easier to fix than almost anything else. So long as I could focus on the memory of what my healthy self had been like, I could restore my body. In fact, the body I had now wasn't even my original one, it had been produced using a significantly riskier process by Gareth Gaelyn. At one point I had looked like his twin. I had had to modify it to return to my accustomed face and form. I could easily do so again, once I could use my power.

"Good," she said, nodding. "I don't think I could make it without you." She squeezed my hand so tightly it was painful.

I could hear the depression in her voice, so I tried a joke. "Don't worry. I'll be fine. I might even use the opportunity to get rid of this belly, maybe add some more muscle."

She flinched, and I felt it through her grip on my hand. Inadvertently, I had struck a nerve. Or was it an accident? Had my remark been born of some subconscious desire to hurt her?

"About what happened…," she began.

I interrupted her, "I'm sorry. It was my fault."

Her breath hissed between her teeth angrily, "Shut up. None of it was your fault."

"I lost," I said simply.

"We didn't go there to fight. None of it was your choice," she responded bitterly. "Lynaralla told me what happened. You had already won. You hurt yourself to keep from killing him."

"I was weak, and he played on that weakness," I answered. "He anticipated my hesitation, and he used it to crush me like a bug—and then." I stopped, unable to say the words. After a second I tried again, "And then he—and then I—I couldn't protect you."

"Just stop," she ordered. "I love you because you aren't a murdering monster. Don't pretend your kindness is a weakness. We wouldn't be here if you were any other way. If anyone was weak, it's me."

"No…"

And then her tears began to trickle down her nose, dripping onto the bed next to me. "I couldn't stop him. No! I *could have*, but I didn't. I should have put that sword straight through his withered black heart!"

"You were scared…"

"No! And yes, I was scared, but I've faced worse. I wasn't afraid for my life. I knew he wasn't going to kill me. I was paralyzed, but not by fear. It's like my body betrayed me. I couldn't fight him." The self-loathing in her words was so strong it burned in my ears.

"Penny, you did the right thing," I insisted. "You couldn't have killed him. The krytek would have killed us. You knew if you stabbed him, we would both die."

"That's not it!" she said, choking out the words. "I didn't know that. I wasn't thinking about that. There was no thought at all. I was horrified, scared you might be dying. What he did to you was awful! But when he grabbed me, I—I—all of that just vanished!"

Suddenly a thought occurred to me, and everything made sense. "Penny, do you remember when I told the kids about his life story?"

"What?" she said, sounding confused and angry at the change in subject. "Some of it, why does it matter? I wasn't there for all of it."

"He raped over a dozen women, but not by force. He used his power to manipulate their bodies and emotions," I told her. It made perfect sense now.

"You said only a Centyr, like Moira, could do that." There was a hopeful sound in her voice.

"Only they can control people's minds, but any mage can induce sensations, emotions. Back then, Tyrion had his way with those women by inducing a powerful feeling of lust. Whatever you felt, it wasn't *you*. It was *him,* screwing with your head!"

The air left her lungs suddenly as she exhaled, a weight having been lifted from her shoulders. Then her lips were against mine. After a moment she pulled back, relief written in her features. "That's so evil! I was sick with guilt! I haven't slept since we returned…"

I smiled and squeezed her hand, wishing I could sit up and hold her. "He screwed with both our heads, one way or another."

Penny clenched one hand in a tight fist until the knuckles turned white. "I despise that bastard. How can such filth survive in this world? I've never wanted to kill someone so badly in my life."

The fury in her eyes was real, yet it comforted me. I had never loved anyone the way I loved her, and every year, every day, the feeling seemed to grow stronger, despite all the shit life threw at us.

We talked for a while longer, but our conversation was more relaxed now, our thoughts no longer dark with guilt and shame. After a bit she helped me up, so I could relieve my overburdened bladder, something else she had to help me with in the past. She had nursed me back to health so many times.

Later, she left, but she leaned down to give me another kiss first. I felt the weight of her pendant fall against my chest. The silver pendant I had made ages ago, to protect her from the shiggreth. Darkness descended over my thoughts once more, but I kept smiling until she had left.

***

The next day was worse than the first. Bruises are like that. They fool you the first day, make you think perhaps it won't be too bad, but as soon as you lower your guard, they pounce. I could hardly move, and when I did it was only to relieve myself. My urine was dark brown, a propitious color.

My entire family took turns hovering over me, watching me breathe, sleep, and continually trying to force unrealistic amounts of water down my throat. All part of Elise's sadistic plan to keep my kidneys functioning until they had a chance to recover. I had always known she had it in for me. She knew I was the mastermind behind the thefts of her blueberry tarts, which Dorian had nobly taken the blame for. I told everyone who would listen that she was trying to kill me, but they paid me no heed.

The second day Rose appeared.

Lady Rose Thornbear, or more officially, Lady Hightower, was an old friend. She had been married to my friend Dorian, and she had been through dark times with Penny and me. I trusted her as much as anyone in my family. Honestly, in my mind, she *was* family.

I didn't trust her today. "What are you doing here?!" I demanded when she crossed the bedroom threshold. As usual her long dark hair was immaculately braided and coiffed on top of her head. She had foregone wearing one of her more usual elegant dresses in favor of a plain linen shift. She looked suspiciously like a nurse.

Her lips quirked into a half-smile when she saw me. "Penny had to go to Gododdin, since you are still not well. I volunteered to take

Mordecai-duty today. Have you had any water yet?" She lifted the pitcher from a table along the wall.

"Help! She's here to kill me!" I shouted half-heartedly at the now closed door. Lady Rose was Elise Thornbear's daughter-in-law, it was a good bet she was in on the plot.

"That's enough of that," she snapped playfully. "Your children told me you were a handful, but I didn't expect you to be this bad."

I turned my head away from her petulantly. "If you try to offer me a cup of water, I'll bite your hand," I mumbled. "I already feel like an overfull wineskin." I tried to lift a hand, so she could see my sausage-like fingers, but it hurt too much, so I gave up.

Rose moved closer and sat down on the chair next to the bed, then leaned over to look down at me. "How low the mighty have fallen." She graced my forehead with a light kiss before resuming her seat. "How do you feel?" she asked.

I grimaced, "How do I look? Multiply that by ten, and you'll be close."

A look of concern flickered across her face, but it vanished almost as quickly as it appeared. Most would have missed it entirely. Lady Rose was a consummate actress, and few ever saw the depths that hid behind her perfectly composed expression. "You always did like to whine," she said, needling me. "When was the last time you relieved yourself?"

I gave her a look of mock embarrassment. "You haven't even given me flowers yet, and you already want to know about my bladder?"

"Mort," she said warningly.

"An hour ago," I lied.

Her blue eyes flashed, "Your daughter said it was last night."

"I snuck out of bed this morning when she stepped out. It was too embarrassing to do with her there."

"You can barely move," she observed, and then, without the least bit of embarrassment, she bent down and retrieved the chamber pot. I felt my face flush as she removed the lid. "And *this,* is empty."

"I poured it out the window."

She gave me a severe look. "It sounds like more dandelion tea for you, milord." Then she placed her hand on my brow. "And perhaps some willow as well, you feel hot."

"Traitor," I hissed. Both of those tasted horrible, and I shuddered to think what the flavor would be if she mixed them.

Rose smiled. "I've been called worse. Do you think you can pee if we get you up out of that bed?"

She was a slender woman, and despite her towering personality, she couldn't possibly hope to hold me up. "We?" I asked suspiciously.

"Alyssa is waiting outside to help, if needed," she informed me.

Alyssa was one of my household servants, as well as Lady Rose's future daughter-in-law. She was also extremely young, less than twenty if I had to guess. The girl was incredibly athletic, a natural warrior, and I had no doubt she could have carried me by herself. "If you drag her into this you may never have grandchildren, Rose. Think of the trauma the girl will suffer if I have to drop my trousers in front of her!"

She patted my leg through the bedcovers. "You aren't wearing trousers, and I survived the experience, I'm sure she will as well. This isn't my first time playing nursemaid to you, remember?"

I did. In fact, I had had to help nurse her back to health on one occasion too. The more I thought about it, the more I realized how many life-threatening injuries I, and everyone around me, had been through. It was a sobering thought. It was also part of what made Rose family.

I stared at her for a moment, studying the faint lines around her eyes, the silver streaks that had begun to sneak into her hair. Rose was getting older, just as I was, but it only seemed to enhance her beauty. "Rose, if I don't make it...," I began.

"None of that," she barked firmly. "You will get better Mordecai Illeniel, so that I can torment you for years to come." Standing, she headed for the door. "I'll fetch Alyssa and then we'll see if you can fill that pot."

A mischievous thought occurred to me as she was leaving. "Rose, wait. This is embarrassing, but I'm too weak. It's a heavy burden that I bear, I don't think I can lift it. I think perhaps I'll need more assistance than you might anticipate." I gave her a wicked grin.

She clapped one hand in front of her mouth and feigned shock. "Oh no! If that's the case I am sure my slight strength will be insufficient. Perhaps I should call Gram to hold it for you?"

"Nevermind," I replied instantly. "I feel my strength returning already." Honestly, Rose was no fun sometimes, and she had an evil sense of humor.

A minute later she returned with Alyssa, but despite their best efforts they weren't able to get me on my feet. It hurt too much, and my legs wouldn't take my weight. The day before I had managed it with only Penny's help, but I had grown weaker. After some struggling, and one or two painful screams on my part, they gave up. Instead they rolled me onto my side and brought the chamber pot to me.

It was a thoroughly humiliating experience. After a quarter of an hour I hadn't managed to accomplish much, but they relented and took the pot away.

The dandelion and willow bark tea came after that, and while I didn't like it, I drank it with a minimum of complaints. She hid it well, but something in Rose's posture told me she was worried, and the tea was the only thing I could do to help relieve that, so I swallowed it quickly.

I slept for a while after that, and when I awoke again I opened my eyes slowly. Rose was still there, sitting at the bedside. Her hands were busy, tatting lace I realized after a moment. She couldn't cook (I knew from experience) but Lady Rose was a product of her upbringing, she spent every spare moment keeping her hands busy. Over the course of a year her dexterous fingers would produce a prodigious amount of lace to be used on collars and ruffs.

Silently I watched, admiring her skill. When she spoke it surprised me, for I didn't think she had noticed my wakefulness. "Want to tell me about what happened on the island?"

"I'm sure you heard it all from Penny."

Her hands continued moving, and her eyes never wavered from their work. "Enough to know how much the entire thing upset her. One look at you is enough to understand why, but I'm sure she didn't tell me everything."

Lady Rose had a keen intellect and a knack for observation and inference. Despite being without magesight, she always knew more about what was going on than any ten people that I could name put together. It was sometimes frightening how much she knew. On occasion I had wondered if she had some secret ability to read minds. What's more, she only spoke a fraction of what she had observed or figured out, so it was always a safe bet she knew far more than she said.

When I didn't say anything she prompted, "Fill me in on what happened."

"Why? I'm sure you already know as much as I could tell."

"Because you need to," she responded.

She was right, and there was no better confessor a man could find than her. If anyone could understand, she would be the one. I felt trapped by my isolation, so I began to talk. A half an hour passed as I slowly detailed what had happened, describing everything, leaving nothing out, at least not until the end. When I stopped there, she picked up the thread for me.

"And then he kissed her, and she dropped the sword," she finished for me. "You weren't going to say it, were you?"

"She told you."

Rose nodded. "She was very relieved when you told her about his ability to influence emotions, but that wasn't the whole truth, was it Mordecai?"

Dammit. I had known this would happen. The woman missed nothing. "No, it isn't."

Reaching into her collar she lifted out her own pendant, the same one that every resident of Castle Cameron and Washbrook wore. "I am not a wizard, but from what I remember of your explanation, these prevent that sort of manipulation."

I had given that explanation to her and others well over fifteen years ago, but she had not forgotten. The enchanted pendants weren't perfect or foolproof. A Centyr mage, like my daughter, Moira, could get around their protection with a small delay, but a non-Centyr, like Tyrion, or myself, could not. "Did you tell her?" I asked simply.

She pursed her lips. "No. I think you did well to leave her with that comfort, though one caveat would be, if she realizes this on her own, things might be worse."

"What would she do?" I croaked, my voice having become much thicker.

Rose stared sharply at me for a moment before her eyes softened, "Idiot! Is that what you think of her? She would do nothing, except perhaps secretly hating herself. For all your brilliance, there are times when you surprise me with your stupidity, Mordecai."

My vision went blurry, and I couldn't respond.

"She loves you. She always has, and she always will. What happened to her was an instinctive physical reaction, something we are all prone to suffer from." There was a hint of bitterness in her voice.

Everything stopped. I stopped. My world, the internal spiral of doubt—stopped. In her words, I could sense something new, something that puzzled me, something that might turn my perceptions upside down. I glanced at Rose, waiting for her to continue.

Her eyes bored into mine, while an unknown time passed. Behind them was a burning intelligence so bright it would have been frightening, if it had not also been tempered by an equal amount of compassion. Something passed between us, some understanding or feeling, though if I was asked to put words to it, I would not know what to say. It was deep and subliminal, a feeling of comfort, of understanding, coupled with a certain wistfulness. Eventually she reached out and wrapped my swollen hand with her soft cool fingers, her touch a balm for my nerves.

"Humans are complicated creatures, Mordecai," she said at last. "We are not any one thing, but several at once. We can describe ourselves in terms of our animal desires, in terms of our rational decisions, and in terms of our higher emotions, the beast, the mind, and the heart. I'll use those labels to describe them, but remember, they are just words. In reality, in the deeper truth, they are all part of a single thing, a thing we cannot describe without losing some of its meaning.

"The best part of us, is our heart, the place where our love comes from, and love is a thing that has many forms, but they are all the same. Whether it is love for a child, love for your wife, or love for a friend, it's the same thing. We use different names for those relationships, not because the love is different, but because there are other elements tied to them, the lust of our inner beast in some cases, and the framework and rules imposed by the mind."

I had said something similar once, but often the truth means more when heard from the lips of another. Rose squeezed my hand and nodded, as though she could hear my inner monologue.

Then she continued, "Remember when Elaine was chasing you?"

Internally I winced. Elaine Prathion was the daughter of my good friend, Walter. For a time, I had been her mentor and teacher. She had idolized me, and in her early adulthood, that admiration had become something more intense for her. A lovely young woman, she had done everything in her power to force me to acknowledge her womanhood. Until at last I had been forced to confront her, to explain why that physical attraction would never be answered, why there were some boundaries that I wouldn't cross. She had been hurt and embarrassed, but my firm words had put an end to an infatuation that could have only led to pain.

I smiled ruefully, "I should have known that couldn't have slipped by unnoticed by your eyes."

"Not just mine, Mort. Penny knew as well, I have no doubt. I can still remember the day when you crushed poor Elaine's hopes."

I pursed my lips, it hadn't been a good day. Hurting people wasn't something I enjoyed, even when it was necessary. "You even knew the day, eh?"

Rose nodded. "I wasn't there. I didn't see it, but it was apparent from her behavior, and I can guess what happened. You were under a lot of pressure at the time, sick with worry, and as usual, you were keeping it from everyone. She probably approached you at some point, when you were alone, and offered her comfort in a very direct fashion. When you rejected her, it sent her into an angry depression."

It hadn't been quite that simple. The facts were correct, but too plain. I closed my eyes.

She squeezed my hand, "That was the easy version—in reality, you wanted her."

"No."

Rose tapped my forehead with her other hand, and then my heart. "Not in here, or here, no—but the beast, the animal that lives within men and women, it wanted her. I'm sure you struggled with it, but in the end, you did the right thing.

My breath escaped in a long sigh. Rose was *far* too perceptive.

"In some ways, that was similar to what happened to Penny, but not in every way," said Rose. "With Elaine, you had other feelings as well. You loved her as a student, as a pupil, as a friend. But in Penny's case, there was not even that. She was caught, trapped like a wild animal by a dangerous hunter. As a woman, she suffered a momentary surge, but there was no affection, no thought of betrayal, only fear and an involuntary rush of hormones. Rather than the pain of rejecting someone, as you experienced with Elaine, she got a sample of something far darker and more painful. She was nearly raped, and whatever reaction she had in those initial seconds, what followed would have been painful and destructive."

Silence followed, until finally I spoke, "Thank you, Rose."

"You already knew all that," she replied.

"I needed to hear it, from someone who's heart and mind wasn't clouded by anger."

She smiled faintly. "Glad I could help, but don't make the mistake of thinking I'm completely objective. I suffer from the cravings of my inner beast, and the longings of an irrational heart as well, just like everyone else."

Fatigue was wearing on my consciousness, but I couldn't help but wonder, "Even you, Rose? I have never known anyone with an intellect as clear and insightful as yours. I always imagined you lived without doubt, secure in your decisions, perfect in your composure."

A shadow crossed her face, but was quickly gone. "Ever the poet, aren't you, Mort? Even half dead you string your words together like pearls. You flatter me, but you know just as well as I do, that a towering intellect is as often a curse as it is a blessing, and it is certainly no protection from the whispers of the heart."

Her words faded in and out for me. Sleep would take me again soon. Too relaxed, I asked a question I would never have dared voice normally, "Were you ever tempted, Rose? When Dorian was still alive, or after?"

She sighed. "Dorian was perfect, in every way, more so than I could ever be. I was infatuated with him as a girl, I loved him helplessly as a young woman, and nothing that life ever threw at us made me love him any less. I was devoted to him, and the years since he died have been long and hard."

She fell silent, and I fell asleep, my heart finally free of the guilt that had plagued me.

In my dreams I felt a ghostly touch on my lips and Rose's voice echoed through the mists, "But I'm only human, Mort. I've been tempted, both before and since, but love is not so simple. My love is for my family, for your family, and it is too strong to allow me to hurt one of them for want of another."

CHAPTER 11

When I awoke Rose was gone, but Alyssa was there—with more of that wretched dandelion tea in her hands. Penny returned soon after, and the late afternoon was a steady progression of family members, in and out of the room. My mother, Irene and Conall, Moira, and even Humphrey was brought in for a brief visit.

It was an awful lot for someone as sick as I was to manage, but I didn't complain. Instead I asked Penny about the one notable exception, "Where's Matthew?"

She sighed, "He's working on a project."

"Ah."

"For you, actually," she added.

"Me?"

"The portal to the Queen's chambers in Albamarl," explained Penny. "I mentioned it to him and he took it upon himself to handle it for you. He won't admit it, of course, but I think it's his way of trying to help. Checking something off your list of obligations…"

A knock came at the door. Penny rose and opened it to find Elise Thornbear standing outside.

"Time to check on our patient," said the old woman with an easy smile.

I groaned from the bed.

Penny motioned her in with a wide sweep of her hand. "I'll leave him to you then. I have a few things to take care of. Let me know when you finish, and I'll come back. We've been trying to keep someone with him around the clock." She stepped out and closed the door before I could protest, leaving me alone with the fiendish old crone.

I would never have called Elise a 'crone' out loud, though. She was Dorian's mother, and when we were younger such a phrase might have earned me a strapping. She had had a firm hand with discipline back then, whether it was her child, or in my case, someone else's.

"Good evening, Lord Cameron," she said in a bright tone. The formality was a ruse, as was the cheeriness. It meant she had something terrible in store for me. And Penny had left me alone with her! This merely served to confirm my suspicions, all the women in my life were in on it together. They were out to get me, and Elise Thornbear was their leader and chief torturer.

"I drank all the tea they gave me," I said defensively.

"Mm hmm," she said neutrally. Then the fiend pulled the covers up from the foot of the bed, exposing my feet to the cold air. She eyed my feet clinically while I shivered, then replaced the covers. A reasonable man might think that was enough, but she pulled the blankets from my chest next. "Turn onto your side for me," she ordered.

I tried.

When I failed, she assisted me, her long bony arms both stronger and gentler than one would expect. With her help I made it, though I groaned loudly several times during the process. She pulled up my shirt and studied my backside for a minute. Then she began lightly prodding me with her fingers, placing them here and there. When she reached my lower back I let out an involuntary scream.

She stopped and pulled my shirt down. Then she eased me onto my back and covered me, tucking me into the bed as though I was a small child. She sat down and said nothing.

The silence drew out for a while, making me slightly uncomfortable. Elise Thornbear was something of a force of nature, hard-willed and indomitable. In her youth she had been a Lady of the Evening, poisoner, prostitute, and assassin. Later she had married Gram Thornbear and rejoined the respectable circles of polite society and the nobility, but she had never forgotten the lessons she learned. As Lady Thornbear she had never feared to get her hands dirty, and she had frequently used her skills to treat the wounded and ease the pain of the dying.

But looking at her now, she just looked old—defeated. Hers wasn't the demeanor of a lady trying to cheer or tease a patient to keep their spirits up.

"How is your mind, Mordecai?" she asked suddenly. "Are your thoughts still clear?"

"Clear enough," I answered. "I'm sleeping a lot, but I'm good for short sprints of conversation, if that's what you're asking."

"Many physicians wouldn't tell you what I'm about to. They'd talk to your family first," she began. "Then again, I think most of them are fools. If you're still clear headed, then you should be the one to make the choice."

"Listen, Elise…"

"Shh!" she snapped.

"Yes, ma'am," I responded immediately. The habits of childhood die hard.

"This isn't easy for me. I've lost too many, more than any woman should, my husband, my son, Marc, Ginny, James, and too many other friends to count. Every time is different, but one thing I've come to realize over the long years, is that when possible, it's best not to pretend. Honest conversation and honest good-byes save a lot of regret for those left behind. Do you understand?"

"Wait, Elise," I said. "This isn't as bad as it seems. Whatever you think, in a week, or maybe a little more, I'll be able to fix this."

"You don't have a week, Mort," she said bluntly. Lifting my hand, she showed me how swollen my fingers were. "Your kidneys have shut down."

I frowned, "They weren't injured."

"Doesn't matter," she responded. "Massive trauma can cause it. Breaking down and reabsorbing blood, from bruising or internal injuries, is very taxing for the kidneys. Yours have been overwhelmed. That's why you're swelling, that's why you can't piss. Your blood is turning into poison. In a few days you'll be delirious and in tremendous pain. From there it's just a horrid waiting game, but two or three days more and you'll be dead. The worst of it, is that there isn't anything I can give you at that point that will ease the symptoms. Only death will release you, and your family won't be able to do anything but watch."

"I've been dead before," I said callously.

"That's not the point," she replied. "The point is how much your family will suffer watching it. That's why I'm talking to you now, while you're still clear enough to decide for yourself."

I didn't say anything, preferring instead to stare at the ceiling.

"Word has been sent to Gareth Gaelyn," Elise informed me. "Matthew said he could possibly do something…"

I interrupted her, "He won't come."

Elise nodded, "Matthew said the same, but your wife sent word to him anyway. Are there any others that might have some ability to help?"

There were. Lyralliantha, if she possessed the She'Har's knowledge of spellweaving techniques for healing, but she was a tree now. She couldn't travel, and even if she could, it would take weeks just to pose the question to her. The only other possibility was Tyrion himself, and I would rather die than accept his aid. Even if he was willing to come, there was no telling what horror he would ask for to repay him.

I shook my head negatively.

Elise bowed her head sadly. "I expected as much." Reaching into her pouch she pulled out a glass vial. "In a day or two you'll start to itch all over. When that happens, you'll know it's almost too late, madness will follow soon after. Talk to your family, give them peace, then drink this."

Pulling my eyes away from the ceiling, I looked directly at her. The tough old woman had tears on her cheeks. This had to be incredibly difficult for her. I remembered all too well how hard it had been for me, when I had 'helped' my own father die peacefully.

"Elise," I said quietly. "Thank you. You've done the right thing. Remember that, in the nights to come. I haven't quite given up yet. I've cheated death too many times to believe it's my time, but if the worse comes, this will make it easier."

She wiped her face. "Gram and I always wanted more children, but it just didn't happen. You and Marc helped fill that gap. The two of you were like sons to me. If my husband were still here, he would tell you to be proud. You've done well with what you were given." She rose to her feet and walked to the door. "Remember, when you start to itch all over, delirium will follow soon after. Wait too long and you'll lose the choice."

Then she was gone, and it was hard to ignore the itching in my hands. *Dammit.*

***

Another nap and I found Penny sitting beside me again. *How long did I sleep?* Time wasn't my friend anymore, if it ever had been. "I need to see Mother," I told her.

"What did Elise say?" asked Penny, concern in her features. "She said you would tell us what you talked about."

Even dying, I was more worried about my wife's reaction than I was the grim reaper showing up on my doorstep. I could see no way this conversation would end well. "She said to use my time well."

Her hands tightened into fists. "I'll kill him."

"Penny…"

"This is no idle threat," she said, cutting me off.

"You can't."

"Maybe not alone," she admitted. "But I'm not alone. Do you realize how much raw power sleeps under this roof? How many dragons we have?"

"You'd start a war," I cautioned.

"I don't care!" she yelled. "Don't forget the Queen either. If we don't have enough here, I'll see to it that all of Lothion goes to war with us. We'll burn every tree on that fucking island, and when that's done I'll see Tyrion gutted like a fish!"

"No, you won't," I said tiredly. "Are you planning to kill Lynaralla's mother too? She's innocent. The She'Har are innocent. Even Tyrion didn't mean for *this* to happen."

"There has to be some way," she muttered, her voice thick.

"Several," I replied, "but none that allow me to remain human."

Her eyes lit with hope, but I shook my head immediately. "No. I've been a monster before. I'd rather go gracefully than accept that," I told her.

"But you came back," she insisted. "You could do it again."

She was referring to the immortality enchantment. The magic that had once trapped me in an undying body. I had been forced to steal life from the mortals around me to retain a semblance of humanity. *And I'm not sure I came back last time,* I thought. *At least not all the way.*

"With the help of two wizards, and one of them an archmage. Gareth won't be doing me any more favors, and I wouldn't ask it of him if he were willing. They got lucky last time. It could just as easily have been all three of us dead."

Penny wasn't listening. "Can Matthew do it?"

"Not with my consent."

She smiled through her tears. "We'll just wait until the delirium sets in."

"The enchantment creates a snapshot of the mind at the moment it goes into effect. You'd be stuck with a madman," I told her. "Come here." I waved my hands vaguely, urging her to draw close. When she leaned in, I kissed her cheek. "There's still hope, but I'm not doing anything stupid. If it comes to it, I want you to be strong and accept whatever comes."

The dam broke, but Penny didn't cry long. After a few minutes she pulled herself together and stood straight. She sent for my mother first, and I spent a considerable time visiting with her.

I didn't tell my mother I was dying. That was too much, even for me. But I'm sure she sensed it in my words somehow. We spent an hour talking, and over the course of that period I made certain I left none of my feelings unspoken. She had to know what she had meant to me.

My kids were a different matter. They had no inhibitions about blurting out what their intuition told them. Irene was the worst. No matter how cheerful I was, she wasn't buying any of it. She was inconsolable, and she cried all the way out the door, tearing at my heart.

Conall took the news quietly, but he too was a mess by the time he left. Moira kept her composure, but like her mother, she insisted on proposing an outlandish scheme to preserve my mind, if not my life.

I rejected her idea outright. I had no desire to die and be replaced by some sort of spell-copy, which is what her plan amounted to.

Matthew was the last to visit me, long after the sun had set. He had waited until last because he was caught up in his newest project. Or perhaps he was merely reluctant.

When he entered his expression was blank. "The portal to Albamarl is almost done," he informed me.

I nodded, "That's a load off my mind."

He laughed lightly. "I'm sure you have bigger things to worry about."

I smiled. "Maybe, but I can't think of anything."

"Everyone thinks you're dying," he stated bluntly. "The whole house has gone crazy."

"But not you," I observed.

He sighed. "I don't know. It doesn't feel real. Maybe later. I'm not going to run around the house crying and screaming, though."

No, you'll ignore it until it bites you in the dark a few weeks later, I thought. *And that's why I worry about you more than them. You'll try to face your grief alone.*

"Gareth has refused to come," said Matthew.

"As expected."

He walked to the window, looking out at the fall scenery. "Elise says it's your kidneys that are the problem."

"Yeah," I replied. I wanted to say more, to say a hundred different things. But I didn't know how to talk to him. In some ways he was like my father, he communicated through actions and ideas. Feelings were not part of his vocabulary.

My son tapped his temple, "The She'Har had ways to cleanse the blood. It's all in here. We could study and adapt their spellweaving, create an enchantment to do the same thing."

And it would take weeks, if not months. The information was there, but understanding it, converting it, and using it, those were much harder things to do. "Possessing knowledge is one thing, using it is another," I said simply.

He nodded. "Then I'd better get started." He walked toward the door but paused before he reached it. Walking back to the bed he leaned over and hugged me briefly.

I grinned. "If I had known dying would get me hugs, I'd have done it sooner."

Matthew smirked. "Don't get used to it. You'll be better soon."

CHAPTER 12

The next day I was miserable. Despite my exhaustion I hadn't been able to sleep. The itching that had started in my palms had spread, first to my feet and then to my legs and torso. It was maddening. Desperately, I longed to leap from the bed and throw myself into a cold bath. That was the only relief that I could imagine would stop the hot itching sensation that crawled over my skin.

Today I was planning to meet with my friends, Cyhan, Chad, Peter, and several dozen others. Then I'd spend the last hours with my family. I was trying to decide which to call for first when I heard a commotion in the hall.

"Who let you in here?!" That was Penny's voice. "He's sick. Too sick for this."

The reply came in Chad Grayson's rough tones, "Yer daughter did. An' I need to speak to him if he ain't dead yet."

"I told you no this morning!" shouted my wife.

"An' yet, ye ain't done a damn thing," he responded.

Listening to them, I worried for fear she might decapitate the surly huntsman. Penny had never been particularly fond of him, and she was highly stressed currently.

"I have to think," she answered.

"Lancaster is missing, ya crazy bitch! Someone's got to decide what ta do!"

What?! I knew I must have misheard him, and the last part—I listened hard, expecting to hear steel being drawn. Prickly as he was, even Chad wouldn't normally speak to Penny like that.

Penny's response came in a measured tone, "My husband is dying."

"Then let him decide," said Chad, his tone bitter and wry. "He probably needs somethin' to take his mind off it."

The slap that followed was loud enough for me to hear through the door, and a momentary silence followed.

"Could you people shut up! I can't focus will all this racket!" That was Matthew. The sound of feet told me that the rest of the household was probably emerging to join the ruckus.

"Get Sir Gram and Sir Cyhan," said Penny. "Take your hunters as well. Examine the area and report back."

"This needs a wizard, milady," said Chad gruffly. "I just returned an' I can't make heads or tails of it. What about him?"

Matthew's voice answered, "I'm busy."

A flurry of suggestions followed, but Matthew shot them all down. "I said no. I need them here."

Moira spoke then, suggesting they send one of the Prathions.

I missed the rest of the argument because just then a purple cloud came through the window with a roar of wind. The sound drowned out their voices. It was so sudden that I was alarmed, but Dorian stood up from the chair beside the bed. "Get out!" he yelled at the cloud.

It didn't listen, but Dorian had brought the bellows from my father's smithy. Setting up at the foot of the bed, he proceeded to pump it until the rushing air pushed the cloud back out the window.

Once that was done he sat back down. "Now, where were we?"

I smiled at him, "We were talking about Marc."

Dorian shook his head sadly. "I told you, he's gone. He disappeared when Lancaster vanished."

That made no sense. Looking up I watched the geese flying overhead. "Then why are the birds still there?" I asked.

The rest of the day was confusing. It seemed as though hundreds of people came and went, and there were always at least twenty people in my room, all talking at the same time. There was no quiet until sundown. As the sky turned orange and the sun began to vanish behind the mountains, everyone left, until only Elise remained, staring down at me with sad eyes.

"You waited too long," she said sadly. "Now it's too late."

I tried to answer, but my voice wouldn't work. *It's not my fault. It's these ants, they're all over me!*

And then darkness covered my eyes.

***

A faint light irritated me. When I tried to look at it, it faded, but as soon as I turned my head it followed, keeping me from resting. There was something I had forgotten, something I needed to do.

Penny's face came into focus. She sat huddled beside the bed. Her head turned, and the candlelight caught her eyes for a moment, so I knew she wasn't asleep. What bothered me more was that the shadows were moving behind her. They were long and distorted, but I could see the knives in their hands.

Trying to warn her, I opened my mouth, but whatever I managed to say, it wasn't enough. She couldn't see the shadows.

The door opened, and light exploded into the room, setting my eyes on fire and sending the ants that covered me scurrying for cover. I might have screamed, but I heard nothing. After an eternity the flames died down, and I saw my children against the wall. No, there were too many. And some of them weren't mine.

Why is Gram here, and Alyssa too?

They were staring at me with empty eyes, and that was when I realized they were dead. Desperate, I scanned their faces, Irene, Carissa, Conall, Gram, Alyssa... all dead. Even Rose was there, but Matthew and Moira were missing. *Maybe they escaped...*

I stared at their dead bodies, slumped along the walls and in the corners of the room, and when my heart could take no more, I began to cry. Some of the bodies moved, rising from their eternal rest. They had become shiggreth. I struggled to rise from the bed, but a demon was pressing me down, forcing me onto the mattress.

It had Cyhan's face, but none of his gentleness. Its hands were burning brands that seared me wherever they touched, but I didn't have the strength to escape them, so I ignored the pain and relaxed.

My hand found something under the covers, something cool and hard. Drawing it out, I saw a glass vial between my fingers. The liquid within shone golden in the candlelight. Hope blossomed in my chest. Sitting back up, I called for Penny, but my cry was answered by the demon, and this time it had a helper just as big, wearing Gram's face like a skin-mask.

They forced me down, but I held on tightly to the vial, to my salvation. And then they vanished, their darkness fleeing before the light that shone around Penelope. Evil could not bear the sight of her, or remain in her presence.

"What is it Mort?" she asked, her face hovering above me, too far to reach. Her eyes were wet, and her cheeks red. *Did they hurt her?*

Holding out the vial, I tried to explain, "I found it, Penny. Help me drink it. It's magic. I can save us, there's still hope!"

She smiled, and sunshine broke through the window, cascading over us. "Of course," she whispered. Pressing it back into my hand, she helped me lift it to my lips and something cool trickled down my throat, fire made into liquid ice. My power swelled within me, and I raised my hand to the ceiling, strong once more. Blasting a hole through the roof, I took Penny's hand in mine, and we flew.

A door opened in the heavens, and I saw Moira ahead of us, blocking our path to freedom, except it wasn't her. It looked like her on the outside, but within I could see a monster, a serpent that had eaten her up, from the inside out. It smiled, showing me fangs and leering at me with serpentine eyes.

Father, can you hear me? It was her voice, but now I could see there were two of her.

Let me go! I ordered, for there were shackles on me now, dragging me down and binding me to the bed. Matthew stood behind me, hidden in a black robe, while Lynaralla stood to my right. The two Moiras were on my left, and Conall and Irene were at my feet. All of them were in robes, and I realized then that they meant to sacrifice me.

I would die in the same way that Tyrion should have, at the hands of my children. Lynaralla leaned over me, her silver hair falling across my chest, almost hiding the silver dagger in her hands. It glittered in the light as she lifted her hands to strike.

The blade hovered there as she chanted in Erollith, "So that the Illeniel may live, you must die." Then she plunged it into my chest, and agony screamed in my heart and through my veins.

Powerless even to cry out, I stared into the eyes of my murderous offspring as the world dimmed around me, my life leaking out of my chest, a river that they were devouring like feral beasts.

Unlike an ordinary murder, this one went on for ages, my heart somehow pounding around the blade in my chest, while I slowly died in silent steps. Despite their betrayal, I forgave them, and as my life bled away, I spoke my final words, "I love you." Thankfully, oblivion found me after that, the sweet embrace of death.

CHAPTER 13

The afterlife turned out to be more pleasant than I had expected. I floated along for some time on a white cloud, while the trees shed their leaves like rain. Warm sun and cold wind competed for my skin's attention. I stared at the scenery, unable to comprehend the beauty before me.

A young man walked in front of me, my son, Conall. I wasn't certain until he turned his head to look back at me. Then he spoke, but it was Chad Grayson's voice that emerged. "How long are ya goin' to keep droolin' like that? Ya look like a fuckin' idiot."

I frowned. Conall's lips hadn't moved. Something wasn't right. Had he spoken in my mind? On impulse I tilted my head back. My vision was filled by the sky, a grey and blue masterpiece filled with clouds rushing in the wind. In the center of it was Chad's face, staring back at me.

"Yeah, those are clouds, asshole," he said to me.

Then Conall chimed in, "I really wish you wouldn't speak to him like that."

Chad waved a hand dismissively. "He doesn't know what I'm sayin' anyway. We'll know he's really wakin' up when he gets pissed off."

I started laughing.

"See? He's got no clue. He's still a moron," said Chad.

It wasn't a cloud I was riding on, but a palanquin of sorts. Really it was more of a cushioned bed on two poles, and the two of them were carrying me, though they had since stopped. We were in the meadow below my house on the mountainside. I still felt weird, but my mind was functioning. It was obvious I wasn't dead.

Looking up at Chad again, I spoke, "If this is heaven, should you be here?"

Conall snickered, and I winked at him. Meanwhile Chad's eyes narrowed as he studied me, wondering if I were really regaining my self-awareness. Finally, the hunter replied, "Ye're right about that. This ain't heaven. Not a tavern in sight. 'Swhy I brought this." He held up a small metal flask and unscrewed the top, taking a swallow.

"Why are we on the mountainside?" I asked. It seemed a strange place for a sick-bed.

Conall answered, "Elise thought you might benefit from some sunshine."

Chad chuckled. "More like yer wife got sick of lookin' at that dumbass face of yours."

Despite his rough tongue, I found myself smiling like an idiot. "Is she alright? How about everyone else? How long have I been out of it?"

Chad summarized quickly, "She's fine, they're fine, and you've been a gibbering idiot long enough to piss me off pretty good." He addressed my son next, "Since he's talkin' we best get him back to the house. The Queen will want to know."

Conall picked up his end of the litter, and they started trudging back uphill while I pondered what had been said. "The Queen, is she here?" I asked.

"Yeah," said Chad. "While you were sick they all got together an' decided to throw ya a fuckin' party. They're up there now, plannin' decorations and decidin' which noble pricks to put on the guest list."

"Master Grayson!" snapped Conall, outraged. Then he spoke to me directly, "Matthew finished the portal to Albamarl, and Her Majesty came to observe your recovery."

Nodding, I looked back at Chad. "While I was sick I had some interesting dreams. I thought you tried to see me, but Penny wouldn't let you in. Something about Lancaster having vanished…"

The huntsman winced. "That was no dream. She damn near broke my neck."

"And Lancaster?"

Conall broke in, "That's why he's so mad. It's gone. He and Sir Cyhan, and a lot of the hunters went to scout the area after that. Most of them didn't come back. Sir Cyhan was badly wounded, and he says the missing are either dead or…"

He stopped, so I prompted him, "Or what?"

Chad finished for him, "Or eaten. Somethin' bad came out of the forest, though I'll be damned if I could tell ya what it is."

"Walter and Elaine were with them," Conall informed me. "They haven't come back either."

Alarmed, I asked, "When was this?"

"Four days ago. Same day yer wife tried to break my neck," answered the old archer. "Arrows had no effect on 'em. Their hides were tougher than granite, an' they just about ignored everything that old Walter an' his daughter threw at 'em too."

"Tell me exactly what happened," I ordered.

"One of my boys came back that mornin', told us that Lancaster was missin'. Walter checked the World Road portal, and tried the teleportation circles, and none of 'em were workin'. After yer wife nearly killed me, I went back with Cyhan and a group of scouts, along with the two wizards," began Chad. "When we got there, there wasn't no sign of what shoulda been there. Lancaster was gone, just as neat as ya please. The road just dead ended against a forest the likes of which I ain't never seen. Trees as big across as two men layin' head to toe. Huge ferns and grass so thick ye'd think no one'd ever been there before.

"I sent two men south and two to the north, to try and see how far it went. The rest of us went straight in, tryin' to reach Castle Lancaster, or at least see if it was still there. We barely got five hundred yards in before somethin' jumped out and about tore poor Sammel in half. Damn thing was as big as a bear, a really big fuckin' bear, but it didn't have fur. Its skin was hard and crusty, like it was covered in gravel.

"It ripped into the guys in front, an' nearly had me fer dinner, but Cyhan ducked in and took one of its legs off midway down. It fell forward, and then slapped him with its other paw and pitched him ten foot into a tree. Damn near killed him, armor or no armor. I had my bow out by then, but arrows didn't do nothin', didn't even piss it off.

"That one was too hurt to follow though, so we started backin' outta there, 'til it's mate showed up and bit Fergus's head clean off. Walter's girl hit it with lightin' an' he tried to burn it, but it just started roarin' and tearin' into everyone. I was dragging Cyhan by the feet, so I couldn't do much. We just ran—everyone left anyway.

"We didn't stop until we were gone from there and a hundred yards more besides. That's when I noticed Walter an' Elaine weren't with us." Chad stopped then, his features hard.

"But they weren't all dead, not yet. We could still hear 'em," he said slowly. "One of 'em kept screamin' fer almost a quarter of an hour, like it was eatin' him alive. An' we just kept walkin'. Couldn't look back, couldn't even look at each other. That was four days ago, an' ain't no one gone near there since." The old hunter fell silent at last.

I didn't know what to say, but Conall spoke up, coming to the master hunter's defense, "They wanted to go back. Mom and Gram were going to go with the house guard and the hunters, but the Queen showed up first. She wouldn't let them, not without magical support."

As much as I hated the thought of my children going into harm's way, I didn't understand. Even with Walter and Elaine missing, there were still George Prathion, Lynaralla, Matthew, Moira, and even Conall. They could have gone back with the troops, Sir Gram, and the dragons. If they had returned immediately, the chances they could recover some of those lost would have been much higher.

My son must have seen the confusion on my face. "They were sick, well, a lot of them anyway, Gram, Irene, Matthew, and even Lynaralla."

The odds of that didn't seem likely. "All of them at the same time?"

Conall nodded, "Off and on, they took turns."

We were almost to the house, but I motioned for them to stop. I wasn't ready to face everyone yet. I had already noticed that my magesight was back. It had taken a moment because it was such a normal part of my life that it was usually easier to notice its absence. Examining myself, both with my eyes and my arcane senses, I could see that I was a wreck.

The swelling in my hands and feet was better, but still present, and my skin was an ugly mess of red blotchy areas and lighter patches. My hair was remarkably well kept, a sign that someone had been grooming me, but I had no doubt there would be bags under my eyes, if I looked in a mirror. Trying to rise had shown me how weak my arms were, and I knew without trying that my legs wouldn't hold my weight.

"Go wait by the door," I told my keepers. "I'll join you in a minute."

"Dad!" protested Conall. "You can't walk yet. You'll fall for sure."

Chad put a hand on the teen's shoulder. "Leave him be, lad. It's every man's right to make an ass of himself. If he falls and breaks somethin', we can just laugh and pack him back onto his bed here." He leaned in and whispered in my ear, "I'm hopin' you know what ye're doin'. If you do hurt yerself, that mad dog wife o' yours will have my balls." He led Conall away while I grinned.

What I was about to do was about the simplest form of metamagic, returning my body to its former healthy state. Unlike most other things an archmage might do, this didn't require me to become anything other than myself. My mind didn't have to encompass something foreign. In comparison to the difficulty of healing using ordinary wizardry, it was absurdly easy.

But I didn't want to just return to my most recent former health. I wanted to make some improvements, and that could be tricky. The body, or rather the part of the mind that represents our body to us, has a strong memory. Returning to what you were moments before an injury was simple, but to deliberately alter something was much harder, and if an archmage should let his focus waver for an instant, the result could be unpredictable.

Years of good food and little exercise had produced predictable effects, effects that were firmly set in my mind. But I didn't care. Or maybe it was my recent encounter with Tyrion. Being beaten half to death by a lean, muscular, and disgustingly handsome man, while my wife looked on—there was every chance that it factored into my decision. But I'd be damned before I admitted it.

Closing my eyes, I imagined myself, not as I was now, but as I had been two weeks ago. I concentrated until I could feel it, believe it, and then I began to retouch the image in my mind. The grey hair I kept, there was no need to be obvious. Besides, I rather liked it. If anything, for a man, grey hair was a blessing. Rank and station aside, you got more respect with some grey in your beard.

The belly needed work, though, and my muscles, but not too much. I had no intention of trying to imitate that sweaty muscled barbarian I had recently fought. No, this wasn't because of him at all. Definitely not.

I tried to remember what it was like to run without being out of breath too soon, the vitality of just ten years past. The memory of it was easy, but keeping it solid in my thoughts was more difficult.

My face and skin I left mostly unchanged, I had always been content with my features, and age had been kind to me thus far. The faint lines and whatnot were welcome. If anything, they had improved my looks. The only thing I altered was removing a small mole that had appeared near the corner of one of my eyes a few years back.

The soreness in my back and shoulder, which had become ever present in recent years, I had no mercy or regret over those.

Once my vision, my self-delusion, was complete, I touched it and let myself flow into it, letting it become reality. When I opened my eyes again, it was done. I took a deep breath and stretched, enjoying the sensation. I felt better than I had in years. Why hadn't I done this sooner?

The answer was simple, for Penny. I wanted to grow old with her, and I hoped I hadn't screwed that up too much. I'd know for sure when I found a mirror, but for now my magesight seemed to confirm that things were as they were supposed to be.

From what I knew, mages tended to live substantially longer than most of their non-magical peers. Wizardry allowed the healing of many minor wounds, and even those not skilled in healing seemed to do something, perhaps subconsciously, that kept their bodies working long after most people started to bow beneath the weight of their years. Archmages however, didn't even need to worry about that. Some in the past had chosen to remain eternally young, right up until the day they fell over dead.

The aystrylin, the source of one's life-force and aythar, that was the true limit. When that eventually gave out, you died, whether you were a wizard, an archmage, or a regular person like my deceased friend, Marc. Most people possessed an aystrylin that would still have plenty of life left in it by the time their bodies gave out, and mages tended to have even sturdier aystrylins than most. It was possible, barring a horribly violent end, that I might live to be very old indeed.

The sad truth was that someday I'd likely have to watch my wife pass while I was still hale. But until that day came, I intended to wear my years proudly.

Today was an exception, I told myself. *And I only did enough to recover from my illness and make myself healthy enough to deal with that asshole Tyrion if it becomes necessary. As long as I still look old it should be fine.*

Standing in the sunshine, I hardly noticed the cold autumn wind. "Damn this feels good," I said to no one in particular. *But I won't do it again,* I assured myself. Still, even the thought felt false. How long would it be before I gave in again, and how would Penny feel if she was forced to watch me remain young while she slowly crumbled over the decades to come?

No, never again. Not until the terrible day that I became a widower, and maybe not even then.

"Knowing my luck, I'll be killed in some particularly awful way long before she died," I said aloud, and then I laughed at the thought. Despite my newfound vitality, the wind *was* cold, and I was naked. I could have removed a blanket from the litter and wrapped myself in it, but since my power was back I created a bubble of warm air around myself.

To solve the 'nobody-wants-to-see-that-scary-naked-middle-aged-man' problem, I added illusory clothing. Close fitting black trousers and doeskin boots that almost reached the knee made a nice counterpoint to the loose white linen shirt covering my torso. Well, most of my torso, I left it unbuttoned in the front. I was feeling wicked.

Using my power, I created a reflective pane of air in front of me so I could check my appearance. *Damn, I do look good,* I thought appreciatively. All I needed was a rose clenched between my teeth, and

I'd be ready to see Penny. I dismissed the idea, though. As funny as it was, it was too much.

Leaving my litter behind, I walked up the slope to where Conall and Chad were waiting.

"Dad?" said Conall, his voice quavering slightly.

Chad's response was more colorful, "Well, fuck me…"

"I'm feeling much better now," I told them. "Let me go in first. I want to surprise them." I stepped past and opened the door without waiting for a reply.

My mother and Elise Thornbear were sitting in the front room, while Alyssa served them tea in small cups. The three women noticed me immediately and their reactions were all the reward I could have asked for.

My mother was first. "Mordecai?"

"I don't believe it," added Elise.

Alyssa's reaction was the best, though. Unlike the other two, she noticed my clothing first, and as her eyes traveled up my partially bare chest her cheeks colored slightly, and she nearly dropped the teapot. "Milord," she said quickly, dipping her head forward respectfully.

Their welcome was immediate and confusing. After a rush of questions, I stopped them. "I'm alright. I woke up. I healed myself…" My mother ignored all that and rushed to hug me.

I leaned much farther forward for the hug than I usually would have, and as her hands found my bare shoulders she understood why. "I haven't had a chance to dress myself yet," I told her.

Elise was also on her feet, but she stopped a few feet away. "I guess the hugs can wait then. Go get dressed. I'm starting to blush just thinking about it, and I'm far too old for that."

I winked at her and then asked, "Where is everyone?"

Meredith answered me, "Irene and Lynaralla are in bed. They've been very sick today. Moira is looking in on them. Matthew and Gram are out, scouting the area around Lancaster from dragonback. Rose and the Queen have returned to Albamarl to inform the high council of recent events…"

"And Penny?"

"She just got back," said Elise. "She's in your room, getting out of that smelly armor."

"Armor?"

My mother and Elise exchanged a quick glance. Then Mom spoke first, "She's been in the castle yard all day, getting the men ready for the expedition or sortie, whatever you want to call it."

I raised my brows questioningly.

"They're planning to take back Lancaster," Elise added. "You have a lot to catch up on." She started to tell me more, but Meredith interrupted her.

"Go see Penny. She needs to see you first, and she can tell you the rest." Mom made a shooing motion at me, directing me toward the hallway.

Needing no further encouragement, I headed for the master bedroom. I opened the door and found my wife with her hands in the air and her head covered. She was trying to shimmy out of her mail and padded gambeson unassisted which, while possible, was an awkward undertaking. Currently the chain shirt and gambeson were half off but her arms were still trapped in the sleeves. She was bent over the bed, shaking her body from side to side and trying to get them to slide loose.

At the sound of the door she jerked and yelled, her voice slightly muffled by the gambeson, "How many times have I told you to knock?! I'm changing!"

I grinned. She thought I was one of the kids. Ignoring her warning, I closed the door and stepped up behind her. Then I leaned forward to slide my hands up her sides in an attempt to help lift the armor from her. It wasn't an innocent attempt either, I made certain to enjoy her curves along the way.

Surprised, she jerked, spinning in place. The heavy arms of her mail coat slammed into the side of my head, and I fell sideways. "What the…!" she yelled. "Who is that?"

The impact left my head reeling, so I sat on the floor while I collected my wits. Meanwhile, Penny finished discarding her armor and grabbed up her sword before turning to face me. She froze when she realized who it was sitting before her. "Mort? How? Oh, gods! Are you alright?"

Her hair was sticking up in random directions, thanks to the armor she had just removed. She was clothed now in a linen undershirt, but she still had on the mail leggings, secured to a waist belt. Reaching down she pulled me to my feet and then wrapped me in her arms.

Being naked, I found the cold rough texture of the mail unpleasant against my lower half, but I kept my complaint to myself. Much better was her second surprise. Finding my back bare beneath her hands, she slid one down until it reached my buttocks.

"You don't waste any time, do you madam?!" I proclaimed with a lopsided grin as she pushed me back slightly.

"You're naked!" Penny had always been very observant.

My grin grew wider, and I added a lascivious leer. "You should know, since I'm sure you were the one who undressed me."

Her face took on an evil expression. "Actually, it was Elise who undressed you. I was in no state to manage it at the time."

My smile turned sour. "Why did she need to?"

"Bed bath," said Penny. Sensing her advantage, she added, "She was very gentle." Penny enjoyed my grimace, but then she started asking questions. "How are you like this? You were deathly ill a few hours ago."

I gave her a brief explanation. She was already familiar with my abilities, so I didn't have to say much. While I talked she finished removing her armor and sat down on the bed, clad only in her linen undershirt now. I sat beside her and put my arms around her. She leaned into me, resting her head against my shoulder.

She was dead tired, I could see that at a glance. Resting my chin on her head, I could smell metal and sweat in her hair. Not the sexy kind of sweat, mind you. Women often think they smell bad when in fact their perspiration can sometimes be almost an aphrodisiac. This was not that sort of smell. It was the smell of sweat that has soaked into a linen head covering, then been allowed to grow old and stale. Combine that with the pungent scent of iron and you begin to approach the stench of it. Anyone who has worn armor is familiar with it, and no one has ever called it pleasant.

She sniffed my chest. "You stink."

If that wasn't the pot calling the kettle black, I didn't know what was, but her nose was probably blind to her own aroma. "You need a bath too."

Years ago, inspired by the baths in the palace at Albamarl, I had built something similar for our mountain home. In fact, I had built two baths, one for the family, and a separate, private bath just for Penny and me. The water was provided by a spring-fed cistern some distance up the mountain side, and I had added an enchantment to heat the water coming from one of the pipes.

The family bath was small, accommodating only one person at a time, but ours was large enough for two, though we usually took turns anyway. Today, we bathed together, washing each other's hair while she caught me up on recent events.

"I heard Irene and Lynaralla are sick," I said as our discussion began.

"Which is why you are not," responded Penny.

The strange visions I had seen during my madness came to the fore, and I wondered what had been real and what had been delusion. "What did they do?" I asked.

"I've never been so proud of our children, Mort," said Penny. "I couldn't do anything, but they—they pulled together and found a way."

Dying of curiosity, I wanted to rush her, but I held my tongue and waited.

"It was Matthew's idea initially," she continued. "Something you said got him started. He talked to Elise, and then Gary, questioning them about how the body works."

Gary was not human, he was a man-like machine Matthew had brought back from another dimension, an android. I could well imagine he might have a different viewpoint on the knowledge that the She'Har might have.

"He came up with some sort of plan, but only Lynaralla could do it. It required She'Har spellweaving, but she didn't know how. So Moira forged a link between them, something beyond the normal telepathic communicating you all do sometimes, not that there's anything normal about the things the rest of you do. Somehow it enabled him to control her seed-mind directly."

What she was describing was fascinating, and I already knew what he must have used her spellweaving to do. They had probably created a spellweave to cleanse the blood. Some of my fever dreams made sense now. The 'ritual' I had imagined had probably resulted from that. The spellweave would have been used to slowly remove my blood, filtering it and returning it to my body.

"But it didn't work," continued Penny.

"Why not?"

"It was too slow, and we feared you would die before it could do you enough good. So, using a trick Gary told them about, they tested everyone's blood to see if it was compatible with yours," explained Penny.

"A trick?"

She nodded. "Matthew will explain it to you when he sees you. I didn't understand it, but the end result was that your blood was compatible with some of us, but not others. If they had used the wrong person's blood it would have killed you."

I was confused now. "Use it for what?"

"To replace yours. Conall, Gram, Irene, Matthew, and Lynaralla all had blood that could be used. I wanted them to use mine, but it wasn't compatible, nor was Moira's."

Gradually, I understood what they had done, and I couldn't help but think it was a brilliant idea. If my kidneys were in shock or not functioning, they had used their own to do the work for me. Rather than wait on the spellweave to filter my blood, they had exchanged blood directly with me and let their own kidneys cleanse it.

"Conall and Gram were first," said Penny. "They each exchanged roughly half their blood with yours, but afterward both of them became violently ill." She saw the look of alarm in my eyes and rushed to add, "But they're fine now. They got better after a day or two.

"You were still raving and very ill, though, so Matthew repeated the process using only himself the next day. They thought since you'd already had some done that maybe it would only take one person, but he got even sicker. He was throwing up until last night.

"Irene insisted they use her the next day, which was yesterday, but to make it more tolerable, they included Lynaralla too. Both of them became ill, but it was much less severe than what the others went through. They'll probably be right as rain by morning." Penny gave me a worried look. "There's a catch, though. Elise warned me that we might be wasting our time. You might seem to get better, but your kidneys might not recover. If so, you'll get sick again. We might have to keep doing this indefinitely, or watch you die."

Smiling, I leaned over and kissed her. "Don't worry. Whether my kidneys recovered or not, what I did today reset my entire body. I'm fine."

She exhaled slowly, letting the last of her tension leave her body. Penny had been holding that fear back the entire time we had been talking. "I hope you're right."

I held her tightly, feeling her shoulders shake. She didn't cry out loud. There had been too many tears over the past week, so this spell passed quickly. I wanted to do more than just hold her, but I could tell she was tired. So we dried off and went to bed.

The sun was still up, it was only late afternoon, but Penny was exhausted. Even so, she had trouble sleeping, so I used my power to give her a gentle push, easing her into a restful slumber. I wasn't actually tired, but I stayed with her until the peace and quiet overcame my newfound energy, and I drifted off beside her.

She woke me a few hours later. Night had come, but the intensity in her gaze told me she wouldn't return to slumber until a more basic need had been satisfied.

When I returned to sleep a while later, it was with a smile on my face.

CHAPTER 14

We woke early, very early, with nearly four hours until dawn, but that's what happens when you go to bed before the sun has finished setting. It isn't something I would normally recommend, but after being in bed for over a week it hardly mattered to me.

Penny was shrugging on her armor and buckling straps before I had even finished wiping the sleep from my eyes. Aside from the smell, she looked pretty good in it. Well, she always looked good to me. In all honesty, mail isn't a good look for anyone. It sags in places, even if it's well fitted, which hers was. It also completely obscures the form of whoever is wearing it, muscles, breasts, whatever you like about yourself, it won't be discernible. Forget the romance paintings, real people wear a padded gambeson underneath, and it's so thick it's almost like sewing pillows together and then making a coat out of them.

The gambeson is more protection than the mail itself, truth be told, and if you had to forgo one for the other, it would be the mail. A good gambeson could stop most arrows all by itself, and it was the only protection you had against blunt force attacks, mail or no mail. That's the power of fifteen plus layers of linen.

The mail she wore was enchanted, which made it impossible to cut or pierce it. It also protected the metal rings from rust and reduced the weight, but even with those advantages, it was the gambeson that did most of the real work of protecting my wife's precious body.

I was glad I didn't have to wear that rubbish. Being a wizard has a lot of perks.

Not to be outdone, I started putting on my dapper black and red hunting leathers. They were stylish as well as enchanted to provide *some* protection. From what Penny had told me the day before, today was the day that our expeditionary force would ride out to confront the matter of Lancaster's sudden jungle disappearance.

"What do you think you're doing?" asked Penny, her eyes sending a clear message that I was once again doing something terribly wrong.

I assumed it was my decisions to come, despite my recent stint at death's door. "I'm healthy as a horse. I'm coming with you."

"Not wearing that, you're not."

"You prefer my naughty courtier look from yesterday?" I quipped.

Lifting her scabbarded sword, she pointed it at the armor stand in the corner.

"Oh, no! Not that! I'd rather go naked!" I stated bravely. She was pointing at my enchanted plate. It was some of the first armor I had ever made, and it was a match to the armor that my friend Dorian had once worn. I probably hadn't put it on in over a decade.

Now, before I go on, let me state one thing clearly. Plate, even a full set of plate, is more comfortable than mail, lighter too, even if it isn't enchanted. It still requires a padded gambeson, but the gambeson doesn't need to be quite as thick. It also provides considerable freedom of movement, despite how it looks. I had long intended to make a set for Penny, but life always had more pressing matters for me to attend to.

"You'll wear it, or you'll stay home," said Penny evenly.

Having just woken up, my good sense and good humor were paper thin. "Remind me again, which one of us is the Count di' Cameron here?"

I flinched inwardly when I saw her face harden. Marching toward me, she gathered the front of my shirt in her fist and pressed me back until I felt the wall behind me. "You're not the Count of anything until we walk out that door! You're my husband! How many times have I seen you injured or nearly killed? How long was I a widow, thinking you dead and gone for good? This past week was just a reminder of that. How many more times do I have to be scared to death, thinking I've lost you? Do you care?"

And if I didn't feel enough like an ass, she added, "Put it on, please— if you love me."

Several of Chad Grayson's favorite phrases came to mind, but they were all directed at myself. I nodded, and unsure how to apologize I said simply, "You're right."

So, I put the damned armor on, with her assistance of course. Despite its many advantages, putting plate on by yourself isn't a practical undertaking. It's possible sure, but it takes twice as long, and you're likely to wind up with some of the straps too loose.

She gave me a kiss when we finished getting it all secured, and despite being a middle-aged man, I felt like a very good boy.

I fastened my belt of deadly surprises, took up my staff, and we went out the door. It was time to face the world.

The rest of the house was just beginning to stir. There would be no breakfast at home today, we'd be eating in the castle with the rest of the armsmen. Every single one of my children intended to come, and we allowed it, except for poor Irene. She was too young, and still hadn't come into her power yet, and she didn't have armor, or any training.

If Penny had had her preference, none of them would have come, and I felt much the same, but today wasn't a day for half-measures. Plus, we intended to keep some of them in 'reserve' rather than putting them in harm's way. There was another, smaller argument, when they were all forced to wear armor.

Conall was fine with it, though he didn't have enchanted mail. He wore a gambeson and normal mail. Matthew objected to his magical armor, arguing that his enchantments and other devices provided far better protection already, but I overruled him immediately. Moira and Lynaralla had no armor at all, but we found gambesons that would fit them, and they were destined for the reserve portion of our force anyway.

By the time we reached the main hall in the keep it was bustling with activity. The kitchen had been hard at work for an hour already, and the food was beginning to come out, even though dawn was still almost an hour away. Armsmen were everywhere, sitting down, moving around, entering and leaving, it was organized chaos.

At the center of it all were Sir Gram and Captain Draper. As a nobleman, and the only knight present, Gram was nominally in charge of the men, but Captain Draper was far older and more experienced. Carl Draper had been the captain of my guard for years and with Cyhan wounded, it fell to him to organize the men. Gram assisted primarily by standing nearby and paying close attention. On any matters that came up for debate, he settled them by supporting the captain's decision.

The hall fell temporarily quiet as I and my family entered. During normal dining activities everyone waited to sit until I had arrived, but this was no normal breakfast. Raising my voice, I addressed them, "Forget about formalities for now. Finish your preparations and fill your bellies. We leave in less than an hour!"

Gram nodded to me, and Captain Draper resumed talking to the knot of men around him. The noise and clamor returned to its previous volume. Penny and I sat at the high table and began eating.

Chad Grayson appeared moments later, clad in the mail I had crafted for him years ago. I couldn't remember the last time I had seen him wear it. There was an enchanted sword on his hip that I didn't recognize and a heavy warbow in his hand. A quiver of arrows rode at his hip and my magesight could detect still more bundled away in the pack over his shoulder. All of them had enchanted metal points.

"You almost look heroic," I told him as he sat down beside Conall.

His face puckered in a sour expression. "I feel like a jackass in all this shit. My only consolation is seeing you all dandied up in yer fancy plate like a prize show horse."

I couldn't think of a decent reply, so I just whinnied at him instead. A few of the kids were kind enough to laugh, though it wasn't funny enough to warrant it.

An hour later, we were on the road, well some of us were. My fifty men at arms were on horseback, led by Captain Draper. Conall and Lynaralla rode with them. Penny was on dragonback, and I sat behind her, marveling at how large Layla had grown. The beast was as long as four wagons placed end to end. Matthew was mounted on his dragon, Zephyr, who though he was relatively newly hatched, had grown large enough to support a single rider. Gram and Chad were astride Grace, and Moira rode her dragon, Cassandra. Their dragons were nearly as large as Layla.

We made an impressive sight, fifty horsemen on the road and four dragons flying above them. Just as impressive, though not visibly so, was the fact that our group included no less than five wizards. Penny and I weren't taking any chances today.

The dragons could fly much faster than the men on horse could travel, so we went ahead to examine the edge of the newly arrived 'jungle'. It would take the soldiers almost four hours to reach that point, but on dragonback it was just a matter of a quarter of an hour's flight.

We landed a good distance from the edge, and I relayed my orders to the others. "Moira, you and Cassandra fly back to the riders, let them know the road is clear, then return. The rest of you hold this position until they get here. Penny and I will fly over and get a good look at things from above."

Gram objected, "My lord, I don't think it wise for you and the Countess to do the scouting. You should let…"

I cut him off, "Noted, Sir Gram, now do as I command."

"Yes, milord," he responded.

That was rude, said Grace, Gram's dragon, projecting her thoughts to my mind.

The same goes for you, I told the dragon. Whenever I heard her thoughts or voice I couldn't help but remember her as a stuffed bear, which is how she had started her life. She had been a spellbeast created by Moira to animate one of her toys, but our family had grown so fond of her that she was later used to give life to one of the new dragons. *This is a military expedition and I expect everyone to follow orders,* I added.

She sniffed mentally. *Well I, for one, am not a soldier.*

I didn't respond to that, and Gram must have started talking to her, for she said nothing more to me. Penny sent the command to Layla and with several great downstrokes of her wings, we were airborne once more.

"How would you like to do this?" asked Penny, leaning back and yelling into the wind.

It was easier for me to reply, since I could put my mouth close to her ear, "Take us up a thousand feet or so, then fly east. Stay just beyond the boundary."

She did, and we flew that way for several minutes while the miles vanished beneath us. One thing became immediately apparent. The boundary between the new jungle and the old land that we expected to see was impossibly straight, as though it had been drawn by a giant hand with a ruler. In a few spots the massive trees at the edge looked as though they had been cut in half by a razor, perfectly obeying the boundary line. Then at some point, the line changed, angling away from us in a northeasterly direction. Again the line was perfect, and it met the previous one creating a precise angle.

Maybe a hundred and twenty degrees, I guessed mentally.

We followed this new direction for a while, and after traveling a similar distance it changed again, heading to the northwest. If there was a similar shift ahead it would take us west, parallel to the first part of the boundary we had seen. I tapped Penny on the shoulder. "I have a hunch. Turn Layla around and follow the same route we came. I'm going to fly above and see if I can get a better view."

She wasn't fond of my plan. "We should stay together."

"This will only take a few minutes. I can do it much faster this way." Then I stood and let the wind sweep me off of Layla's broad back.

Sometimes being me is pretty damn awesome. I used my power to shape a shield around me, catching the wind, and then I caught the air itself with my aythar, directing it according to my will. I spun head over heels in a graceful loop and then rocketed straight up toward the grey clouds above.

It might have been an overly showy move, but I had spent the last week terribly ill, skirting the line between life and death. I felt I deserved a moment to show off. Picking up speed I was already a thousand feet above them when I looked down to see Layla slowly banking to the right, making a wide circle to take them back in the direction they had come.

My power drove me ever higher, as I raced toward the limits of the sky, the ground dwindling beneath me. As the air began to thin I changed my shield to keep a heavier bubble of air around me. As I went higher still I felt the pressure inside begin to press outward. My altitude now was such that it would probably be impossible to breathe without my shield, and I knew I was limited by how much air I had with me. I couldn't stay this high for too long.

The view below had already revealed what I suspected, though. The bizarre foreign forest had arrived in a precise geometric shape, that of a hexagon. *The question, is why?* I thought. There was something about the shape that tickled a memory in the back of my head, but I couldn't yet put my finger on it.

Lancaster Castle should have been in the northwestern portion of the hexagon, but I could see no sign of it, or of the lake that was associated with it. Even with those huge trees, the lake should have still been easily visible, but it wasn't. The piece of land beneath me simply wasn't the same one that had once held Lancaster.

Putting that question aside, I began my descent. I was so high I could no longer make out the massive dragon, but soon enough she appeared, a tiny dot below. I angled my flight to meet them and slowed when I was almost there. With a flourish I turned over and dropped lightly onto Layla's back, exactly where I had been before.

Penny nearly jumped at my touch. "I will never get used to that!" she yelled over the rushing wind.

I laughed, and we flew on, returning to where we had left the others. They were anxious to hear whatever news we had, so I explained what I had seen. Matthew frowned as I described the hexagon I had seen, and his eyes met mine for a second, a question in them.

"Why would it be that shape?" wondered Gram aloud.

Chad wiped his mouth, slipping a small flask back into his pack, ignoring the look of scorn Penny gave him. "Fuck if I know," he commented. "Maybe the gods have a weird sense of humor."

"There aren't any gods left," said Penny.

Layla spoke, her deep rumbling voice rolling across us, "Could it be a spell?"

I dismissed her words, "No wizard could do such a thing. It's too big. I wouldn't even begin to imagine how it could be done. Growing trees of that size, in less than a day, over such an area?"

"What about an archmage?" asked Grace.

Matthew shook his head. "No, there are traces of magic at the boundary."

Gram's dragon nodded, "So it could have been an archmage…"

I interrupted, "That's not what he means. What an archmage does isn't really magic. It's more like persuading the universe to do what we want. If this was an instance of an archmage remaking reality, there wouldn't be any traces of strange aythar at all. Besides, if someone like me managed to do this, it wouldn't be a hexagon. It would be circular, or even irregularly shaped. The human mind doesn't usually imagine things in perfect geometric forms like this."

"What if it wasn't a human archmage?" asked Grace.

Chad spoke up, mildly annoyed, "He already said it wasn't an archmage."

"There aren't any non-human archmages anyway," I added. "Tyrion was the first, and the She'Har had never encountered the phenomenon before he was discovered."

"Does Tyrion even count as human anymore?" asked Gram. "I thought he was supposed to be She'Har now. Wasn't he a tree?"

Penny grimaced, "Not the last time we saw him. He seemed entirely too human then."

Matthew had been silent the entire time, deep in his own thoughts, but I had an idea what he might be thinking. There was one type of magic that used the hexagonal shape in everything it did. He looked up at me. "Do you think Tyrion can spellweave now?"

Everyone fell silent, watching us as I replied, "I don't know. Even though he was or is a She'Har elder, I'm not sure it's possible. It requires a seed-mind."

The seed-mind was the main thing that distinguished She'Har children from regular humans. Their bodies were fully human in every respect, but within their brains was an extra, non-human organ, a small structure of vegetable matter. It was this structure, the seed-mind, that eventually became a She'Har elder, a tree. It recorded all the events of their lives, preserving the information and giving them perfect recall. It was also what produced their spellweaves, transforming their thoughts and aythar into a highly structured form of magic.

What few knew, was that that magic was formed entirely of tiny hexagons. The shapes were so small that few mages, She'Har or human, could perceive them. Tyrion had seen them once, two thousand years ago, and I had observed them myself when I had occasionally encountered She'Har spellweaves.

Penny broke the silence first, "You think Tyrion did this?"

"I don't see how he could have," I answered. "Or why he would, for that matter. He would have had to travel here right after we fought. And that still leaves the question of how he would have done it. The amount of power that would be required to do this—none of it makes sense."

"This was translation magic," pronounced Matthew.

Translation was the term my son had coined for his own special gift, the ability to manipulate dimensions and travel between them. It was an ability that had once belonged only to the Illeniel She'Har, but it had been passed on to him through an inconceivable series of seeming coincidences. Coincidences planned by the Illeniel She'Har in their bid to preserve their species. He had inherited his magic from me, but while my last name came from Tyrion, neither I nor my ancestor possessed the Illeniel gift. No, my son had acquired the Illeniel gift from his mother, Penny. She had always had the gift of foresight, a gift that appeared to come from some unknown Illeniel ancestor.

In my son, who was also a human mage, the gift had finally come to fruition, granting him the ability to manipulate dimensions and to sometimes predict the future. He didn't describe it as foretelling, though. His explanation was that he saw into closely related dimensions, dimensions advanced in time compared to our own. From that he was able to predict what would 'probably' happen in our own.

He also had little conscious control over that aspect of his ability. From what he had said, in times of stress or danger it allowed him to avoid attacks before they came, but he had never had prophetic visions like his mother had, or like the She'Har elders did.

"You're sure?" I asked him.

Matthew nodded. "I am. It's also the only thing that makes any sense. Growing giant trees and changing the landscape doesn't seem rational. The land didn't change. It's been replaced. The jungle we are looking at came from somewhere else."

"An' what about Lancaster?" put in Chad.

Matthew shrugged, "If this is here, maybe it's where this came from?"

My wife rephrased her question with more emphasis, "So it had to be Tyrion who did this, right?"

"As much as I'd like to blame him, he doesn't have the Illeniel gift, and he probably can't spellweave either," I told them.

"Lyralliantha does," said Matthew. "And so does Lynaralla, along with any other children the new She'Har have produced."

"Then they have betrayed us," concluded Gram. Penny's face echoed the anger in his words.

Holding up a hand I cautioned, "We don't know that yet. There's no apparent reason for them to do something like this. It makes no sense."

"Unless the She'Har planned this as a way…," began Matthew.

"Matt!" I barked, a bit too sharply. "No more speculation for now. We need more facts." I turned to the others, "I don't want any of you discussing this when the others get here, either. I'll investigate the idea further when we return home."

"Fuck that!" said Chad, spitting at the ground. "Lynaralla's one of 'em. Walter and Elaine are probably dead, an' she could be a traitor. I say we make her tell us exactly what she knows."

I gave him an imperious glare. "Master Grayson, you will do exactly as I have commanded."

The archer held my gaze steadily, rebellion in his eyes, but after a time he eventually responded, "Fine—for now."

Penny spoke up, "I don't want to believe she has anything to do with this, but he has a point, Mort."

Facing my wife, I put my back to the others before mouthing the words, 'not now'.

After a second she added, "I agree, though. We should keep this quiet."

A sigh of relief escaped my lips. I couldn't have them descending into argument and accusations. My son had almost blown the entire thing wide open with his remark, and I already knew what he was thinking. What we were looking at could be the result of some long-hidden plan of the Illeniel She'Har. It was possible they had hidden a part of their grove, tucking it away in an extra-dimensional space. What we had found could be part of it, if there were Illeniel elders tucked in amidst the massive trees, or it could be some kind of side effect.

Either way, if it turned out the Illeniel She'Har had some hidden plan, the knowledge could spark a war. I wasn't ready to allow rumors and speculation to start that war, not until I knew more. I sent a private thought directly to my son, *Say no more of this, to anyone. If you have any ideas save them for my ears only.*

He nodded, and then sent a reply, *If this is something done by the Illeniel She'Har, why don't we know about it?*

Because the loshti Tyrion stole was tailored by them. Whatever their full plan was, they kept all knowledge of it from him, and by extension, his descendants, I answered.

We waited in silence after that, as everyone pondered their own thoughts. It would be another two hours before the soldiers arrived.

CHAPTER 15

Moira arrived first, her dragon Cassandra coming down in a long glide to land near us. An hour and a half later the horses could be heard and soon we were all together once again. Thankfully the others heeded my command, and no word of our prior speculation was brought up.

"Captain, pick twenty-five of your men to go with us under Sir Gram's command. The other half will remain here with you as a reserve force. Lynaralla, Conall, and Moira, you will stay with them," I ordered, announcing my plans.

Conall stood up in his stirrups, "But Father!..."

Penny cut him off, "Conall! If you want to be on any more military exercises, then you'd best learn to obey commands."

None of the others dared protest after that.

Once I was sure I had their attention, I went on, "The rest of us, along with most of the dragons, will enter the forest. We will blaze a path and search for survivors. If possible, we will make our way to where Lancaster was, or where it should be. If things go badly, it will be the responsibility of those here to either haul our asses out of the fire, or fight a holding action while we retreat. Am I understood?"

Captain Draper saluted, "Yes, my lord!" Almost comically, Lynaralla saluted along with him, unaware of the fact that since she wasn't technically my vassal, or part of the military, she wasn't required to do so. A few of the men chuckled at her overly serious demeanor.

There's no way she's part of some plot or scheme, I thought silently.

We entered the forest with the three dragons leading the way, Layla, Zephyr, and Grace. Their massive forms created an easy path for the rest of us. The largest trees they avoided, but everything else, smaller trees, bushes, and underbrush, they trampled and tore through. Gram and five of the soldiers followed them on foot, while five took position on either side of us. The remaining ten men kept to our rear. Chad, Penny,

Matthew, and I remained in the center. The horses remained with the reserve force as the terrain was too unpredictable.

Using such a wide formation wouldn't have been possible in such thick growth, were it not for the wide path created by the dragons. With their help it was easy going, almost easy enough for us to have brought the horses, but the destruction they left in their wake included a vast amount of broken limbs and uprooted saplings, which would have made for treacherous footing.

Matthew and I kept our magesight trained on our surroundings, searching for some sign of Walter or Elaine, or any other survivors. From what we had heard, I doubted we would find any, and if the Prathions were alive, they might well be veiling themselves from even our senses. We could only hope that the incredible noise of the dragons tearing through the forest would alert them to our presence so that they would signal us in some way.

I detected no animals in our vicinity at all, other than small rodents and the occasional bird. Nothing like the monstrous bear-like creatures presented itself within my range. That might have been because of the dragons, though. The sound of their passing was incredible, and I could well imagine that any large predators with even an ounce of intelligence would be quickly heading in any direction but toward us. It was almost disappointing.

If anything did attack, though, it was bound to learn the error of its ways quickly enough. Dragons were not to be messed with. After an hour of traveling, stepping on and over broken limbs, I was convinced there would be no attack.

"I don't like this," muttered Chad, who walked beside me. Of our entire group, he had the least trouble with the unpredictable footing. He was at least as old as I was, but his feet were sure.

"If you say, 'it's too quiet' I'll laugh," I replied. The noise of our passing was deafening. During the moments where the dragons did pause, it was quiet, but that was to be expected. The creatures making our path were predators large enough to scare away *everything*.

"Very funny," he said sourly. "Nah, it's not that. It's these trees, the grass—all of it. I don't recognize any of it."

"That's a pine," I said, pointing at one of the larger trunks we were bypassing.

"Yeah, but what kind of pine?" he remarked. "There are dozens of different kinds, and this ain't like any of the ones I know." Bending over, he snatched up a leaf with an irregular star-shaped leaf, "An' yeah, this is a hardwood, but what kind? I don't know it."

I had never taken him for a botanist, but that was the thing about the greying woodsman, he was full of surprises. People often dismissed him because of his rough phrases and uncouth demeanor, but underestimating him was a mistake. I knew for a fact he was just as sharp as his arrows.

"An' every bit of it is too fucking old, too damn big," he continued. "This is like a primeval forest. Trees don't get that big unless they've been left alone for a really long-ass time."

"What are you getting at?" I asked.

He sighed. "I'm a hunter. I spent my whole life in the woods, and in all that time, I knew I was the biggest, meanest thing there. Well, 'cept maybe for a bear, but even they know to steer clear of humans. This place makes me feel small, an' somethin' tells me I ain't the most dangerous animal in these woods."

"At least we're the smartest," I said lightheartedly.

The veteran archer wasn't amused. "Are we, Mordecai? We don't know a damn thing about this place."

"Well, if we aren't the smartest, at least we brought the biggest with us," I said, nodding toward the dragons.

"Bigger ain't...," he started to reply, and then chaos broke loose.

I felt it only a second before it happened, multiple flashes of aythar appearing around, and more crucially, below us. They weren't the sort of flash you would see when a mage used his power, no, this was much more subdued, as though a host of living creatures had appeared where only inanimate dirt and soil had been before.

Two of Captain Draper's men, Daniels and a fellow whose name I didn't know, vanished as a flurry of dirt flew upward. I could still see them with my magesight, struggling only a foot or two beneath the surface with monsters that had entirely too many legs. They had been dragged under.

At the same time, attacks came from both sides of our party. One man on either side was drawn under while a large number of the unknown beasts swarmed over the dragons.

All of this was merely the backdrop for what had my personal attention, though. The ground had shifted beneath me, and something with fangs, clawed insect-like legs, seized my legs. I was flat on my back and halfway underground before I fully registered what was happening. Matthew was in similar straits.

Dragons roared, and men screamed, but before I could help anyone else I had to do something about my own situation. Seconds later, as the initial shock passed, I struck out at the thing holding me with a powerful bludgeoning strike of pure aythar. The results were less than impressive. It shed aythar like a duck shed water. My power hit, but slid away, doing minimal damage to the creature, if any at all.

Simultaneously, I flailed with my arms, legs, anything that would move. That part was purely instinctive, and not very manly, when viewed from an objective standpoint. But it wasn't a matter of thought, I was overwhelmed by the raw terror that anyone would feel at being seized by a giant man-eating spider.

Terror was an old friend of mine, though, and some part of my mind kept working, just not the part that managed kicking and screaming. Since my power was ineffective against the creature, I directed it at the ground instead, creating a rock-solid foundation beneath me to halt my descent. Then I used the earth like a fist, clenching it around the thing trying to bite through my greaves.

A short struggle ensued, but after a moment I was able to force my body and the spider's apart, though my leg was bruised and twisted in the process. I opened the earth above my head and glorious sunlight spilled down on me, a welcome sight. Penny's hand reached for me, but before I could take it, the thing beside me broke free, scrambling over me and surging toward her.

Her sword stabbed downward, passing through its head and all the way into its body, spraying me with ichor. Scrabbling to get out from beneath it, I finally emerged into the daylight where a scene of madness and horror greeted me. Spiders the size of ponies were clambering over and under the dragons. The soldier's who had been spared the initial ambush attacks were backing in around us, forming a desperate circle.

Gram had been the first to react. His unusual training granting him a near instantaneous reaction time. His sword, Thorn, had cut through the cephalothorax and legs of the spider that had tried to grab him, and then he had turned to help some of the others.

Matthew had also responded quickly, if less gracefully, by virtue of his precognitive gift. He struggled a few feet away, his enchanted metal hand holding a spider's fangs at bay while he anchored and supported himself in place with his power. The arachnid's forelegs battered him several times, but the claw-like tips weren't able to pierce his mail. Gram's sword swept in and bisected the lower half of the creature before Matt had a chance to do anything else.

Everything had happened in a span of less than ten seconds. Penny leapt over me, soaring through the air to land in front of one of our defenders who had just been mauled. She came down in a crouch, driving her sword point first through the spider beneath her feet.

Help the dragons, I told my son mentally. *I'll help the soldiers.*

His answer was terse, *Got it.*

The men had good discipline, and now that their nightmare enemies were visible and in front of them, they were better able to defend themselves. But the four who had been taken underground were beyond their aid, so I focused my efforts there first.

Releasing my power in a surge, I used the earth itself to grapple the spiders that had taken them under. With four men to save and little time, I could no longer afford to be as gentle as I had been when extricating myself. One after another, I ripped the men free and pulled them up, crushing the monsters holding them as I did in a vice of soil.

Almost beneath my awareness, was a constant thrumming noise, and it was then that I noticed Chad Grayson standing beside me. The sound came from his bow, which had been working steadily since the beginning. Unlike his previous trip here, this time he came armed with war arrows from the castle armory, which were tipped with enchanted bodkin points.

His shots were well aimed, and the arrows penetrated deeply, most of them sinking into the spiders until only the fletchings were still visible, but the arachnids were slow to die from such wounds. Slashing cuts from the swords of the soldiers were quicker to have visible effect, though most of them lacked the strength to cut deeply, except for Penny and Gram.

My wife was fury incarnate. Outside the circle of defenders, she went from place to place, cutting away legs, fangs, heads, anything that came with reach.

Gram on the other hand, I had no words for him. In his size and form, he reminded me of Dorian, especially with Thorn in his hands, but his movements were unearthly. Dorian Thornbear had been a knight and a great swordsman, but his son did not fight like a swordsman. At times I could have sworn he had magesight. He used Thorn almost entirely for offense, while his uncanny movements sidestepped every striking claw or leaping body, whether they were in his field of view or not. Thorn's long blade swept through his enemies, leaving only dismembered pieces in its wake.

Most of Chad's arrows had been fired at the spiders clinging to the dragons. They were at a serious disadvantage against their smaller opponents. They thrashed and rolled, trying to dislodge their nimble attackers, but without much luck. Matthew was finishing them off by using his power to smash them loose with heavy rocks and small boulders he had ripped from the ground.

"Everyone inside the circle!" I commanded, yelling mainly for Penny and Gram's benefit. They withdrew, almost reluctantly, into the relative safety of our small defensive line. Once they were in, I shouted my spell, *"Grabol ni'targoth, mai cieren, forzen dantos nian!"*

The earth was ripped from beneath the spiders harrying the soldiers, creating a ten-foot-deep trench around us in a circle. The newly liberated soil rose on the outside like a massive dirt wave that crashed down over the falling monsters. I put all my anger and fear into it, and the soil slammed down on them like a hammer, crushing and smothering them in darkness. All thirteen remaining spiders were swallowed up by the savage spell.

Silence fell over us, but it lasted only seconds.

Chad Grayson reached down and angrily ripped an arrow from the body of a dead spider within the circle. "As I was fuckin' sayin'," he grumbled loudly, "bigger ain't always better! Not that I needed these cocksuckin' whoresons to show up an' prove my damn point!"

After a moment a few of the men began to laugh, though it was more a hysterical tittering born of adrenaline and nerves, than genuine relief.

Of the four I had dragged from underground, three were dead. Daniels was the only one who remained alive, and he was badly injured. His leg was torn and twisted, the bones shattered. I attended to him first, since he was bleeding so badly he would die within minutes otherwise.

I could hear deep moaning rumbles from the dragons while I worked to seal the blood vessels in Daniels' leg. The skin and muscles had been mangled, and despite my best efforts I had a feeling he might never have use of his leg again.

Three others were injured, and one had been bitten. The bite looked bad, and the man who had suffered it was sweating and crying out in pain. Each beat of his heart caused agony to surge through him. The fangs had passed through his gambeson and punctured his forearm, and the flesh there was already purple and shading toward black.

We removed his mail hauberk and cut away the sleeve before using it to apply a tourniquet to his upper arm. I hoped it would keep the poison from spreading farther, but the man's eyes were already twitching. I had a bad feeling it was too late already.

Of the dragons, both Layla and Zephyr had suffered several bites apiece. Given their size and powerful constitutions, I didn't think it would kill them, and anything that didn't kill them, they could recover from, given time. For now, though, they were both in incredible pain.

All eyes were on me.

This was one of those moments, the sort that had bothered me greatly during my early years as the Count di' Cameron. My decisions had consequences, people were dead, and some of those that survived would have lifelong injuries. As a young man I had bulled through these moments by necessity, while suffering from my doubts and what-ifs after the dust settled.

Not much had changed, but it was easier. I would still feel guilt later, but not quite as much as I once had. It wasn't that my doubts had grown smaller, just that I no longer believed in perfect choices. Whatever I did, someone would suffer. And just as then, confidence was more important than perfection.

"Can the dragons fly?" I asked firmly.

"Layla can," answered Penny.

Matthew nodded. "Zephyr should be able to make the edge of the forest at least. After that, I'm not sure."

"They'll return to the reserve force's position then," I ordered. "Matt, I want you to ride Grace and take the wounded men with you. Once you reach them, share what has happened here and return.

"Tell Conall to prepare a temporary circle to take the wounded back to the castle. Then have Moira and Cassandra return with you, along with five more men. Captain Draper is to stay with the men, along with Conall and Lynaralla." I stopped, scanning their faces and looking to see if there were any questions. When I didn't see any, I finished, "Get moving."

Once they were on their way, Gram had the remaining soldiers clear the ground of debris, piling it up to create an impromptu barrier around our location. Then he stationed them around it in a broad circle.

Gram approached me then. "Do you think we should position a few lookouts?"

Before I could answer, Chad spoke up, "Do you want to go stand out there? I fer damn sure don't."

"He makes a good point. Besides, in the absence of an enemy we understand, like other soldiers, putting our men outside the immediate area only exposes them to risks we can't anticipate. I'd rather keep them together. My arcane senses should provide us with forewarning should something attempt to sneak up on us," I told them.

Penny didn't look happy. "Like it did with the spiders?"

That was something that already bothered me, but I had been thinking about it. "The spiders had some method of lowering their ambient aythar, so they appeared more like inanimate objects rather than living creatures, but when they moved to attack their aythar became brighter."

"What if something out there can do the same while movin'?" asked Chad.

Shaking my head, I responded, "I don't think it works that way, but even if something could, the movement alone would be enough for me to see it. These things surprised us because they were still and underground, where we weren't paying close attention."

The huntsman nodded and removed his pack, opening it to remove one of his stored bundles of arrows. The quiver at his hip was empty. During our short battle he had managed to put at least one shaft into nearly every spider we faced, and two or three in some of them. "I hope nothin' else shows up," he muttered. "Or I'll be out of arrows." He finished his preparations by taking another long pull from his flask.

"What bothers me most," said Chad, "is that those spiders, besides bein' fuckin' huge, didn't act like normal spiders."

I was busy scanning the area around us with my magesight, but I listened carefully as he spoke. It was Gram who asked the first question, "Lots of spiders hunt. And I've seen a trapdoor spider before, they use ambush tactics. Wasn't this similar?"

"Trapdoor spiders build their trap long before the prey shows up," said the woodsman. "These fuckin' bastards dug in here just to get us. They saw our route and planned ahead. Not only that, they worked as a group. I never heard of any spiders that were pack hunters, an' that scares the *shit* outta me."

"We should just burn this place to ashes," observed Penny. "When the dragons get back, they could do it. Imagine if something like those spiders got loose and started breeding."

She had a valid point, though I wasn't sure we could do that without risking a wildfire that would spread far beyond this strange forest. Plus, we didn't know yet whether there might be survivors from Lancaster here, or from our own first group of explorers.

My thoughts ended there. A flash of aythar in the distance had caught my attention. Holding up my hand, I alerted the others while I focused my magesight in that direction. In the best circumstances, my magesight could see things more than a mile away, but the armor I wore interfered. The enchanted plate blocked aythar as well as mundane threats. The helmet and gloves were specially crafted so that I could make them permeable, allowing me to sense things and use magic while wearing it, but it still wasn't ideal.

I removed my helmet, earning a frown from my wife, but the look on my face silenced her before she could complain. *There.* I sensed it again, clearly this time, a pulse of aythar, like a brief beacon. I recognized it as well. "Elaine."

"She's alive? You can see her?" asked Penny, a hopeful look on her features.

Nodding, I raised one hand and created a similar pulse, an answer of sorts, to make sure she knew where we were. Elaine would also recognize my aythar, so she would know it was me. "She's not quite a mile from us, in that direction," I said, pointing to the east.

Then the trace of aythar vanished, not just Elaine's signal, but *every* hint of her. "She's veiled herself," I announced. "She's probably been in hiding for the past few days."

"We need to get to her," said Penny.

Chad shrugged. "She's lasted this long. Best to wait for the dragons to return. It'll be tough goin' to try and get through this place without 'em."

Walking to the edge of our position, I lifted my staff, holding it horizontally and then crouching so that it was close to the ground. Drawing a deep breath, I pulled in my will, letting my strength build in my chest. Then I exhaled and forced the aythar down the length of the rune channel carved in the wood. A line of red incandescent energy shot forth. Sweeping it from side to side, I cut a path through the thick forest that extended nearly a hundred yards. Two of the giant trees were in that path, and both were now falling.

We had the beginnings of a path now, though it wouldn't be nearly as easy to walk as the one the dragons had created. My method had cut away everything in our way, but most of it, aside from the largest trees, had simply fallen where it had been, creating a tangle of brush, limbs, and downed saplings.

I raised my staff again and began selectively cutting the worst of the tangle near us, then I turned to the others, "Let's go."

CHAPTER 16

Lady Rose stared out over the battlements from the top of Castle Cameron. She stood alone, for nearly every man at arms within the keep had gone with the Count and Countess on their expedition to Lancaster. Just five guardsmen remained, and those were posted at the gates.

If anyone had been there to observe her, they would surely have been taken by the sight of her. Rose Thornbear was not a tall woman, but her bearing left most with the impression they had met a towering beauty after meeting her. Now in her middling years, the traces of grey in her black hair did nothing to detract from her looks.

In spite of her striking features and petite form she had rarely suffered from being seen as unintelligent, as so many beautiful women were. A single glance from her icy blue eyes left most men in no doubt that they would be quickly outdone should they dare match their wits against hers.

Outwardly she was composed, but internally she was a tangled knot of emotions. She had been here many times before, it was one of the repeating conditions of her life. *First my father, then Dorian, now Gram—and Mordecai...* Over and over she had been forced to watch the men in her life march off to risk themselves, leaving her to keep vigil. She hated it.

Her father and her husband were both dead, but neither had died while she had been waiting, expecting the worst. Not that that helped.

At times like this she envied Penelope. The Countess had been born a commoner, and though Rose had spent years helping train her friend in the ways of the nobility, the woman had never taken to some of the rules. *And now I get to worry about her too,* thought Rose wryly.

Rose's frustration grew until at last she reached up and began pulling at her hair, removing pins and undoing braids until it hung freely down her back, nearly reaching her hips. There was no one to see her anyway. With most of the men, as well as the Count and his family gone, the majority of the castle staff were enjoying the quiet in their quarters.

A stiff breeze picked up her hair and tossed it behind her. It was a rare sensation for her, but she couldn't enjoy it. *I'll be forever combing out the tangles.* Her irritation only increased. She returned to the stairwell and descended, heading for her apartments.

Though the chances were extremely small, she still encountered one of the castle maids in the hall, a young woman named Daphne. The girl's father had been a shepherd, and her mother had passed away just a year ago. She had two younger brothers, and she sent most of the money she earned working at the castle to her father. Rose knew everyone who worked in Castle Cameron, and she made a point of knowing the details of their lives as well. That held true not only here, but at her residence in Albamarl and within the Hightower keep that guarded the capital city.

Daphne's mouth gaped when she saw Lady Rose, startled by her wild appearance, but after a brief hesitation she curtseyed. "Milady."

Rose barely glanced at her, but her mind had already made several connections. Ordinarily she would have asked after the girl's family, or if she was busy, she would have passed by with only a brief nod. Not today, though. "Relax, Daphne, your secret is safe with me." Then she resumed walking.

Idiot! Rose reprimanded herself. *Why did you say that? Now the poor girl will be stricken with anxiety the rest of the day.* She had let her irritation get the best of her. Rose didn't care in the least that Daphne was heading to a secret assignation with one of the young men who worked in the kitchen. *And yet I tormented her.*

Most saw her as the perfect example of nobility, but Rose knew better. She was just as flawed as the rest of them. *And entirely alone.* She had been a widow for too many years. *And now I've grown petty.* For a moment a man's face flickered through her mind, but as so often happened these days, it wasn't Dorian's.

Ruthlessly she pushed the image aside. She was far too disciplined to allow such things to distract her.

The door to her empty apartment loomed in front of her. She entered and passed through the front room before stopping in the main living room. She felt restless and had no appetite for any of her usual pastimes. Often when she felt this way, she would travel to Albamarl. As *the* Lady Hightower she had no shortage of duties to attend to there. Her title made her responsible for overseeing the protection of the capital city itself.

But today she was trapped. Mordecai had left her in charge of Castle Cameron and if she abandoned it, that would place the burden squarely on his underage daughter, Irene. Peter, the chamberlain, was there to help if any serious need arose, but Rose wasn't about to leave Irene in that position without a good reason. She might be a Thornbear now, but she had been raised a Hightower, and a Hightower never shirked their duty.

An errant air current blew a stray bit of hair across her cheek. Annoyed, she brushed it back behind her ear. For a brief instant, she froze in place, but she resumed moving again almost immediately, crossing the room to check the hearth. Her eyes surreptitiously examined the room as she did so.

The shutters that covered the lone window in the room were ajar, and the small table beneath it was sitting at an odd angle, no longer even with the wall. The flower vase that sat upon it had been shifted as well.

Someone had entered the room while she had been gone, and they had probably come through the window. On its face, that fact was almost absurd. Her window was on the fourth floor, and barely wide enough to accept any but a child or a very thin man. The wall outside would also be difficult to scale. Though it was constructed of stone, it wasn't rough, the available handholds would require a climber to have incredible finger strength.

They entered, and either stumbled over the table or were forced to move it. Afterward they tried to put everything back in place, she noted silently. *Then they entered my bedroom.* She had already observed that that door hadn't been firmly shut.

The question that made her heart flutter with cold fear, was whether they had left. *Stay calm.* Her mind raced through possible scenarios, theft, espionage, or assassination being the top three that presented themselves. She had already discarded the notion that her maid had disturbed the room. Angela knew her habits and preferences well after years of service.

After stirring the fire, she straightened back up and re-racked the andiron. Though she was reluctant to release it, she didn't want to give away her hand, if someone was watching her. Better to feign obliviousness. She had other weapons close by.

She needed to get out of the apartment, but the only possible hiding place in the main room was the wardrobe, and it was positioned close to the door that led to the front waiting room. *I never should have placed it there,* she thought regretfully.

Aloud, she said to herself, "It's still too chilly in here. Where did I leave my housecoat? Probably in the front room." Then she moved purposefully toward the door. She hoped that, if there was someone in the wardrobe, they would wait for her to return before springing their trap. Assuming they did wait, she would simply leave through the main door and return with several large bodies to search the apartment.

As she passed, the wardrobe doors sprang open, and a someone leapt toward her.

Most of Rose's dresses had a hidden opening in the skirt, allowing her to reach a long knife strapped to her leg. She altered them herself if necessary. Already alerted, her hand was on the handle when her attacker emerged. Pulling it free she brought the blade up at a low angle and drove all nine inches of sharpened steel into the stranger's body, just above the groin.

She was momentarily shocked to see the stranger was a lithe young woman with short-cropped hair and wearing men's trousers. Rose's second surprise came when the assassin didn't crumple or flinch away from the pain of her wound. Instead, her attacker's hand dropped down to grip her wrist, preventing her from striking again.

Rose screamed, deliberately pitching her voice to its highest volume. As empty as the keep was it was unlikely anyone would hear her, but there was always that chance. Jerking backward, she tried to pull free of the invader's hold, but the woman's hand held onto her wrist with a grip of iron.

Though the assassin was slender and small boned, she was still taller and heavier than Rose. Awkwardly, the strange woman tried to slam her hand into Rose's head.

Dropping low, Rose avoided the punch, while continuing to twist the knife still lodged in the woman's abdomen. As she went, she reached into her bodice and drew out her second weapon, a small stiletto, and drove it into the first available target, the assassin's knee.

The strange woman fell forward on top of Rose, driving the knife even deeper into her own belly, and they struggled together on the floor. Blood was everywhere. Rose managed to keep her left hand holding the stiletto free. She stabbed again, and again, while the other woman scrabbled at the floor with her own free arm.

Eventually she managed to get free. Rose slid and almost fell getting to her feet, for the floor was slick with dark blood. The woman was still trying to rise, to reach her, but she had grown too weak to manage it.

Then two hands gripped her shoulders from behind, pulling her backward. Rose screamed again, and this time her cry was born purely of instinct and fear. Twisting, she pulled forward, but the hands had caught the neckline of her dress. The fabric gave way before she did, and she wound up tangled in her own clothing, her arms caught in the material that had previously covered her torso. She still held the stiletto, but it was impossible to bring it to bear.

The new attacker was male, and inexorably he twisted her body around. When she resisted, he kicked her legs out from beneath her and followed her down to the floor, landing atop her.

For a moment she thought he meant to rape her. Even as the nightmare unfolded, her mind had continued working. Neither of the two intruders had had weapons, or sought to use any. It had to be rape, or possibly kidnapping—or both. Then, as the man pulled his head away, she knew it wasn't rape.

The look in his eyes was dead, empty. Not once had he glanced at her exposed chest. *Kidnapping, then,* she thought, but something still didn't feel true about even that. As her assailant moved to secure his hold on her she brought her knee up, slamming it into his groin.

It had been a desperate measure, one she hadn't expected to work. Most men guarded their precious parts instinctively.

This man simply ignored the move, and when her knee connected, he didn't flinch.

One of his hands slipped behind her, grasping her unbound hair by the roots, jerking her head back at a painful angle. She gasped at the pain, and then his mouth opened as he leaned in to kiss her.

Something metallic glinted within.

***

Gary stood quietly in Matthew's workshop. His eyes were closed, and his body in a low power mode meant to preserve energy, but his mind was active. It wasn't something he did when humans were around, for it only served to highlight his mechanical differences. If he had to rest in sight of humans, he would lie down and pretend to sleep, but Matthew didn't seem to care about his uncanny strangeness.

Matthew was gone today, so there was little for him to do, other than think. At least that was true until he began receiving the signal.

The android opened his eyes and returned his body to normal function levels, listening in his own special way. It was a sense unique to him in this world, though he hadn't ever expected it to be useful here. There was nothing to hear.

Until now.

For all the apparent power and special senses that the mages of this world employed, none of them could have detected this. *But what is it?* he wondered. His higher functions had already turned the signal over to his multi-point computational unit, which in turn was running it through a variety of specialized signal algorithms.

Thus far it was just noise, but it wasn't natural noise, it was highly organized and discrete. It was coming through on a low frequency shortwave bandwidth. *Almost too low for me to detect,* he realized.

Spreading his arms wide, he maximized the distance between his hands while applying a mirror repetition filter to the signal. It wasn't a perfect technique and could be prone to error, but it allowed him to simulate having a much longer antenna. The signal became stronger, but he could detect clipping at the edges. The distortion would make it impossible to decode, even if he knew the encryption code.

Then the signal ended.

But who sent it, and who was it for? Pure deduction couldn't answer the question. A shortwave signal could cross vast distances, so the location of the intended recipient would be nearly impossible to determine. And without an active signal, as well as a much larger antenna, he couldn't know from what direction it had originated. It could easily have come from hundreds of miles away.

Inductive reasoning produced significantly more information. Based on his prior experience, he knew of only one entity likely to be on this world that would use such a signal. ANSIS. The weaponized artificial intelligence he had helped create in his home dimension. Matthew had already told him about its incursion here.

The humans here had hoped it had been eliminated, but this signal proved that to be a false hope. Someone needed to be notified, but who? Matthew, along with his father and the rest of the ruling family here were absent, except for one. Irene.

Gary finished his analysis and decision making in less than a fraction of a second. Moving to the door, he opened it and began walking toward the keep that was the heart of Castle Cameron. There was only one guard at the main entrance to the keep. The rest were probably stationed at the outer gatehouse.

The man recognized him immediately, his body language broadcasting his unease at seeing the artificial man.

Gary smiled to help alleviate the human's anxiety. "Excuse me, where is Irene Illeniel? I have important news to relay to her."

The guard looked at him suspiciously. "You'll have to wait here. I don't think the Count would want you anywhere near his youngest while everyone else is gone. I'll send for the chamberlain."

Gary decided that would be acceptable. The recipient of the signal was probably far from here. The humans wouldn't be able to react to the news in any meaningful timeframe.

And then he heard a new signal, this one on an entirely different wavelength, a high frequency radiowave. This one could transfer information at a much higher rate, but only over short distances. Almost immediately a second signal became active. Two ANSIS units were talking to each other.

Fortunately, the higher frequency and short range also meant he could detect the direction of the signal source. Taking quick steps, he walked a triangle in the yard, taking measurements at each point, then he triangulated the source location. *Roughly fifty feet above and to the left,* he noted. That put the source somewhere in the living areas used by some of the castle inhabitants. *They're inside the castle!*

The matter was considerably more urgent than his first estimate.

Returning to the guard, he spoke, "I am afraid that there is an enemy within the keep, probably the same one that the Count and his daughter faced in Dunbar. If we do not act quickly, I do not know what may happen."

Those words got a more appropriate reaction. The guard stepped within and rang a bell, then he abandoned his post, running down the main hall. Gary took this as an invitation to enter. Guessing that the guard would be heading for Irene, he followed the man.

***

Irene Illeniel sat in the main hall, trying out her father's seat. It was unlikely she'd ever be the Countess, since she had two older blood siblings. But she couldn't help but have a fascination for the seat of authority. Besides, there was little else to do with everyone gone. Her closest friend, Carissa, was away in Albamarl.

In short, Irene was bored.

In theory, being left in charge sounded exciting, though both her parents and the chamberlain, Peter, had made it clear that Lady Rose would be the actual arbiter of any important decisions. The reality though, was that she had been left behind with nothing to do and a babysitter to make sure she didn't cause trouble. Irene let out a long sigh, wishing something, *anything,* would happen.

"Lady Irene!"

The doors at the end of the hall were flung back as one of the guards, the only guard in the keep in fact, entered. *What was his name?* she tried to remember. *Stevens, that was it.*

Irene felt self-conscious at having been caught sitting in her father's seat, but she pushed the feeling aside and straightened her back. "Yes, Guardsman Stevens, what is the problem?"

"Your brother's creature, the one they call Gary, is outside. He claims there are enemies in the keep!"

The young lady's heart jumped in her chest. Excitement was one thing, an attack was something else. She still had nightmares of the day that she had been kidnapped. Behind the guard she could see Gary walking into the room.

Stevens turned around, alarmed at the android's presence. "I told you to stay outside!"

Irene frowned. She hadn't particularly liked Stevens' referring to Gary as her 'brother's creature', nor did she think his reaction now was appropriate. "Stevens!" she called out. "Stand down. Gary is a friend of mine as well. You should have let him in immediately."

Stevens bit his lip, but kept his sword sheathed. He didn't particularly like taking orders from a young girl, especially one whose judgement he doubted, but until Lady Rose appeared, he had no choice. "Yes, milady. Forgive me."

Irene addressed the machine-man, "Gary, what is this news of yours?"

Gary didn't waste time beating around the bush. "ANSIS is here. I can detect signals coming from two of their units above us and in *that* direction." He pointed at the ceiling, angling his arm to the left. "Given my readings since entering the building I am certain of their height now, which places them on the fourth level."

Irene froze. His statement terrified her. All too vividly she remembered the assassins in her home, the fighting and the blood. The murder of Lily. What should she do? There were no guards, other than Stevens. It would take ten minutes or longer to recall the other four from the outer gate. Anything could happen in that time. Her hands began to tremble.

Peter entered then, coming through one of the side doors. "What's going on?"

This was her moment. Irene knew it. She had to say something, otherwise Peter would take over, and she would be ushered off to someplace the chamberlain decided would be safe. "Peter," she said loudly. "Send for the guards at the gate. Have them meet us on the fourth floor."

Unsure of what was happening Peter glanced at Stevens, but the guard merely gave a slight shrug. "Certainly," he answered. "I'll send someone for them and follow you up."

Irene was already standing, though her knees felt weak. Marching forward, she headed for Stevens and Gary. "Let's go." *Do I really mean that? I can't do this.* Her legs continued to move despite her doubts, however.

The walls seemed to close in around her as they went, enclosing her in a dark tunnel. Something terrible waited for her at the end, and Irene's heart began to pound harder with each step. Deep down she wanted nothing more than to stop, to turn away—to run. Gritting her teeth, she kept moving. *No! I have to face this.*

Her hands were sweating by the time she reached the fourth floor. Gary led the way, and she was glad he couldn't see her face, she was sure her fear must be written across it.

"It's this way," he told them.

Stevens sped up to walk in front of her as well, and from behind Irene could hear steps on the stairwell. Glancing back, she saw Peter emerge. He was panting, and she guessed he had probably been running to catch up after sending a messenger to the gate. The chamberlain held a short mace in his hand.

It should have comforted her. Irene had three defenders now, but the sight of the quiet chamberlain grasping a weapon only served to highlight the gravity of the situation.

Gary stopped. "This door, they're in there."

Irene stared in horror at the door he had chosen. *No, no, no, no—not this door, not her. This can't be happening again!*

"That's Lady Rose's chambers," said Peter in alarm.

The guard tried the door handle, but the it wouldn't move. The chamberlain pushed his way forward, "Hang on, I have the keys for it." Fumbling with his ring, Peter tried several, his anxiety and haste only serving to slow him down. When at last he got the right key in, he realized the door was already unlocked.

"It isn't locked," he announced. "Someone has barred it from the inside."

A heart wrenching scream coming from within pierced their ears.

"Get it open!" yelled Irene.

Stevens threw himself against the door, but it was made of heavy oak, bound with iron.

"Get it open, now!" Irene yelled again, her voice rising to a near hysterical pitch.

Gary turned to her. "These doors are too heavily constructed. Neither my body nor the guard's has sufficient mass to break or dislodge the bar on the other side."

Another scream came from within, a cry of desperation and fear. Irene stared at the door and the world shrank around her until she could see nothing else. Her mind went blank, and the world vanished in a white blaze.

When her vision returned the door was gone, and everything was bathed in a strange golden light. Irene felt as though she was swimming. A dead woman lay in front of the door, but she hardly noticed her. Across the room and through a second door she could see Rose on the floor, her dress covered in blood, while a man lay atop her, twisting her head back at an odd angle.

Irene's throat erupted with a shriek of rage and denial, and everything turned first red, and then black. Her knees folded, but she never felt herself hit the floor.

CHAPTER 17

The forest around us was foreboding, but then again, when had anything in my life not been. I was certain I had been born under some cursed star.

With Penny on my right, Gram to my left, and Chad leading the rest of the men behind me, I felt well protected. Even so, I kept my senses tuned to the environment. Using my staff to clear the path was effective, but it still took time, time I used to make sure we didn't fall into another ambush. Now that I knew what to look for, I didn't think the spiders could surprise us again.

Still, a dragon would have been nice. Dragons are always nice—as long as they're on your side.

A quarter of an hour passed, and we had crossed perhaps a third of the distance, when I sensed something new. "Something is coming," I warned the others. "Two of them."

They were big, much bigger than the spiders, though nowhere close to the dragons in sheer size. I followed them with my magesight, as they ducked between the larger trees and smashed through the underbrush. They were roughly the size of very large brown bears, but they weren't furry.

I pointed my staff in the direction they were coming from, and Gram and Penny moved forward and to the sides. Looking back at the men, I ordered, "Fan out. They're too big to hold with a defensive line. If they get past, you'll need to try and surround them."

"How big?" asked Chad.

"I think they're the same thing you fought before, when you first came here," I told him. "Bear size."

The ranger nodded and after a brief search, began climbing a tree.

One of the soldiers shouted at the archer, "Shouldn't you be down here with us?"

The hunter tapped the long-knives strapped to his hip. "These ain't gonna be much use against somethin' that big. It'll be easier to use my bow up here, than if I'm down there gettin' my arse mauled."

The men looked nervously at one another, and I wondered if they might break and run. I had to do something. "Stand your ground," I commanded. Then I raised a wide shield between us and the direction the creatures would be coming from. I colored it blue to enable the soldiers to see it. Penny and Gram were on the other side, and I hoped they would be up to the task. "The shield should protect you, but if Sir Gram or the Countess have trouble, I'll release it, so you can back them up."

Penny gazed at me through the shimmering field for a moment and our eyes met. Then she nodded and turned to face the dark woods. We had come a long way over the years. In our early days, I would never have allowed her to face such a thing without protest, even though it had often been her job. But I had learned to respect her strength and resolve. We each had our part to play, and whatever happened, I would be there to haul her ass out of the fire if these things were more dangerous than we expected.

Had I made the right choice? There was no more time to consider options, for the massive creatures were upon us, bursting from the underbrush and leaping toward me.

Now that I could see them with my own eyes, they did indeed look bear-like. Stony skin covered massive shoulders and flanks. Their limbs ended in a multitude of glassy claws the size of meat cleavers. They roared as they came, ignoring the two warriors in front of them and instead charging toward the middle of my shield, trying to reach me.

An arrow sprouted from the shoulder of the one on the left, but it didn't seem to slow it in the least. Gram ducked under and brought Thorn up from below, cutting deeply into the side of its chest. The sword stuck there, and rather than struggle to free it, he bent his knees, dropping below a great sweeping paw. Then he stood and put his hands against the thing's shoulder.

It looked almost like magic. Despite Gram's considerable strength the beast outweighed him by at least an order of magnitude, yet he hardly seemed to exert himself when he pushed, toppling the monster over sideways.

Penny wasn't quite so lucky.

As the beast on her side charged toward my shield she sidestepped and cut at its front leg, hoping to cripple it. Her lighter arming sword failed to cut deeply, though, and as she dodged out of the way the beast crossed the remaining distance to slam into my shield.

My defense held, but it was slipping. Something about the very nature of these creatures made them difficult to deal with using pure magic. The strain it put on my shield was far greater than it should have been, even for a creature of its size and mass. After the first shock of contact it withdrew slightly and then brought its claws to bear. In spite of my efforts, they tore through the shield as though they were enchanted.

Unprepared, I felt the feedback from the shattered shield like a hammer-blow to my mind. I swayed on my feet, and only by clinging to my staff was I able to remain standing. An arrow appeared in the beast's throat, and two of the men behind me stepped forward, stabbing at the monster, but it seemed to feel none of it.

Standing on its hind legs, it towered over me like the shadow of death. Its massive forelimb swung forward in a sweeping attack that seemed certain to rip my head from my shoulders.

And then Penny was back. Jumping in front of me, she stabbed upward with the point of her sword, catching the inside of the creature's foreleg and using its own momentum to help drive the point through. It screamed in rage and then dropped down to snap at her with its teeth.

She should have moved. Her sword was trapped, and the thing was just too damned big to face in a stand-up fight, but I was still behind her. Rather than move, she threw up her left arm to keep the massive jaws from reaching me.

The monster's maw clamped down on her arm, encompassing it from just above her elbow all the way to her wrist. The deadly teeth weren't able to pierce her mail, but I heard her bones cracking as the jaws snapped shut. A tortured scream came from her as the beast jerked its head to one side, whipping her off her feet.

My vision was clearing, and I saw two more arrows standing out from its shoulders. The rest of the soldiers were around it now, stabbing in at it with their swords. They didn't have the strength that Penny or Gram had, but their blades were enchanted, and given time I was sure the beast would die.

But time was something my wife did not have.

Somehow, she had drawn her dagger with her right hand, but the beast that held her had begun shaking its head like a dog with a toy. Her body was thrown back and forth, and only the unyielding strength of the mail encasing her arm kept it from being ripped from her shoulder.

Pushing through the pain in my head, I tried to grip the creature directly with my power, to stop its violent thrashing, but it was like trying to hold a greased pig. Desperate, I used the air itself, pressing it inward, compressing it around the monster's skin. The dirt beneath it would have been better for the task, but I had no time.

Air is a poor medium to try and hold something with, but I put everything I had into it, until the air was as hard as steel, and it immobilized the beast holding Penny. Gritting my teeth and crying tears of rage, I continued to squeeze. There was a brief pause as the pressure mounted, and then the monster's chest collapsed inward. Its jaws opened, and Penny dropped to the ground as blood fountained from its mouth.

The men were all around us, but I had spared none of my attention for them. The only thing in my sight was Penny's crumpled form on the ground before me, her arm twisted across her body as though it was made of dough rather than bone and flesh.

Her heart was beating, I could see her chest still rising as she breathed, though the pain had rendered her unconscious. Frantic to help her, I needed to remove her armor, but it would be a long and terrible process. The mail was twisted around her arm as well as her chest.

Without thinking I applied my power to it, ripping the welded and riveted links apart with thought alone. It shouldn't have been possible to do it that way. Enchanted mail is incredibly strong, and regular wizardry isn't normally up to such a task. If I had been in my right mind, I would have used the rune channel in my staff to cut it, but I was beyond sanity.

Yet the mail came apart like tissue under the force of my will. Beneath it, her flesh was a horror of blood, twisted flesh, and shattered bone. Her arm was a ruin, nothing could salvage it, and her ribs and collar bone were broken as well. The skin across her chest was red and purple, and in places where the mail had been driven through the gambeson, it had been torn.

My mind was blank, and my heart cold with fear, but I didn't hesitate. Reaching down with my right hand, I created a tightly focused line of gold fire at the tip of one finger and used it to remove the tangled flesh that had once been her arm, cutting it off close to the shoulder. Then I sealed the artery and closed the skin.

That done, I began reconstructing her ribs and collar bone, relieving the pressure on her lungs and internal organs. Minutes passed while I worked, moving quickly and efficiently to save her life. There were no words in my mind; it was an empty place that only had room for quick decisions and fast action, but eventually there was nothing more I could do.

And then reality came rushing in at me. *Why didn't she have enchanted plate?* If she had been wearing the sort of armor I had on, the damage would have been far less. *Why didn't I ever make any for her?* I had always meant to do so, but it was time consuming. I had been busy. There was always something more important to do. *But I wasn't always busy. I could have made the time.*

I covered my face with my hands, hiding it from the men around me. Seconds ticked by; I could feel their eyes on me. I had to say something, I was in charge. They needed me to tell them what to do, but all I wanted to do was curl into a ball and die. Lifting my head and squaring my shoulders, I spoke to them, "We'll hold this position until the dragons return. Sir Gram, you're in charge of the men while I attend to the Countess."

Staring down at Penny, all I could do was watch her heart flutter in her chest. Her body had suffered a massive shock, but I had done everything possible for now. My eyes kept drifting to where her arm had been. Stifling a silent scream, I pulled my eyes away. *Don't look. Don't think about it. You have to keep it together. Everyone's counting on you,* I told myself.

Someone stood beside me, though I was too overwrought to recognize who it was at first, then the figure spoke, and Chad Grayson's voice found my ears. "Whatever yer thinkin' it wasn't your fault."

The urge to lash out, to strike him, was almost overwhelming. "Shut—the—fuck—up."

He held out a hand toward me, "Here." After a moment I realized he was holding his flask. I took it and unscrewed the top. Whatever he had in it burned as I swallowed.

"The dragons are back!" said one of the men loudly.

Glancing up I saw Grace and Cassandra descending, my son and daughter on their backs. I ignored their arrival, though I couldn't help but listen as Gram filled them in on everything that had happened over the past half hour.

"Mother!" That was Moira, running toward Penny, Matthew right behind her.

I said nothing while they examined her with their own eyes and magesight. Then Matthew put his silver hand on my shoulder. It was rare for him to seek physical contact, though perhaps he was only trying to remind me that losing a limb wasn't the end of the world. "We'll make her a better one," he said quietly. "Take her home, Dad. Moira and I can find Elaine."

Something clicked inside me as I listened to his words. "No. You take her home." Then I turned to Gram, "Take the men back. Moira will teleport home with the Countess. Matthew and the dragons will stay with you until you reach the reserve force."

Sir Gram's eyes flicked uncertainly toward Matthew, as though seeking confirmation.

"Dad!" broke in my son. "No. You are in no state to do anything. Let us finish this. I'm the best equipped for this place."

He was right, of course. My head was still tender from the feedback, though it wasn't nearly as bad as what I had experienced in the past. I was functional, but my emotional state was in disarray. I also didn't give a damn. "I'm not risking any more of my family today. Do as I say."

Gram nodded, "Yes, milord."

Matthew wasn't having it, though. "You aren't the only one with family at risk here. Do the smart thing and go home." Moira stood beside him, clearly agreeing with him.

"I've made up my mind," I told them.

Moira started to speak, "Dad, this is insane. Listen to him…"

Grinding my teeth, I ordered them once more, "Do as I say."

Both of my children looked at me as if I had lost my mind. Perhaps I had, but mad or not, I was *certain*. Certain no one else would be hurt. I turned away and began to walk in the direction I had last sensed Elaine's aythar. "I'll see you when I get home."

As I walked I heard Chad's voice behind me, speaking to Matthew and Moira. "Ease up, he'll not listen to you. I've seen that look before. Best we get out of this damned forest as quickly as we can."

I left them there, and since I was now alone, I didn't bother cutting a path. Instead, I sought relief from the pain in my head by slipping into the mind of the stone. In the years since my abilities had first awakened, it had gotten easier. Opening myself to the world around me, I became more than what I had been, a larger entity that encompassed some of my environment while retaining the majority of my humanity.

It was like walking a tightrope, but with practice, balancing had become second nature. Language was still possible, I kept my ability to reason, but my emotions were distant. The ground beneath my feet was a part of me, as was the air I breathed. The trick was keeping my focus on the fragile human body in the middle of it all. The aching in my head was still there, but it was a thing too far away to hurt me.

Branches and limbs bent and swayed, pulling aside to let me pass.

In the mind of the stone, there was no physical danger that could touch me, only the constant danger that any archmage faces, the risk of losing himself. I continued toward my goal, letting the world slip past. I felt as though I moved without walking, though I was quite aware of my legs taking steps beneath me. The truth was more that the world ahead *became* me, while what was behind passed into the land of the *other*, that which was no longer me.

How long I walked was a mystery, for time had little meaning. Things moved in the shadows, some large and some small. For those that entered my domain, I had no mercy. Rather than allow them to join me, my body moved to destroy them. Vines and underbrush strangled the smaller creatures, and when larger ones came, the trees themselves tore them apart.

I remained untouched, as the world passed beneath my feet, changing to become the place I had set as my goal.

A light flared before me, not a light of the eyes, but of the spirit. There was a space, an opening beneath one of the great trees, and within was a creature burning with life and vitality. For a moment I considered destroying it as well, but then I recognized it. Blond filaments floated around its head. *Hair,* supplied the voice in the back of my mind. *This is Elaine.*

Death hung close to it, a dark shadow that would not be dispelled despite the creature's fierce life force. It spoke to me, and at first I failed to comprehend it.

"Mordecai!" it repeated. No. *She* repeated. Elaine was a woman. *A human being, like me.* "Elaine?" I asked.

She looked at me strangely, "Yes, Elaine. Snap out of it. Help me."

At last my mind collapsed, like a bubble breaking. My thoughts fell inward, and the world shifted. I stood deep within the depths of the forest. I had found Elaine, huddling in a small cave-like place under a tree. There was a man with her. I hadn't registered his presence before, probably because he was already dead, his body beginning to decompose. He was one of the soldiers who had entered with Elaine and her father, Walter.

"Get inside," she told me, urgency in her voice. "If you stand out here long, more of them will come."

I stepped in and darkness enveloped us, a veil of invisibility, blocking both visible light and aythar. I could still see Elaine within the veil, but only with my magesight. "Is there anyone else?" I asked her. "Your father?"

"Dead," she answered in a voice numb with fatigue. Elaine looked gaunt and drawn, with dark circles under her eyes. Her skin seemed tight, stretched across her features and frame. "He drew them off, so Brent and I could hide."

Brent, I assumed, was represented by the body of the soldier at the back of her hiding place. He smelled bad, but there was no sign of bloat yet. A small hole in his abdomen explained that, though if it was the result of an injury or whether she had done it herself, I had no way of knowing. Now was not the time to ask.

His body was partly covered with loose soil and leaves. Judging by the black dirt beneath Elaine's nails, it looked as though she had been trying to bury him using only her hands. That made little sense, she could have accomplished the task much quicker with her power.

Her arms went around my armored chest, despite the fact that hugging a man in plate armor wasn't a pleasant thing. "Where are the others?" she asked. "Are you alone?"

"I sent them back. Penny was injured, and we had lost a number of soldiers."

She released me and sank to her knees. "So, you're trapped too. Do you have any food?"

"Trapped? No. I came to take you home," I told her. Her face changed at those words, new hope replacing the despair in her eyes. I still didn't understand everything, though. "Why didn't you teleport back?"

Elaine looked down, "I couldn't remember the keys. I had them written down, but I lost my belt and pouch during the chaos of the first attack."

I sighed. "I made you memorize them when you were a student. How could you forget?"

"That was years ago. Some things get fuzzy with time…"

"Then you should review them," I said, regretting the harsh tone in my voice almost immediately. My own recent failure to protect Penny had left me bitter, and it was coloring my reactions. Unlike Matthew and me, other people didn't have perfect recall. It was easy enough for me to judge, but reviewing details like that was something I never had to do. "I'm sorry," I said quickly. "This is not the time. I'm tired and upset myself."

Now that I was no longer in the mind of the stone, my head throbbed, but I ignored it and used my power to clear away a level place in the middle of her hideaway.

Anxiety gripped Elaine, and she warned me, "Careful. Any use of power draws them."

"They can't see our aythar inside this veil of yours."

She shook her head. "It doesn't matter. Even the veil draws them. They sense the aythar it uses, even if they can't see exactly where we are. Too much power and you'll draw a lot of them, eventually one will stumble into the entrance."

"What have you been doing all this time?"

"I kept my mind closed, my aythar damped down as much as possible. I only used the veil when I heard something getting close. Dad and I hid the first day using veils, along with poor Brent here. But they kept finding us. Dad finally figured out it was the diffuse aythar of our veil that they were homing in on, but it was too late. When the wolves found us, he ran, drawing them away."

Walter, killed by some kind of strange wolf? It was hard to believe.

Elaine went on, "I think he killed the wolves somehow. I saw him coming back, but the spiders caught him." She stopped briefly, her throat struggling to say the words. "I saw—everything."

I felt sympathy for her, but even that emotion was blunted. "You say 'them', but what do you mean exactly? The bears, or something else?" I asked.

"All of them," she answered. "The bear things, the spiders, the wolves—there are even large serpents that hunt in this forest. All of them are drawn to any significant amount of aythar." Then she pointed at me, "Right now you're drawing them to us. That's why I put the veil back up, but if you don't close your mind, seal your aythar inside yourself, they'll find us eventually."

A noise outside caught our attention, leaves rustling beneath heavy feet. Elaine seemed to crumple, shrinking back toward the back wall of her hiding place. She motioned toward me with her hands, begging me to come with her.

"We have to make a circle," I told her, refusing to lower my voice. "Get started. I'll deal with this."

"Magic doesn't work..." she began, her voice almost a whisper. "You have to use something else."

I nodded, "I know. Rocks, dirt, whatever is close at hand. Start the circle, I'll finish it and add the keys when I get back."

Stepping back through the veil, the shadowy light of the forest floor was still bright enough to almost blind me. Luckily, my magesight didn't suffer the same problem, for standing not ten feet away was a giant man.

Well, 'man' wasn't really an appropriate description, but it was humanoid. Covered in pebbly grey skin and standing somewhere close to fifteen feet in height, it had two arms and two legs, though they were twisted and lumpy compared to human proportions. The head that sat on its shoulders was thick and short with almost no neck, and it was crowned by a massive black horn in the center of its forehead.

"Damn you're ugly," I muttered. Looking at the horn I felt sorry for the mother that had birthed it. Then again, I realized on second thought that the horn had probably grown in later.

CHAPTER 18

The ogre and I stared at each other for a second. I thought of it as an ogre because I had no idea what else to call it. It certainly looked like a monster from some demented writer's fairytale. Since I was no longer in the mind of the stone, I couldn't expect my surroundings to deal with it for me, but I had plenty of other options.

Plus, I was still dealing with a lot of pent up anger and self-loathing.

The ogre twisted at the hips, whipping the massive club it had been dragging behind it into the air and swinging it toward me with one large lumpy arm. Perfect.

I didn't bother directing my power at the monster, since it likely had the same protection all the creatures here had. Instead, I seized its club, which was in fact a moderately sized tree that appeared to have been recently uprooted and trimmed of its upper limbs.

My iron will and seething power gripped the club, stopping it only a foot from my still tender head. Then I wrenched it around in the air, which sent its former wielder flying into the nearby bushes.

It roared with rage and seconds later it was back, covered in twigs and leaves. I met its call with the rooted end of the club, driving it into the ogre's head like a battering ram. "It's time to improve your looks," I muttered.

And then, I beat it to death.

There was nothing glorious or romantic about it. It couldn't even be called a battle. The ogre never had a chance. The first blow had stunned it, and after that it was just a brutal succession of hammer blows while I smashed its body into a twitching pile of flesh and broken bones.

Even furious as I was, the sight of what I did made me sick. Finished, I placed the club in front of the entrance to Elaine's hiding place, in case I needed it again. And as I walked inside, I couldn't hide from one particular thought, *If I had done that earlier, rather than rely on Penny and Gram…*

My stomach knotted within me.

Elaine had the circle half done. I finished the rest and added the destination key, before doing a calculation to assign the present location key. Once that was done, we returned to Castle Cameron, taking Brent's body with us. It would do him no good, but at least we could give him a decent burial, unlike poor Walter.

Matthew, Moira, and Conall were there ahead of us, having brought Penny back via a similar temporary circle as soon as they had left the forest. The others were still on the road with the soldiers.

Moira and Conall embraced Elaine, while Matthew looked on. He wasn't one to give hugs when they could be avoided, but as his siblings had released her, she reached out and pulled him in anyway. From my vantage point, he looked uncomfortable, but then the dam finally broke within Elaine and her shoulders began to shake. Matthew's face softened, and he held her tightly while she cried.

Moira looked to me, mouthing Walter's name in a silent question. Bowing my head, I answered with a negative nod.

Leaving Elaine in their care, I found Peter, my chamberlain, waiting for me. I directed him to Brent's body, which we had left outside. "Send word to his family and have him prepared for a hero's funeral."

Peter started to speak, "My lord, I have…"

Ignoring him I asked Conall anxiously, "Where's Penny?"

"The men just took her upstairs. She should be in bed by now," he replied. "Elise went with her."

I started for the stairs, but Matthew called out to me, "Hey, old man!"

That brought a frown to my face. "What?"

"Don't do that again. I don't want to be Count any time soon."

"Oh really? You should be so lucky," I told him.

He nodded. "Really. It seems like a very inconvenient job. I have better things to do with my time." Then he grinned.

I hadn't thought about the matter in a long time. I had been declared dead once before, and Penny had held the title in my stead, but she wasn't a Cameron by blood. She could only hold it until one of the heirs was of age. If I had died, it would have fallen to him. Conall and Irene were in line after him, since Moira was adopted and not my natural born child.

"You'd better use your time well then," I said. "One of these days it will be your turn, whether you like it or not."

Peter spoke up once more, "My lord. Things have not been quiet here. I have bad news."

I was in no mood. I needed to be with my wife. "Haven't you already told them?" I asked, waving my hand toward Matthew and the others.

The chamberlain shook his head. "They arrived only moments before you did, and with the Countess in such a state, I haven't had the chance."

"Whatever it is can wait…," I began.

"It's Lady Rose, and your daughter, Irene," interrupted Peter. "There were intruders in the castle."

"What?! How? Are they alright?" I rounded on the chamberlain with something approaching panic.

"Lady Rose was rather shaken, and Irene—I'm not sure what happened. She's asleep now. Gary understands more of what happened, but I'll give you the details of what I know."

I listened for several minutes, and then headed for home.

***

"How is she?" I asked Elise.

The old woman looked at me with tired eyes. "First you, now her, I'm convinced you two are trying to work me to death before my time. She's breathing, and you seem to have done a good job with her bones. I can't tell if there are more serious internal injuries, though. I don't have your sight."

"She isn't bleeding inside," I told her. "Everything is in its place—except her…," I stopped, unable to say the words. *Except her arm.*

Elise got up from her stool at the bedside and wrapped her thin arms around me. "You did well, Mort. If you hadn't removed the arm immediately, she would have died. Don't blame yourself for it."

"I'm going to fix it," I said suddenly, firming up my conviction.

She misunderstood me. "I'm sure Matthew can build her an arm that will be better than the original."

I stepped away from her. "No, I mean I am going to restore it."

Elise frowned. "Can you do that? I thought your unique form of healing was limited to yourself."

It was, if the archmage attempting it was sane, but I had done it twice before, once when Penny had nearly died after being struck by a ballista bolt meant for me, and once when Elaine had been near death years before. It was something I had never intended to do again.

Using metamagic to become another human being, essentially resulted in a merging of souls. It held a risk unlike that of becoming earth or wind, but no less dangerous. Separating again was difficult, and afterward you could never be sure who you had been originally, the healer or the patient. I still wondered occasionally if I was really Elaine, and whether she was walking around with my soul instead of her own. There was no way to know.

But for Penny, any risk was worth it. And if I had to become another person, there was no one else I would rather be. *I'd feel a little sorry for her though,* I thought. *I wouldn't wish being me on anyone.*

In answer to her question I nodded. "I can. I'll wait until she has recovered, though."

Elise's eyes narrowed. "Is it safe?"

"Certainly," I lied, before changing the subject. "What was your impression of Irene?"

She threw up her hands. "What do I know of magic? Her body is whole, but I couldn't wake her. Whatever she did sent her into a comatose state."

It was obvious that Irene's power had finally awoken, and if her body was unhurt, I was fairly certain she would be fine. It went differently for everyone and usually occurred sometime after puberty, and often during a moment of stress. With me it had happened around sixteen, to save a friend's horse from drowning.

At least Irene, unlike me, would have plenty of people to help her learn and adjust to her new abilities. A splashing sound from the adjacent room drew my attention. I did my best to ignore it.

After they had settled Irene's unconscious form into her bed, Elise had brought her daughter-in-law to my room to use the bath. Nearly alone, the old healer had had a lot of patients to look after, and they hadn't expected me to return so soon.

Most of the bedrooms in my hidden mountain home were warded for privacy, but the large bath that Penny and I shared was warded *with* our bedroom. Which meant it was entirely open to view with my magesight while I remained by Penny's bedside.

A natural question to ask would be, why did it matter? In my everyday life I dealt with people constantly, and clothing was no more of a barrier to magesight than walls were. I, and my children, were all accustomed to that. For myself, I usually just tuned it out. Peering through clothing and searching out the shape and form of other people's bodies gets old quickly when it's part of your everyday life.

Also, it wasn't quite like sight. There was no color, only form. For example, in a pitch-black room I couldn't read a book. I could detect its shape, look at the pages, but the writing was not easily apparent, unless it was writing imbued with aythar. I could potentially read it, but only by focusing intently on it, inch by inch, to detect the difference in places where ink was present and where it wasn't, but such a thing would take forever.

Similarly, examining people's skin beneath their clothing didn't reveal too much more. Usually their general shape was already apparent from the lay of the cloth anyway.

A woman bathing nearby though, was a little different, though it was mainly a psychological thing. Fortunately, I had developed a lot of discipline, and age and maturity helped as well.

I couldn't help but see a bit, but the main thing was to keep my attention focused on other things closer at hand.

One other point, while aythar doesn't show true color, that doesn't mean it doesn't present other information to the mind beyond simple form. The problem is that the human brain wasn't designed with this extra method of perception in mind, so it borrowed from our experience of the other senses to interpret what was observed. The aythar of individuals was unique, and the mage's mind often presented that difference as a taste, a scent, or a color.

Through long association I could easily identify the aythar of my friends and family. Someone like Rose, whom I had known for well over twenty years now, was no exception. Not being a mage, her aythar was far dimmer, and it clung closely to her body. To my mind it possessed a pleasant scent, and it was entirely feminine.

At times like this, as she stretched and stood to rise from the bath, it rippled across her skin, highlighting the shape of...

"Goddammit," I said out loud.

"What is it?" asked Elise, looking at me strangely.

Leaning over, I kissed Penny's sleeping face. Standing, I took a few steps and then answered her, "Nothing, I just need to go check on Irene for a while." It was a relief when the door shut behind me, and with it the ward.

Irene was unchanged. I had been in her room only a short while before, to look in on her before checking Penny. I hadn't really expected to find anything changed yet. She still lay quietly, her breathing and heart steady. Most importantly, her aythar seemed intact, though it was still turbulent. She would probably be nauseous when she awakened.

A knock came at the door, and then Matthew entered without waiting for me to answer. Gary stood behind him in the hall. "Dad, we need to talk."

"What have you learned?"

"Quite a lot, actually. Gary has been able to give me some important insights…"

He didn't finish the sentence, for another voice interrupted him. "I hope you gentlemen weren't planning on having this discussion without me." Lady Rose stood in the hallway, her hair in a towel and clad in one of Penny's nightgowns. The garment was entirely too large for her.

"You should probably rest," I argued. "You've been through an ordeal, Rose."

She nodded, "I couldn't agree more. I don't enjoy being attacked and having to wash that much blood out of my hair was almost as unpleasant. Nevertheless, before I sleep, I'd like to know the meaning of it. Otherwise I won't be able to rest."

Gary spoke up, "Actually, it would be helpful to have your account of what happened before we arrived."

Since they were all making sense, I agreed, and we adjourned to the living room.

CHAPTER 19

Rose followed the others, and I was behind her. Before entering the main room, though, she turned back toward me. "I need something, Mort. Just a moment if you don't mind."

Matthew looked at me questioningly, but I waved him on. "I'll be right there."

Lady Rose smiled at him and after a second, we were somewhat alone. Rose turned to me and looked up. "I am not well."

Concerned, I asked, "What's wrong?"

Then her façade cracked, and her face twisted. Burying her head against my chest she threw her arms around my waist and held on tightly. I hugged her back, worried. Rose was a woman of famous self-control. In the twenty plus years I had known her, I had only seen her like this on a couple of occasions.

She wasn't crying, but I could feel a tremor in her shoulders and a strangled noise came from her throat. She was screaming silently into my chest.

After a minute she took a deep breath and released me, composing her face and wiping at her eyes with the sleeve of the nightgown. "How do I look?" she asked me.

I gave her a once over and made my pronouncement with a wink, "Better than me, as usual."

She nodded, making a brave face. "Thank you, Mordecai." Then she turned toward the living room.

I followed her in. "Don't thank me, Rose. That's what family is for."

After that she found Alyssa and set her to making tea for us. Then we all settled in and got comfortable.

Conall walked in before we could start. "What's going on?"

Matthew looked at his younger brother with frustration, but after a moment he sighed and answered, "Actually, go find the others. We may as well do this once, so everyone can share what they know."

Conall left, and a few minutes later he returned with Gram, Moira, Elaine, and Lynaralla. There weren't quite enough seats, but that was a common problem in our house, which was why we had an abundance of cushions. Elaine took the last chair while Moira, Lynaralla, Gram, and Conall made themselves comfortable on the floor.

Matthew addressed the room, "I'll start, since I think Gary and I have the most to add." Leaning over, he waved his hand at the android. "Gary can detect ANSIS. He can hear their means of communicating with one another."

That produced a stir in the room.

Matthew went on, "He can detect types of light that are invisible to us. One type he detected today is used for long distance communication, but it generally requires a long piece of metal called an antenna to be used. He also detected a different type of communication that is faster, but only effective over shorter distances of a hundred feet or so. That was why he led Irene to Rose's room."

Elaine spoke up, "Did you say this was a type of light?"

Gary answered her, "It is, and before you ask, yes, your invisibility veil blocks it. When you went to my world with Karen and Matthew, that was why I had to have you open holes in your veil, so I could communicate."

She nodded. "I just wanted to be sure."

Matthew smiled. "What Elaine is considering is an important point. The Prathion abilities could conceivably be used to block or interfere with ANSIS's ability to communicate. With her and her brother George's talent and the judicious use of specialized enchantments, we could create areas that prevent them from communicating."

Lynaralla broke in, "If you can use the short-range signals to locate them, can you also use the long-range signals to discover where they are hiding?"

Gary answered, "Yes and no. It is possible, but I am barely able to detect those signals at all, given the size of my physical body. Also, because of the potential distances accurate triangulation would require me to measure the signal from at least three separate locations simultaneously. Those locations would need to be separated from one another by a significant distance. We would have to build antennae in different cities and find some way for me to connect to them all at the same time to monitor for the signal."

"If you can hear them, what are they saying? If they don't know anyone can listen, they might give away their secrets," said Conall.

"Encryption," said Gary.

Before he could launch into an explanation, Matthew interrupted, "I'll explain that to you later Conall. The important point is that their messages use a code that we can't break."

"I'd like to know why they were targeting my mother," said Gram.

Rose sighed. "That's obvious enough, son."

Gram shook his head. "No, it isn't. Sure, you're important to me, and you're important to Lothion, but we are dealing with machines from some foreign dimension. Why would *they* be interested in you?"

"Strategy and tactics are always based on similar principles no matter what the nature of the mind behind them," explained Lady Rose. "In this case, they wanted eyes inside the castle, and they sought to implant one of their metal bugs into me for that purpose. They couldn't target Irene because she was too close to Mordecai. Moira has already shown them that wizards are capable of detecting their presence in human hosts. They wanted someone important enough to learn valuable information, but far enough away from the Count's family to avoid detection."

I watched Rose carefully as she spoke, and as usual I couldn't help but be impressed at her objective calm as she discussed the possibility of her own body being used as a host for the enemy's body controlling machines. I also noticed that she tucked her hands into her sleeves, to hide her trembling.

Moira spoke then, "I don't understand how this connects with what happened to Lancaster. None of it makes sense."

I looked at Lynaralla, my gaze steady as I spoke, "It doesn't. I think we're dealing with two completely separate events."

Lynaralla met my gaze without flinching. If anything, there was a question in her eyes. I honestly didn't think she knew anything, but if she did have any guilty thoughts, I didn't want to miss the signs.

Moira frowned. "Why are you looking at her?"

"I believe the Illeniel She'Har are responsible for what happened at Lancaster," I responded. Then I let my eyes move to Moira's face. "But I have no idea how, or why."

That statement produced another commotion as everyone began asking questions at once. Questions we had no answers to. Eventually, Matthew got control of the conversation again. "He's right. What I sensed at Lancaster was definitely translation magic, and the hexagonal shape of the land that shifted was a likely indicator that it was done with spellweaving. The problem, is that we don't know of any current She'Har with the numbers or power to do something that large."

"Could there be some hidden group neither of you know about?" asked Rose.

"Doubtful," I answered. "And it had to be Illeniel She'Har. Only they have the gift to accomplish it."

Lynaralla asked the question everyone was wondering, "Do you think it was my parents?"

"Can Tyrion spellweave?" I asked. "How long has he been in human form?"

"Only a few weeks," she replied. "He was still an elder when I returned to the Grove. As an elder he could spellweave, but as a human—I have not seen him do so."

"So, it could have been him," said Conall. "He had time to travel to Lancaster."

"How did your mother react to him abandoning the grove?" I asked simultaneously.

Lynaralla answered carefully, "He never left while I was there, and though he took human form, his elder body remains. It still provides pollen for mother's flowers, but it has no mind while he is apart from it. I do not think he could have done this."

As much as I wanted to blame her murderous psychopathic father, I was inclined to agree with her. Which left, what? "We're going in circles," I said at last. "We need more information."

Rose nodded agreement, and after a short discussion everyone agreed, so we moved on to other things.

I stood up. "For now, we have a number of things we can do. Matthew, you and Gary need to come up with a plan for these antennae he mentioned. Ring gates would probably solve the distance problem, but I want you two to determine what locations to build the antennae, and I'll need a detailed accounting of what materials and support you will need. Elaine, I want you to work with Gary as well. See if you can create a veil that only blocks the signals that ANSIS uses. If you can, then perhaps we can ward the castle in such a way to create a dead zone for them here.

"Conall, I need you to go to Arundel. Tell George he needs to come here. It's no longer safe for us to be in separate locations. I want as many mages as possible here, so we can watch and guard one another. The last thing we need is for something like what almost happened to Rose to happen to one of us.

"Moira…"

"I know," she said with a smirk. "Spellbeasts. You want as many as possible and you want them stationed with the guards and in Washbrook to help make certain ANSIS doesn't get a foothold here."

It was disconcerting having a daughter who could read my mind almost at will, despite whatever mental barriers I put up. I grimaced but let it go. Then I added, "I'd like one or two in Albamarl also. The Queen will be staying with us much of the time, but she will have to be there during the day, and I don't want to leave Ariadne unguarded."

"Gram, you've personally been host to one of ANSIS's bugs before. We've kept a lot of that information quiet to avoid a panic, but you need to have a discussion with Captain Draper. Tell him everything you know. I want the two of you to prepare our guards for this threat. They have to know what to expect.

"Rose, you and Carissa are moving. You will live with us. Your apartment is unlivable at present, and I don't like the thought of you being anywhere without appropriate protection."

Conall put a hand up. "Dad, I don't think we have enough room."

"Then we'll make room. Lynaralla can construct an additional temporary room or two from nothing but spellweaves. In the meantime, you can assist the workmen in building a permanent addition to the house."

"What about Albamarl," suggested Matthew. "Our house there is better guarded than this one, other than the fact that its location is well known, and that's gotten to be less of an advantage these days anyway. Why don't we build a gate between it and here? We could use both together as though they were one house."

That was actually an excellent idea. "I like it," I said, beaming at him. It was definitely simpler than what I had been thinking. Recently I had started considering the idea of using his interdimensional abilities to create a home within a pocket dimension. If it could be done, it would provide us with a place completely secure and unassailable by any...

A shiver ran down my spine as my thoughts came together. *Of course!* Pieces began to fall into place in my mind. There were still plenty of gaps and things I didn't understand, but I knew where to look now. Most importantly, I knew who was responsible for what had happened at Lancaster, and just as importantly, I know who wasn't.

"Mordecai?" asked Rose, studying me. "You have something to add?"

Damn, she was almost as much of a mind reader as Moira. "No," I lied. *Not yet.* Later I would need to talk to Matthew, Lynaralla, and Gary. The three of them together might be able to shed some light on my suspicions. Facing the room again, I finished, "Let's get to work."

As everyone started moving, Elaine made as if to follow Matthew and Gary, but Rose called out to her. "Elaine, not today, you need rest, and food. Your part can wait a while."

The young woman looked at me, and I shrugged. "She's right."

Moira took Elaine by the arm. "You can sleep in my room."

"I don't think I can sleep," protested Elaine.

"You will," said Moira firmly, "and I'll make certain you have no dreams either." Then she took Rose's hand as well. "You too Lady Rose. You need sleep even more than Elaine does."

Rose wasn't having it. "That's ridiculous. I have too many…"

"Rose," I said, interrupting her. When I had her attention, I leaned over and kissed the top of her head, while at the same time touching her pendant and cutting her off from its protection. *"Shibal,"* I whispered, sending her into magically induced slumber. I caught her as her body slumped.

Moira grinned at me. "That was a dirty trick. You should have let me do it. I could have gotten past the pendant without the extra showmanship." Then she looked pointedly at Elaine.

Elaine held up her hands. "I'll come along quietly, no need to force me."

Together, Moira and I levitated Rose and escorted Elaine to Moira's room where we tucked them in for a long rest.

CHAPTER 20

The next few days passed peacefully, full of work and activity. Irene and Penny both awoke after the first day. My daughter was confused, but otherwise normal. She did indeed suffer a significant amount of nausea, but we all assured her that it would pass within a week. It would just take a while for her brain to adjust to the new input from her magesight.

Penny was more difficult. She didn't talk much at first, which was certainly unusual for her. She rejected every effort I made to discuss what had happened to her, and I sensed an underlying anger within her.

Naturally, I felt she must be angry with me, but Elise took me aside and counseled me otherwise.

"Losing a limb is like losing a loved one," she said. "The survivor goes through a process of grieving, and in the beginning, that often means anger and denial. It isn't you she's angry with. It's the world itself."

I still felt responsible, and that made it hard for me to be objective on the matter, so I did much the same as my wife. I didn't talk about it. Penny was keeping her thoughts to herself to avoid inadvertently hurting me with her inner anger, and I kept my mouth shut to avoid burdening her with my selfish guilt.

In short, we weren't a lot of fun to be around.

Other than that, things at home were busy, hectic, and at the same time comforting. With Rose, Elise, Carissa, and Gram living with us, there were always people around. It almost felt like a holiday. Irene in particular loved it, once she began to get over her constant vertigo. She was probably the most outgoing of anyone in my family, and Carissa was her best friend.

Rose even got into the domestic spirit of things and attempted to cook a meal. When I got word of this I tried to discourage it, but Moira and Conall had already told her it was a great idea.

Lady Rose Thornbear was many things—diplomat, politician, strategist, chess player, and a wise counselor—but I knew from experiences during our younger days that she was no cook. Raised from birth as a noblewoman, she had never been expected to perform such mundane tasks. She could sew, tat lace, and innumerable other things, but cooking was not in her repertoire. Brewing the occasional cup of tea when her maid had a day off was about the extent of her skill.

Penny and I had both been raised commoners, and as such, we had both learned to cook a variety of things from an early age. Penny really enjoyed it, and she often sought to arrange her official duties so that she would be able to cook a breakfast or dinner for the family now and then. I did the same, though not quite as often, and consequently all of our children had learned the basics, along with the joys of washing dishes.

Seeing them take turns at the task inspired Rose to try her hand at it, and I knew things wouldn't end well.

What I didn't factor into my calculation was Moira's ability to read people. She not only encouraged Rose, she offered to assist, and with her advice and help, things didn't turn out too badly.

I sniffed at my bowl of pottage suspiciously when it was put before me. Everyone else began eating immediately, and I didn't hear any sudden outcries of agony or vomiting. "What's in it?" I asked casually.

"Lamb, barley, carrots, and onions," answered Rose immediately from the other side of the table.

Glancing at Moira, I saw her wink at me. *How bad is it?* I asked her, sending a silent thought to her.

It's fine, Dad, really, came her reply.

Then I spotted a grimace on Conall's face. *I knew it! We're going to die, aren't we?*

Moira stifled a laugh, then wiped her face. *The meat was seared a little too much, that's all. Try it.*

"Is something wrong with your dish, Mordecai?" asked Rose sweetly.

"Oh, no," I said quickly. "I was just lost in thought." I popped a quick spoonful into my mouth. My first impression was that it lacked salt, and someone had gotten a bit heavy handed with the thyme. The meat was tough, and it had been slightly burned, imparting a faint bitterness to the broth.

But it was edible. In fact, compared to her last attempt at cooking over a decade ago, it was practically a miracle. Encouraged, I took a bite of the bread she had made and regretted it. It was as dry and tough as hardtack. I dropped one end into the stew and hoped it would soften, but it appeared impermeable to the liquid.

I focused on the stew after that. Matthew finished his first and asked for seconds.

Delighted, Rose filled his bowl again. "You ate quickly, Matthew. Do you like it?"

"Not really," he answered with brutal honesty, his tone matter-of-fact. "I'm just very hungry today. I skipped breakfast."

Rose flinched but kept her composure. Moira's response was quick, though: "Matt! What is wrong with you?"

"What?" he asked in confusion. "She asked. I'm just being honest. There's nothing wrong with it. It's not bad, it just isn't good either. It's edible, though."

The table erupted in loud talk and argument as everyone began offering their compliments or condemning Matthew for his remark. Meanwhile, Rose took her first bite. After a moment she spoke, "Well, he's right. It isn't very good, but it's edible." Then she laughed and patted him on the arm. "Thank you for being honest, Matthew."

Things quieted down after that, and everyone finished at least one bowl. The bread was a lost cause, however. "I appreciate everyone letting me try my hand at cooking," said Rose, "but perhaps I should leave it to others from now on."

My first instinct was to agree with her, but after a moment's thought I said, "Actually, if you enjoyed it, you're welcome to try any time you like. Everyone improves with practice."

Irene piped up, "Like Conall's eggs! They used to be awful, but now they're only moderately bad!"

"Hey!" said Conall, outraged. "They're pretty good now!"

Gram spoke up, "I hope so, because I remember when you brought your first batch down and tried to give it to Cook to add to his slop bucket. Even the pigs wouldn't eat them."

Everyone laughed and as things quieted down Rose stood up, a faint smile on her face. "I'll take a bowl to Penny."

"Let me do that," I protested.

Rose held up a hand. "No, I'll do it. If it's too bad, I'll accept responsibility."

***

I finished the second portal to Albamarl in just under two days. Both of them appeared to be normal doors that opened from the back wall of a small room at the end of the central hallway in our mountain cottage. For security, I added an attunement enchantment to the room itself that would deactivate both portals if it failed to detect the aythar of one of the people I had chosen. I did the same thing at the other end of each of them.

The one that opened into my house in the capital was located within the chamber of circles. I merely coopted one of the circle niches and built the portal doorway within. The one in the palace opened into a closet in Ariadne's bedroom.

Since the portals were an inherent risk, I kept the number of people attuned to them small. The list included myself, my family, Ariadne, and the Thornbear family. My initial design still had a flaw, though. A hostile enemy could potentially use one of the attuned people to keep the portals open while they or others passed through.

Matthew suggested adding a second enchantment to alleviate that problem. After some thought, I agreed with him. This additional protection would shut down the portals if the aythar of anyone *other* than those attuned entered. Since this would also make it impossible for us to allow anyone else through, I added a password that would bypass the second enchantment's effect.

This meant that an enemy would have to have one of the attuned people *and* know, or at least know about, the password. If someone learned it, for example, by hearing it spoken while being allowed through on one occasion, they would still require the presence of one of the attuned people to use it. I also made certain I could easily change the password, in the event that I knew someone outside the family had learned it.

Of course, even with that, nothing was perfectly safe. If the enemy knew about the password and already had possession of one of us, they could torture that person to force them to reveal it and then use it and that person's living body to pass through the portal.

To minimize that, I made sure only a few of them knew that a password even existed: myself, Penny, Rose, Matthew, and Moira. I told the rest that the portal could only be used for themselves and left the extra protective measure out of my explanation.

Was I paranoid? Damn right I was. I had been for years, and despite my best efforts, my enemies had managed to harm me and my family. Just a few months prior, my daughter Irene had been kidnapped from my supposedly secret mountain home.

While I had been involved with that project, Elaine, with Gary's help, had learned to create a privacy ward that would specifically block a wide range of signals that ANSIS might potentially use. Since it was a type of barrier, rather than a type of invisibility veil, she was also able to teach it to the rest of us, which she did with the exception of Irene. Irene was just beginning to learn to shield herself, so she had a ways to go before she could attempt anything as complicated as warding or creating enchantments.

Once we understood the technique, I gave Elaine the task of adding her special privacy ward to the enchantments that protected my home, and when that was done, she moved on to Castle Cameron itself. Gary suggested creating interior barriers as well, so that if any ANSIS units managed to enter, they could not coordinate with one another.

It was a large task, since it meant she would have to create enchantments to protect each room within the castle, but it would effectively limit them to communication distances as small as whatever room they were in.

Was it overkill, especially considering we didn't have any known enemy in the castle? Damn right it was. As I said earlier, I'm paranoid, and for good reason.

I would have had Conall assisting her, but Matthew had already appropriated his younger brother to help with the antennae that he and Gary were building.

Since I was finished with the portal, I decided to check on them and see how they were progressing. I found Conall in Matthew's workshop in the castle yard, but his older brother and Gary were absent.

When I entered the building, which had at one time been my father's smithy, I saw that Conall was hard at work. A modest pile of copper nuggets sat by on one side, while still more had been loaded into a crucible that was just coming out of a newer furnace that Matthew had built the year before.

My father, Royce, hadn't done much in the way of smelting, but Matthew's projects often required considerable volumes of fresh metal and occasionally an alloy.

As he brought the crucible out, Conall immediately began siphoning out the liquid metal using his aythar. The copper began to cool quickly as it left the crucible, and he stretched and formed it into a wire that was nearly a quarter of an inch thick. As it solidified, he looped it and shaped it into a coil on the ground a few feet away.

To be fair, we could have bought copper wire from the foundries in Albamarl, but the cost was high, and the supply was small. There wasn't a lot of demand for it, and if we had made an order, it could have taken months for them to fill it. Copper itself was very valuable, so purchasing the raw material would have been exorbitant as well, even if we planned to produce the wire ourselves.

Fortunately, precious metals were not a problem for me. Many years before, when my children were still young, I had nearly been bankrupted after agreeing to pay a vast weregild to the survivors of the Duke of Tremont's estate.

Prior to that, I had been trapped in the body of an undead monster, my actions controlled by an alter-ego that was slowly going mad. My alter-ego, aptly named Brexus, or 'payment' in Lycian, had sent a horde of shiggreth to the Tremont estate with horrifying results. Thousands had been murdered and the lands there were still uninhabited. People thought they were haunted.

In any case, the weregild, or payment for the wrongly murdered, had been massive. Lady Rose had defended me in court and had found a loophole that would have allowed me to avoid punishment, but I refused to take that route. After my conviction and subsequent flogging, paying the fine had used up nearly all the wealth I had inherited from both the Cameron estate and from the Illeniel family. Before that, I had been one of the three richest men in Lothion.

These days I was only in the top ten, but that was mainly by choice. As an archmage I had used my abilities to manipulate the earth, and it had provided whatever I desired. If I had wanted, I could have brought forth enough gold to wreck the market.

Instead I had varied which metals I produced and how much of each I released into the market. Initially I had been a bit malicious, releasing quantities designed to ruin a few of my nastier political foes who relied on mining for their fortunes, but after that I had moderated myself.

Now I only produced small amounts, and only rarely, except for instances like this, when I had a particular use in mind.

Matthew and Gary had told me they would need a substantial amount of copper, so I had provided it, but from the look of what remained, they might need more soon.

"How is it going?" I asked Conall as he finished his current batch of wire.

Wiping his brow, he gave me a look that said 'pity me.' "It's awful," he complained. "I'm just slave labor here."

I grinned at him. "What you've done would have taken dozens of men and many hours to do in the normal fashion."

"At least they would have been paid for it," he said with a sigh.

Contrary to popular belief, wizardry is work. It might be much easier, more efficient, and capable of wonders, but using one's power all day long was exhausting. *Which is why it's good I have four capable children.*

"You are being paid," I told him. "Your work is helping to protect not only you, but your family, and hopefully the entirety of Lothion. Isn't that sufficient reward?"

"Heh," he muttered. "There are one or two in my family I am starting to rethink protecting. In fact, I have a particular brother I might be willing to sell to the enemy if they offered me a decent price right now."

Nodding, I sighed and looked off into space. "I know what you mean. I was once offered a vast sum by Nicholas of Gododdin to adopt one of my children. You were just an infant at the time. I've often wondered if I should have taken the money."

Of all my children, Conall was the most gullible, and while he had learned to mistrust the things his older brother told him, he still treated most of my pronouncements with quick belief. "Really?" he asked, astonished.

I waved my hand at him. "A lot of noble houses would kill to have a wizard in the family. You would have been very valuable to them."

"I would have been a prince!" exclaimed Conall.

"Should I send him a message and tell him you're interested in a late adoption?"

He heard the hidden laughter in my voice then and his eyes narrowed. "Dammit, Dad! It's bad enough when Matt does it."

I hugged him as I laughed, ignoring the dirt on his clothes. "Sorry, I couldn't help myself." In fact, I probably could have sold my children. There were a lot of wealthy families that would have paid for the opportunity to have such power in their grasp, but none of them had ever dared offend me by making such an offer.

And I would have refused…probably.

"Where have Matthew and Gary gone off to anyway?" I asked him.

"Malvern," responded Conall. "They're starting work on the antenna there."

"So old Malvern agreed," I commented. I hadn't heard that news yet.

My youngest son nodded. "You'll have to take the World Road if you want to check in on them, since we don't have a circle there."

"Where will they be?"

"Lord Malvern is letting them put it atop his keep."

"I guess I'll go check on them, then. I haven't been to Malvern in a long time." I headed to the transport house and took the circle that would put me on the World Road. After that, it was just a short walk to the Malvern portal.

CHAPTER 21

Malvern was a sunny, coastal city. It wasn't as big as Albamarl of course, but it was significantly larger than Washbrook. There were at least ten or fifteen thousand people living in the city and surrounding areas.

The city itself wasn't walled, and it was a long way from the border with Gododdin, so war had never been a problem for the inhabitants. It was a modestly prosperous port, but the Count that governed it kept a strong fleet to protect it.

Count Malvern's keep stood on a hill that overlooked the city. To the west the keep looked over a steep cliff that plummeted straight to the sea, and to the south of it was a small road winding its way into the town proper.

The castle wasn't particularly impressive. There was no outer wall or towers, just a tall square keep that rose perhaps eighty feet in height with battlements at the top. A wide flight of stairs led up to a heavy oak door broad enough for two men to enter side by side.

From the portal that opened near the city, I flew to the keep. From my height, I could see activity on the roof, and my magesight confirmed it as soon as I was within range. Gary and Matthew were there, constructing something.

Unfortunately, I didn't want to insult the lord of the castle, so I needed to pay him a visit before heading to the room. The Count, Stephen Malvern, was a decent fellow, close to my age. I had met him on several occasions. He had lost his first wife during the first year that the shiggreth had plagued Lothion. In fact, while I had been 'dead,' Penny told me that he was one of the suitors that Rose had tried to convince her to marry.

I didn't hold that against him, though. He had since remarried, and he had always been polite when I had met him. Now, I was glad we had no bad blood between us, since his keep was apparently an ideal spot for the antenna that Gary wanted to build.

A servant ushered me in to see the Count, and I found myself being escorted up a series of stairs. It turned out my host was already on the roof, watching Matthew and Gary's work. He greeted me as I stepped out into the stiff, salty breeze coming from the shore.

"Lord Cameron! It is good to see you again," he said, offering his hand to me.

I shook it, replying, "Malvern, you're looking well."

"Call me Stephen," he insisted.

I agreed and returned the offer, and then he began peppering me with questions. "Can you explain this thing to me, Mordecai? Is it some sort of wizardry?"

Gary and my son were mounting a long wooden support pole, and next to them they had several substantial coils of Conall's heavy copper wire.

"There's no magic involved in this, Stephen, not as far as I can tell. As I understand it, the copper wire will enable us to capture signals that our strange enemy uses to communicate. You've been informed of what went on in Dunbar, correct?"

Count Malvern nodded. "Yes, some sort of mechanical foe, I heard. I'm not sure how this relates, though."

"They use an invisible type of light to communicate," I began.

He interrupted me almost immediately. "If it's invisible then it isn't light."

I sighed. "Whatever you call it, it's the same sort of thing light is; you just can't see it. The metal will resonate and produce an electrical current when the signal strikes it…"

Stephen frowned. "What kind of current?"

"Electrical," I repeated. "You're familiar with lightning. This is the same sort of thing except…"

"How dangerous will this thing be?"

The rest of our conversation was frustrating, and it was mostly incomprehensible to the Count of Malvern, but he did at least accept my assurance that we weren't endangering his castle. He gave up trying to understand after a while and left me to talk to Gary and Matthew.

Gary smiled at me, his android face almost perfectly imitating the human expression. "I listened to your conversation. It is impressive how quickly you've learned the principles of electromagnetism."

Still irritated from my talk with Count Malvern, I ignored the compliment. "What I'm really curious about is how you plan to locate the enemy with this. I understand how you'll detect the signal, but from what you've said you won't be able to determine a direction. If that's the case, you can't triangulate."

"Correct," said Gary. "However, we will have multiple receiving antenna and the signal strength will be different at each location. Using that information—"

I interrupted him, "Even if you had accurate signal strength, that would only give you an approximate distance, but you don't have that, because you don't know how strong the signal is at its source."

"Very true," he answered. "But, I can compare the signal received at each point and get a ratio, that, when combined with the known distance between those points, will give an approximate distance."

Clever, I thought. *With three approximate distances, he can create circles and trilaterate the source.* "That only works if the signal originates between receivers, though, and you'll need three signals to determine a rough location, assuming it is inside the area of the triangle."

"That is why I would like to create more antennae at other locations, such as Surencia," said Gary. "But I also have a method to determine location even if the signal comes from a place beyond the outer boundary between receivers. If I measure the difference in time of arrival of the same signal at widely separated locations, I can also get an approximate distance, even if the source is not between them."

I thought about that a while, digesting what he had said, before finally asking, "What about speed?"

"Pardon?" said Gary.

"To estimate distance from time, you need the speed the signal travels," I clarified. "Right?" I was in over my head, but I was determined to understand.

Matthew spoke up, "That's the easy part. The signal is composed of light, so it travels at the speed of light."

"The what?" As far as I knew, light didn't have a speed; it was instantaneous. Then again, it hadn't been that many years ago that I had thought the same thing regarding sound.

Matthew grinned. "I did some reading back in Karen's world, and Gary's explained a lot more since. We can go over this later, but trust me for now, it does have a set speed. The problem, for us mere humans, is that it is so great that it seems instantaneous, even over large distances. Luckily for us, Gary can measure time in very tiny increments."

Things got more interesting from there, and I was amazed at the precision and scope of the knowledge people had possessed in Karen's world. After a while, though, it was obvious that I was slowing them down, so I curtailed my questioning and bid them goodbye.

Gary stopped me. "One moment, Mordecai. I wonder if I can get your help with a small experiment."

"Sure."

A moment later, the android handed me a straight metal rod. "Today the weather is clear, and visibility is almost perfect. Since we are by the ocean it's the perfect place to do this."

"What do you want me to do, exactly?" I asked.

"Take this rod, which I've measured to exactly two meters, and fly out over the water. Matthew will stay with me on the beach at the water's edge, and communicate with you telepathically. When you are nearly over the horizon, I'll have him ask you to stop and place the bottom of the rod at the point where the wavetops are just touching it. From there I will have you keep moving away until I can no longer see the top of the rod." Then he handed me the small rectangle that I had first talked to him through.

The rectangle was a device from Karen's world that she called a 'PM.' It was an item of technology, just as Gary's body was. In the past, he had spoken to us from it. "What's this for?" I asked. "And what's a 'meter?'"

"A meter is a unit of measurement from my world, one much easier for me to work with. This will help me determine our exact distance to you. I cannot communicate with you through it from that distance, but I can measure the signal it emits to determine distance. Ideally, that would be unnecessary, but I have a hunch I may need the extra information," answered the machine.

"What are you trying to figure out?"

"The exact curvature of your world," said Gary.

I laughed. "I have that information in my library. Mariners and navigators have already done all of this. I can show you the charts tonight."

The android was insistent. "Nevertheless, I would like to do this. We can compare the figures from your charts with my results this evening."

***

When I got home a few hours later, I took a bath. I hadn't really gotten dirty, but the sea spray had left me feeling sticky and smelling funny. Penny was feeling stronger, and everyone else was out of the house, a rare quiet moment. She was moving around the house, which I took as a good sign.

I had just finished drying off and had donned a long tunic when I heard a yell from the direction of the kitchen.

Running, I was there a few seconds later, and I found Penny sitting on the floor by the counter, crying, carrots and turnips scattered around her. Her favorite kitchen knife was embedded in the mantle over the door.

"What happened?" I asked worriedly.

Her head was down, staring at the floor tiles. "Go away," she said quietly, a warning in her voice.

Ignoring years of marital experience, I approached her anyway. "Talk to me, Penny."

My wife's answer came in a growl, "Go away!"

"I can't help if you don't talk to me."

"Isn't it obvious!" she yelled. "I only have one damned arm! I'm useless! I can't cook. Do you know how many things you can do with only one fucking hand?! I can't even peel a gods-be-damned turnip!" There were tears of rage and frustration in her eyes.

I wanted to get closer, to hold her, but she jerked when I started to move. "Don't!" she warned. "Leave me alone. Can't you see my hand? I'm holding it up to tell you to stay the fuck away." She was pointing at her missing arm with her right hand. "It's still there. I can feel it. Do you see it now? I'm waving at you."

"It's hard, I know," I said soothingly. "It will take time to adjust…"

"Adjust?" she croaked. "I can't dress myself. I can't undress myself! Do you know how humiliating it is to have to ask Moira or Irene to help me when I have to relieve myself? How am I supposed to live like this?"

Without a good answer for that, I simply sat down myself, across the room from her. What could I tell her? Was this the right time to suggest I could heal her?

"I think there's a way to restore your arm," I said finally.

Penny didn't look at me. "Matthew told me. It sounds better than this at least." Her voice was flat, empty. "Who knows how long it will be before either of you have time to waste on something like that…"

"First, you aren't a waste. You've never been a waste. You're far more important to this family than I am. You're far more important to me! And second, I wasn't talking about a metal arm. I think I can restore your flesh and blood arm."

She looked up, and her face shifted through a range of complex emotions. First, hope, and then suspicion showed in her eyes. "What does it cost?"

I shrugged. "Nothing."

"Then why haven't you done it already? Don't play games with me, Mort. I know you better than that."

"I wanted to wait until you were fully recovered."

Penny picked up a carrot and tossed it up onto the counter. "There's no such thing as fully recovered, not while I'm missing an entire arm."

"I meant your health."

Wiping her eyes, she replied, "I know what you meant. And you're still not telling me everything. It's dangerous, isn't it?"

"Everything I do is dangerous," I said. "Everything involving my unique abilities anyway. I would have to become you, like I did when you were hit with the ballista bolt. We could both vanish, or wind up a single person, fused together. In the best case, it works but we never really know who was who to begin with."

She exhaled, releasing a dark laugh. "I can't blame you for not wanting to be me."

Grinning, I replied, "I'd feel worse for you, if you wound up stuck as me."

"That sounds grand to me," she said. "Do you have any idea how much I envy you sometimes? No, of course you don't. Remember when we were little? There wasn't much difference between us then. You were just this awkward, skinny kid. No one understood you back then, but I did. I saw your heart, your kindness. I loved you, and I didn't care that you were nobody. I was nobody.

"Then you became a wizard, and suddenly you were at the center of everything. And I was still nobody, but for some reason you loved me anyway. And lo and behold, it turned out you were the lost heir of the Camerons, *and* the Illeniels. Everyone wanted you, or wanted to kill you. You were *important*. But who was I? I was just the plain girl you refused to let go of.

"For a while I was your bodyguard, and I had some purpose. At least I was able to stay with you. But I could hear them talking. Did you ever wonder what I might hear with these inhumanly sharp ears you gave me? How many of those fancy lords and nobles might say things without knowing I could hear them? They felt sorry for you, or worse, thought you were a fool for wanting to marry me.

"But you married me anyway. How could I refuse? You were all I ever wanted, but I still felt ashamed. I should have let you go, pushed you away, but I was too selfish, too stubborn to let anyone else have you.

"Now I spend my days pretending—pretending to be something I'm not, pretending to be important, pretending to be a leader, and all I really want is to be invisible. I wish—I—I wish you were nobody, so we could go back to those days." She finished with her head resting on her knees, staring at the floor.

"Penny…"

"I know," she interrupted. "I'm wallowing in my own self-pity. Just let it be. I'll be the *Countess* tomorrow. Right now, I just can't do it. I'm tired."

Standing up, I crossed the room and sat down beside her, putting one arm around her shoulders. "I want the same thing," I told her. "So many times, I have wished we could just forget about all of it and run away. There's only one thing in all of this that keeps me going, one consolation that makes it bearable."

"If you say it's me, I'll knock you across the kitchen," she said ruefully.

"No," I answered. "At least, not the you I first fell in love with. You were sweet back then, but it's the woman with me now that makes it worthwhile. The Penny I knew as a kid; she wasn't anybody, but I loved her. But that isn't who you are anymore. You're the girl who refused to give up on me, the one who didn't care if I was a nobleman or not, a wizard or not. The one who didn't listen to all the stuck-up assholes who thought they knew better than I did about what was good for me.

"Maybe you think you're pretending, but no one else does. You've held this place together when I wasn't there. You've fought for our children when they didn't know what to do themselves. You've saved me from my own bullshit so many times I can't even count them. The only thing that's kept me going is *you*, watching you refuse to give up. You've always been too damned stubborn to let them beat you down. That's why I love you."

She gave me a strange look. "Because I'm stubborn?"

"There's nothing so precious as the love of a stubborn woman," I said, smiling through my own tears now.

Penny didn't say anything, and after a while she leaned over and kissed me softly.

"Are you going to knock me across the kitchen now?" I asked afterward.

She chuckled lightly. "I haven't decided yet." Then she stood and offered me her hand to help me up.

I took it, and after I had risen, I started to leave the kitchen, pulling her along with me.

"Wait," she told me.

"What?" She glanced around, and then I realized the kitchen was still a mess. "Oh, yeah," I said glumly.

The Count and Countess di' Cameron spent the next several minutes picking up vegetables and cleaning the kitchen.

CHAPTER 22

"**O**pen it," I commanded.

Peter Tucker, my chamberlain and long-time servant, stepped forward with the keys. I could have opened the lock myself, with or without a key, but I had learned never to use magic in front of regular folks unless it was necessary. For one, it startled them, and sometimes left them confused, but even worse than this, it was a constant reminder of the difference between someone like me, and them. It also sometimes led people to strange expectations. Why should they do anything if I was present and could do it easier and faster?

While Peter shuffled the keys, Sir Gram moved up beside him, putting himself between me and the doorway. Lady Thornbear's apartment had been locked after the bodies were removed so that nothing would be disturbed. With my magesight, I already knew there was nothing living within, but Gram took his duty seriously, and besides, our new enemy didn't fit the traditional category of 'living.'

Before Peter found the key, Gram voiced a quiet word and the enchanted tattoo on his arm flared to life. Metal scales flickered into existence and fluttered around him briefly, like a cloud of shining silver butterflies, before settling and locking into place. In a few short seconds he went from being unarmored to being better protected than any man in the entire kingdom.

His armor was unique, a product of my son Matthew's special genius. It covered him from head to toe like a metallic, reptilian skin, but unlike traditional scale mail, it suffered from no weaknesses. The individual pieces moved freely with him, but when confronted with an exterior force, such as a sword blow or an arrow, they locked in place, becoming more rigid than a solid plate of steel. It formed not only armor for his body, but his head as well, and the parts that covered his face were invisible, allowing him to see.

The armor's wonders didn't end there, however. The enchantment also included his sword, which had been re-forged from his father's greatsword, Thorn. The sword could take several forms, that of a greatsword, twin arming swords, or a sword and a large heater shield. It could even be commanded to take on its original broken form, before it had been remade.

With just the tattoo on his forearm, Gram could go from being unarmed and unarmored, to thoroughly equipped with a variety of weapons depending on the situation.

If Penny had had armor of a similar sort, she wouldn't have lost her arm. But I had never found the time to bother repeating my son's feat of enchanting. For now, Gram's sword and armor were unique.

As the door opened, Gram eased Peter aside and entered the room, surveying it quickly before continuing on to check the rest of the rooms. Personally, I thought his insistence on so much caution was excessive, but Gram was much like his father in this regard—rigid, loyal, and stubborn to a fault.

"Clear, milord," he called to me.

I already knew that, I grumbled internally. As I stepped into the small waiting room, my eyes confirmed what my arcane senses had already reported—Rose's living quarters had been destroyed. The floor was covered in dried blood, and sunlight entered from the direction of her bedroom, where a wide hole had been created in the wall.

The doorway from the sitting room to the living room was largely gone. Irene's blast had removed it, along with portions of the wall on either side. The wall between the living room and Rose's bedroom had entirely collapsed, giving a clear view of the round hole in the exterior wall.

The man that had been atop Rose was gone. All that had been recovered of his body was part of his right leg—the ankle and foot. The rest of him had been blown out of the room and seemed to have been incinerated in mid-air. Only ash and rubble had been found in the castle yard.

I had already examined the female assassin's remains, but that had left me with more questions than answers. Her name had been Mary, and she had been the young wife of the tanner in Washbrook. The tanner himself was missing, so the obvious conclusion was that he had been the male assailant, though we had no way of confirming that. Both Mary and her husband had been well liked and respected in Washbrook.

I hadn't known them well, but I had seen them at least twice a year at the feasts I held for the villagers of Washbrook, one of my duties as their liege. I had liked them both.

From Rose's account, I had expected Mary Tanner's body to harbor one of the metal parasites we had encountered in Dunbar. There had been no sign of one, nor had there been any tissue damage to her throat or neck. If she had been harboring an ANSIS parasite, I could find no sign of it.

Had she been acting on her husband's behalf? Was he the only one being directly controlled? I couldn't believe that either. The evidence pointed to both of them having scaled the wall to enter Rose's apartments through the window. Mary Tanner was a healthy woman, but she hadn't had the strength to do such a thing, and neither had her husband. No rope or other climbing tools had been found.

Also, Rose's description of their behavior pointed to them having been controlled. Normal humans don't ignore fatal wounds as Mary had. Normal men don't ignore a solid knee to the groin.

Gram started toward the door that led to his own bedroom, but I cautioned him, "Don't."

"I thought we were going to search everything," he observed.

"Give me a few minutes. Don't touch anything," I ordered. "I want to examine it carefully before we start moving or touching anything." To illustrate my point, I closed my eyes.

Giving my full attention to my magesight, my focus roamed through the apartments like a disembodied ghost. *Clothes, jewelry, teapot, cups…* Mentally, I catalogued each room, searching through every nook and cranny. Everything seemed normal, everything was mundane, except for one small oddity.

There.

In the corner of the main room, near the hearth, there was something metallic that I couldn't identify. It was flat and irregularly shaped, conforming to a small niche in the brick that enclosed the hearth. I moved toward it, with Gram following close beside me.

Bending my knees, I stared at the space where I had located it. There was nothing visible, though my magesight still showed it there. *Something invisible?* Stretching out one hand, I was surprised when it moved. I jerked my hand back. It had risen slightly, as if it meant to meet my fingers. Still, my eyes had seen nothing.

"There's something here," I muttered.

Creating a probe of pure force, I extended it, attempting to touch whatever it was, but as soon as it made contact, the seemingly liquid metal surged toward me. It struck my legs, but my personal shield kept it from making contact with my clothing or skin. Exhaling with a sharp hiss, I changed the shape of my probe, using it to envelop the metallic thing.

"Got you," I exclaimed. Lifting it into the air, I was amazed to see it become visible within my globe of force, a thick, viscous glob of what appeared to be liquid metal. There wasn't much of it; in total it comprised perhaps a cup of liquid. Within my magical sphere, it shifted and moved, searching for an escape.

"What is that?" asked Gram, his eyes growing wide.

"Nothing good," I answered.

***

I stood in the yard outside of the smithy that Matthew used for his workshop. "Is that enough?" I asked. A large pile of copper in irregular chunks and pieces lay on the ground in front of me, the product of another exercise of my connection to the earth.

Gary glanced at Matthew, and after a moment they both nodded. "It should be plenty," said the android.

"I still don't understand why it takes this much material," I confessed.

"It wouldn't," began the machine, "but we don't know what frequencies the enemy may be using, so I have to construct antennae of a variety of sizes and orientations to make certain we detect whatever ANSIS uses."

"Orientation," I muttered. "Is that why they use a cross shape?"

Matthew jumped in, "Exactly. If the transmitter is using a vertical antenna then a horizontal one would miss the signal, and the opposite is also true."

"What if they use a diagonal antenna?" I mused.

"We would get a half strength signal," said Gary confidently.

"And why do you need different sizes?" I asked. "Wouldn't the largest antenna pick up everything the smaller ones would?"

Matthew started to speak but then deferred to Gary. Gary explained, "It depends on the wavelength of the signal. If the antenna is a quarter, a half, or the full length of the wavelength, you get a good signal, but if it's much larger or smaller you won't. We have to match the resonant frequency length of a wide variety of possible signals..."

He went on for a while, and I found myself following much of it, but it was too much, too soon. The topic was fascinating, but I already had too many other things to think about. I decided I would have to trust his expertise.

Even so, I listened, storing his words away for further study. When he finally ran down and stopped, I was ready with my next question. "So, back to the functional end of this. You're going to use these small ring gates to put the output leads from each of these antennae in a central location here, and then connect yourself to all of them?"

Both of them nodded, then Matthew added, "We'll also make sure that each lead has exactly the same distance from the antenna to its connection with Gary."

"Why?" I asked.

"To make sure he receives each signal at approximately the same time," said Matt.

Gary held up his hand. "Well, I won't get them at the same time, but I intend to measure the difference in reception time for each antenna, and I don't want a disparity in the antenna lead length to confuse that."

I felt stupid then. I should have remembered from our earlier discussion about trilateration. "Got it," I said. "By the way, I found something today. Take a look." Reaching into my pouch, I drew out the glass container holding the silver metal I had found in Rose's rooms.

The glass had been open on one end, but I had used my power to heat and seal the open end, and then for good measure, I had enchanted the glass to make it nearly unbreakable. I wasn't taking any chances.

Matthew frowned, and Gary simply stared. Neither said anything.

"Any idea what it is?" I asked. "I found it hiding in the wreckage of Lady Rose's living room."

Finally, Gary answered, "I think it's ANSIS, a piece anyway."

Matthew muttered, "Grey goo."

"They finally made it work...," added the android.

Their responses were cryptic and frustrating. "Anyone care to explain? I get tired of mysterious answers."

"It means we have already lost," declared the android.

I fought the urge to choke him. I doubted it would do any good anyway, since he didn't breathe. Instead I waited; my patience had improved with age. After a minute he began to explain, "They've created programmable matter. That glass container holds a vast number of impossibly small machines, each communicating and coordinating. Together they can create almost anything you can imagine—larger machines, for example. Assuming that that is indeed them and not just a container of quicksilver."

I held up the glass. "So with this amount they could construct a teacup, or something similar in size. How does that equate to us having already lost?"

"Self-replication," said Matthew. "If it works the way it was described to me back on Karen's world, it can create more of itself. It could potentially convert the entire world into more of itself."

Gary nodded. "My creator, the original Gary Miller, worked on the software for ANSIS, but there were several other related departments trying to create something very like this. As far as I know, they made some progress but never fully succeeded."

"Then where did this come from?" I asked.

"ANSIS is much smarter than those who created it," said Gary. "It may have succeeded where they failed. However, I misspoke earlier. We should not give up hope yet. We don't know the properties of this new nanomaterial. It may not be able to self-replicate, as Matthew mentioned. It might still require larger facilities to produce it."

Matthew spoke up, "Why didn't you detect it? You were following its signals when Rose was attacked. How did it escape your notice afterward?"

Gary tapped his temple, "No signal. It isn't attempting to communicate. When the attack failed, it probably ceased signaling to avoid detection. Let me try something." He held out his hand for the container.

Somewhat begrudgingly, I handed it to him. The android held it in his hand without speaking, while he merely stared at it. A minute went by and nothing happened.

"What are you doing?"

"Trying to talk to it," said Gary. "Let me focus. I'm trying a variety of different short-range radio signals."

Nothing happened, but after a minute the android spoke again, "There it is."

"What did it say?" I asked.

He gave me one of his unsettling smiles. His mechanical body was an almost perfect human imitation, but it showed its artificial nature in certain expressions and gestures, and smiling was one of them. If questioned, I couldn't have put my finger on exactly what it was, but something about the expression didn't ring true and it never failed to leave me feeling uncomfortable. "I have no idea," said Gary. "ANSIS uses a variety of encryption methods, methods for which I do not have the key, otherwise I could attempt to alter its programming, or at the very minimum spy on its communications. This sample is communicating in the two-point-four gigahertz band."

We had already been through several discussions about the meaning of radio bands and wavelength, so I understood the gist of his statement, but I wasn't sure what it might imply. "Does this help us?"

"Yes and no," said Gary. "It means I have a good reference for detecting their local communications, the signals they use to communicate within a few hundred feet. Unfortunately, I don't think there's any way we can easily build devices that can do that for us, not with the technology and materials you have available."

Matthew chimed in, "So the only way we can detect them at close range is if you yourself are within the vicinity."

The android nodded affirmatively.

I ground my teeth. *Great.* Before I could verbalize my frustration, I heard the distinctive sound of the alarm I had created years before, during what scholars had retroactively labeled the God-Stone War.

CHAPTER 23

The bell tower was ringing. Rushing out into the courtyard, I looked up at the nearest tower. A vivid blue light shone there, emanating from the enchanted crystal mounted atop it. A similar light was shining from all the wall towers, as well as the smaller towers protecting Washbrook.

Everyone in the yard—stable grooms, men-at-arms, washerwomen, craftsmen—they all stood still, staring at the towers. It was as though the world was holding its breath. After a second someone yelled, and they all began to run at once, heading in various directions.

In the sky above, I could see the shield was up, visible only to my magesight, a faintly glowing dome that covered the entirety of Castle Cameron and Washbrook. The people around me were heading for their assigned positions, which for most of them in the courtyard meant the keep itself. The castle denizens were supposed to muster in the great hall. In Washbrook a similar process should be taking place, though it was likely a bit more chaotic. Most of the townsfolk would be heading for the tavern, the Muddy Pig, to take sanctuary in the hidden shelter built beneath it.

There was an anxious feeling in the air, but it stopped short of panic. Since the time of my battle with the Shining Gods, we hadn't needed to use the defenses, but I had insisted in keeping up the practice of having a yearly drill, usually right before our mid-winter festival. Thanks to that the people knew how to respond.

What I couldn't fathom, though, was *why* the alarm had been sounded. Was it ANSIS? Had Tyrion decided to make war on us with the She'Har? Neither seemed likely, at least not yet.

Matthew started to run past me, but I stopped him with a yell, "Where are you going?"

"The control room," he answered immediately.

I shook my head. "No, that's my job. You take position at the main gate."

"What about me, Your Excellency?" asked Gary.

"You head to the great—no, scratch that. You stay with my son. If this is ANSIS, you might have some insight to offer him," I ordered. Without waiting to hear their responses, I lifted myself into the air and shot toward the doors to the main keep. They had already been thrown wide to accept the influx of castle servants and rather than mingle with them, I flew over their heads.

It was a short trip down the hall and around a corner before I reached the hidden door to the secret chamber that controlled the castle's defenses. Pressing my hand against a certain spot on the wall, I stepped through the door that opened in front of me. Elaine was already inside, which meant she was the one who had activated the castle's shield.

"What's happening?" I asked.

"We're under attack," she replied immediately.

"Who?"

Elaine waved her hand at the wall. "You tell me. I don't recognize them."

The wall she indicated was covered in large panes of enchanted glass. The enchantment on the glass was just to protect it, making it incredibly strong and hard to break. The glass covered small portals that opened on the exterior walls of the towers around Castle Cameron and Washbrook. Without the glass, an enemy could fire projectiles directly into the control chamber through the viewing portals when they were active.

Most of the portals showed nothing unusual, but those on the towers flanking the gate of Washbrook showed what appeared at first glance to be a small army.

On second glance, I decided it was definitely an army, but it didn't look like any army I had seen before. Heavyset men in some sort of strange plate stood in vague lines in front of the gate. Their heads and chests were covered in some sort of metal plate, but their legs and arms were less protected, covered only in some kind of heavy leather. Or was that their skin?

I revised my initial impression. They weren't men, at least none I had ever seen before. They were short, perhaps only four and a half feet in height and close to being as wide as they were tall. Judging by their thick arms and legs, they were probably very strong. Most of them carried steel-rimmed square shields. Those in the front ranks had one-handed axes while those behind had some sort of polearm similar to a halberd. *No, more like a bardiche*, I corrected myself. The weapons were mounted on long hafts eight or nine feet in length, with a long blade with a wicked tip at the end, making them suitable for both chopping and thrusting. The rear ranks carried crossbows, though they were far heavier than any I had seen troops carry before.

They looked dangerously brutal. Having faced an army at the gates before and being familiar with the distances between the wall towers, I was able to do a rough calculation of the enemy's numbers. *Seven, maybe eight hundred men, or whatever they are,* I thought. Certainly, they far outnumbered the men guarding Cameron and Washbrook.

People often made the mistake of thinking that lords kept small private armies within their castle walls, while nothing could be further from the truth. Castles usually had only the staff required to keep them running and a relatively small force of guards. Men-at-arms were expensive to feed and maintain. The real point of a fortified castle was that it didn't take *that* many men to defend. Ten or twenty men with strong walls could hold off a force of hundreds for long periods of time.

In fact, I had nearly sixty guards within the walls of Castle Cameron, but only because we had made our recent expedition. Otherwise half of those would have been elsewhere, tending to their homes and families. In times of war I could muster perhaps two hundred levies, peasant soldiers, but that took at least a week's advance notice.

With over fifty men, we could defend the castle from a force this size, even without a magical shield and wizards, but it was unlikely we could keep them out of Washbrook. Fortunately, that wasn't a concern. The magical shield protecting the village as well as the castle was designed to withstand even the forces and powers of a god.

But I didn't intend to wait within our perfect defenses. The enemy at our gates would soon realize they couldn't breach the shield. What would they do then? Historically, the answer was that they would then burn and pillage everything that they *could* reach. The mill, herders, and tenant farmers, all would pay the price for our neglect. Most of them were still in the surrounding countryside, and even those that had retreated into Washbrook would lose their homes, crops, and property.

No human army, local or otherwise, would have dared present themselves before my gates. The last army to do so, a force of nearly thirty thousand from Gododdin, had been burned, crushed, and then drowned. In my overzealous desire to make certain no one forgot the lesson, I had killed them all to nearly the last man. The only reason I wasn't called the 'Butcher of Battle Cameron' was because I had committed more memorable atrocities in the years that followed.

"What will you do?" asked Elaine, interrupting my thoughts.

I shrugged. "What else? Parley. If that doesn't work, I'll get rid of them." Before I stepped out the door I added, "Watch for my signal at the Washbrook gate. When you see it let me through, then close it behind me."

"But—," she started to protest, but I ignored her, closing the door after me.

A variety of people yelled for my attention as I headed toward the keep entrance. Sir Gram and Captain Draper were the first I addressed, "Gram, you're coming with me. Captain Draper, assemble all but the sentries near the Washbrook gate. I'll be going out to parley."

Penny was next. She stood by the door, already in her armor. The empty sleeve of her mail hauberk pulled tight and tied in front of her. "You aren't going out there," she said firmly. "Someone else can talk to them."

I met her brown eyes, staring into the dark depths of her resolve. How many times had we faced similar situations together? Every case had been different. Sometimes she had been my guardian, and other times she had been forced to take other roles. If I didn't take her with me, there would be hell to pay later. In my youth I had often agonized over my decisions.

I was not that man anymore.

"Organize those sheltering in the keep, reassure them," I told her. "I don't think there is any real danger to them, but a panic would be dangerous. If something does go wrong, I trust you to do whatever is necessary."

She started to argue, but I held up one hand, cutting her off. Penny's face blanched at my brusqueness. *I will definitely pay for that,* I sighed inwardly.

"Matthew, Moira, you will come with me to the gate in Washbrook. Conall and Irene, you will take positions at the castle gatehouse. Captain Draper, make sure they have at least two guardsmen with each of them. They will be responsible for managing any threat that gets through Washbrook," I commanded. With those words, I began walking again.

Gram and my two children fell in behind me.

"Thank you," said Moira.

I assumed she meant because I had brought the two of them along. "Don't," I told her. "You'll both be staying inside the walls, acting as reserves in case I do something stupid and get myself killed or incapacitated. Only Gram and Myra will accompany me outside."

"What about the dragons?" prompted Matthew.

I glanced up and over my shoulder, toward the eyrie that lay in the mountains behind us. The dragons were currently up there, outside the protection of the shield over Cameron. "They're safe where they are," I noted. "I don't intend to drop the shield to bring them in."

"They could strafe the enemy with dragonfire," suggested Gram.

"Our guests have rather formidable looking crossbows," I informed him, since he hadn't seen the enemy yet. "The damn things are like small ballistae. I'm sure the dragons could inflict serious harm, perhaps even rout them, but I'd rather not risk them being injured."

Five minutes later we stood in front of the town gate. Several nervous-looking town militiamen stood close by. The first to approach me was Simon MacAllistair. Technically, he was in charge of Washbrook's small citizen guard, but he was a cobbler by trade. "Milord," he addressed me, bobbing his head respectfully. "Washbrook stands ready."

His serious tone almost made me chuckle. The Washbrook militia was made up of older men, those too old to serve as soldiers if I had to call up my levies. Many of them had some past military experience, but all of them were long past their prime. They were intended as auxiliaries, in the event that my actual soldiers were absent or if they had been overwhelmed.

I knew better than to dismiss him, though. However old he might be, Simon meant business. "Have your men hold their positions in the towers," I ordered. "Keep your bows ready. Let Captain Draper's men handle the walls and gate if it comes to a melee."

Stepping up to the gate, I raised my voice, "Open it, and be sure to close it tightly after we're through."

They did, and seconds later the massive oaken timbers of the gate began to move, swinging inward. Moira had already released her alter-ego, Myra, and she and Gram followed me closely, one on either side. Matthew and Moira followed a short distance behind. When we had reached the shield, which stood some five feet from the walls, I turned back to them. "When I signal Elaine to open the shield gate, stay here. Do not have her open it again until we return. If things go wrong, don't open it unless we're close and you think you can get us back safely. Remember, there are hundreds of people in Washbrook. Their lives are more important than ours."

Neither of the twins looked happy. Matthew's expression was one of disappointment, while Moira's face spoke clearly of her opinions. *She thinks I'm an idiot,* I noted. At least she had the sense to hold her tongue.

"I think you're an idiot," she said aloud, echoing my thoughts.

"Captain Draper should be the one to do this," added Matthew, agreeing with his sister for a change.

Already full of tension, I found myself unable to muster any anger at their verbal mutiny. "Your objections are noted. Now, do as I say." Then I held up my hand and made a vertical slash in the air. Elaine was watching through the window portals, and that was my signal to open the shield.

A second later, I felt an opening appear in the air in front of me, twenty feet wide and twenty feet high. I stepped forward, leading Gram and Myra.

The first thing I noticed was the wind on my cheeks. It had been conspicuously absent before, since the protective dome had enforced a calm over Washbrook. There weren't many clouds, and the sun warmed the side of my face that wasn't being buffeted by the breeze. It felt good.

It was always like that during these moments. Anxiety and adrenaline drive the mind and body into a state of hyperawareness, and often the things one notices most, are the small impressions that are frequently ignored during everyday life. In the air I could smell the trees from across the field, as well as a hint of sheep dung.

The enemy was less than a hundred yards away, watching us carefully. I began walking toward them as the shield closed once more behind us. Gram was silent as he walked by my side, a moving statue of shining metal. Speaking to Myra, I asked, "Can you get anything from here?"

Being a spell-twin of Moira, she possessed the same gift of the Centyr that my daughter did. "Their minds are strange," she responded. "They don't speak our language, and there's an odd resistance, as though they are shielding their minds. I can feel their wariness, but little else. They think this might be a trap."

That was pretty much what I'd expected, though the language problem was a new twist. We kept moving until we had reached the midway point, and then stopped. Since the strangers hadn't attacked yet, I held up a hand and waved at them.

"We should have brought a white flag," observed Gram.

"They aren't even human," I replied. "They probably wouldn't recognize it. We don't even know what their custom for parleys might involve, or if they have one."

A rapid-fire series of metallic clicks rang out from the enemy, as though all of them had tapped on their armor in quick succession.

Myra answered my unspoken question, "That was some sort of signal, an order to stand ready but not to attack—yet."

"Can you tell where their leader is?" I asked. Standing at ground level, I could only see their front rank, and even that was largely covered by their shields. With my magesight, I searched through the ranks behind that, but I couldn't detect any obvious movement or arrangement that indicated who their commander was.

"There are around twenty of them that radiate some degree of authority, scattered throughout," said Myra. "Near the left of the center there are three that stand close together. One of them seems to be directing the other two."

Try as I might, I couldn't figure out which three she meant.

"Let me link with you," said Myra helpfully. "I can show you." She reached out toward me with her hand.

Slowly, I took it. Moira had given her enough of her power to allow Myra to create a form with physical substance. Her hand felt real in my grasp, though my magesight could easily detect that it was merely a construct of aythar. Lowering my mental shield, I touched her mind and images began flowing between us.

There, she told me. *Those three.*

Magesight was a thing of form, almost touch. There was no true color in it, and when there was, it was a product of the human mind interpreting different 'flavors' of aythar. The three Myra was indicating lit up with mental colors, two of them red while the one between them seemed golden.

Studying them for a moment, I made a note of their aythar, ensuring I could recognize them in the future, then I broke the link between Myra and myself. "Thank you," I told her.

Seconds later there was movement. One of the three began to make his way forward, and two others bearing shields and axes followed on either side of him. "That's the second in command," relayed Myra. "The leader and third in command are staying behind while he comes to meet us. He's bringing a small honor guard with him."

I could have guessed as much, but I nodded my thanks to her, keeping my eyes on the soldiers in front of us. A gap opened in the front rank and their sub-commander and his two guards strode toward us.

"Any instructions?" asked Gram.

"Try to look intimidating," I replied.

Gram straightened, tightening his grip on Thorn. "Yes, my lord."

"That was for Myra," I said with a smirk. "I only brought you to look pretty, Gram."

He gave me a bewildered look that reminded me so much of Dorian it made me want to hug him, while Myra stifled a laugh.

Mentally, I reached out to Myra, creating a new link without taking her hand. *You're much better at reading thoughts. Since we don't share their language, I'll need you to try and interpret for me.*

Her reply was a warm glow—I could feel her love and trust. *Of course.* Though I had only recently learned of her existence, I realized she truly considered me her father. It was a humbling sensation, and I began to doubt my decision to bring her with me. My intention had been to use her for this in order to protect my 'real' daughter. Now I felt as though I had just substituted one family member for another.

Don't worry, came Myra's mental voice, *the body of a spellbeast is much harder to destroy than one of flesh and blood. You made the right decision.*

The strangers finished their walk, stopping five feet away. I met their sub-commander's eyes squarely, though they were nearly two feet lower than my own. Most of his face was obscured by a metal helmet that covered his head and cheeks, leaving only a wide gap for his eyes and mouth. His skin was a dark brown and appeared thick and rough, almost like cow-hide. When he opened his lips to speak, a long series of clicks and strange staccato sounds emerged.

He greets you as an unknown enemy of indeterminate social standing, Myra told me.

"You are also unknown to me. I would like to know why you have entered my lands in such a threatening manner," I said aloud, but before Myra could attempt to relay my meaning the sub-commander gasped, his eyes narrowing as though I had offered some offense.

He seems shocked, Myra explained. *He thinks you have used a type of language reserved for intimate communication with a lover.*

Well, that's inconvenient, I replied. *So, they do use words of some sort, but not for day to day talk?*

Myra nodded. *That seems to be the case.*

Spreading my arms wide in a gesture meant to convey peaceful intentions, I spoke again, "We mean you no harm."

That earned me a rapid-fire burst of strange sounds between the sub-commander and his two guards.

They're trying to decide if you're deliberately insulting them, said Myra.

This was pointless. *Try to connect directly with his mind,* I told her. *We'll never get anywhere like this. You can relay my thoughts directly to him.*

I felt her aythar begin to move as a thin line stretched out to connect Myra to the enemy sub-commander, but before anything could be relayed, the man began to scream.

It wasn't a scream in the human sense, for it sounded more like the squeal an injured pig might make, high pitched and ear-piercing in its volume. Without hesitation, the two enemy guards stepped forward, their axes flashing toward me and Myra.

Thorn knocked one axe away before it even reached my shield, and Gram's backstroke dipped down below the enemy shield before flying upward. Both of the strange man's arms were severed, and a portion of his helmet went flying as the impossibly sharp sword, driven by Gram's unnatural strength, tore through his flesh and armor.

My reaction was slower, but not by much. I used my power to slam all three of them away with a blast of pure force, but the result was underwhelming. My magic should have struck them like a battering ram, but instead it fell apart, skittering across their bodies and draining away like water from a duck.

The other guard's axe slammed into Myra, ripping through her shield and cutting her magical body nearly in half. I felt her pain screaming in my head as she collapsed. Then I saw him lift the axe again, glaring at me with coal-black eyes.

Enraged, I let a single word fall from my lips, *"Pyrren."* Burn. I already knew my magic wouldn't touch him directly, so I ignited the air around him, pouring my strength into it until the heat threatened to blister my skin just from standing so close to him.

The guard screamed briefly as his body was charred and blackened, but the heat stole the breath from his lungs almost immediately. He slumped, dying in front of me, and I saw that the sub-commander had fled during the commotion. Gram stopped short of chasing him, for the enemy crossbowmen were leveling their weapons at us. Muttering a command, Gram changed his greatsword to a one-hander and shield.

That bastard isn't getting away! I cursed mentally. Reaching toward him with one hand I used my power to rip the earth upward from beneath the sub-commander's feet in a solid chunk. Then I used it to propel him violently back toward us. The enemy leader sailed through the air over our heads to slam into the castle shield fifty yards behind us. He struck the solid wall of magic and slid to the ground, unmoving.

Pain flared in my left leg, below the knee, then again in my right shoulder. The sound of missiles striking metal rang in my ears as Gram's shield stopped the majority of the crossbow quarrels fired at us. Looking down I saw that two had gotten past him; one had gone completely through my leg while the other was buried in my chest. The enemy crossbowmen were spread out in a line that was far too long for Gram to protect me from those firing from the ends.

Somehow the missiles had passed through my personal shield without breaking it. *How did they do that?* There was no time to think, though. The front line was charging toward us, hungry to avenge their fallen sub-commander.

That suited me just fine.

The sight of a large armed force charging directly at you isn't something most people ever see. In fact, it's a profoundly frightening experience, but my life was such that it wasn't my first time to witness it, and I was too angry to give a damn. I didn't let my rage make me stupid, though. I had a number of possible actions I could take, ranging from reckless to ineffective. Tossing those aside, I dipped one hand into my pouch and brought out a large handful of my old favorites, the iron bombs. Flinging them into the air, I used my power to spread them in a wide arc, settling them in amongst the enemy before I detonated them.

It wasn't the most devastating thing I could have done to them, but it cost me little and it would buy me time.

The explosions sent shockwaves through the air and sent bodies flying in every direction. In the seconds that followed, only Gram remained on his feet, for I had fallen unceremoniously on my ass. To my right I saw Myra struggling to rise, her aythar body having already reformed. She looked weaker, but she was intact. I just needed to get her to safety.

"Back, Gram! We need to get back to the wall!" I shouted, but the young knight didn't react to my words. *He can't hear me,* I realized. From long experience, I had learned to always shield my own ears when using the iron bombs, but Gram hadn't had the benefit of that protection. He was probably deaf. Fortunately, Myra realized it just as quickly.

We're retreating, Gram, she announced, broadcasting her thoughts to both of us.

Then I saw the enemy scrambling to their feet. A few of them didn't rise, but only those that had been closest to the blasts. Most of them were getting up. It was hard to believe how incredibly tough their bodies were. Behind me, I felt the shield gate open. Matthew or Moira had decided to open it, probably to rescue us.

It'll be a bloodbath if they get in, I thought. With my children fighting, we might win, but the cost would undoubtedly be high. Pushing Myra ahead of me, I started toward the gate. Knowing my stubborn offspring, they wouldn't close the gate again until we made it back.

The enemy was not only resilient, they recovered faster. Charging toward us on their short, thick legs, they would reach us before we made it.

Gram came to the same conclusion, and he turned to buy us time. His sword and shield blurred again, becoming the greatsword once more. The enemy axe-men reached him first, but he didn't hold his ground, otherwise they would have wrapped around him and been on Myra and me in a second. Instead, he skipped backward as he cut down the ones who reached him first.

It was hard to believe such a large man could move like that, and I wondered what Dorian would have thought, if he could have seen his son dancing with the blade. *He'd have thought it was weird as hell, but he'd have also been proud.*

His movements were graceful and fluid, with sharp, whip-like counterpoints. At first glance, he appeared almost weightless, floating across the ground as he moved, but an experienced fighter would have noted how his feet were firmly set just before each strike, allowing him to deliver the maximum amount of power and then absorb the recoil.

Gram—*no, Sir Gram*—for the young man was every inch the knight his father had been—danced backward, staying within a few feet of us as we retreated. Thorn's reach in his hands was close to ten feet, and none survived who entered that space.

Then the crossbowmen lifted their weapons again. They had taken the longest to recover, having had to not only regain their feet, but also to reload. Despite their distance and everything else going on around him, Gram noticed their preparations. Just before they loosed, he switched again, from greatsword back to arming sword and shield.

Realizing I had to do something, I did what I should have done half a minute sooner. I shouted a word and released my power, creating an almost instantaneous fog to cover us and the enemy, obscuring their aim.

Gram leapt in front of me as the first quarrels shot through the mist, catching a number of them on his shield. Several struck his legs and head, but his armor held, though the strike to his head sent him stumbling, half stunned from the force of it.

We needed something big, or we weren't going to make it the remaining twenty yards to safety. Pushing Myra hard, I yelled, "Keep running!" Then I stopped, letting my focus drift as my mind sought the silent strength of the earth. I was done playing nicely. If these new strangers wanted us dead, I would bury them instead.

More crossbow bolts flew through the fog, and my concentration was ruined as they found me, first in my right thigh, then my hip. The pain was so intense I hardly felt the one that tore through my chest, piercing my heart.

My heart stopped, and with it, the pain vanished.

CHAPTER 24

The voice of the earth faded as the pain struck, but when it ended, another voice became much louder, drowning out everything else. The void howled around me, and releasing my fears, I claimed it.

My perception changed. My magesight was still there, but it tasted different. The aythar of my enemies became brighter, and it called to me, tempting me like a glass of water set before a man dying of thirst. Rising to my feet, I began to walk toward the buffet that had been laid out for me.

Gram was the first that I passed in the fog, close enough that he saw me. "Mort!" he shouted. "That's the wrong way. Go back!"

I paused, fighting the urge to take him. His heart beat strongly in his chest and his life force shone brighter than that of anyone else on the field. More quarrels struck his armor, and I distantly felt another embed itself within my chest. Struggling to draw breath with my damaged lungs, I growled hoarsely at him, "Run." Then I continued on toward our foes.

The first was only a few feet away, blazing at me through the fog like a lighthouse on a stormy night. Unable to restrain myself, I lashed out at him before I was close enough to touch him. A thick umbilical of black power sprang forth, latching onto his head and neck. In less than the span of a heartbeat, I ripped the life out of him, gasping with pleasure as the energy flooded into me.

I walked on, my stumbling gait becoming a confident stride.

The next two I found at the same time. Moving quickly, I placed one hand on the nearest, who had just raised his axe. I smiled as his eyes glazed and the weapon fell from his fingers as he sank to his knees. His friend chopped at me from the side, the power of his blow driving his axe almost halfway through my chest. I ripped the life out of that one without even looking at him, then resumed savoring the slow death of the one kneeling in front of me.

My chest began healing as soon as I pulled the axe blade out. Then I removed two of the crossbow bolts, but more appeared almost as soon as I had. I decided not to bother since they didn't particularly hinder my movement. I could take them out later.

I killed more, reveling in the joy as the fire in my chest burned brighter. Gram was following me, cutting down those that approached me from the left, and I began to grow annoyed. Each life that died at his hands was one less for my feast.

At last I could take no more, so I turned on him. The young knight nearly severed my arm before recognizing me, not that I'd have cared. I moved close, my face only inches from the transparent steel of his helm. "I told you to run."

Gram's face showed shock, and perhaps—fear. "Mordecai, your eyes!"

I placed my palm on his chest. My patience was done, but the enchanted steel resisted my effort to draw out his life-force. Snarling, I pushed, and then he was airborne, flying across the field and back to the open shield gate. I didn't bother watching to see how he landed, but I felt a faint pang of regret. *He's not my enemy,* I thought. *I shouldn't hurt him.*

Something flew out from the direction of Washbrook, a spinning plane of strange power almost two feet in width. It passed some thirty feet to my left. It was at waist height, and I could feel the aythar attached to it, guiding it through the mist. Matthew was controlling it, and the spell sliced through air and enemies alike without slowing.

Frustrated at the loss of yet more prey, I focused my attention on the gate into Washbrook. Matthew stood there while some of the men-at-arms helped Gram and Myra through. He held his metal hand out in front of him, and he projected a wide flat plane of utter blackness from it, absorbing everything that the enemy fired at them. *Is that a newer version of his fool's tesseract?* I wondered. If so, did he mean to blow the enemy away, me included?

No, that couldn't be it. He would be fully enclosed if he had that sort of intention, and it would probably be too dangerous to risk so close to the town.

Moira's mind reached out to mine, bridging the distance between us. *Father, come back.*

Tell your brother to get back inside the walls! If he kills any more of my toys, I'll come and rip his soul out by the roots, I snarled mentally.

What's wrong with you? she replied anxiously, and then I felt the link began to change, driving more aggressively into my mind, trying to seize control.

Rather than fight it, I latched onto the connection and began to pull, drinking in her vitality. She would release me or die.

The connection broke almost instantly. My daughter was no fool. A dark feeling akin to pride washed over me, knowing that she hadn't been weak enough to let me kill her. Seconds later, the opening in the shield that protected Washbrook closed. My wish had been granted.

During my brief pause to deal with the rebellion, I had apparently killed several more of the enemy, but more of them were closing on me. Aythar was flashing in the air, and my fog began to disperse. The enemy had spellcasters.

If the mist vanished, the enemy soldiers might be able to overwhelm me. I doubted they could kill me, but being hacked to pieces would probably hamper my ability to kill them. But I wasn't new to this game. I knew what I needed to do.

Reaching out to the void, I touched the faint lines of darkness that still connected me to my recent victims, and then fed a portion of the dark power into them. As one, they began to rise from the ground, lifting their axes and turning on their former brothers-in-arms. The battle raged, and though I was outnumbered at first, the enemy soon realized that their advantage was a delusion. More of them fell, both at my hand and at the hands of my new servants, and each that fell rose again moments later, ready to serve.

Strange clicks and noises rang out across the field as my foes began to cry out to one another in alarm. Their bizarre clicking was augmented by animal-like squeals of terror as panic began to spread among them.

I directed my new helpers in an unorthodox strategy. Whereas most battlefield commanders were concerned with casualties and preserving their force, these things were not my concern. It didn't matter whether my servants were hacked apart. All I cared about was making certain that none of the living escaped. Therefore, I directed most of my troops to the edges of the field, herding their former comrades in toward the center, where I and a small knot of my guardians waited.

Covered in blood, some my own, some that of others, I reveled in the slaughter. My wounds were gone. I had removed the last of the bolts from my body, and the holes had vanished as I basked in the deaths of my foes. It was like standing beside a bonfire on a winter night. The cold dark swirled at the edges of the light, but the burning light of my enemy's dying heart-fires surrounded me in warmth.

In the beginning, when there were many of them, I didn't bother going slowly. I sent black whips out to grasp them, ripping their lives out and filling me with a violent ecstasy. But as their numbers dwindled, I slowed my pace, taking them one and two at a time to prolong the fun. The last ten I kept prisoner, struggling in the grip of my dead soldiers while I approached them individually. A hand on a cheek or throat and they began to wilt before me, crumpling one by one as I devoured their lives.

I paused when I reached the last one, their proud leader, now reduced to a terror-ridden lump of trembling flesh. *I should make this one special,* I thought. With a mental command, I had those holding him step away. To his credit, he bravely struck at me, but I caught his thick wrist in an iron grip. He began to weaken immediately, but I avoided killing him quickly. *Perhaps I should open his throat, let the warm blood out.*

Some part of me rebelled at that thought. This wasn't normal. This wasn't me. *Kill him and go home.* That was all I needed to do. Clenching my will, I tore his life out and released his arm. Then I turned my back and walked toward Washbrook.

My family was waiting.

As I returned, I could see that all eyes were on me, whether it was the soldiers and militia on the walls and towers, or those gathered within the city gate. Matthew and Moira were just outside that, but the shield remained closed as I drew near. Gram stood with them, though I could tell by his stance he was still nursing a few injuries.

When I stopped a few feet from the barrier enchantment, they merely stared at me.

"Open up," I commanded.

"I don't think that's a good idea, Father," said Matthew, his tone neutral.

I smiled, knowing he must be afraid I meant to kill them. While the thought had crossed my mind, it had passed as my bloodlust dissipated. They were my children, not my prey. I just had to convince them of my peaceful intentions. Glancing down at myself, I realized I was quite literally covered in blood. That combined with the gruesome scene they had just witnessed had probably unnerved them.

"I'm fine now," I said. "I'll admit I suffered a turn of battle madness, but it has passed now."

"That was more than battle madness," said Moira firmly. "Something happened to you, something bad."

Then I noticed that the men on the walls were gone. In fact, no one was visible other than my two children and Gram. Was this some sort of trick? "What's going on?" I demanded, struggling to keep my growing irritation hidden.

"His eyes turned black on the field," said Gram. "I saw them, just before he hurled me at the walls."

"Mom will be here in a minute," announced Matthew. "She wants to talk to you before you come in."

"Just open the shield gate," I said. "This isn't necessary."

Penny stepped out from the town gate. "I'll be the judge of that, Mort." She nodded at the three of them and they withdrew, leaving us alone. Moving as close as she could, she stood just a couple of feet away, with the thrumming power of the barrier enchantment standing between us. The heavy wood of the city gate closed after Gram and my children passed through it.

I stared at her, and despite the heavy pulsing aythar of the shield between us I could see her heart-flame, her aystrylin, flickering within her. Compared to that of the others, it was a pale wan flame. She was healthy, physically, aside from her missing arm; even the level of her aythar was what one would usually expect for a normal human, but her aystrylin was dangerously weak. In contrast to her outward health, her aystrylin resembled that of an extremely elderly woman.

It wasn't something I had noticed before. Normally I only saw people's aythar. Discerning the aystrylin was only possible for me through a tight link, such as that formed for deep healing. I should have been paying closer attention to her.

She never fully recovered after the battle with Mal'Goroth. At one point she had given most of her life to me, feeding me her vitality to strengthen me while I struggled inside the She'Har spellweave that held my soul captive. It had nearly killed her, and she had been deathly ill for weeks afterward.

I had wanted to believe she was the same. I should have made sure.

"I saw the fight from the chamber in the castle," she said, breaking me out of my reverie. "It was terrible. What happened to you? How is this possible? Did you become one of *them* again?"

No! That wasn't it, it couldn't be, but even as I denied it to myself I knew the truth. I had been hearing the whispering voice of the void for years now, ever since I had regained my humanity. Today I had let it fill me. By *them* she meant the shiggreth, undead monsters we had spent years fighting.

"Of course not," I answered hastily.

"Gram said you took a crossbow bolt through the heart," said Penny, her voice hard.

I nodded. "I did. It nearly killed me, but I healed it."

"Like the shiggreth?" she accused.

My anger from earlier had vanished, replaced by fear, not of *her*, but for her—fear of myself. "No," I declared, staring down at my hand. "I'm still in control of myself. What happened was temporary, like when I listen to the wind, or the earth. I'm still human."

She pointed, directing my attention over my shoulder. "What about them?"

Behind me, forgotten, stood an army of inhuman soldiers. Dead soldiers. With my magesight, I could see the black cords binding them to me, connecting them to my silent, still heart. "Oops," I replied convincingly.

The corner of Penny's mouth rose briefly, just a hint of a smirk at my poor attempt at humor, but it vanished as soon as it appeared. "I need better than an 'oops,' Mort. A lot of people depend on us."

Focusing my will, I severed the links and an army's worth of man-like soldiers collapsed to the ground behind me. Meeting Penny's eyes again, I spoke, "You're right. I wasn't even close to normal. I'm still not there. Give me a few minutes."

Surprisingly, she lifted her arm over her head and gave the signal to open the shield gate. The barrier between us vanished. "I rejected you once," said Penny. "Do you remember? I swore I'd never do it again. You sound like yourself to me."

She started forward, as if to embrace me, but I stepped back quickly. "Wait. It isn't safe yet." I could still see her faint aystrylin, and I feared that even a moment's touch would kill her.

I needed to restore myself. I was still wrapped in the void. I could force my heart to beat, but that wasn't enough. If I released the connection, I would probably collapse. *Or maybe I would start living normally,* I thought. I really had no idea. There was nothing physically wrong with my body anymore, but my intuition told me that I might just fall dead if I released the void too suddenly.

Perhaps if I replace it with something else first. Opening my mind, I listened, finding the deep, slow sound of the earth beneath me. I put all my attention on it, and it became louder. I forced my heart to beat and filled my lungs with air, and then I sank into the mind of stone. Pain shot through me but faded as quickly as it came, dulling into insignificance as I expanded to become *more*, until my body comprised not just a human form, but the soil it walked upon.

I studied that body. Its heart had grown still again. It needed something more. Drawing it down, into myself, I transformed it, filling it with stone and fire. Then I contracted, making myself smaller, until that hot, rocky lump was my only flesh. Clawing my way upward from the darkness, I stood above ground once again, staring out at the world with alien eyes.

My memory was fading, but the animal in front of me reminded me what I wanted. I wanted to be like it. Gradually, I rebuilt the image of the—what was it again? Then I saw it, a man. *That was me. That is me.* I let it flow into me, and the world changed. Colors gained new meaning, and I felt the air on my skin. The woman—Penny—Penny was close by. Breathing, I felt my life moving within me and my thoughts became fluid again.

I watched her for several minutes, taking stock of myself and remembering who I was. Penny was patient, but eventually she spoke, "Mort?"

"I'm pretty sure," I said after a moment. When she came at me again, I held up a hand. "Let me be sure." Then I bent down and put my hand on a patch of green grass, watching it to see what happened. I felt no life transfer, and when I removed my hand, the grass still looked green.

Glancing up at Penny again, I realized I could no longer see her aystrylin. "Yeah." I nodded. "I think I'm me."

She took my hand, and then she hugged me. Together we walked back into Washbrook.

CHAPTER 25

"Where is everyone?" I asked Penny. The town was empty, devoid of people.

She laughed. "In the castle courtyard. I told Elaine not to open the Washbrook shield until everyone was safely within the castle shield. That way if you really were insane, they'd be safe."

I frowned as I looked down into her brown eyes. "What about you?"

Penny patted my cheek. "I'm with stupid."

"Hey!" I muttered, mildly offended, but she cut me off.

"Live or die, Mordecai, I'm in it with you. After everything that happened before—with the shiggreth, the Dark Gods, all of it—I promised myself I would never turn my back on you again."

I growled, "That's a dangerous philosophy. With all the weird things that happen to me, I'd rather you think more about yourself. What would our children do if—"

Penny interrupted me again, "Stop and turn that sentence around. I've made my decision. If you want them safe, if you want *us* safe, then you had better be more careful what you do—or become."

Watching her from the corner of my eye as we walked, I knew I wouldn't win this argument. The wind tossed her soft brown hair and made me want to sigh, while her empty sleeve made me wince. She had suffered so much for me over the years, and yet I still couldn't protect her—not from pain, not from the world, sometimes not even from *me*.

"I don't deserve you," I muttered.

She released my hand to signal to Elaine to open the castle shield gate, then looked up at me. "Shut up. You deserve more than you know. Nobody talks about my husband that way, not even *you*."

My guardsmen saluted as we entered, but kept their eyes on the ground, fearing to meet my gaze. I couldn't say I blamed them. What I had just done was gruesome. Gram and Matthew stood in my path.

"We took the sub-commander prisoner," Matthew informed me. "He's unconscious, but once he wakes, Moira can learn a lot from him."

I nodded, and then looked over his shoulder at Gram. "I'm sorry for what I did to you. How badly are you injured?"

The young knight shrugged. "A cracked rib, nothing more. Moira already took care of it."

I held his gaze. "Forgive me, Gram. You didn't deserve that. I was... not myself."

"It's already forgotten, milord," he responded.

Maybe for you, I thought, *but I have to answer to your father in the next life. What would he think of my actions?*

The silence was broken when Gram spoke again, "About the bodies..."

I stifled an inappropriate chuckle. I should have had them bury themselves before I released my newly created shiggreth. Penny answered before I could, "Send a wagon and some men to strip the bodies, then organize the townsfolk. They can dig a trench to bury them."

"What about our guardsmen?" suggested Gram. "They should help."

Penny responded in a neutral tone, "We have met our duty to defend them. There are far too many for our men to deal with. You can detail half of the guards to assist, but keep the rest ready in case there are more enemies nearby. Make sure everyone is prepared to retreat within the walls if there's any sign of another attack."

I nodded in agreement. My wife had the right of it, though I had been unable to say it myself. I was still in shock from what I had done, and I wondered what should be done next.

Matthew took the lead. "No one has had lunch. After all that excitement I'm sure everyone is hungry. Let's eat."

Of course. I should have thought of that, though perhaps part of the problem was that I was the farthest thing from being hungry. Unlike most battles, I had emerged from this one feeling better than when I had entered it. I was practically bursting at the seams with energy. Food was the last thing I needed. *Because you already ate enough for several lifetimes,* I thought darkly.

***

While everyone ate, I went home. I needed to think, so I left our mountain cottage and took to the air, flying up until the peaks of the Elentirs were beneath me and the world appeared small. It helped, seeing the world that way; it made my problems seem smaller, less overwhelming.

Visions of what I had just done kept creeping into my thoughts, but I pushed them aside. They weren't helpful, and I knew from long experience with such horrors that I would have plenty of time to revisit what had happened in my nightmares.

"I'm a long way from the simple boy who lived at the smithy," I said to the landscape far below. "Every passing year seems determined to dye my soul a darker shade."

That wasn't helpful, so I decided to list the current problems. *A mysterious forest appears where Lancaster used to be, and somehow, it's tied to the ancient Illeniel She'Har. A new race of people arrives and promptly attacks us, for reasons I don't understand. Intelligent machines have invaded the world, secretly attempting to enslave all of humanity, or maybe just to remake our world according to their own vision. Meanwhile, the She'Har I resurrected are led by my ancestor, who has no discernible morals, and may or may not be on our side.*

It was human nature to seek a pattern. I wanted to believe all my problems were connected in some way that made sense, but I cautioned myself it could be a non sequitur. Some of these things could be entirely coincidental.

The She'Har initially came here to escape from an ancient enemy. Tyrion's suffering and eventual holocaust was part of their long game to find a way to save themselves. I and my children were one result of that. The Illeniel She'Har had been brought back as a result of our actions. Now ANSIS, the ancient enemy of the She'Har, was here, and ironically my son had discovered during his recent travel that they were probably created by humanity as a response to a She'Har invasion.

Those things, fantastic as they were, had some sort of cause and effect, or perhaps even a circular cosmic cycle, but the disappearance of Lancaster and the appearance of this new enemy didn't seem to fit. It seemed possible that the new enemy came from the primeval forest we had found, or from someplace like it. Those things might be connected, but they didn't fit in with the rest of it.

Except for the fact that my son had detected translational magic at the borders of the strange territory that had replaced Lancaster. That implicated the Illeniel She'Har, indicating it might be some sort of result of their millennia-long plan to protect themselves from ANSIS.

Then again, it might be something they had done that was unrelated to that plan. Yet, if they had done it, and I was ignorant of it, then it must have been part of the knowledge removed from the loshti. That would tend to indicate it was part of the She'Har's secret plan.

Now that I've established that I'm essentially clueless regarding current events, what can I do to gain more information? I reminded myself. *Focus on what you can do.*

Interrogating the prisoner was obviously our first and most promising source of potential information. Continuing Matthew and Gary's project to locate ANSIS was equally important. I could also ask my son to investigate the magic around the border of the strange forest. It might help if we knew where it came from.

It might also help to talk to Lyralliantha. She hadn't received the loshti, but being the last of the original Illeniels, she might have some knowledge that would shed light on what their plans had been. I didn't relish the thought of another trip to their island, though, or the fact that even asking simple questions of her might take weeks of valuable time.

You need to delegate more, stupid, I told myself.

Moira was the obvious choice for extracting information from our prisoner, although I hesitated to put her in a situation in which she might break more of the rules the Centyr had created to protect themselves. She might also be able to speed up the time it took to gain information from Lyralliantha, or discover answers the She'Har meant to hide.

Am I willing to put my own daughter at risk? I was only one man, but I had incredible resources at my disposal, if I dared to use them. It really came down to whether I prioritized the safety of the world, or my family. My first instinct was to keep them safe, to try and do everything myself, but was that really in their best interest? My oldest children were grown, but if I didn't allow them to leave the shelter of home, they'd never become true adults.

Honestly, the same was true of the Queen and the nation of Lothion. My actions in the past had been founded on the assumption that only I could protect them. They needed to be given the information and power to do so for themselves. My only previous attempt to do that had been the creation of the Knights of Stone, but they were gone now.

There were only a few surviving members of that order, Cyhan, Harold, Egan, William, and Thomas, and none of them had the earth-bond any more. After a period of years, it became too dangerous, slowly converting the men so bonded into golems of earth and stone. I had broken their bonds when they began to show signs of the change.

We needed them back. I wasn't willing to subject more people to the earth-bond, but the dragons I had created were the perfect solution for that. I had just been too cautious to use them, giving them only to a few family members and the Queen. "That will change," I muttered.

Having resolved myself, I dropped from the sky, stooping toward the ground and only slowing myself just before I reached the doorstep of my home. Conall was standing there, and he opened the door for me. "I wish you'd teach me to do that," he said.

"It's too—"

"Dangerous. I know. You tell me that every time," he groused. "But *you* learned it."

I frowned. "I don't think you want to go through what I did to learn it. Sooner or later, everyone who has tried flying this way has wound up dead—usually *sooner*, rather than later."

"But you keep doing it," Conall reminded me, as he led the way. "Elaine and Elise have been examining the prisoner. They want you to come see him."

I followed my younger son, thinking on what he had said. My flying skill was such that it was unlikely I would kill myself, unless I lost consciousness while in the air, but today's events made me wonder. Could I die? I had just been shot through the heart, and here I was wondering about it. Had my internal transformation only been possible because I was already starting to listen to the earth when it happened? That might have made it easier to touch the void.

What if I was killed while unconscious? What if I was decapitated while conscious? I was pretty sure those things would be fatal, but I couldn't be entirely certain, not anymore. There might be nothing more between me and becoming a monster than the beat of my heart.

When I had been trapped as a shiggreth before, it had been an artificial copy of myself making the decisions, while I was trapped as an observer within the She'Har immortality spellweave. That was not the case anymore. *I* was the one who had crossed the line this time, and it hadn't been easy to come back. If it happened again, I wasn't sure I would *want* to come back. It had felt so good.

It was like being drunk. My inhibitions had been gone, leaving me free to indulge my darker impulses. Pain had been a thing of the past and killing had felt natural, pleasurable. Even now, the void was only a heartbeat away, waiting for me to listen to it, to give it power and expression.

The example of Gareth Gaelyn was a warning. An archmage could easily lose control, giving themselves over to the impulses and drives of whatever they became. In his case, he had become a dragon, and after slaughtering his enemies, he had turned claw and fang on his friends and allies. It had taken him a thousand years to regain his humanity.

I was on the precipice of something far worse.

Conall pulled up short in front of me. "They're inside."

We were at a stone enclosure in the castle yard, near the barracks. It was originally a small storage building, but it had been repurposed as a jail cell. During a previous war, I had felt a lack for not having a dungeon, but once peace returned I hadn't bothered to build one. On the few occasions I needed to lock someone up, I usually borrowed Lancaster's facilities.

A guard opened the door and inside there were two more, along with Elaine Prathion and Elise Thornbear. Their 'patient' lay on a small cot. He was still unconscious, but his hands and feet were chained to an iron ring set in the wall as a precaution.

"What have we learned?" I asked them.

As usual, Elise didn't mince words. "I think he's human."

"He's got two arms and legs, two eyes, all of that," I responded, "but beyond that he seems too different."

Elaine piped up, "He has all the same internal organs we do."

"So do bears," I countered.

"It's more than that," said Elise waspishly. "I've had Elaine examining him carefully, comparing his internal body structures to mine for comparison. While he's different in stature and proportion, everything else is too similar. Even the patterns of hair growth on his body are the same."

"Hair?" I mumbled.

Elise raised one brow. "Want me to undress him and show you?"

I gave her a hard glare. "That won't be necessary. You're telling me that he's deformed, like a dwarf or midget?"

"He isn't misshapen," said Elise. "And there are seven hundred other bodies out there on the field that are just like him. I think he's from some race of men that we've never encountered before."

"And they just appear on our doorstep, ready for war?" I muttered. "None of this makes sense. Perhaps we'll learn more when he's awake."

I left, and found Penny and Moira waiting for me outside.

Penny smiled briefly. "Learn anything?" Her expression was normal, trusting, but Moira's eyes studied me carefully. I could sense her wariness. She was probably still wondering if I was safe, and I couldn't blame her. I was wondering the same thing.

"Elise thinks he's human, but other than the fact that they're very similar to us, we don't know much," I told her. Then I added, "I'd like Moira to sift through his mind when he wakes up."

Penny glanced between me and our daughter, a look of concern showing in the lines of her face. "Is that safe for her?" Though she didn't understand the particulars of what Moira had done in Dunbar, she knew that messing around in the heads of others was what had gotten our daughter in trouble.

I decided to be honest. "I doubt Moira Centyr would agree, but I am inclined to trust her."

My daughter's eyes locked onto mine. "According to her, I'm already a monster." Deep down I could almost hear a silent addition to her reply, *and you might be one too.*

"Your choices are your own," I told her. "I firmly believe that. Monster, human, whatever labels we call ourselves, what matters is our actions. In the end, it's our actions that define us, not the opinions of others."

Penny looked back and forth between us. "Dramatic statements like that don't really do much to reassure me. I hope you realize that."

Moira's features softened. "I'll be alright, Mom." Then she asked me, "How far do you want me to go with this?"

"I'll trust you to make that decision. Do whatever you feel necessary, whatever you can do without damaging yourself."

My daughter nodded, and then without warning she took my hand. I felt the beginning of a tentative link and I allowed it. After a brief inspection she spoke in my mind, *Thank you.*

What for? I replied.

Trusting me, and allowing me see your mind. I couldn't be sure you were still you until now.

I smiled. *Actually, I was wondering the same thing. You've set my mind at ease.*

Moira dropped my hand before announcing, "I'll stay here then. The prisoner is starting to come around."

"He's awake?" I asked.

"No," said Moira. "There are levels to consciousness. When we first brought him in, he was still out cold, and his mind was silent, but I can feel it now. He's dreaming again. Now he's like one who has fallen asleep."

Penny and I left her there, but as we walked back to the keep Penny asked me, "Are you sure she'll be safe?"

I shook my head. "Nope." Her face turned to worry before I could add, "But it's the right decision. You convinced me of that."

"I did?"

"Mm hmm," I answered. "Your little speech after I came back to my senses."

"I told you to be more careful with yourself," she growled. "Not to take more chances with our children."

"You also told me you trust me, no matter what," I responded. "I did some thinking and realized I need to apply that same reasoning to others. Matthew and Moira are grown now. We have to let them take risks, or they'll never be anything more than children."

"And if they make terrible mistakes?" asked Penny.

"Then we do what parents do. We pick up whatever pieces are left and clean up the mess," I told her.

CHAPTER 26

That evening Penny and I sat in the living room of our mountain home, enjoying a moment of peace. We were about to have a second cup of tea when the Queen of Lothion entered the room, surprising us. Well, technically, she surprised Penny; I had seen her enter through the portal down the hall about twenty seconds earlier. Interestingly, she didn't come alone.

The man that followed after her was above average in height, perhaps five feet and eleven inches. He had broad shoulders and a muscular build that matched his thick mustache and beard.

I jumped up to greet them while Penny scampered out the other door with a strangled 'eep' as she sought to find something better to cover herself. It wasn't that she was exposed in any way, but she must have thought her ratty old housecoat inappropriate for such high-ranking guests.

"Egan!" I cried, before giving the man a bear hug. "I haven't seen you in ages!"

Sir Egan had once been one of my knights, and though he now paid obeisance to the queen, he was one of the few remaining Knights of Stone. In fact, he was a member of two orders of knighthood, being also a founding member of the Knights of the Thorn. The Knights of the Thorn were an order created by the Queen herself, and they were so named to honor Dorian Thornbear's sacrifice.

A rough-looking man by all measures, Egan stiffened in my arms. "The Queen," he hissed in my ear.

I laughed. If we had been at court, my greeting him first would have been a major breach of protocol. I held onto him, winking at Ariadne over one of his shoulders. "Don't be so shy, Egan! I see little Ari every day almost, but it's been ages since you came to visit." I pushed him out to look at him from arm's length and then used my hands to ruffle his thick beard playfully. "Damn, you look good! Aren't they feeding you? A man of nearly forty should have little extra around the middle by now."

Sir Egan stepped back, turning to address Ariadne, who was openly laughing at his discomfort. "My Queen, please forgive…"

The Queen grinned mischievously at him. "Egan, I told you once already. This is an informal setting. Mort's my cousin, and he's been sharing his home with me. Let the etiquette and protocols go for a while."

To emphasize her point, I swept Ariadne into another hug and then kissed her soundly on the cheek.

Sir Egan gave me a thoroughly disapproving look. "I see now why you aren't encouraged to come to court more often."

It was at that point at which Penny returned. She still wore a housecoat, but this one was longer, heavier, and embroidered. It wasn't formal wear by any stretch of the imagination, but it did at least look like something a noblewoman would wear at home.

Egan's face lit up at the sight of her and he almost forgot himself. He ducked his head respectfully toward the Queen, who was now standing comfortably next to me, tucked under my arm. "Your Majesty, if I may?"

Ariadne frowned. "I told you to relax."

The gruff knight nodded, and then stomped across the floor to embrace my wife. "Penny! How have you been?" His demeanor on meeting her was completely different from his manner with me.

Ariadne looked up at me, a question in her eyes, but I merely shrugged, as if to say, *How should I know?*

Penny seemed equally enthused to see him, and the two of them nearly forgot about us as they greeted each other. They seemed so excited that I thought for a minute they might begin to hold hands and hop around in circles, but they managed to restrain themselves.

Then Egan focused on Penny's missing arm. "I heard the terrible news. I only wish I could have been there to help," he told her, half apologizing.

Penny pursed her lips before replying, "What's done is done. Let's not talk about it. Would you like some tea?" Then she remembered the Queen. "And you too, Ariadne, of course."

It was a testament to her fortitude that she managed not to call her 'Your Majesty.' Over the past week, Ariadne had worked hard at making Penny more comfortable with her presence. She had only partially succeeded, primarily in getting Penny to drop the honorifics.

Both of them nodded affirmatively and my wife started for the kitchen, but Sir Egan quickly followed her, offering his assistance. Ariadne and I were left alone, so we sat down.

"I had no idea they were such good friends," observed the Queen.

"They fought together through some hard times, while I was—away," I noted. "Sharing a battle makes close friends of men who've fought side by side. I would think it's the same for men and women." By 'away,' I was delicately referring to my exile as an undead monster. Egan and Dorian had fought shoulder to shoulder with Penny to help extract my family and the Thornbear family from Albamarl while the Duke Tremont had occupied it.

Ariadne patted my hand affectionately. "That's true, but he didn't seem nearly as happy with your welcome."

I sighed. "I don't think he's ever been completely comfortable with me after our encounters back then." In fact, Egan had been guarding my family on two separate occasions, and he had been forced to protect them from *me*. In one encounter, he had nearly burned me to ash with his sun-sword, and in the second I had wounded him badly, before sucking some of the life out of him to heal my injured son.

Despite the fact that I had been his first liege, and the one to knight him, Egan had plenty of unpleasant memories regarding me. I really couldn't blame him if he still felt uncomfortable around me.

After a few minutes Penny and Egan returned, carrying a tray laden with cups. They sat and made themselves comfortable, but before the conversation could begin Lady Rose appeared. "Did I smell freshly brewed tea?" She stiffened at the sight of Sir Egan in the room.

Egan stood and bowed respectfully. "Lady Hightower."

Rose recovered from her surprise almost instantly. She crossed the room and found a chair, but before sitting, she answered, "Sir Egan, I see that you are well."

I watched her studiously. Rose wasn't the only one capable of careful observation, though I was far more prone to lapses in judgement than she was. It had been so long since any of Dorian's fellow knights had visited that I had almost forgotten her dislike for them.

It wasn't that she nursed an active grudge, but the events surrounding and following her husband's death had left her with a certain amount of prejudice against them. It had been Egan who held her back when she tried to join Dorian beneath the monolith that crushed him. She had forgiven him for that, but later, when the Order of the Thorn, had been created she had been vehemently against their use of some of her husband's things as memorials in their chapterhouse.

In particular, her husband's broken greatsword, the same one her son now wielded after Matthew had remade it, was practically considered a relic. She had refused to let Sir Harold have it, even though the Knights of the Thorn had been named after it.

The most telling sign of her distraction was the fact that Rose was so focused on Sir Egan that she didn't notice the Queen until she began to sit. Despite the enforced rule of familiarity in my house, she wouldn't dare sit down before at least addressing her monarch, not intentionally at least. She jerked to a halt as her eyes lit on Ariadne. "Your Maj—Ariadne, my apologies. I didn't see you there."

Ariadne smiled. "Don't worry about it, Rose. Sit down."

Penny started to rise to fetch Rose a cup, but Egan beat her to the punch. When he returned he took it upon himself to fill the cup before handing it to Rose.

"Since you're here so early, I'm guessing you already heard of our doings today," I said, beginning the inevitable conversation.

Rose coughed lightly, and I got the sense I had made a mistake, then Ariadne answered, "Actually, no. We've had our own troubles today, but please, fill me in. I'll share my news afterward."

I glanced at Penny, and I could see she was just as clueless as I was, but the look in Rose's eyes held a distinct message. She had already observed something. She had probably known that Ariadne had some news and thought I was foolish for speaking first. It was too late to correct that, however, so I launched into a concise retelling of the events of the day.

I spared little as I recounted the details, other than summarizing my victory over the invaders as a major feat of magic. Ariadne would probably get a grislier account later from others, but I had no stomach for it. I included the fact that we had a prisoner who spoke no known tongue and Elise Thornbear's speculation about his humanity.

Ariadne's face was graven with disapproval when I finished. "I know we're being informal here, but I'm sorely tempted to put my crown on and make a formal decree after hearing that."

"Am I not allowed to defend my citizens and holdings?" I asked sincerely.

"That's not the problem, Mordecai, and you know it!" declared my cousin, the Queen of Lothion. "How would you feel if I went to war and led the charge against an army?"

"I'm not the Queen, Ari, you are," I replied sharply. "It's not that uncommon for noblemen to take the field."

"You aren't some lowly knight or small baron," stated Ariadne.

Leaning back, I answered in a dismissive tone, "That may be true, but it isn't unheard of for even the greater lords to take the field."

Ariadne's eyes took fire. "I don't need a history lesson from you, Mort! And you weren't leading an army, you went out to parley—alone! And *then* you fought a major battle by yourself."

"I had some help," I insisted, but Penny ruined my statement by punching my shoulder.

My wife gave Ariadne a sympathetic look. "I agree with you. He took almost no support with him."

Ariadne smiled at her. "I should probably command him to stay off the battlefield if this happens again."

Penny nodded enthusiastically. "You should!"

I glanced between the two of them, and then at Rose and Egan. There wasn't a sympathetic face in the room. "You can order whatever you like, but I'll do as I see fit according to the situation," I said defiantly.

Sir Egan choked on his tea, and after a fit of coughing he spoke out, loudly, "That's open contempt for the crown!"

The Queen stared him down. "Egan, don't make me repeat myself again. This is a meeting of friends and family. Don't ruin it for me."

Rose sniffed. "Politics is a poor topic for family and friends, but if we're going to speak of it, I think there are a few things you should consider, Mordecai."

I took a deep breath. "I'm listening."

Rose looked at the Queen. "You'll forgive me if I speak frankly?" Ariadne nodded, so Rose continued, "Mordecai, while your rank as the Count di' Cameron puts you in the lower upper end of the peerage, you are in reality the most powerful nobleman in the kingdom. You are very nearly as important as the Queen herself."

Egan choked again, and Ariadne began pounding on his shoulders as if to help him, though I suspected she was also hoping to cut off his outraged response.

"You're overstating things, Rose," I argued.

Rose's brow went up. "No, I am not, and I believe the Queen agrees with me. What do you think would happen to Ariadne's position if you were to die suddenly?"

"Not a damn thing," I declared confidently.

"Her position as the first ruling Queen in Lothion's history would be in jeopardy. It was never a popular decision to put her on the throne. It was merely the least distasteful option. She has been in power long enough now that most have grown accustomed to it, but dissent could grow quickly if you were to disappear," explained Rose.

"I am not the only wizard in Lothion anymore," I countered. "And every wizard in Lothion is firmly in her camp. Not only that, but Matthew would support her. No matter what happens to me, she will have Cameron behind her. And she has a dragon. The lords wouldn't dare turn against her."

Rose dipped her head deferentially. "I'll grant that the dragon was a masterful stroke, and it does indeed strengthen her position, but your son is an unknown in the world of politics. He does not command the same respect. You are the most feared man in Lothion. Your mere existence does more to silence the Queen's critics than every other factor combined."

I chuffed, "I doubt they fear me that much."

"Then you'd be wrong," said Egan honestly. "Your deeds are the stuff of legend."

More like the stuff of nightmares, I thought, but I was grateful for Egan's tasteful wording. I leaned forward. "Even so, Egan, you make a point in my favor. Today was yet another of those *deeds.* Once the story gets out, they'll be reminded that I haven't lost my teeth."

Penny surprised me by setting her teacup down firmly. It startled me more that she *didn't* break it, which was more her style when upset. Instead she was calm and composed, and when she spoke it was in a fashion I would have expected from Rose, rather than my wife. "Please forgive my husband," she said, directing her words to the rest of the room. "He is almost certainly the most frustrating man I have ever known." Then she set her eyes on me and continued in a fashion I was more familiar with, "I often dream of strangling him and putting myself out of my misery."

Everyone laughed, but I had to correct her. "No, you'd have to strangle yourself to put you out of your misery."

"*You* are my misery," Penny said firmly. "It would put me out of my misery whether I was strangling you or whether I was strangling myself."

More laughter followed, and I chuckled. "Still, it would be clearer if you said—"

"Don't be a pedant, Mordecai," Rose abjured me. "It isn't very becoming of you."

I sighed, looking around me. I couldn't win. "Fine, you're all right. It was stupid of me to go out there today," I admitted. "However, I reserve the right to be stupid in the future. There's no help for it."

"How so?" asked Ariadne innocently.

"Well, I wouldn't expect any of you to understand, not being wizards, but my magic is founded on stupidity. If I tried to change that, I would lose my powers," I told them grandiosely.

"Oh, is that so?" asked Penny incredulously.

I nodded. "I'm pretty sure it is. In fact, I am pretty sure that the motto of the Illeniel line of wizards is 'stupid never dies.'"

There was more laughter, and Rose snorted in decidedly unladylike fashion before speaking up, "What a bold liar you are! The wizardly lineages don't have any mottos, not that I've ever heard of."

"Well they do now," I declared. "I'll just need to add it to the banners."

The mood had lightened, but after a minute Sir Egan brought us all back to the seriousness of the present. "Your news regarding this attack is disturbing, and unfortunately it seems it may connect with what the Queen has to share."

"Have there been other attacks?" asked Penny.

"We aren't sure," said Ariadne. "In Albamarl we have several reports of small villages being attacked by strange creatures. While most of them aren't enough for me to fear some sinister plot, there have been several deaths. What concerned me most is a report from the Duke of Cantley, stating that the entire populace of the market town, Brodinton, has vanished."

"Vanished? Like Lancaster?" I asked worriedly.

Ariadne shook her head. "No, the place is still there, but the inhabitants are missing. Being a market town, this was noticed almost immediately, as people go there to trade daily. Our best guess is that this happened some three nights ago and was discovered the following morning. Duke Cantley sent a force of men to investigate, and they reported signs of a struggle, but no bodies were found."

"Where is Brodinton?" Penny questioned.

"A day and a half east north east of Cantley, on the northern bank of the Surrey River," I answered. Geography was an important subject of study for the nobility, but I had the advantage of my near perfect memory.

Rose broke in, "Now I understand why Egan is here. You sent Harold to Cantley?"

Ariadne nodded. "I dispatched two units of the royal guard. Sir Harold is in command, and his fellow knights, Sir William and Sir Thomas, are with him."

"I drew the short straw," said Egan sourly. Then he glanced at the Queen and his cheeks colored. "Forgive me, I meant no disrespect."

The Queen laughed. "I know guarding me is a boring task, but maybe you drew the lucky straw. You never know. I could be attacked at any time."

"You shouldn't say such things, Your Majesty," protested Egan, "not even in jest."

Ariadne frowned at him. "Egan…"

"Ariadne," he said, correcting himself. "Forgive me. I can't get used to addressing you like this. It isn't right."

"How many men were in these units?" I asked suddenly.

"It was two companies," answered Egan immediately, clarifying the Queen's earlier remark.

So, three hundred men, assuming the two companies were at full strength. It wasn't enough, not if they encountered a force the size of the one that had attacked us today. "They need more support," I announced.

"We only have three more companies in Albamarl," Egan informed us.

Penny leaned forward. "Why so few?"

"We've had peace for many years now. A standing army is expensive," said Ariadne. "Given a few weeks, we can raise many times that number, but I can't justify keeping thousands of men in arms when there are no threats to the kingdom."

"You need to put out the call to arms," I said suddenly. "We have an unknown enemy in Lothion. Have the lords prepare for war."

Ariadne focused on me. "You think I should call for levies as well?"

For thirty seconds or so I was silent, thinking hard. "No, but make sure they're ready to do so if needed. Don't have your vassals rally at the capital either. Tell them to activate their reserves but keep them in the major cities. We don't know yet where the enemy is, but if there's a force the size of the one we faced today, they could overwhelm even a city the size of Cantley if they aren't prepared."

"How strong were the ones you faced today?" asked Egan.

"They were tough, not superhuman, but they were seasoned fighters, well equipped and fierce. If I had to guess I would say they were veterans. A force like that could handle many times its own numbers in peasant levies and would be difficult even for professional soldiers. Individually they were more like our knights, but they worked together as a unit," I explained.

"You're saying you were faced with the equivalent of seven hundred knights today?" asked Egan incredulously. "Yet you destroyed them with relative ease."

"I didn't say it was easy," I replied. "They were resistant to magic, and they had some magic-users of their own. I can't be everywhere. If your two companies meet a similar force near Cantley, they won't stand a chance."

Ariadne rose to her feet. "It appears we will need to return to Albamarl then, since there's more work to do."

"I'll come with you. Whatever force you send will need magical aid," I told her.

The Queen glared at me. "Absolutely not. You've already fought one battle today. Do you even remember the conversation we just had?"

Everyone stared at me, agreement on their faces. I sighed. "Fine, but let me send Sir Gram and another wizard in my place."

Rose blanched almost imperceptibly at my suggestion, but she held her tongue. I had just offered to send her son into harm's way. Penny's reaction was less restrained. "Wizard? Which one? Elaine?"

Elaine was still recovering from her ordeal and the loss of her father. There was no way I would send her, and it surprised me that Penny would even suggest it. Of course, our children constituted all the other available wizards. "Matthew," I told them. "He and Gram will take their dragons along as well."

Penny's face paled slightly, but she merely clenched her jaw. She clearly wanted to argue, but when she saw Rose's quiet fortitude she kept her silence. I had a feeling I would be hearing about it later, however, once we were behind closed doors.

Ariadne nodded, but before she and Egan could leave, I caught Egan's arm. "Once this issue is resolved, tell Harold to select suitable candidates. The Order of the Thorn will need to grow. You, Harold, William, and Thomas will be dragon-bonded, along with another ten according to the Queen's choosing."

Egan was momentarily stunned, but he recovered quickly. "Shouldn't that be the Queen's decision? The Order of the Thorn answers to her."

I turned to Ariadne. "Do you agree?"

She nodded. "It will be as you say."

"What about armor and weapons?" asked Egan. "We still have the sun-swords, but it took you months to produce the enchanted armor we once wore."

He was referring to the fact that the old armor couldn't be worn by new knights. While Egan, Harold, and William still had theirs, any new knights would need armor made to fit them. Even the remaining pieces we had from their deceased brothers couldn't be used, since the enchantment made it impossible to re-forge them to fit new wearers.

"We can work out those details later, but I will trust the Queen's armorers to handle the task. They can produce armor to match yours for the new men and I will enchant it afterward," I told him.

Ariadne and Egan left after that, and less than a half an hour later, Matthew, Gram, and their dragons followed.

CHAPTER 27

The next morning found me up and moving before the sun rose. 'Bright eyed and bushy tailed,' as my mother was fond of saying. It wasn't my usual mode of operation, but I was still brimming with energy from the battle the previous day. I probably could have foregone sleep altogether, but I knew from long experience that the mind doesn't work properly without rest, no matter how much energy you have.

I spent the hours before dawn in my private workshop, which was down the hill from my home in the mountains. There, I worked on a new set of armor for Penny. It was an old project, and one that had long been put aside. It had never seemed urgent enough when we had no enemies to fight. Most of the major pieces had already been formed and shaped, but a lot of finishing work remained, and there would need to be some modifications since she had lost her arm. I called up a brisk wind to blow away the dust and set to work.

Much of the work was rote, allowing my mind to wander freely while my hands and my power performed the necessary tasks. Mentally, I took notes on the enchantments that would be laid down at the end, considering how I would make the process neater and more efficient. Once the Queen had set her armorers to work, I might potentially have more than a dozen suits to enchant in a relatively short period of time. With proper planning and a standard design for the enchantment, I should be able to do the work much more quickly than I had in the past.

I also thought about some of the things Matthew had done. He had been extremely clever over the past few years, and I was immensely proud of that. Most importantly, he'd taught me a lesson: I shouldn't limit the scope of my ideas to only include my own capabilities. Some of the enchantments he had crafted for his journey to an alternate reality had included special additions from both Moira and Elaine.

Thinking along those lines, I thought I should plan on using some aspects of my son's special 'translation' magic in both Penny's armor and the armor I enchanted for the new knights. Producing something like what he had done with Thorn wasn't practical—that had been a work of art requiring vast amounts of time—but some of the ideas could easily be adapted to make the new works more practical.

As the sun began to peek over the horizon, I sighed and put down my work. It was time to eat. I still wasn't hungry, but some tea might be welcome.

Alyssa was in the kitchen when I arrived, a knife in her hand as she cut bacon for breakfast. A sudden thought struck me. "Come here," I told her.

Frowning, she set down the knife and moved to stand before me. I studied her up and down for a moment, but the dress she wore was too bulky for me to measure her properly with my eyes. "Take off the dress," I ordered.

"Sir?" she answered in surprise.

"Hurry up and take it off, but keep your nightclothes on. I want to examine your figure," I explained.

Her cheeks colored slightly, but Alyssa was no shrinking violet. She was a fighter with skills to match Gram and her father, Cyhan. She began shucking the heavy wool while I searched in my pouch to find what I needed. Once I had it, I began issuing orders. "Lift your arms straight up." Standing behind her, I reached around with my hands and pulled my measuring tape snug around her waist, noting the number. Then I repeated the action, measuring her bosom, the breadth of her shoulders, and her hips.

Alyssa's body was smooth and curved, but beneath her deceptively feminine figure was a lot of muscle, the product of a lifetime of training and exercise. On her physical merits alone, it was easy to see why Gram was attracted to her, but her body was probably the least of it for him. The mental training she had undergone was what made her such a deadly warrior. That was probably also a plus in Gram's mind, though to me, her intelligence and other talents were equally impressive. Alyssa had infiltrated our household originally on the strength of her acting ability, serving as a spy for her uncle.

I measured her upper arm, the length of her elbow to the wrist, and the circumference of her wrist, and then I moved to her ankles. "Stand with your feet apart a little bit," I told her.

"What are you measuring me for?" she asked finally.

"What every knight needs," I responded vaguely.

It was about then when my daughter, Irene, wandered in. "Dad?" she said querulously.

"Oh good, you're just in time," I responded. "Come here, Irene. I need your help. This part would have been a little embarrassing."

My youngest daughter understood my meaning pretty quickly when I asked her to take Alyssa's inseam and thigh measurements for me. That done, I told Alyssa to put her dress back on and get back to work.

"You should measure me too," suggested Irene.

"I don't think you're done growing yet," I clucked. "Also, this sort of armor can be something of a hindrance for a wizard."

"Oh," said Irene, sounding disappointed.

"What's a hindrance for a wizard?" asked Penny, having just appeared in the doorway. She looked somewhat disheveled, but I didn't detect the irritation I had feared after my decision to send Matthew to Cantley the night before. Sleep is a wonderful thing. Then again, she probably hadn't had time to think through the previous day's events yet.

"Morning, my sweet," I responded. "Come here and take off your housecoat, and the dress too, if you don't mind."

Penny looked disgruntled. "It's too early for these shenanigans. I haven't even had my tea yet."

"I want to remeasure your torso," I explained, waving at her to come closer.

Irene piped up, "He just finished measuring Alyssa too." She made sure her tone was suggestive too, the little scamp.

Luckily, Penny and I had been together for too many years for her to fall for such obvious baiting. She knew me too well. "What's this all about?" she asked, but she was already removing her housecoat.

"I just wanted to compare your bust size to Alyssa's," I answered flippantly.

Penny gave me a feral look. "Careful, it's still morning. I bite."

I kissed her on the cheek. "I hope so."

"Eww!" exclaimed Irene. "You're ruining the innocence of my youth."

Chuckling, I explained, "Actually, I decided to finish your armor, but I need to remeasure a few things due to your…"

"Disfigurement?" said Penny, trying to finish my sentence.

"I was going to say, 'swelling bosom,' but if you prefer disfigurement, so be it," I replied.

My wife's eyes narrowed slightly. "Now you're suggesting I've gotten fat."

I sighed. "There's just no way to win." Finishing up my measurements, I put my tape away. "Have you seen Moira this morning?"

"Not yet," answered Penny, "but Conall tells me she ate in the main hall already. She wants you to come visit the prisoner."

"I'll go find her then."

"What about breakfast?" asked Penny.

"I ate earlier," I lied, giving her another kiss. Then I headed for the door.

***

It turned out that my daughter was already coming to find me. I ran into her as I descended the stairs of the keep. "Dad!" she said as soon as she spied me.

I smiled. "Did you make some progress?"

"Of course," replied Moira, seeming almost insulted. "You know me better than that."

"Don't get your feathers ruffled. It's just a phrase to start a conversation," I responded. "Let's go see him."

When we reached the bottom floor, I turned toward the main entrance, but my daughter stopped me. "He's in the hall."

"Why isn't he locked up?"

She smirked at me. "He's no longer a threat. He's eating there, but I left a guard with him."

Confused, I asked, "Not a threat, but he needs a guard?"

Moira nodded. "To make sure none of the men try to kill him. They don't trust him yet."

I stopped outside the door to the great hall. "Explain what you did and what you've learned before we go in. Are you sure he's safe now?"

"His name is Sanger," began Moira, "and his people are called the Ungol. He has absolutely no idea how his people got here. They think it's probably something we did. As for where he came from—"

I interrupted, "No, explain *what* you did, so I'll understand how it works, what the limits are."

"Oh," she said, glancing briefly at the floor. "I explored his mind first, before he woke, to see how it works and to examine some of his memories. As Elise said, it seems very human in most respects, although their language is unusual. They use two different languages, or maybe I should say it's one language with two different modes of expression.

"One is similar to ours, in that it uses sounds for words that are much like ours. The grammar and vocabulary are different, of course, but we could learn it. The other mode of speaking uses clicks and harsh guttural sounds to convey the same meanings. They use that in business, the military, and dealing with strangers—basically everything except communicating with friends and family.

"I think it would be difficult for anyone not raised with it to emulate that way of speaking, and because of their cultural differences, it would be hard to convince one of the Ungol to learn our language, so I used a workaround," said Moira.

"What sort of workaround?" I asked.

"I broke the rules," said Moira, hesitantly.

I nodded. "I expected you to."

Moira went on, "I've done something similar once before, for a girl I met who couldn't speak. I created a specialized spell-mind, essentially just the part that I normally use to give my spellbeasts the ability to speak, and then grafted it onto Sanger's mind. It will allow him to speak and understand our language."

"How long will it last? Will it run down like a spellbeast over time?"

My daughter shook her head. "No, it's attached to him in such a way that it is sustained by his aystrylin, as if it were a part of his natural body and mind. It will last as long as he lives, or until it is removed."

"Could any mage remove it?" I asked. "For example, one of their magic users."

Moira grimaced. "It's possible, but if anyone other than a Centyr tried, it would likely render him insane. It might even kill him."

"That's comforting," I muttered. "What else did you do?"

"To make him 'safe,' I had to alter his personality to a degree, reversing some of his values. He now regards us as allies, and his own people with mistrust. I didn't change his memories, since we need that information. Instead I changed his fundamental reaction to those memories. It was a lot simpler than making a lot of subtle alterations, but it's bound to cause some problems for him.

"He's loyal to us now. He's even aware of what I did to him, but he sees it in a favorable light. Over time, the internal conflict between the artificial values I've implanted, and his normal values, will probably tear him apart. He might go insane, develop headaches—I don't really know," Moira admitted. "But I've created a contingency."

"How so?"

"The spell-mind fragment that handles language for him does more than just that. It also monitors his thoughts. If he becomes violent, or somehow begins to contemplate betraying us, it will kill him," she finished flatly.

The sweet child I had once raised could never have done such a thing. It was a stark lesson for me in how much the ordeal in Dunbar had changed my daughter. What she had done was evil, pure and simple, and I had sanctioned it. No, I had *asked* her to do it.

"Don't be," said Moira suddenly.

"Don't be what?"

"Sorry," she explained. "Don't be sorry. This wasn't your fault."

I rubbed my face to relieve some of the tension that had built up. "I was the one that put you in this position. How much did this hurt you?"

"It isn't like physical pain," said Moira. "It doesn't work like that. It just gets easier each time, and harder for me to stop myself. But this needed doing, and I'm already a monster, anyway."

We both are, I thought silently.

"That's true," said my daughter. "I got a glimpse of what happened inside you yesterday."

I almost shuddered. "I wish you hadn't."

"It made me feel better, if we're being honest," she replied. "I'm not the only one. We've both done terrible things, but we're doing them so other people won't have to. We'll take on the burdens so the rest of them can sleep in peace, so they can stay sane."

"That still doesn't justify our actions," I argued.

She nodded. "No, but we're doing it anyway, so let's make a pact."

"What sort of pact?"

"We watch one another. If you go too far, I'll take care of it. If I go too far, you can squash me with a boulder or something."

As much as I disliked the idea, it had a few glaring flaws. "If I know you're about to kill me, you won't stand a chance," I pointed out.

Moira patted my cheek, her eyes sad. "I'll make sure you don't see it coming."

"The other problem," I went on, "is that you can pick up my thoughts too easily. If I decided you needed to be put down, you would know about it long before I could trap you."

She shook her head. "I had Myra insert a compulsion in my subconscious over a month ago. If you decide that, if you even *think* it, I will submit, regardless of how I feel on the matter. I also can't alter your mind, or that of anyone else in the family. Not anymore."

This had to be the most disturbing conversation any father and daughter had ever had, but somehow it put me at ease. Maybe it was simply knowing that despite the dark changes she had suffered, Moira was still thinking about her family before herself. Unable to restrain myself, I leaned over and kissed the top of her head. "We may be monsters, but we'll protect those we love. Won't we?"

Moira jerked her head in a quick motion that was taut with barely suppressed emotion. "We'll be monsters, so they don't have to."

CHAPTER 28

O ur prisoner sat at a table on one side of the great hall, eating a
large bowl of stew with a spoon in one hand and a large hunk
of rough bread in the other. One of my guardsmen stood close
by, watching him carefully, but he wasn't alone. Every man and woman
eating there also stared at the stranger.

The dwarfish prisoner looked up at me as I stopped beside him.
Dropping his spoon, he stood and executed a quick bow. "My lord,
forgive me, I didn't see you until just now!" He spoke with a deep voice
with no accent, in spite of the fact that he had never used our language
before today.

I could see the traces of my daughter's magic buried in his skull,
and while it chilled me to see how effective it was, I couldn't help but
be impressed with how flawlessly it granted him command of a new
language. "What is your name?"

"Sanger, my lord," he answered quickly.

When he spoke his name, I could hear a strange lilt to his tongue,
and I guessed that must be because it was spoken without any
assistance of my daughter's magic. "Why did your people attack
us?" I asked abruptly.

"They thought you were responsible for stealing our land, my lord,"
he responded. "Though I understand now that they were wrong. I was
wrong to help them."

"And you will help us now instead?"

"Of course, my lord. I will do whatever I can to help you," said
Sanger emphatically.

It was bizarre hearing such obeisance from a man who had so
recently been determined to kill us, but thus far it appeared Moira's
alterations were working just as she had said, so I pushed further.
"Why should I trust you?"

Sanger lowered his eyes to the floor. "Lady Moira has changed
me. The world is different now. Somehow, I can speak your strange

language, and I also know that I will do as you wish. I don't really understand it, but it is true."

"Tell me about your people then," I commanded. "Describe how you came to be here."

"They are not my people, my lord," answered the dwarf. "Not any longer."

I raised one brow. "Oh, then to what people do you think you belong?"

"None. I am of no people, but I belong to you," returned Sanger.

The absolute devotion in his eyes was disturbing. "Tell me about the Ungol, then, who were once your people."

"They are a proud race of warriors, far greater than the weak men I have seen here in your fortress," said the dwarf honestly. "The tribe I was born in, the Talbrun, were nearly two thousand strong."

"Tribe? Aren't they part of some larger nation?"

"No," said Sanger. "The Great Ones decreed long ago that we must not gather or form greater alliances. Each tribe lives alone in their place within the mountains, though they trade some. Any who defy this rule are destroyed and their names wiped from the scrolls of the ancestors."

Now my curiosity was piqued. "Are the Great Ones some sort of tribal elders?"

"They are not men," insisted Sanger. "Their power and wrath are not to be questioned."

Moira sent me a silent thought, *I picked this from one of his memories last night, but it will clarify. The leader of these Great Ones is known as Mal'Goroth.*

My mind reeled at that revelation. Were the Ungol from the place the She'Har had created to hold the Kionthara? Was that possible? I had no idea what it was like. I knew the Dark Gods had been kept within another dimension, one meant to protect ours from external threats, specifically ANSIS, but I had always imagined it as an empty place.

Further questioning revealed that Sanger's world was much like ours, with forests, plains, and mountains. The Ungol lived primarily in the mountains, in widespread villages from what I could understand. After taking him outside and asking him about directions, it seemed that his village had somehow been relocated to an area about a day's travel north of Arundel, just across the border between Lothion and Gododdin.

"How many more of the Talbrun are left in your village?" I asked after a while.

"A thousand perhaps," answered Sanger. "Mainly the women and children, along with the old warriors."

In other words, nearly all the adult males of his community were now dead. Once, such a realization would have crippled me with guilt. These days, though, while I felt remorse, it was only one more addition to the pile of regrets I kept in the dark storage of my soul. Misunderstanding or not, they had threatened my people, they had attacked first, and I was no longer kind enough to spend much time beating myself up over it.

"What will happen to them?"

Sanger's face twisted momentarily, as conflicting emotions warred within him. I wondered for a second if Moira's magic would break under the strain. If so, would he die in front of me? Then his face smoothed and he answered, "They will starve. The food stores were lost when the village was transported. The crops are gone. Most of the hunters were in the warband. The warband itself was a last-ditch effort to find or take a reliable food supply."

***

At the other end of Lothion, Matthew and Gram rode at the head of a group of fifty mounted soldiers. They had arrived in Cantley via the World Road sometime in the darkest hours of the night, not long after midnight. Not wasting time, they had ridden out immediately, Matthew and Gram astride their dragons, Zephyr and Grace, while the soldiers were on horseback.

With their enhanced eyesight, not to mention Matthew's magesight, the darkness wouldn't have been a problem for the dragonriders, but for the men and horses it was a more significant obstacle on a night with no moon. Hence, Matthew had kept a set of ten glowing orbs floating above their heads to light the way.

Carrying lights at night was a risk in its own right, for a military expedition. It meant they were well lit for whatever enemy might be waiting ahead in the dark—perfect targets, but this was mitigated by Matthew's confidence that he could detect any hidden enemies long before they were in range of missile weapons.

For now, it was most important that they catch up to the Queen's companies before they encountered whatever foe had destroyed Brodinton.

Those they were trying to catch up to had left the previous morning. If they had ridden for eight hours, then they were probably still four or five hours ahead of them. With luck they could reach them before they broke camp in the morning.

It was still several hours before dawn when Matthew sensed movement ahead of them. Holding up one hand, he called for a halt while he examined what his magesight was showing him. Then he announced, "A large band of men are heading this way. Almost all of them are on foot, and some carry torches."

"The Queen's men?" asked Gram tensely.

"It's hard to tell at this distance," said Matthew. "They're still over a mile distant. I'll know in a few minutes." Reaching out with his power, he spoke a single word, *"Haseth!"* and the light globes hanging above them vanished. They were in total darkness, and the men began to grumble. Facing a possible enemy while effectively blind was not to their liking.

"We don't want to give away our position," said Gram, his voice calm but loud enough to be heard. "This will also allow our eyes to adjust to the dark."

"Don't matter how much they adjust. It's pitch black," muttered someone in the ranks.

"I'll light the field when they are almost upon us. It should surprise them," said Matthew. Then he studied the terrain. The River Surrey lay fifty yards to their right and the edge of Cantley Forest was on their left. Their group rode on a small market road that followed the edge of the river almost half the way to Albamarl.

"We should move into the forest," suggested Gram. "With the trees and darkness to hide us, we can make the decision to ambush or aid whoever is riding this way in relative safety. If it's an enemy, we'll catch them by surprise, exposed on the road with the river to their backs."

Matt agreed, and so they began leading the horses carefully into the trees and underbrush on the north side of the road. He could see those approaching more clearly now, and he was certain they were men. Normal men, and therefore probably the Queen's guardsmen. He relayed that information to the others.

Then he spotted those that they ran from, a mass of squat, heavyset foot soldiers. The short-legged pursuers ate up the ground between them and the Queen's men in steady, powerful strides. Matthew studied them for a while, feeling something was strange about their movements, until he finally realized.

They carried no torches, or magical sources of light, and yet they moved with surety in the darkness. The Queen's guardsmen, by contrast, were struggling and stumbling, even with their torches in hand. "They can see in the dark," he muttered.

"What?" said Gram, slightly alarmed.

"There are several hundred of those short invaders chasing the guardsmen. They carry no light, and they seem to be moving better than our allies," explained the young wizard.

"How many of the Queen's men are there?" asked Gram.

"Fewer than we have with us," said Matthew darkly.

Sir Gram began swearing, a bad habit he had picked up sometime in the past from one of his teachers, Chad Grayson. After he recovered himself he spoke again, "If the Queen's men are running ahead they've probably been routed. If we try to help them in this darkness, they'll have no clue what's happening. They'll keep running. That leaves us and our fifty men to handle several times our number. Yet if we do nothing, they'll be run down and slain."

Matthew didn't reply, brooding silently.

"But, we have a wizard, and two dragons," added Gram.

Absently, Matthew replied, "And you. You count for more than you realize." Then he sighed. "The enemy have mages as well. I can spot them now—four, no, five of them."

Gram growled in the darkness, "This is ridiculous!"

Quietly, Matthew said, "It seems that way. What do you want to do?"

"If it was just me, I'd walk down there and stand in the road. Cut down as many of the enemy as I could manage—"

Matt cut him off, "It isn't just you. Don't be stupid. We're going to do this together. I'm asking how you think we should arrange our forces for an ambush."

Gram bit his lip, thinking. "Their mages will see us, even if we hide, right?"

Matthew nodded. "Probably. Since they're running, they might not notice as much as if they were moving slowly, but they'll detect me and the dragons for sure. We stick out like beacons to magesight."

"How about me?" asked Gram.

"Once you call your armor, the enchantment will be just as visible. Until then you look almost like a normal person," answered Matthew.

Gram made up his mind quickly. "Take the dragons and fly back the way we came. I'll wait in the road and greet the Queen's men as they run by. When the enemy reaches me, I'll armor up and slow them down while you and the dragons circle around to come at them from the river. Once the fighting starts, our men can charge in from this side and turn it into a real fight. They'll be too busy with us to prepare for the dragons when they see them. Strafe them with fire and we'll clean up the rest."

After listening, Matthew nodded. "That sounds good, but I'm going to drop in during the first flyover. I can do a lot more from the center than I can in the air."

Grace chimed in then, speaking silently in both their minds, *That's stupid. You can't risk yourself, Matthew. For that matter, Gram shouldn't be out there alone either.*

Gram agreed, partly. "You shouldn't risk yourself."

"Too bad. You don't get a say in what I do," replied the wizard. Then he launched Zephyr into the air and Grace took wing behind them.

***

Gram was waiting in the road when the Queen's guards ran past. They spotted him in the torchlight and veered, running past him on both sides. He could see panic and fear in their eyes, though most were unhurt. The wounded hadn't been able to run, or if they could, they had fallen behind long ago. He waved at the men as they ran by, ignoring the warnings that some of them shouted to him.

Then someone recognized him. "It's Gram!"

The one who knew him slowed down to a walk and then made his way back, followed by one other. Both wore the distinctive armor crafted years ago for the Knights of Stone. It was Sir William and Sir Thomas.

His vision was sensitive enough to see the onrushing enemy, and the sound of their feet pounding toward them was audible even for William and Thomas. "Follow your men," said Gram loudly. "It's too dark for you to fight yet, but the sky will light up in a few minutes. When it does, get as many as you can to come back."

"But what are you...?" began Sir William.

"Run!" shouted Gram. Then he whispered a quiet word and Thorn appeared in his hands, while a cloud of metal scales whirled around him, settling into place.

At fifty feet he could see his enemy clearly, and by the enthusiastic looks on their faces, he knew they could see him as well, or perhaps even better. Seconds later, they reached him, axes swinging toward him from several different directions.

Thorn was longer, and he didn't wait for them to get close enough to make deep cuts. Gram's first sweep of the blade caught three of them, delivering a shallow cut that was only inches deep, but it served its purpose, forcing them to pull up short. More piled into them from behind, forcing the first Ungol warriors closer while others streamed around him on both sides.

He didn't try to halt the greatsword after his first swing; instead he followed it, while at the same time darting forward and to the right, twisting his body full circle as he went. Thorn's second arc cut deeply, severing limbs, ribs, weapons—anything that interfered with its path. Several fell dead, becoming obstacles in the path of those coming from behind, and while it was tempting to stay there, where his presence had begun to slow the enemy, Gram kept moving, heading toward the forest side of the road.

His intent was to cross as much of the front line as possible, to leave enough bodies to stop the overall rush of the Ungol. He made it twenty feet before he was inevitably forced to a halt. Gram was surrounded, and the Ungol were too fierce to give him the room he needed to continue. Dancing with the great blade in his hands, he killed ten, then fifteen, but he couldn't kill enough to gain the room he needed.

Stepping back to dodge an axe swung at his face, he stepped on the arm of a man he had already slain. That momentary loss of balance was enough. One of them managed to grab him from behind, wrapping thick hands around his right arm.

He released the hilt, and leaving Thorn in his left hand, he picked up the stout warrior with his right and tossed him toward the Ungol in front of him. As he did, he managed a sideswipe with Thorn that killed another on that side, but two more managed to grapple him from the right side.

Gram ripped his right arm free, but the two became four, and then six as the heavyset warriors swarmed over him. They couldn't compete with his strength—even two or three couldn't bind his movement—but they bore him down with sheer mass. Soon he was at the bottom of a pile of men, his sword all but useless.

On the ground, they kicked and punched at him, and occasionally one managed to find enough of an opening to slam an axe into him, but his armor held. Gram gave better than he got, though, his steel-clad punches breaking jaws, ribs, and cracking a few skulls. If the fight had stayed like that, a simple brawl, he might have still broken them all, one punch at a time, but then something that felt like a battering ram slammed into his head.

Probably an axe, he thought, struggling to organize his limbs. Dazed, more blows rained down on him as his opponents made room for others to bring their weapons to bear.

Gram's armor was virtually impenetrable, at least against anything a man might do with two arms and a piece of metal, but he was still flesh and blood beneath the enchanted steel. Heavy impacts, for example, those from axes and maces, could still bruise and batter him. Too many blows to the head might even kill him.

But then his body was lifted into the air, and the grasping hands fell away. He found himself suspended, face down, six feet in the air. Looking around, Gram could see one of the Ungol standing close by, but this one was dressed differently, in robes. The newcomer carried a long spear in one hand, its head sharp and dripping with green fire.

Slowly, the Ungol mage lifted the spear, taking it in both hands and pointing it at Gram's shoulder as though he would drive it through. There was a smile on his broad face.

Where was Matthew? Where were the dragons? Those thoughts flashed through Gram's mind, but the thought that stayed was the memory of his father. *Was this how he felt, unable to stop what was killing him?* No, Dorian had died protecting his family. *I'm just going to be spitted like a pig.* It wasn't fair. He had earned a better death than this. *Sorry, Alyssa...*

And then the world exploded.

The sound and light crashed over him, over all of them. It was so immense that it didn't even register as a sound; it was more like a punch in the gut that erased all hearing, and the light was so intense it left the world a smeared blob of orange, as though he was staring at the sun through his eyelids.

Deaf and blind, the Ungol couldn't see the fire that followed, falling on them from the sky like a searing rain—but they felt it. They screamed at the agony, but even that sound was denied their wounded ears.

Are you alright? It was Grace, her voice echoing in his mind.

I think I'm dead, replied Gram mentally. He tried to lift himself from the ground, though he had no memory of landing on it.

Stay down, cautioned Grace. *I'm standing over you and I don't want you to poke me with that sword.*

You were supposed to strafe them, not land in the middle of it, Gram complained.

I changed the plan when we got close enough to see what was happening, answered his dragon.

Where's Matthew?

***

Matthew stood about ten feet to the left of Grace, who was crouched protectively over her fallen rider. Fifty feet behind him, their soldiers, along with some of those who had previously been running, were fighting with the Ungol. Most of those in front of him were burning and dying, a result of Grace and Zephyr's dragonfire. A hundred feet above him, an artificial sun burned in the sky, turning the night into day.

But there were still hundreds left, and once the flash blindness wore off, the fight would get nasty. He didn't intend to let things go that long, though. Raising his left hand—the metal one—above his head, he clenched his fist and sent a command to it with a thought and a whisper of power. Some of the runes etched into the metal glowed briefly, and two metal triangles appeared in the air above him, summoned from the pocket dimension he kept them safely housed in.

Reaching out with two tendrils of finely wrought aythar, he grasped them, holding them in place and activating the enchantment built into them. Shimmering planes of absolute black sprang outward, until the two triangles were each three feet wide, from point to point.

And then they began to spin.

With a thought, he sent them flying in two different directions, racing outward, only two feet above the ground. Unerringly, the dimensional blades cut through the air, and they found the Ungol mages first, before they could recover from their shock. After those targets, the weapons continued on, sweeping across the field, back and forth, according to Matthew's will.

Some of the warriors were recovering, stumbling toward him, half-blind, but a withering blast of dragonfire from Grace put an end to most of those. Several from the end that hadn't suffered as badly from his flashbangs lifted massive crossbows, but Matthew sidestepped just before each bolt was fired. He didn't bother with a shield. The Illeniel gift alone was enough. Nothing could touch him.

He was careful to keep the dimensional blades away from the active fighting behind him, lest he inadvertently kill or maim his own men, but the rest of the field was fair game. The Ungol died, and the earth became a thick, red mud, saturated with their blood. Matthew stared over the battlefield with cold, passionless eyes.

Without warning, a highly focused beam of green power lanced toward him, but again, Matthew simply leaned to one side. More attacks followed, and he realized he had somehow missed one of the enemy mages. The short man was standing some fifty yards away, near the forest's edge, surrounded by a knot of Ungol warriors.

Calling his spinning blades back, Matthew advanced toward the mage, taking long strides punctuated by sudden jigs as he dodged crossbow bolts and magical attacks.

His enemy was powerful, stronger than any wizard Matthew had met before, save for his father. The Ungol mage was taller than his guards, standing slightly over five feet in height, with a grey beard and an elaborately embroidered stole across his shoulders.

At ten yards, Matthew stopped and then sent a broadly branching web of lightning bolts forth to clear away the enemy wizard's defenders. His opponent was quick, however, and a wide shield appeared around the entire group, protecting them.

Matthew's lips curled into a faint smile. He had hoped for that response. With a thought, his spinning dimensional blades flashed forward, cutting through the shield and the men behind it. The Ungol wizard reeled as his shield was destroyed, and he struggled to hold onto consciousness. Matthew called back his dimensional blades and dismissed them before finishing off the remaining guards around the dwarf with a series of precise bolts of force. He didn't want to risk killing the wizard by accident. Then he struck at the wizard with a broad stroke meant to batter him more than wound.

The Ungol wizard tried to defend himself, but the feedback sickness from his broken shield had robbed him of his strength. He was knocked flat, and then Matthew seized him with his will.

"*Shibal!*" shouted the young man, driving the force of his power against the Ungol's dazed mind.

In general, attempting to put another wizard to sleep was a futile exercise, unless they were already greatly weakened. After a brief struggle, Matthew's spell won out, and he smothered the Ungol's consciousness, sending him into a deep and dreamless sleep.

The battle was over.

CHAPTER 29

Oddly, I didn't have anything urgent to do. Oh sure, the kingdom was under threat of war from a strange new enemy, the She'Har might have turned against us, and ANSIS was hiding somewhere, plotting to remake all of humanity, but I didn't have anything to do myself, not today.

The Queen was back in the capital, sending out the orders to call up the levies to every noble landholder, and Egan was presumably drawing up a list of candidates for Harold to consider for knighthood. Gary was working on his antennae. Penny was checking the granaries with Peter, and Moira was overseeing our prisoner.

Matthew and Gram were dealing with the danger in Cantley—and me, I was sitting at home, pondering my existence. In the middle of so many urgent matters it was an unusual feeling for me.

Even Irene and Conall had something to do. They were out in the yard, where Conall was giving Irene some instruction on how to manage her newly acquired power. Lynaralla had gone with them, though whether as a spectator or as an advisor, I wasn't sure.

There would probably be a lot of decisions to be made soon. Calling up the levies and preparing them for war was no small task, but Captain Draper knew his work and my chamberlain, Peter, knew the ins and outs of Castle Cameron and its doings better than I did. Penny had been the sole ruler of my estate for a year back when everyone thought I was dead and gone. She knew the right decisions to make as well as I did.

In fact, it might be better to leave most of it in her hands. Having lost her arm, she was dealing with a lot of internal turmoil. If I felt useless, she probably felt the same by a factor of ten. Rather than push her aside and handle everything, I figured it would do her more good if I let her bury her self-doubt in the work of running the castle.

But what should I do?

"Something brilliant," I said, answering my own question with more enthusiasm than I truly felt. *Except, I have no idea what that is.*

My thoughts returned to Penny. I could solve her arm problem—probably—but my recent vision of her dwindling aystrylin had put the seeds of doubt in me. I had seen something like it once before, in my best friend, Marcus. He had died a year later.

Using my power as an archmage to meld with her might put a considerable strain on Penny's aystrylin. It might kill her outright.

But she expected me to do it. I had told her I could.

"Time to lie," I said with a sigh. Perhaps I could put her off by claiming it would take longer than it really would, or by exaggerating the danger. *Well, it is dangerous,* I reminded myself. *One or both of us could be lost entirely during the merger.* In honesty, though, that wasn't my greatest fear. Now that I had seen how weak her aystrylin was, my fear was that I would succeed, and she would promptly die after.

Then I realized what I should do. *Matthew suggested it already. Make her an arm.* Once she had a functional solution, the urgency would be gone. Penny might even refuse to let me attempt to replace her natural arm simply on the grounds that it wasn't worth the risk.

Getting to my feet, I started for my workshop. As I passed the kitchen I yelled at Alyssa, "Go find Moira. Tell her to meet me in my shop."

Things were coming together in my mind too rapidly for me to put words to them. I had assisted Matthew with some of his work creating his artificial hand, so I already had a good feel for the complexities of articulation that went into such a task. More importantly, I knew what the biggest problem would be.

Creating a functional arm wasn't enough. The user had to be able to control it. In my son's case, this wasn't a big problem. He was a mage. With time and practice, he was able to control his new hand with just his aythar and his thoughts. He didn't even think about it consciously anymore.

But Penny wasn't a wizard. Her new arm would have to move itself in accordance with her thoughts.

My drafting desk was in front of me now. I pulled out a large sheet of parchment and began sketching. "Long and slender," I muttered as I outlined a female arm. "Slightly smaller than her real arm, of course, to allow for a covering."

I'd need her present, so I could match the dimensions of her remaining arm, but it wouldn't take me long to shape the metal. As an archmage I had a considerable advantage over Matthew in that regard.

Along the bottom of the sheet I began listing the functional requirements for the enchantment. Each point of articulation would need a separate enchantment, and each of those enchantments would need to be functional across a gradient, to allow Penny to use her arm with precision and delicacy. Those separate enchantments would need to be coordinated to make the movements smooth and natural.

"I should include one to warm the metal as well," I muttered. With a soft doeskin covering, the entire thing it would feel almost human. The leather would also serve to hide the runes engraved into the metal. *There will need to be sensory feedback as well,* I thought to myself. *Pressure and gross mechanical force can be reported by the metal structure, while temperature, texture, and pain can be reported by the leather covering.*

Lost in thought, the sheet of parchment was soon covered in runes and designs. An hour, perhaps two, passed without notice, until a voice called to me. "Dad?"

I turned around. Moira stood a few feet away. "Oh! There you are! I need your help."

Looking over my shoulder, she took in the drawings. "You're making an arm for Mom?"

I nodded. "Something like your brother's hand, but with a more artistic touch," I replied.

She smiled approvingly. "What do you need me for?"

"Your mother isn't a wizard," I began, before explaining the need for her new arm to communicate directly with Penny's brain. I finished by telling her what I hoped she could do. "You created a sort of spell-mind to translate for our Ungol prisoner. Can you do the same for this?"

"Built into metal?" asked Moira uncertainly.

"Yes. I need it to translate her mental impulses into motive commands for the arm's enchantments, as well as provide sensory feed back from these enchantments." I pointed to indicate the enchantments I was referring to.

She pursed her lips, thinking for a moment. "I think so. What is this part for? It's not connected to the rest."

"A permanent illusion," I explained. "If everything works properly, it will feel a lot like a real arm, *to her,* but it won't look like one. This will cover it in an illusion, so it will appear to be a normal arm to everyone else. It won't make it feel completely normal to someone else touching it, but with the warmth and the soft leather, it shouldn't feel too strange."

"That's a nice touch," said Moira, "but it will still need to be connected so she can turn the illusion off sometimes."

I frowned. "Why?"

"So she can clean it. It's hard to clean something if you can't see what it actually looks like."

"Oh." That hadn't occurred to me. Two minds were definitely better than one.

***

I had almost finished my plans when another presence appeared in my shop. This one had no living aythar, just a moving body. It was Gary. I looked up as he entered. "How are things going?"

He shrugged, making a passable imitation of the eminently human gesture. "The array should be ready to test in a week or two."

"That's good news," I replied. "It would be nice to be ahead of the game for a change."

"I've been thinking," said Gary, pausing at the end of an obviously open-ended statement.

I said nothing for a moment, letting the silence drag out. "About something other than ANSIS, I presume."

He smiled. "That's what I like about you."

I lifted my brows. "Hmm?"

"You're more perceptive than most organics, whether from my world or yours. No, let me correct that. You're more perceptive than most humans, organic or digital."

Despite being a machine, Gary obviously enjoyed conversation. Otherwise he wouldn't have bothered dragging out the conversation, so I played along. "Is that a compliment?"

"You should take it as one," answered the android.

"Talk to Lady Rose. You'll find she's even more interesting—if you're looking for clever conversation." I winced inwardly as I said it. It wasn't a fair statement. Rose was more than just a conversationalist.

Gary stopped beating around the bush. "The measurement you helped me with a few days ago, the curvature of the world..."

"Yes?"

"It wasn't what I expected," he finished.

I could make a lot of different assumptions based on that one statement, but I wasn't in the mood to speculate. So I simply asked, "What did you expect?"

"Your world's gravity is identical to mine," said Gary. "Assuming they have a similar density, they should be roughly the same size. If so, they should have a similar curvature, since they would be spheres of almost the same size."

Our worlds were analogues in different dimensions. From what Matthew had told me, they should probably be nearly identical in almost every respect. "They aren't?" I asked.

"No," said Gary. "They aren't. But the way they are different is so specific it arouses my suspicion."

I waited, knowing he would go on.

"Based on the curvature, your world has precisely half the surface area that mine does," he declared.

That surprised me, but what interested me was why it surprised Gary. As far as I knew, he didn't know that our worlds should be nearly identical. "So it's smaller. What's unusual about that?"

Gary frowned. "Don't play innocent. Even you should find that unusual. Based on simple math, that means your world should have roughly two-thirds the volume of mine. Unless the density deviates greatly, the gravity should follow suit."

I had worked that out already, but I knew relatively little of what constituted 'normal' when it came to the density of a world. "I'll admit it seems strange, but isn't it possible that our world is just that much denser, enough to make its gravity stronger?"

"No," said Gary. "It isn't. Assuming that the physics of your universe are similar to the physics of mine, then no. The density of rocky worlds in a solar system should fall somewhere within a small range. This would put your world far outside that range. It is also strange that the total surface area would factor out to be exactly half of what my world is. There are too many coincidences here. I don't know how, but somehow these figures are deliberate."

I thought hard for a minute. Doing a bit more math in my head. "If your world were divided in two, the surface areas wouldn't be halved. They would be smaller. And the gravity would be halved, not the same. Perhaps you're looking too hard for meaning where there is none."

"That's why none of this makes sense!" said Gary emphatically. "If this was something as simple as that—say someone could divide a world in two, but keep the surface area of each half the same—then the interior would have to be partly hollow. And again, as you said, the gravity would have to be half of what it is."

Turning back to my design, I let my eyes scroll across the page. I didn't have time to ponder the mysteries of existence. "If the numbers don't match expectations, then the conclusion is simple. Your assumptions were wrong. Maybe this is just simply a smaller world, with a much higher density than is found in your universe."

He left after that, but I could tell he wasn't ready to accept such a simple explanation as a brute fact. For that matter, neither was I. His words rolled around in the back of my mind, and though they eventually dropped below the level of conscious thought, they still bothered me, like an itch I couldn't scratch.

CHAPTER 30

The next morning, I had Penny come to the workshop, so I could take detailed measurements of her surviving arm. Then I spent the rest of my morning shaping the metal structure that would be her new arm.

This was one aspect of crafting in which I had an enormous advantage. As a wizard I could shape metal with heat and force, forgoing even the use of a forge if I wanted to do everything with magic, but it was exhausting and time consuming. As an archmage, though, it was simpler still. I didn't have to force the metal into shape; I could coax it into taking the form I desired.

All that was required was temporarily sacrificing a bit of my humanity. Working with something as small as that wasn't hard, and compared to other things I did regularly, was nearly as safe as riding a horse.

The silvery metal that lay on the bench before me wasn't iron. Gary probably had a name for it. Maybe I would ask him later. I had made my desire plain to the earth and it had provided. The substrate for Penny's new arm was just as strong as the best steel, but it only weighed half as much. Once it was enchanted, it would be far stronger.

Knowing Penny, it would need to be. I made a mental note to remind her to be even more careful about hitting people with her new arm once it was finished. She was already used to the fact that her dragon-enhanced strength sometimes made casual blows dangerous when she struck normal people, but having an arm made almost entirely of metal would make an impulsive strike even more dangerous.

I shaped the upper portion of metal into a rounded cone that would fit over both what was left of her arm as well as some of her shoulder. I wanted it to be comfortable, and once strapped into place it would need to be able to transfer a lot of force to her shoulders and skeleton, otherwise it wouldn't be very effective while fighting. I wanted her to be able to use just as much strength with this arm as she could with her other one.

From there it tapered, slightly smaller than her other arm, to allow room for the leather covering, until it reached the elbow. The joint there was particularly clever—in my humble opinion, at least. The lower portion was all one piece, instead of being two separate bones like a normal arm, so in order to facilitate rotation as well as bending, I used a ball and socket joint.

I did the same at the wrist, but for the hand itself I copied the structure of a normal hand more closely. The finger bones had hinge-like connections, though. I didn't have the option of relying on tendons or ligaments to hold them together.

Once I was satisfied with the basic structure, I began engraving the motive enchantments, leaving room for the final portions that would incorporate Moira and Matthew's specific contributions later. I didn't have the time necessary to do anything as fancy as the armor that Thorn could summon, but it would be an easy matter to have Matthew add a function to summon a shield.

When all of that was done, I realized I had made better time than I expected. I wasn't ready to work on the leather covering yet. I still needed to go into Washbrook and see about acquiring the materials first. So instead I started working on Penny's armor.

If I could keep at it for another week without significant interruptions, I could probably finish the armor and her arm. Better late than never. My wife would be as well-equipped as any Knight of Stone had ever been, perhaps better.

I would have liked to incorporate an offensive enchantment into her arm or weapon, something similar to the fire that the sun-swords could produce, but I didn't. Though the necessary power could be drawn from her dragon-bond, it would still require her to exert her will in a manner that might strain her aystrylin. That was something I couldn't allow. I hoped she didn't ask me for such a thing later. Mentally I ran through the excuses I could make. I didn't want to tell her my secret fear, that her time was limited.

Gritting my teeth, I growled softly. I hadn't been able to save Marc, but I would be damned if I didn't find a way to save her.

My thoughts were interrupted by a knock on the door; Lynaralla stood outside. She remained still when I opened it, but I could see something different in her usually unperturbed demeanor. "Come in," I told her.

She did, her deep blue dress whisking softly as she moved past me. My newly adopted daughter was a beautiful study in contrasts, with shining silver hair falling past her shoulders and framing startlingly sapphire eyes. Like all the She'Har, she was almost ethereal, as if she were a spirit made manifest in the flesh.

My own eyes were blue, and people sometimes commented on them, perhaps because they were highlighted by my dark, nearly raven-black hair, but Lynaralla's were so vivid they stood out even against her pale skin and shining tresses. "What's on your mind?" I asked her.

Without changing expression, her lips moved and she said, "I want to thank you. I also want to thank Penelope, and if you will allow it, I think I can help."

I frowned at her words. It wasn't that she never thanked anyone, but it was rare. The She'Har girl was never deliberately rude, but she was always honest, sometimes brutally so. Because of that she was frequently misunderstood. While she did possess emotions, they were so muted as to seem nearly absent. In many ways Gary the android was more human than she was. "What are you thanking me for, precisely?" I asked.

Her gaze was fixed on mine with an unsettling intensity. It was like looking at a painting. "I am thanking you for not teaching me what my fa—no, my progenitor, wanted me to learn."

"He's still your father," I hurried to correct her, "even if he says—"

"No," she interrupted. "He is not. Since coming here, I have struggled to understand you. I have struggled to understand everyone. Your emotions, everyone's emotions, are so intense, and frequently irrational, that I initially dismissed their value. Tyrion was responsible for my conception, but he has never been a father to me. For that, I am grateful. When he renounced his claim to me, when he named you my father—I felt relieved."

Her words were so straightforward I found myself embarrassed, while at the same time fighting my instinctive urge to hug the girl. From past experience, I knew that such gestures were often awkward for her. "You don't need to thank me," I said. "It has been an honor to have you in the family."

Lynaralla's aythar shifted in a manner that in another person would have made me think they were upset, or perhaps agitated, but I knew such was unlikely in her. Then I noticed a tremor in her hands. Her arms moved with a slight jerk, spreading slightly, then stopping, as though unsure what they were supposed to be doing. "Please, do not imitate me," said the young woman. "I would rather become more like you and Penelope, not that you become like me."

"Imitate you?" What was she talking about? Then she took a short step toward me. I watched her carefully, trying to analyze her body language and failing. My brain wasn't up to the task, but then my heart gave me the answer. *She wants a hug, stupid.*

Silently cursing myself for my slowness, I stepped forward and swept her into my arms, squeezing her tightly against my chest. I had absolutely no idea what to say. None of the phrases I might use with my own children seemed suitable, so I kept silent.

Lynaralla didn't let go, even after I relaxed my grip to allow her a chance to step back. She held on and kept her cheek pressed firmly against my chest. "It wasn't until you and Penelope came to get me that I realized I had learned to love."

My vision blurred, and I kissed the top of her head. "I'm proud to call you my daughter," I whispered.

She finally released me and stepped back, smoothing the front of her dress before taking a seat on the only stool in my shop. "It is thanks to you and your family that I have learned these things. It has also helped me to recognize the love I received from my mother."

"By mother, you mean…"

"Lyralliantha," she finished for me. "She is still my mother, though I consider myself lucky to have two now. Penelope's example, and yours, helped me to understand the warmth I felt from her. Given the nature of She'Har elders, I have only been able to communicate with her directly on a few limited occasions, but there was always something in those conversations, something I felt but could not name. Now I understand what it was.

"I have never felt the same from Tyrion," she added a second later. "I have thought a lot on it since I returned. I have replayed what I know of his past, over and over in my head. Despite knowing the story, and even with your recital of it from his perspective, I find myself confused. I am still not very good at understanding these matters, but his actions then, and even more so now, do not make sense to me. They run counter to everything I have seen here with you. If you are both human, if you both feel the same things, how can he be so different from you? Would you have done the same if you were in his place?"

Lynaralla's voice was calm, but I could detect a faint undercurrent of pain in it, and it tore at my heart. I hadn't paid much attention to her recently; she was always so quiet. It was easy to dismiss her as an observer, as emotionless, or perhaps unaffected by those around her. But the truth was far different, silently and without troubling those around her, she had been struggling to understand the paradoxes of the heart all on her own, using the only tool she had, her intellect.

She needed an answer that I didn't have, but there was a burning resolve within me to help her. There was a hidden plea in her eyes, a secret desperation to understand. *Tyrion, you bastard!* I swore internally. *You wanted me to teach her the harsh reality of betrayal, but she needs something else. She needs a father.* I hadn't considered her my daughter before, not truly. She was too different, too alien. But I would do my best.

"Do you know what wisdom is?" I said, answering her question with one of my own.

Lynaralla tilted her head slightly, reminding me of Humphrey a little. "Wisdom is the use of reason to discern the most efficient course of action to effect the desired outcome. In general, it is referred to when looking at long-term consequences as opposed to short-term gain."

I shook my head. "No." Actually, I thought her answer was close, but it had missed the key ingredient. "What you just described is a function of intelligence, and it is similar, but wisdom is the attribute that allows us to discover what is *right*. Wisdom is the application of intelligence and emotion, together, to solve moral decisions. Right and wrong do not exist in the realm of pure intellectual reason—they can only be illuminated by applying the heart as well as the mind.

"Tyrion is an intelligent man, but he failed when it comes to wisdom. I do not know what I would have done in his place, but I cannot believe I would have arrived at the same place he is now. Most humans have similar emotional responses to violence, betrayal, torture, and all the other things he suffered, but through the lens of wisdom, we do not all react the same," I explained.

"What would a wise man have done in his place?" she asked me.

"All people suffer, men and women alike," I began. "It's a part of living, as much as breathing is. Some internalize it, make it their reason for being—they shape their suffering into a dark reason to continue, vengeance. The wise accept their suffering and seek something else entirely. They search for ways to solve it, to minimize the suffering of others, even if it requires them to suffer more themselves.

"I have suffered more than most, perhaps not as much as Tyrion, but I have chosen not to let my suffering define me. Instead, it helps me empathize with others. It drives me to try and help them endure their hardships and trials. It's what is at the heart of a true family, the desire to help one another in the face of adversity, rather than just blindly trying to hurt those who have wronged them." I stopped, letting my words sink in.

After a while, Lynaralla spoke up, "I still do not understand him. What was the point of his brutal training? If he did not care for me, why did he put me through so much pain to teach me to fight?"

"He didn't care for you because he does not care for himself. You were an extension of his pride, a tool to increase his power. He probably doesn't understand himself, either," I said sadly.

Lynaralla's eyes caught mine once more, boring into me. "I want to help Penelope. While I was on the island, I believe I learned something that can help her."

I couldn't help but be interested. "What is that?"

"My ancestors created very advanced methods of using spellweaving to heal injuries. One such method could allow the transplantation of living tissue from one person to another. If I can learn the technique, I could give Penny my arm to replace the one she lost," said Lynaralla.

The mere suggestion stunned me. Ever articulate, I responded, "Huh?"

"I want to give her my arm," reiterated the young woman.

"Don't you need it?" I asked inanely. My higher functions were still locked up.

Lynaralla shook her head. "Not as much as she does. I have magic. She does not. With spellweaving, I can create any number of limbs to do whatever I need." To illustrate the point, she promptly sprouted an arm-like appendage composed entirely of spellwoven aythar, emerging just below her left arm. It reached up and patted her on the cheek with a three-fingered hand. "Besides, eventually I will surrender this form and become an Elder. How many arms and legs I have at that point will be moot."

"No," I said firmly, holding up my palms to emphasize my response.

Her eyes were curious. "Is this not wisdom? This arm is not necessary or important to me, but it could provide great benefit to her."

"It's a kind thought, but irrational," I argued. "You would lose an arm and gain nothing for it."

"You just told me that wisdom is about more than reason. I love Penelope. She has given me far more than I can repay. I would suffer little, lose something of only small importance to me, in order to restore her, a small suffering to end a great one. You must agree, this is wisdom!" Lynaralla's voice rose as she spoke, to finish with more emphasis than I had ever heard coming from her.

I wanted to agree. It seemed logical, but I couldn't. "No. There is some wisdom in your idea, but you are ignoring Penny's heart and will. Wisdom must consider more than just the objective good, but also the subjective good. She will not be happy to see you lose your arm. She won't accept this solution, and if it is forced on her she will feel only guilt and remorse afterward."

She bowed her head, letting her hair fall forward to obscure her face. "This isn't fair. I want to help. Won't she understand that?"

"She'll be overjoyed to learn how much you care," I said softly. "That's enough. I have another question, though. Your mother never received the loshti, and from what I understand of her, she was never taught advanced She'Har healing magics. Even if you were given your father's loshti, it holds the same knowledge I have inherited, and I didn't know about this possibility. How did you learn of this?"

"I read it."

Again, I was surprised. "Read it? Where?"

Lynaralla glanced up and smiled, a faintly mischievous light in her expression. "Mother took root in a place where one of the ancient Illeniel Elders once grew. The writings were preserved in a chamber beneath the earth. She allowed me to enter and read, though there were too many for me to do more than scratch the surface of what is there.

"Tyrion does not know of this," she finished, the lines around her mouth firming up.

My mind was racing to absorb the implications of what she had just revealed. The She'Har language, Erollith, was written using three dimensional structures that resembled a small tree or a bush. The writing system was so complex that few humans possessed the patience to learn it, not that there was anyone to teach it anyway. The She'Har children, such as Lynaralla, were born with the knowledge, and I possessed it only because I had inherited the knowledge of the loshti.

She'Har Elders 'grew' their sculpture writings, creating them from *Eilen'tyral,* a wooden material that was as strong as steel and virtually immune to decay or the passage of time. A completed Erollith sculpture had three axes, moving from the past, called the 'roots', into the future, called the 'branches.' The three axes were labeled, personal, objective, and subjective, and they could branch even more as the writing grew, creating a written sculpture that looked very much like a living plant.

I hadn't ever considered where the She'Har might keep such writings, but it made sense that if the Elders grew them they might be located underground, and if that was the case it was possible that there might be a great many such hidden libraries still in existence. Even if they were discovered, humans wouldn't know what they had found.

The fact that Lyralliantha had taken root above one of them was also an unusual coincidence, and coincidence was always highly suspect when the Illeniel She'Har were involved. Had they known she would find it? Did it contain the information removed from the loshti that Tyrion had received?

And why was Lyralliantha hiding it from her mate? Obviously, the Illeniel's millennia-long scheme for survival wasn't finished yet. The knowledge hidden there must be important, or they wouldn't have preserved it. It must also be dangerous to their plan, or they wouldn't have hidden it from Tyrion, who had made no secret of his desire to derail everything they had worked for.

Tyrion thought he had lost. Despite his self-loathing and his desire for revenge, no matter the cost, he felt he had been outwitted, and used to resurrect the She'Har. If he learned whatever was hidden beneath Lyralliantha's roots, he might well decide to use it to destroy them and their plan for good.

And unfortunately, from what I knew of their prophetic plans, that might well mean the end of humankind as well.

I had to do something. *But I'll be damned if I know what it is.*

CHAPTER 31

I kept my own counsel regarding the hidden knowledge Lynaralla had found, though I did share her outrageous plan to help Penny replace her arm. I knew my wife would be flattered, and in fact it moved her to tears. As I expected, she was completely against the idea, but she was touched nonetheless.

The next morning, I went into Washbrook and found the leather and other items I needed to complete Penny's arm, and then I got back to work. We still had no word from Matthew and Gram, but we had to trust that they were alright. Even so, the waiting was driving Penny mad.

I was walking back to the house around dinnertime when I felt a surge of aythar and a figure appeared on the path in front of me, a young woman, standing just in front of our door. Her brilliant aura gave her away as a mage and I discovered I had already strengthened my personal shield reflexively.

What's more, she was cloaked in an illusion, one that hid her true appearance. To my eyes she appeared to be wearing a high-quality linen dress dyed in shades of yellow and blue, but my magesight could tell it was a lie. There was no dress at all; she wore a tunic, trousers, and leather boots, though I had no idea what color they were. Her long blond braids were a lie as well.

After a brief moment of shock, I realized her aythar was familiar, before she glanced at me and vanished, reappearing right in front of me. It was so sudden I almost lashed out with a potentially lethal lance of power, only barely managing to rein in my impulse. A lifetime of deadly conflicts had left me with some instincts that were counterproductive to a natural, peaceful existence.

She was tall for a woman—the illusion could do nothing about that. Even so, she had to look up slightly to meet my gaze. There was a playful sparkle in her eyes when she spoke, "Did you miss me?"

My mind was still recovering from the surge of adrenaline, but somewhere behind the scenes my subconscious had already worked out the answer. "Karen?" I asked. "Is that you?"

"Yep!" she answered cheerfully, in her oddly accented Barion. "Did I startle you? You looked like you were about to do something awful to me for a second there."

I sighed, then took a deep breath, trying to slow my heart rate down. "Just a bit. You don't look like yourself."

"Oh!" she exclaimed, and then the illusion covering her melted away, revealing a young woman with wild, curly black hair and light blue skin. Like Lynaralla she had ears that ended in tapering points, but despite her strange appearance she was fully human. She didn't have a seed-mind, as She'Har children did. Instead she had been born as a result of experimentation by the humans of her world. "Is that better?" she asked me.

I smiled. "Much. How have you been? We haven't seen you in months. We were starting to worry."

"I've been well, adapting to this new world—that sort of thing," she answered, as if it were a small thing. "I've been staying in Iverly for the past few weeks. I love the weather there."

"Somehow I thought you'd be traveling more."

Her face lit up. "Oh, I have! I've just been spending my nights in Iverly. I rented a small house there, but I move around a lot during the day. I've been to every city connected to the World Road, and I've traveled to a lot of the towns and villages around them. Lately I've been exploring the Southern Desert."

"That seems like an unpleasant way to spend your day," I commented.

"It's beautiful!" Karen corrected me. "I don't spend all day there, though. I'll walk for a few hours and then take a break somewhere else. There are some beautiful beaches north of Verningham, or if I need to cool off, the forests of Gododdin are really cold right now. When I feel ready, I can always go back to where I left off and start walking again."

"You said you're renting a house in Iverly?"

She nodded. "The breezes there are amazing. I like it since it doesn't smell nearly as bad as some of the other cities I've visited."

I wouldn't have been surprised if Matthew had given her some money before she had left, but renting a house seemed exorbitant. I wanted to ask how she was paying for it, but the question seemed indelicate. Had she returned to visit, or was she here to ask for money?

She must have read something from my momentary silence, for she answered my question before I could figure out how to ask. "I'm a courier. Whenever I stop somewhere, I ask if they need something delivered. I've just been doing it haphazardly thus far, but I've thought about offering to check certain cities on particular days and times."

Now I understood, particularly since I had often disguised myself as a tinker. People in towns and villages often asked me where I was headed next and would sometimes pay to have messages delivered. Nobles often did the same, and if she was willing to carry things from one kingdom to another, they likely paid her a handsome fee. Ordinary couriers took days to weeks to deliver such things, but she was able to complete such a job in a matter of minutes. It was easy money for a Mordan wizard.

"Well I'm glad to hear you're doing well," I told her. "Everyone will be glad to see you."

"How is Matthew?" she asked suddenly.

Ah, I thought, *I knew it would come around to him.* I smiled. "He was well the last I saw him, though we're worried about him right now. He went to assist the Queen's men in dealing with a new threat. He's probably somewhere north and east of Cantley."

As far as Penny and I had been able to determine, Karen and our son had developed some sort of relationship, though Matthew was far too taciturn to share any of the details with us. When Karen had suddenly decided to travel, we had worried that meant they had decided to go their separate ways. Now I wasn't so sure.

Her expression shifted briefly to one of concern before relaxing. "New threat? Nothing too dangerous, though, right?"

"We aren't certain," I admitted. "We had a large attack here not too many days ago and we think something happened near Cantley. Gram and Matthew went to lend assistance to the Queen's forces, in case things were worse than they expected."

"But he wouldn't be in any direct danger," said Karen, sounding as though she might be trying to convince herself. "I mean, there are soldiers with him, and he's your son, so he wouldn't be directly involved in any fighting."

I wanted to reassure her, but the truth was that Penny and I were both on pins and needles while waiting for news. "He's strong," I told her. "I wouldn't have sent him if I didn't think he was capable of handling it. Sir Gram is with him, and there's no more fearsome knight in Lothion. I trust the two of them to keep each other safe."

"You're sure?"

"There's nothing certain in this world, Karen," I told her. "But I believe in them. Come inside and have some tea. I imagine you're hungry too. Penny will be delighted to see you, and Gary has been beside himself worrying about you. I'll send word for him to join us."

Karen hesitated, wavering between her desire to go find my son immediately and her need to see her father. Gary was an android, but he had been created by her biological father and possessed the man's memories. Her real dad was dead, but Gary loved her as if he was her true father. Finally, she nodded.

She received another shock when she saw Penny. Their embrace became faintly awkward as Karen realized my wife only had one arm to return the gesture. That resulted in a whole new line of questions and explanations.

Alyssa had dinner ready, so we ate before getting too deeply into the subject, but eventually we finished filling our bellies, and we began to talk of more serious matters, filling her in on recent events. Karen became steadily more agitated as we told her of Walter's death, Penny's injury, my near death, and then my desperate battle outside the gates of Washbrook.

The more we talked, the more I realized it had really been a terrible couple of weeks. It was hard to resist the urge to downplay the gravity of everything that had occurred. Of course, with Irene and Conall there, I needn't have worried. Anytime I began to sugarcoat things, they stepped in with some new inflammatory statement to make things sound worse. My two younger children seemed oblivious to my warning glances.

Gary remained calm throughout, and when I thought we were done, he glibly reminded us of the attack on Rose before launching into an explanation of his recent attempts to create a way of locating ANSIS. It made sense, though. As a father, he wanted to make sure she knew as much as possible about the dangers facing us, and by extension his daughter.

That might have been the end of the day, but three men, Matthew, Gram, and Sir Thomas, appeared as we were clearing the table. Matthew and Gram looked tired and dirty, while Thomas was clad entirely in the plate armor I had made for him years ago. That armor always looked clean, since it never rusted, but a rancid smell of sweat and old blood emanated from the gambeson he wore beneath it.

"We're back," announced Gram.

Sir Thomas made a shallow bow when he saw me. "Your Excellency, it has been too long since last we met."

Matthew said nothing.

Chaos descended as everyone in the room began talking at once. Penny reached Matthew first, but the others weren't far behind. Soon all three of them were surrounded while being peppered with questions.

Matthew only endured it for a few seconds before pushing his way free. "I'm tired. You can get the details from Sir Thomas." Making for the exit, he came face to face with Karen, and for a moment the look of annoyance on his features changed to surprise as his eyes widened slightly. His sullen expression returned almost immediately, however. "You're back," he said flatly to Karen, and then he left.

Irene stared after him. "Why is he such an asshole?" Angry she started to follow him, but Moira put a hand on her shoulder.

"Leave him be," Moira told her younger sister. Then she went to Karen's side. "He's upset."

"I haven't seen him in months—," muttered Karen quietly. Her aythar shifted, as though she had reached a decision.

"Karen, wait!" I called to her, worried she might disappear. "Don't leave. I need your help."

"Now?" asked Karen.

"Tomorrow," I replied.

She started to leave again, gathering her aythar, but Moira caught her arm. "We need to talk."

The two young women left together, followed by Gram, who apologized, saying he needed to see his mother and sister. Alyssa went with him. That left Sir Thomas alone with the rest of us.

Thomas shrugged and gave us a faint smile. "Is there anything left to eat?"

***

"Those two saved our asses," said Thomas. "The—what did you call them again?"

"Ungol," I supplied.

The knight nodded. "The Ungol caught us at night, overwhelming our sentries and storming our camp. We were completely routed. We had no idea they could see in the dark. If your son and Sir Gram hadn't shown up, our losses would have been much worse."

"How many did you lose?" asked Penny.

Thomas sighed. "We thought we had lost almost everyone, but once the sun rose and we went back, we found a lot of the men who went in different directions. We still lost almost half of them, though. The Ungol are brutal fighters."

"What about the people of Brodinton?" I inquired.

"We found them the next day. The Ungol had turned north, heading into the forest. They were being kept captive by a smaller group. It appears they were using the people of Brodinton to haul the spoils from their town, mainly food and livestock. We think they may have a village in the forest somewhere, but we caught them before they reached it. The Queen has scouts out searching for it even as we speak."

"I'm glad to hear it. Matthew seemed out of sorts. Did something happen during the fight?"

Sir Thomas rubbed his chin, scratching at the stubble there. As long as I had known him, the man had preferred to remain clean-shaven, other than a modest moustache. He was one of only a few surviving members of my original Knights of Stone, and perhaps one of my favorites for his soft-spoken demeanor and quiet mannerisms. Other than his size and athletic physique, few would realize his martial profession if they met him out of his armor. Thomas had none of the arrogance so common in the nobility, and neither did he have a commanding presence. If he were dressed in simple clothes, a stranger might easily mistake him for a well-spoken commoner—perhaps a dockworker or a smith, given his build.

The knight thought carefully before replying, another trait I liked about him. He never spoke rashly. "The battle your son fought was bloody. From what I saw in him afterward, I would guess it was his first. Is that correct?"

"Actually, he's been in several big fights, though most of them were in another dimension," I explained.

"Other dimensions? What was he fighting?" inquired Thomas.

"Mechanical monsters for the most part, from what I understand," I answered. "A year or two ago, he fought one of the Dark Gods that escaped my original purge. He's shown his metal in some very stressful situations already."

"But he never fought men?" prodded the knight.

"Ah," I groaned, understanding at last. Destroying monsters was one thing, but murdering your fellow man was an entirely different thing. I should have realized immediately. *How jaded have I become that it didn't even occur to me?* "How bad was it?"

Thomas grimaced. "For most of us, it was brutal, like any war. Most of the men saw friends cut to pieces next to them, and it's never pleasant seeing another man's face as you push a sword through his ribs. I'm not sure what it's like fighting with magic. He didn't have to kill anyone with his own hands, but he slaughtered a *lot* of them with some sort of magic spinning blades. Then at the end he cornered one of the surviving mages, cutting down his guards and capturing the dwarf magic user alive. Some of that was pretty bloody.

"The dragonfire was the worst, at least for me," added Thomas. "Seeing men burned alive has to be the most awful thing anyone could see, or hear—or that awful smell."

His description made me wince. "Don't remind me."

Thomas nodded apologetically. "Sorry. If there's one thing I don't miss about the earth-bond, it's being able to use the fiery magic of the sun-sword." He patted the enchanted blade that leaned against the side of his chair. "Anyway, you can be proud of your son. I'm sure he's regretting it now, but he turned it around for us. I honestly thought it was you at first."

I chuckled. "We do look a lot alike."

"Nah, not your appearance, his presence. He dropped out of the sky and just stood there, like he owned the place. Then he lit the sky up, like it was daytime. He ignored everything they threw at him. A few times it looked like he was dodging arrows, if you can believe that. Whatever it was he was doing, nothing fazed him. From the moment he put his feet on that field, you knew it was over. The Ungol had already lost. They just didn't know it yet."

The knight meant it as a compliment, but his description sent shivers down my spine. I had been in that position too many times. Whether he admitted it or not, my son was probably suffering for his decisions. And I was the one who had allowed him to be there. I shook myself to clear my head. "How about Gram? You almost make it sound as though Matthew did everything."

Thomas smiled. "That was a sight to see. It was like the old days had come back. He was the one that stopped their rush, him and that big sword of Dorian's. I knew Sir Cyhan had trained him, but hearing it and seeing it are two different things. Me and William did our best to help him, but…"

As his voice trailed off, I decided it was time to make my offer. "Do you miss the earth-bond?"

"Most days I would say no," answered the knight honestly. "Being a knight is a lot like being a soldier. Ninety-nine days out of a hundred, it's a waste. That kind of strength just isn't needed for living a peaceful life,

but on a day like that one—well, a night like that one—at times like that,
I missed it something fierce. If William and I had been our old selves,
we might have been able to prevent the rout. We probably would have
lost a lot of men still, but we could have stopped it from turning into the
mess that it did."

"I've been talking to the Queen," I told him.

"You aren't thinking about bringing it back, are you?" said Thomas
worriedly. "I don't think any of us would survive very long if we took
it on again." He was referring to the side effects of the earth-bond, of
course. Over time, men bound to a piece of the earth's heart began to
take on characteristics of the source of their power. It started with rough
patches of skin, granite teeth, and a certain rigid way of thinking. If left
unchecked, they eventually became stone golems. I had released them
all from the earth-bond long before it could get that bad.

"I'm was thinking of offering you and William a dragon-bond,"
I explained.

"There are more dragons?" The knight's eyes were wide. I had kept
the number and existence of the other dragon eggs a close secret. Most
people only knew about the ones possessed by Penny, Gram, and the
Queen. Even Matthew and Moira's dragons were unknown to most.

"There are," I admitted. "The Queen and I think the Knights of the
Thorn should receive them. There are too many strange things happening
these days, too many places that need protecting."

"How many?" he asked.

"I won't disclose the exact number. I still consider the dragons a
personal prerogative, but I can safely say that we could provide enough
to give at least fifteen knights the dragon-bond."

"Have you chosen the men yet?"

I shook my head. "That's up to Harold, though I imagine he'll want
you and William to advise him. What do you think?"

Thomas was already on his feet. "Yes!"

I found myself grinning at his obvious enthusiasm. It was rare for
Thomas to show excess emotion. "Want to meet yours now?"

A shadow fell across his face, dampening his excitement. "Harold
should be first."

"We've wasted enough time," I argued. "I'll take you to the
cave. You can use the portal to go back right after. Whatever Harold
is doing, you can take his place and send him along, William and
Egan too. Then, tomorrow, the four of you can start figuring out who
you want to train."

Thomas couldn't restrain himself, and he started following me before he had even given his consent. "While we're at it," he began, talking as we walked, "what about some armor like Gram's?"

I raised one brow, looking at him over my shoulder. "You don't like the armor I made for you?"

He held up both hands. "No, no, nothing like that! It's just—well, it would be handy to be able to take it off and on with just a word the way he does. I was a little envious after seeing it in action."

Laughing, I shook my head. "I'm afraid Matthew made that armor, and it takes a lot of time. You'll have to make do with the plate I gave you for the foreseeable future."

CHAPTER 32

The small audience chamber in Castle Cameron wasn't a place I used very often anymore, but it proved ideal for the small meeting I had planned the day before. It held a table capable of seating twelve, as well as two large windows that allowed in a considerable amount of light. It was also warded for privacy, an improvement I had added years ago, after learning the hard way.

Karen was the last to arrive, and from the annoyed look on her face I assumed she had been visiting Matthew before coming. She exchanged a knowing glance with Moira, who sat beside me, and probably a few private telepathic messages as well. I didn't ask, though. Sometimes a parent just has to trust his children to figure out their own problems.

Lynaralla sat on the other side of me, and Elaine Prathion was next to her. It occurred to me then that the chamber was occupied by every female wizard in Lothion, unless one counted Moira Centyr's shade, but she was technically a magical construct.

"Now that we're all here, what are you plotting, old man?" asked Moira with a grin that bespoke mischief.

"Something I can't manage for myself," I said cryptically.

Elaine spoke up then, "You know, George is starting to think you have something against him. Every time you need something, you call for me."

I winced. George was her younger brother, and technically, she was correct; he would have served my purpose just as well, since he had the Prathion gift. "You're right," I admitted. "Tell George to come see me after we talk. I have something else he can help me with, but for this I think it would be best to keep it between you ladies."

"So what is it?" asked Karen bluntly.

"I learned something interesting from Lynaralla the other day. There's a library of sorts beneath her mother's roots. I think it holds information we need," I told them.

"And you want us to steal it?" asked Elaine. "Isn't that dangerous?"

"Espionage is a better word," commented Lynaralla. "My mother will likely offer the knowledge we need if we but ask. Your part is simply to keep my father ignorant of our presence. Is that correct?" She turned to see if her assumption was in line with my thought.

I nodded. "I'd like to take you, Myra, Karen, and Elaine to the island."

Moira broke in, "Why Myra? Why not me?"

"The more bodies, the more likely you'll be discovered. Myra can ride along inside one of the others and still provide the same benefits you would," I explained.

My daughter sighed. "Let's see, Elaine to hide our presence, Lynaralla to talk to her mother, Karen to return everyone afterward—what do you need the dark talents of a Centyr mage for?"

"Insurance. On the off chance they're discovered by a lone krytek, Myra can rewrite the memories of whoever sees them," I answered.

"Or, if they're caught and slain by Tyrion himself, she can send a spellbeast back to tell you what happened," added Moira, voicing my unspoken thought.

"That's an ugly way of putting it," I protested.

"But a logical precaution," noted Lynaralla. "Also, if I am her host for the trip, you can count on her to report fully on any conversation between me and my mother. She may also be able to glean information from Lyralliantha that I cannot."

If I had been younger, her cold analysis of my ulterior motives would have made me flush with embarrassment. Instead I merely acknowledged her observation. "I trust you, Lynaralla, but that's a valid point."

"I'll do it," said the young She'Har woman. Elaine and Karen were also nodding in agreement.

Moira wasn't completely sold on the idea yet, though. "Don't agree too quickly, Lynn. What are you getting out of it? I understand why Dad wants us to do this, but this sounds like we're just using you."

Lynaralla smiled. "I am happy to be used, if it helps my family. My reasons are the same as yours. Also, I would like to study the writings. If we bring them here, I can read them at my leisure. Many of them probably contain spellweaving techniques that I can learn from. I cannot do that while they reside within Tyrion's demesne."

We talked a while after that, but not for long. Moira left to pass the word along to Penny while we made our way to Turlington. I had planned to use the World Road to get there, but Karen had already made the trip, so she teleported us directly, not to the city, but to the coast itself. From there I gathered them together and lifted us into the air.

A dragon would have been an easier way to fly, but then Elaine would have had to hide it as well once they reached the island. Plus, I could fly faster, getting them to the shore of the island in half the time.

Once Tyrion's island came into view, Elaine shielded us in a veil of invisibility, and after we landed, Karen teleported me back to Castle Cameron before returning to her companions. Now all that was left for me was to wait.

So I went and found Matthew. I needed him for part of the enchantment I was adding to Penny's new arm. Foolishly, I looked for him at home, thinking he might still be sulking, but it turned out he was in his workshop with Gary.

He and Conall were outside the shop, shaping copper to help finish Gary's antenna. The android was looking on silently, but he greeted me with a quiet nod in my direction. I watched without interrupting until they were done. All in all, I stood there for most of a half an hour.

When they stopped, Conall spoke to me, "Dad." Matthew didn't bother speaking; he was still deep in thought.

"Give me a hand for a while, Matt," I said, interrupting my oldest son's reverie.

"Huh?"

"I need you to lend a hand with an enchantment I'm working on," I explained.

Matthew looked at Gary, but the android simply shrugged. "Conall and I can handle the rest. We can test it this evening, maybe. I'll let you know."

With a grunt, Matthew walked toward me, and I led him back to my workshop. He was never much for conversation, but he seemed depressed. It was hard to say. He was hard to figure out at the best of times, and one had to be a mind reader to know anything about his moods with certainty.

When I showed him my design, he dove into the work immediately. It wasn't particularly complex, especially since it was something he had done before. In this case, it was just an addition to the hand that would allow the arm to summon an enchanted shield I had already prepared. He had perfected the designs to do that back when he made Gram's armor and remade Thorn, so it took him less than an hour.

He finished and started to leave, still not having said a word.

"Matt," I said, causing him to stop.

"Yeah?"

"Are you alright?"

He shrugged. "I'm fine."

"Sir Thomas told us about the battle," I began. "He spoke well of what you did, but I wondered if—"

Matthew interrupted, "I'm fine, Dad. It didn't bother me that much."

I wasn't finished, though. "You know I've been through a lot of bloody situations. Of course, none of them are the same, they never are. If you want to talk about it, I'm always..."

He kept walking, waving his hand in the air to forestall my offer. "I know, Dad. I'm fine."

I watched his back as he left. *Liar.* I wanted to follow him, to *make* him talk, but I knew it wouldn't work. He would open up to someone eventually, or maybe he wouldn't. One thing I knew for certain: it had bothered him, whether he admitted it or not.

Being a parent has to be the toughest job in the world, I thought to myself. *I think I'd rather do the account books or send men to war. At least they listen to me.*

***

Karen returned that evening and found me in the main keep, where I was signing documents that Peter had saved up for me. According to my chamberlain, I had been slacking off too much lately, though from my perspective I felt I had been working too hard. We never saw eye to eye on such matters. In Peter's eyes, the only work I did that was worthwhile was when I was sitting at a writing desk.

I looked up when she came in, "Are they alright?"

She nodded. "I just came back to eat and fetch food for them."

"Where are they?"

"We got to Lyralliantha's trunk without a problem. They're huddled up against it, invisible, while Lynaralla talks to her mother. She said it would take a few hours just to get her attention, but after that they could hide underground, in the chamber where the writings are," said Karen.

Assuming nothing stumbled over them before that. I couldn't help but worry. "How soon are you going back?"

"As quickly as I can," said Karen. "They can't move until I return, otherwise I'll arrive somewhere that isn't covered by Elaine's veil."

Reaching over to the edge of the desk, I picked up a small bell and rang it. Peter appeared after only a minute or two. "Yes, milord?" he asked.

"Go to the kitchen with Karen and make sure that Cook gives her anything she wants, and make sure he knows to be quick about it," I commanded him.

Peter frowned. "I hardly think she needs me to—"

I cut him off, "Now, Peter. The faster she gets the food and can go, the better." I knew from long experience how surly Cook could be when it came to unexpected requests for special treatment. Peter would ensure the man knew how important this was. Plus, it was a great way to get back at my chamberlain for sticking me with so much paperwork. I grinned viciously at his back as he left the room.

Peter was easier to harass than Benchley had ever been. He showed his emotions too easily. I hummed a cheerful tune to myself as I signed a few more papers and then turned to review the latest statements from my factor in Albamarl.

Once that was done, I drafted a letter to King Nicholas in Gododdin. Ariadne had asked me to notify him regarding the Ungol village that we thought was inside his borders. While I had destroyed the warriors, neither the Queen nor I wanted to think about their families starving over the course of the winter. Since it was outside Lothion's borders, we couldn't do anything, but I had no doubt Nicholas would probably find a way to help them.

It was late in the afternoon when I finally finished, but before I could hide, Peter appeared. The man seemed to have a sixth sense when it came to whether I was busy or not, or perhaps he had been spying on me secretly. "George Prathion is here to see you, Your Excellency." I could almost hear the smugness in Peter's voice. This was his revenge for my kitchen errand earlier.

Perhaps he had been taking lessons from Benchley. I resolved to check into it later. No good could come of it if he learned from that man's wicked example.

There was no getting around it, though. I had sent word for George to attend me earlier in the day. I had simply forgotten about it in the midst of everything else. "Send him in," I answered.

The young man entered and presented himself with a short bow. "You called for me, Your Excellency?"

"Come sit down, George. No need to be so formal. It's just the two of us." I waited until he had found a seat before continuing, "How are you holding up?"

George looked uncomfortable, and his hands kept reaching up to adjust his jacket. Though his father had been the Baron of Arundel, most of his childhood had been spent as a commoner. He never had grown completely comfortable with the more elaborate forms of dress. "As well as can be expected," he answered neutrally.

"It's never easy, losing a father," I said quietly. "And now you'll be taking his position. I went through the same thing, though in a different order. I know the pressure you must be feeling."

"Elaine is the eldest," grumbled the young man.

"Tradition in Lothion dictates that the eldest male inherits, unless there is no other heir."

"Those are outdated traditions," argued George. "We have a queen regnant now, and Lady Rose has held the position of The Hightower for years without a husband. Even your wife, the Countess, held her position when you were—"

"I'm not arguing that point, George," I said, interrupting him. "Elaine told me that you offered to step aside for her, but she refused."

"But I don't want it," he said emphatically.

"Then you're wise," I agreed with him. "But one of you must, otherwise I'll be forced to grant the title to someone else. Your mother can't take it." Rebecca Prathion was neither a wizard nor nobility, and while those weren't necessarily problems, she was also fairly old and lacked both the spine and the skills necessary to succeed. The other lords of Lothion would never stand for her taking the title.

"Then give it to someone else," said George. "I don't need it. We survived just fine before. I'm not suited to it and I don't—I don't deserve it."

There it was, the guilt hiding just beneath the surface. He wasn't responsible for the death of his father, Walter Prathion, but he felt it anyway. It wasn't logical, but I understood. "That's not the point, George, not at all."

"It seems pretty pertinent to me."

Given my own background, I knew what he was feeling, but I couldn't afford to coddle him. Instead I took inspiration from James Lancaster, the late Duke of Lancaster. James had had some harsh words for me when I had doubted my own right to my title. With a stern look on my face I responded, "That's because you're an ignorant, self-absorbed young man, George, but I have faith you'll grow out of that. You won't be made Baron of Arundel because you *deserve* it, you'll be made Baron because I *need* you. Your personal failings and character flaws are entirely unimportant to me.

"This isn't an honor or a privilege, as most people assume. In truth it is closer to a punishment. The title is a duty, one that will follow you for life. You will not only become my vassal, but most importantly you will be responsible for protecting and feeding the people of Arundel," I said harshly.

"Like I said, I'm not worthy. I'm lazy and my only claim to it is an accident of birth," protested George.

"Do you think I was *worthy*?" I replied in a dangerous tone. "I wasn't. No one is. Did you deserve to be Walter's son, born with power, heir to his title? That's ridiculous. The fact is, there are only a few wizards in this world. Your power makes you useful to me, and it also means you are better able to provide for the wellbeing of the people of Arundel than most.

"Lazy? Perhaps you were, but I don't give a damn. You'll spend the rest of your life wishing you had that luxury again. You'll do your duty and lie awake at night wondering if you've made the right decisions for your people, and if you screw it up, I'll be waiting in the wings to hold you to account. Your life until now has been a happy dream, one that is now over.

"I will take your vow of fealty next week, and as your liege I will do everything I can for you, George. Not because I was Walter's friend, but because I *need* you. I need you to succeed. I need your support. If you have doubts, I will advise you, but forget about being *worthy*. Historians can make up their minds about that after you've found the sweet release of death. Until then, you will suffer, you will work, you will do everything in your power to serve me and your people. Do you understand me?"

"But…"

"Do you understand?" I repeated, raising my voice and adding a subtle undercurrent of implied violence.

"Yes, my lord," George answered meekly.

I smiled and stood, walking over to a sideboard to fetch a bottle of wine and two glasses. Sitting back down, I poured the wine and handed him a glass. "Here, this will help settle your nerves."

George dipped his head respectfully. "Yes, sir. Thank you."

His manner made me laugh. "I scared the shit out of you, didn't I?"

Nervously, he dipped his head again. "Yes, my lord." Then seeing that I seemed to be in a good mood, he added, "You were joking?"

I took a sip of my wine, and after a pause I showed my teeth in a feral grin. "Not at all. I was dead serious, but I'm not mad at you. It was just something you needed to hear. Stop bobbing your head like that, though."

"My lord?"

"Always know the forms required by etiquette, but do not offer more deference than is necessary. Otherwise they'll take it as weakness. Nobles are like wolves, remember that. They'll eat you alive if they smell blood," I told him.

"Oh," mumbled George.

I almost felt bad for abusing him, but I remembered too well what I had gone through in my early days. I had had even less support, and if it hadn't been for James Lancaster and his brutally honest advice I might not have survived. Then I thought of Walter, something I hadn't had much time to do since his death. "Your father loved you, George, and in the years to come, if he can see you from wherever he is, he will also be proud of you. I'm sure of it." I raised my glass. "Let's have a toast for him."

We talked for a while after that, and I tried to make George more comfortable. He needed to find his balance if he was to succeed. It was a delicate balance I had to strike, at least until he found his footing. I didn't want him to turn into a whipped dog, but I needed to be firm. After we finished our glasses, I gave him one final instruction.

Lifting a folded sheet of parchment from the desk, I handed it to him. "I need you to go to Surencia and deliver this to King Nicholas."

"Couldn't a courier handle it?" asked the young baron.

"They could, but I need you to do it. This is a warning for him regarding the Ungol within his borders, but it's also a chance for you to make yourself known to our neighbor to the north. Spend a couple of days there, and don't be afraid to use your unique abilities," I told him.

George frowned. "You want me to spy on him?"

"I trust Nicholas, but that doesn't mean we shouldn't use every opportunity to acquire more information. You may hear things from him, or those around him. Be discreet."

For the first time, I saw a glimmer of confidence in the young man's face. "Don't worry, my lord, when a Prathion doesn't want to be found, a Prathion isn't found," he answered, reciting his family's motto.

CHAPTER 33

I had barely gotten out of my chair after George's exit when my daughter charged into the room. Moira had been rather disappointed about being left out of the mission to Tyrion's island, so after passing her spell-twin, Myra, over to Lynaralla, she had spent the rest of the day looking for ways to occupy herself.

As I soon discovered, that had primarily meant questioning Sanger and sifting through his thoughts.

"The Ungol come from a world that is overrun with ANSIS!" she began, leaning over my desk excitedly.

With a groan, I sat back down. *This chair is going to need better padding if I have to keep sitting in it for hours on end,* I thought miserably.

"Forget about your backside and listen to me," said Moira, referencing my unspoken thought in her usual unsettling manner. "The Ungol have been dealing with ANSIS for several years now."

I frowned at her. "Just years?"

She nodded. "Since the Dark Gods vanished."

Because I had destroyed the Dark Gods, not realizing that they were somehow responsible for protecting our world from the She'Har's mysterious enemy. I put my face in my hands, rubbing my temples. "Why are they still free then?" I asked suddenly. "If ANSIS has been running rampant on their world for years, surely they would have taken control of the Ungol by now."

"They've been in hiding," said Moira. "They've been hiding for generations, for thousands of years. They hid from the Dark Gods first, and now they hide from ANSIS."

And now pieces of their world were appearing in ours. Was it possible that that was how ANSIS had gotten here? Like rats hiding on a seafaring vessel, they had been swept along with some piece of the Ungol's home world?

Moira nodded excitedly. "I think that's exactly what happened."

"Would you let me actually *speak* my thoughts before you answer them?" I complained.

My daughter grinned at me. "I would if you didn't pause for so long to sort them out. It's exhausting, waiting for people to speak their minds."

I sighed. "Is there anything else?"

"That was the main thing," said Moira. "I thought you should know right away."

Rising from my chair, I massaged my sore posterior. "It certainly helps clear up a few things." I started for the door again.

"Matthew is looking for you as well," said Moira before I could leave.

I didn't sense him nearby, so I gave her a questioning glance.

"I felt some excitement from the workshop as I was heading here," explained Moira. "I didn't wait to see what they were excited about since I wanted to find you first, but I have a feeling he'll be wanting to see you."

"Let's go find him, then," I offered.

"I'm hungry," countered my daughter. "It's almost dinnertime."

Exasperated, I gave her a long-suffering look. "Fine, you go eat. Tell your mother I'll be late for dinner." Then I left and headed into the castle yard.

True to my daughter's word, Matthew was just exiting his workshop when I approached. It was obvious from his demeanor that he was about to seek me out, but his eyes relaxed when they fell on me.

"I was just about to look for you," he said simply.

"So I'm told," I answered wryly.

He ignored my remark and gestured toward the workshop, so I followed him into the interior. There I found Gary seated next to the worktable. A number of small ring-gates were arranged across the table, standing on their edges with small stands supporting them. Each ring-gate connected to one of the antenna locations, and all of them had a thick copper wire extending across the table. The wires all converged at the center of the table, where Gary held his arm. The forearm was open, as though it had been partially disassembled, and the wires all connected to what appeared to be smaller wires within it.

If someone without a broad experience of the world, along with the knowledge of Gary's artificial nature were to see it, they might assume it was some sort of diabolical ritual taking place. I merely found it interesting. Gary's right arm held a quill pen, which he was using to make notations on a map of Lothion and Gododdin.

Considering how expensive good quality maps were, that would have been upsetting, but I knew what his purpose was. "What have you discovered?" I asked, leaning forward to look closely.

"First, I would like to note that the distances noted on your maps are not entirely accurate. I have corrected for this by making measurements from each antenna site, but there will still be some inconsistencies. This was expected, however, given the state of cartographic finesse present in your world," said the android.

I smirked. "I appreciate the disclaimer."

Gary went on, "I have approximated the positions of two distinct signals using a fifteen-meter wavelength to communicate, presumably with each other, though I can't positively confirm this without being able to decrypt the signals."

"It's a safe assumption, though. Since there are only two signals, they are almost certainly communicating with each other," I observed.

"Exactly," agreed Gary.

There were two small 'x' marks on the map, one where Lancaster had been and the other in the forest northeast of Cantley. "Are these marks where the signals are originating from?"

Gary and Matthew both nodded. Then Matthew spoke up, "It suggests that one might be where the Ungol that attacked Brodinton came from, while the other is probably in that strange, primeval forest."

"Things are starting to make sense," I declared.

"How?" questioned my son. "One is where some of the Ungol came from, and they gave no sign of being possessed by ANSIS, and the other is from a site we've already investigated. We didn't find any of the Ungol there either. Moira said that Sanger's people came from a spot within Gododdin's borders."

"She just found out that the Ungol have been hiding from ANSIS for the past few years," I answered. "That fact, combined with this, means that ANSIS probably hasn't been arriving here under their own power. They're crossing with parts of the other world as it somehow bleeds into our own. The piece that replaced Lancaster might have held some elements of ANSIS when it came here, and the same is probably true of the area near Cantley. Now they're growing like a cancer."

Matthew frowned. "That fits the observations, but I don't like it. The whole thing is messy. It lacks rationality. Whatever is causing these pieces of that other world to appear, it almost has to be the result of some sort of deliberate magic. If so, why would it be so random?"

"I have a suggestion," offered Gary.

We both turned to stare at him.

"We could talk to them," said the android.

"Then we would give away the fact that we are listening. ANSIS might realize we can locate them. If they do, they might find another way to communicate, costing us a strategic advantage," responded Matthew.

I was confused. Obviously, my son understood the technical aspects of what he and Gary were doing better than I did. "Wait. I thought we couldn't understand them because of this encryption of theirs."

Gary nodded an affirmative. "Yes, but that doesn't mean we can't transmit an unencrypted signal to them. The technology they use is fundamentally based on the same technology that I use. They can understand a message if I send it that way, and if they choose to reply they merely have to respond with a similarly unencrypted signal."

"I see," I replied to fill the space in the conversation while I absorbed what he had said. Then I asked, "If we send a message, will they be able to locate us?"

"Yes," answered the android. "But that will only give them the location of whichever antenna we use for our transmission."

"They already know where we are," put in Matthew. "The attack on Rose shows that, and they probably were spying on us for some period before that."

"Is there any possibility they already know we're listening?" I added.

"A low chance," responded Gary. "We haven't sent any definite messages, but the initial pulse I used to measure the distance between our antennae might have been detected. If so, they might suspect we are trying to listen."

"The real question," I continued, "is whether we have any more information to gain by waiting. You say we won't be able to break their encryption, right?"

"Not a chance," replied Gary.

Matthew spoke up again, "But we might discover more signals. They may be operating from more than these two locations."

"The chances of that are small," opined Gary. "They had no reason to suspect we would try to eavesdrop, given the technology, or rather the lack of technology, possessed by your world. Any other large clusters of ANSIS would almost be transmitting constantly, just as these two are. If there are small clusters, we won't detect them until they become larger."

"Then we don't gain much by waiting," I observed.

"If you're thinking about a surprise attack, then sending a message will only warn them," argued Matthew.

The frustration of a day spent locked indoors, combined with my general dissatisfaction with the way things had gone the past few weeks, made me want to do something definitive. "A warning won't help them," I responded. "We'll wipe out both locations, tonight. The message will just be a statement of intent."

"What will you tell them?" asked my son.

"Nothing complicated," I told him. "How do we do this?"

Gary answered, "Just speak to me as if you were talking to the enemy. I'll record your face and voice as you speak before converting it into a compressed digital signal and transmitting it."

"How long will that take?" I asked.

The android smiled. "It will be done almost as soon as you finish speaking."

"Very well," I said, squaring my shoulders and facing him head on. "Let's begin."

Gary nodded, and then his head and body went still, staring directly at me. "Go."

Recalling desperate times, I put in my voice all the steel that I had once used when facing down the Iron God, Doron. "This is Mordecai Illeniel. As you are doubtless aware after the events in Dunbar, you are not welcome on this world. I am told that negotiation with your kind is pointless, but given your intelligence, I thought I would offer this warning. You will not find success here. If you persist, we will eradicate you. If that proves impossible, I will make certain that this world is worthless to you before I surrender it, even if it costs the lives of every human now alive.

"These are not idle threats, and furthermore, if I am pushed to such extremes I will also destroy the world you hail from. I am told that humanity has already been exterminated there, at least humanity as I recognize it. Therefore, I will suffer no remorse in annihilating your world. This is your only warning. Remove yourselves or face extinction."

I stopped there, and after a few seconds Gary blinked. "That was the end?"

"That's it."

"You think they'll fall for such an obvious bluff?" said Matthew somewhat disdainfully.

I rewarded my son's disbelief with a dead stare. "Bluff? I think you misunderstood."

My son rubbed at his metal hand, polishing an imagined blemish. It was a frequent habit he had developed since replacing his lost appendage. "Yes, a bluff, a strong front meant to scare an opponent, a threat you have no way of carrying out. We only just located them, and within minutes you're trying to intimidate them without even bothering to make a plan."

I had to admit, he was partly right—about the immediately trying to intimidate them part. "Actually, from what you've told me, and what we learned in Dunbar, I don't expect my words to have any impact. But I did not say those things without reason. I have spent most of my spare moments thinking about this. Now that we have something solid to grasp onto, I don't intend to waste any time.

"ANSIS spreads like an infection. Every second wasted only allows them to become more firmly entrenched. We know where they are, or at least the biggest portion of them, so we act quickly, like a surgeon, to cut the infection out. My words were a warning, and a promise, to whatever is left after that.

"If these machines are as intelligent as you keep telling me, they may realize the sensibility of not provoking us further. If not, we'll make good on that promise," I finished.

Gary watched silently, his eyes moving between us, but Matthew wasn't done yet. "Dad, I know you can do things that go beyond magic and wizardry, and I have no idea what happened to you a few days ago, but from everything you've told me there's no way you can destroy an entire world. A city, maybe. A small piece of a kingdom—sure, I could believe that. But I've seen Tyrion's memories too. I remember what he did to eliminate the She'Har, and it won't work on ANSIS. You can't create those wasp-like krytek he used, and even if you did, they can't eat non-living matter. Maybe you could set off a chain of volcanic eruptions like he did, but that won't stop these things. It would only kill *us*."

Matthew had obviously spent some time contemplating the problem, just as I had. For all his flaws, for all the ways he was different than me, I was proud of his thoughtful nature. But he had missed the answer. Probably because he was used to thinking in terms of what *I* could do. He had grown up in the shadow of a legendary archmage, and that shadow had obscured the solution from him.

"I can't do it," I said at last. "But *you* can."

"What?"

I didn't look at him, setting my eyes instead on Gary. "I've spent some time talking to Gary as well, privately. Asking questions, mostly, to confirm my suspicions. Just from that, I bet he knows what I'm thinking. I'm also sure he hasn't said anything to you about it either. Probably because he fears to even put the seed of such an idea in your mind."

Matthew turned to the android. "What's he talking about?"

Gary said nothing, having gone so still he seemed almost a statue.

I moved closer to the machine-man, setting my hand on his shoulder before speaking to my son again, "He doesn't want to answer you. He's afraid to confirm what I said." Then I clapped the android on the back, hard enough he was forced to move slightly to correct his balance. "Tell him, Gary. He'll figure it out on his own anyway."

Woodenly, Gary answered, "The Fool's Tesseract."

The Fool's Tesseract, or FT for short, was a dimensional enchantment Matthew had devised to serve as both a protection and a weapon when he had gone to rescue Gary's daughter from imprisonment by ANSIS on her world. When activated, it formed a six-sided cube, with each side being a one-way dimensional plane that allowed matter and energy to pass in one direction, inward. The matter was directed into a separate pocket dimension, whose size was controlled by the enchantment. The enchantment could be reversed, and depending on how much matter had been compressed within the pocket dimension, it usually resulted in a devastating explosion.

Matthew's eyes narrowed. "I did some calculating in that regard already. Even if the exterior dimensions were set at the maximum size I can manage, it would take billions of years for it to swallow something as large as Karen's world."

I nodded. "He told you about what would happen if you set the interior dimension too small, though."

"A black hole," said Matthew. "But the amount of matter it could absorb in any reasonable time frame would be too small. Once the FT was reversed, the tiny black hole would immediately evaporate."

"I may have understated the effect. The term 'evaporate' may not be adequate," offered the android.

"Explain," said Matthew.

"A micro black hole would evaporate, but it would happen on an unimaginably short time scale. It would effectively produce an explosion." Gary leaned over and picked up a small piece of slag iron from the dirt floor of the old smithy. "A black hole with this much mass would produce approximately 500 terajoules of energy, enough to destroy a large city." Then he picked up a heavy copper ingot that hadn't been used yet. "With this much mass, it would likely destroy much of Lothion." Then he waved his hands around at the entire shop. "Take all the mass in this shop, and perhaps a little more, and it would devastate the world.

"That wouldn't destroy ANSIS, however," continued Gary. "It might destroy all life on a world. But if it were allowed to build longer, long enough to collect a thousand tons or more of mass, it would destroy my home world entirely, including ANSIS. Your Fool's Tesseract could probably collect that much mass in the span of a few hours."

CHAPTER 34

Matthew stared at the two of us. "You're mad."

I pursed my lips, then nodded. "Probably, but we won't do anything as crazy as that. I hope."

"You hope?!" exclaimed Matthew. "You won't do it at all. You can't craft the enchantment, and I'm not certain I want to do this."

"You will," I said calmly. *In fact, I'm sure you already created a new one.* I let my eyes linger on his metal hand for a moment, pondering the runes engraved on it. *He probably has an enchantment to summon it right there. Plus, there's always Conall, or Lynaralla.* Though neither of them had demonstrated it yet, there was a high chance they both had the same Illeniel gift.

"Besides, that's all hypothetical," I said to allay his concerns. "First we destroy them here. Then we see about what's going on in this other dimension that's bleeding over into our own."

"And if it's overrun, the way Moira suggested?" asked Matthew.

Pushing him too far wouldn't be wise. Better to let him draw his own conclusion. "What would you suggest?"

"Well—," he muttered. "If it is overrun with ANSIS, it's just an artificial dimension, right? One created by the She'Har to shield ours. If we're going to destroy something, it would be better to test it there first."

I nodded agreeably. "Then we see what their response is. If they withdraw, wonderful. They'll still have a place to retreat to. If their remnants here decide to continue, then we'll have to consider the more extreme option."

"If it comes to that," put in Gary nervously.

"Of course," I agreed, but deep down, I didn't believe ANSIS would bend under pressure. "For now we need only concern ourselves with the first step. Matthew, you and Gary, along with Moira and Gram, will go to Cantley. There, you—"

"Hold up," protested Matthew. "I don't need that many people."

I shook my head. "You need Gary to pin down the location of the village. He can detect their shorter-range signals. You'll need Moira to examine any Ungol that you find, to make certain they're beyond help before you do anything final."

"And Gram?" asked my son.

"To make sure nothing kills either of you. You and Moira both are a little reckless," I finished.

Matt grunted. "Coming from you, that doesn't mean much."

That earned him a laugh, then I went on, "Meanwhile, I'll go to where Lancaster used to be and turn it into a slag pit."

"And who are you taking with *you*?" countered my son.

"No one," I stated. "I can walk in unopposed, just as I did when I found Elaine. When I start, it won't be safe for anyone near me."

"That doesn't make any sense—," began Matthew.

"Too bad. I'm in charge," I said, overriding his argument. "In case of reprisals, we'll have Irene stay here with your mother. Conall can go and warn the Queen. He can help protect her as well."

"What about George?"

"I didn't expect you'd get a signal this soon. I already sent him to Gododdin on a separate matter," I answered.

Matthew nodded, his face a mask as he thought through my last statement. "This is a surprise attack. How likely do you think it is that they'll be able to manage a reprisal before we can get back?"

I glanced at Gary. After a second, the android spoke, "ANSIS has already made one attempt to infiltrate this place. Clearly they know its location. There's a high probability they have other assets in place somewhere, but we have no way of knowing what or where."

"Then maybe we should wait until we can make sure—"

"They grow by the day, by the minute," I interrupted. "The sooner we strike, the better. If that flushes their hidden forces out into the open, then so much the better."

Gary agreed, "This is true. How soon, though?"

"Now," I told them.

***

Several hours later, I was walking down the road that led to what had once been Lancaster. Flying would have been much faster, but Matthew and Moira would need more time. Though they could take the World Road to Cantley, they'd have to fly on dragonback from there. Then they'd need to actually find their target. All in all, their mission was more complicated than mine.

They had to find the Ungol village and then determine whether to destroy it or attempt to liberate its inhabitants before destroying the area. Moira's gifts would be particularly useful for that task.

My job was comparatively simple. Lancaster was gone. I could do my work without worrying about any loss of innocents, other than the trees and strange wildlife.

The moon was just a sliver in the sky, casting barely any usable light, but I didn't need much. I didn't have dragon-enhanced eyesight, since I had never bonded with any of the dragons, but a simple spell accomplished the same benefit. Magesight alone was more than enough to walk a country road at night, but by enhancing my eyesight I was able to enjoy the quiet scenery.

The land sloped gently downward toward the Glenmae River on my left, while the forest sat dark and brooding on my right as I advanced toward my destination. This was the same road my birth mother had once taken, trying to escape assassins with me in her arms. It was the same road where I had once killed thousands of Gododdin troops, before drowning their remnants in the valley.

It seemed fitting I would walk it as I headed toward my next act of carnage. At least this time I wouldn't be killing human beings.

It was also beautiful. The land was a vast canvas of varying shades of grey as the grass rippled beneath the faint moonlight. Replete with silence, I walked through the night.

Sometime after midnight, I reached the edge of the primeval forest that had replaced Lancaster. Gone was the gentle land of my childhood, replaced by the oppressive presence of arboreal giants. It would take a few more hours to reach the center, but I had no doubts about what I would do there.

Danger was my companion now, and I knew from our first disastrous journey that magesight alone wouldn't be enough to forewarn me of some of the perils in this place. Softly, I relaxed, letting myself fall gently into the state I called the 'mind of the stone.' My existence expanded slightly, the border between self and other becoming something that extended twenty yards beyond my quaint human body.

My emotions died, replaced by a crystalline clarity, but while all within me was still, there was movement beyond. Things creeping, crawling, and flying, both beyond and inside me.

That wouldn't do. Only one thing was allowed to move, the small bit of human flesh at my center. With that decision, I changed, and the sphere of influence that was now me became a malevolent being, inimical to anything that displayed motive force.

Insects were torn apart, worms smothered by the soil that was their home. Birds fell dead as the very air strangled them. Larger beasts were caught by vines and impaled by branches on trees that suddenly became animated.

I walked, and death walked with me.

The world changed around me, progressing in a single direction, as though I was merely a boat floating in a gentle current of indifferent violence. The earth hummed, and the sky vibrated, singing to me, whispering dreams of something greater, tempting me to join them, but I retained enough awareness to avoid that folly. Another voice sang with them, a deep counterpoint to the dazzling brilliance of the living earth, the empty call of the void.

It was a wonder I hadn't noticed it when I was younger, for it seemed painfully evident to me now. It lay in the silence between sounds, the rest between heartbeats, the cold that hovered outside the warmth of living bodies. It was in the space between the tiniest particles of earth and air. And it knew me.

It begged for my attention, but I ignored it, training my awareness to stay with the voice of the earth and air. The void had seen me before, and if I let myself look back at it, it would take me again.

Yet still, I was tempted. If my desire was to kill anything that came within my sphere of influence, the void was far easier. Why crush, tear, and smother, when life could more simply be devoured?

And then I was there, in the center of it all, and I came to rest. I had encountered any number of massive creatures by then—and left them broken and mangled in my wake. Now that I was no longer moving, more of them came to me. Spiders, wolves, massive bears, and things I had no name for all came, and just as quickly died.

Deep beneath me the earth lay eager, waiting to be released, but it wasn't time yet. I had to wait for the signal. *What signal?*

"A light," I said tonelessly, reminding myself as I exercised an almost forgotten human throat.

There was something new in the darkness. Things that moved without life, constructions of metal that were more akin to the void than the earth. I had expected them, but this was when things would become dangerous. These things could destroy me from a distance.

Letting my body expand farther, I called to the earth and it answered, sending great slabs of stone upward to join me, building a huge mass of stone around the fragile flesh at my center. Almost as soon as it was done, parts of me disintegrated, collapsing under the assault of powerful hammer-blows. The enemy was bombarding me.

Within seconds, I knew I was far from safe, so I drew more stone, encasing myself in a small granite mountain. I was large enough now that I could heal almost any damage to my exterior as quickly as it could be done to me.

But there was a problem. I couldn't see the sky. *I need to see the light when it comes.*

Before I could do anything about that, however, something ripped through the stone surrounding me, penetrating deeply. More attacks struck the same place, shattering the outer layer of my defense and driving ever closer to my vulnerable center. The damage was unrelenting. I had to grow larger, or eliminate the threat, otherwise I wouldn't last long enough to see a signal.

They already know I'm here. No point in holding back.

With a sigh, I released my tenuous hold on humanity and reached down, deep into the earth. It had been waiting, like a hungry hound anxious for its master's call. I changed. My viewpoint grew, and the world became simpler. My blood boiled beneath the cold crust of my skin, and I found joy in giving it release.

I brought it up from the depths, letting it spill across the land, swallowing the insignificant metal parasites that had been pelting me. The ground—no, *I* rose up, hot and molten, and everything burned, melted, or turned to ash.

The fire, my anger, grew ever larger, expanding like ripples on a pond, consuming everything around it. Hotter I burned and farther I spread. The forest was gone, and I began to devour the land beyond that, but as I grew I felt my anger, and my will, begin to cool. My awareness was fading, my anger melting away. *Why had I come?*

And then I saw it. The sky flashed, a brilliant light in the distance that illuminated the world briefly. *The signal.*

Somehow, I knew what it meant. It was over. I had to return. Slowly, painfully, I forced myself to contract, to become small once more. It wasn't easy, but I knew what I needed to be. I had been it before; I would be it again. Flesh forgets, but the stone remembers. Even if the stone must become flesh.

Eventually I found myself standing high above the Glenmae Valley, a mountain of burning rock beneath my feet. I had protected myself from the heat, though I couldn't remember doing so. The sky was beginning to brighten in the east, the first sign of dawn approaching, and I had no idea how long I had been standing there.

I felt heavy, as though my arms and legs were bound with iron weights. I was tired. Surrounded by burning clouds of smoke and ash, I descended, using magic to assist when there was no good footing to be found.

After a while a thought occurred to me. *This is stupid, I should be flying.* And so I did, grasping the air with my will and letting it send me in the direction I needed to go. *Home.*

CHAPTER 35

Penny wasn't happy.

Actually, that was an understatement. She had been in a good mood earlier, but that had been shattered when Mort had showed up late for dinner and begun issuing orders with the frenetic passion of a madman. *Or as I like to think of it, the frenetic passion of my husband.*

He had always been like this. It was like being married to two different men. One calm, quiet, somewhat lazy, and introspective to the point of being almost melancholic. The other was the demon that had shown up tonight. Mordecai could dither, debate, and ponder for ages, but when he made his mind up on something, he turned into an altogether different creature.

The quiet philosopher had vanished, and the frenzied madman had appeared. Worse, this time it wasn't just the usual one, the madman who locked himself in his workshop for days on end, pursuing strange projects. No, this one was telling everyone to prepare for war.

He had issued orders like a battlefield commander, with no patience for debate or dissension. She had put up with such from him in the past, but usually it had been at times when it seemed warranted. Today there had been no warning, no foreshadowing, no anticipation of chaos or disaster. They had had some shocks recently, including the unexpected attack by the Ungol, but Penny hadn't expected to be rushing about tonight, preparing for unseen enemies.

No. She had expected a warm cup of tea, some conversation, and some snuggling with Humphrey.

As if he could read her mind, the half-grown puppy beside her began barking again. Humphrey had picked up on the excitement immediately, and he had been dashing about and occasionally jumping, tongue out, ever since Mort had destroyed the evening's peace.

"Hush!" she snapped at the dog. Humphrey yelped and then ran to jump around Alyssa, still hoping to be included in whatever game all the humans were up to.

Frowning, Penny scratched ineffectively at her stump. She was clad once more in a heavy gambeson with her enchanted mail over it. Both had been mended and altered to eliminate the unnecessary left sleeve, but it still itched. Her only solace was that she'd had it washed before being altered, so for once the smell wasn't as bad as usual.

Unfortunately, the new armor that Mordecai had been talking about for the past week still wasn't ready, and neither was the arm he had been crafting. It was supposed to be a surprise, but she hadn't had much trouble figuring it out. Clever as he was, Mort was an open book to her.

"Shouldn't we be staying here?" asked Alyssa, for perhaps the second time. "It's probably safer."

"This place is no longer a secret, as you well know," answered Penny harshly, causing Alyssa to lower her eyes.

Less than a year ago, the younger woman had led enemies to their hidden mountain home to kidnap Irene. She had been largely vindicated of her crime, but her service to the Illeniel family was part of the punishment that had been handed down to her. Penny liked the girl, and ordinarily she wouldn't have snapped at her, but the stress was making her feel waspish.

She didn't apologize, but she softened her tone for the next remark. "Besides, Irene is the only wizard left, and she needs to be in the keep in order to operate the castle defenses if there really is an attack. If my daughter is there, then I will be there."

Less than an hour later, they were ensconced in the family quarters within the keep, a place they almost never really slept. Lady Rose and Elise were with them, seeming determined to keep some sort of all-night vigil.

The castle guard had been notified and at least half the men were on duty, patrolling the walls and taking defensive stations throughout the castle. The town gates were closed, as was the castle gate. Even the portcullis had been lowered.

Rose looked at her over the rim of her latest cup of tea. "Do you really intend to wear that all night, dear?"

She was referring to Penny's mail, of course. Mort's mother answered before she could respond herself. "Of course she does!" said Meredith supportively. "My daughter takes her duty very seriously."

Meredith, being a commoner by birth and upbringing, had very different views on the matter than Lady Rose. As mothers-in-law went, Penny couldn't say she always agreed with Meredith either, but the woman was always in her corner, right or wrong.

"I didn't mean to sound critical, Meredith," said Rose placatingly. "I just worry she won't be able to rest."

"It isn't as if any of us will be sleeping tonight anyway," said Meredith snippily. "Not until the children get back."

By 'children,' Meredith was referring to the fact that with the exception of Irene, all her grandchildren, along with Gram, were elsewhere, facing who knew what sort of danger. Penny found herself smiling faintly. *Actually, she's probably referring to Mort too.* Meredith Eldridge was only slightly more protective of her grandchildren than she was her son.

"You make an excellent point, Meredith," said Elise, chiming in. "None of us will rest easy tonight."

Rose actually agreed with them, but her irritation had made her argumentative. It was a sign of her inner turmoil that she had put herself in a position to be verbally outmaneuvered to begin with. Rather than argue, she gave a small nod and took another sip of her tea.

"I still think it would be better for me to be with Irene," muttered Penny. Her daughter was spending the night in the control chamber, in order to respond if there was an actual attack.

"If anything happens, you're only a couple of flights of stairs and a short run from her side," said Elise. "Besides, Alyssa is with her."

"The girl is a formidable warrior," observed Rose.

That was certainly true, thought Penny. In fact, without armor and a sword in hand, she wasn't entirely sure she could defeat the young woman if she had to. Alyssa had been trained in the same style of combat as Cyhan and Gram. Though she didn't have a dragon-bond, the woman fought with almost supernatural skill. It was ironic that Irene's one-time kidnapper was now her bodyguard.

"Besides," continued Rose, "the most probable outcome for tonight is that we all lose sleep for nothing. In my experience, nothing ever happens when we expect it. Bad things always happen when you're relaxed and feeling secure." By the time she finished her remark, she realized how dark it sounded. "My apologies, I didn't mean to sound morbid."

Elise grinned wickedly at Rose while waving one hand at Penny. "My daughter-in-law is just as anxious and miserable as our armored Countess here." Then she turned to Meredith. "Would you like some wine? I don't think tea is going to be sufficient for us this evening."

Penny gaped at the two old women. "You would drink when there may be an impending attack?"

Meredith laughed. "I'm eighty now. What would I do if there was an attack? I'd rather be useless and tipsy than useless and cranky." Then she smiled. "Thank you, Elise, I think I could stand to have a glass."

* * *

Penny hadn't expected to fall asleep, but when her eyes flew open she realized she must have. Her eyes darted around, finding Rose sitting upright across from her, alarm on her features. "What is it?" said Penny, unsure of what had awakened her.

Both of them were on their feet, rushing toward the window, when a boom so deep it was more felt than heard shook them. "I think that's what woke us," offered Rose. They looked out the window in time to see the outer wall of the castle collapse. Then they felt the floor shake beneath them.

"Take them to the cottage!" yelled Penny, running for the door. By 'them,' she was referring to Elise and Meredith, who had retired earlier. To reach the mountain cottage, they merely needed to leave the apartment and return by the same door, activating the portal. That hadn't been the plan, of course, but Penny's feet had already communicated the fact that the castle was far from safe.

Rose, ever quick to react, was already hurrying to fetch the two elderly women.

Penny ran down the castle hallway, her feet driving her so quickly that she was forced to run two steps up the wall when she reached the end and had to turn. Then she was in the stairwell. Ignoring the steps, she took each flight in a single bound. The observer at the back of her mind commented dryly, *You're going to regret that tomorrow when your body figures out what you've done.* She ignored the thought. For now she felt nothing.

She was almost to the bottom floor when the wall to her right exploded into a cloud of dust. Stone shards ripped through the air, and she felt a stinging pain on her face. Then the walls above began to slide down, sagging now that their support was gone. Stumbling, she made her way through the rubble, moving as quickly as possible, for it seemed the entire stairway might soon collapse. She emerged into a hallway that was now less of a corridor than it was a bizarrely designed, partially enclosed room. The wall on one side had fallen and large sections of the ceiling were now part of a floor that was half-buried by stone blocks, wood planks, and broken support timbers.

People stumbled through the dust, crying and yelling, lost in the chaos. Penny added her own voice, yelling for all she was worth, "Irene!"

She could see the control chamber now, though it had been hidden. One of the walls had fallen away, leaving it exposed. There was no one within, though she ran to it anyway, to make certain her daughter wasn't trapped beneath something. It was empty. A blue light stood out, glowing on the central pedestal.

She activated the shield, Penny realized. *But where is she now?*

Another thudding boom sounded, and Penny saw one of the castle servers vanish as a stone wall behind him disintegrated. People were screaming from all sides. Penny knew she needed to take charge, but it was impossible. She needed to know where the enemy was, where safety was, and where her people were. She knew none of that. Castle Cameron was coming down around her.

Outside. I have to be able to see. But fear for her daughter stopped her. Where was Irene?

Then she heard men yelling from what she thought must be the castle yard. A strange, high-pitched whine grew and then became a roar. The yells of her guardsmen turned into screams. With no better options, Penny ran toward their cries, leaping over broken stone and piles of timber. Seconds later, she found herself outside the walls of the keep, staring at a scene from a nightmare.

Guardsmen lay everywhere, some moaning and others simply dead. The bailey was still intact, the gates closed, but the east wall on one side of it was largely gone. The shield barrier, normally invisible to ordinary eyes, flashed periodically as something powerful assaulted it.

But the worst was inside already. Two large, metal monstrosities stood in the center of the yard. Each stood on three metal legs, and while they didn't appear to have heads, they each had two menacing arms. The roaring noise came from these. One arm on each of them was a blur, as though it was spinning, while spitting flashes of light.

Their torsos rotated slowly in a circle as they targeted the remaining guards, who were trying to find safe cover. Most were already down.

Penny had never seen such things before, but she knew of them from Moira's story of the battle outside of Dunbar. She even had a name for them, from Matthew's journey to Karen's world: 'tortus.' Strictly speaking, they weren't alive, they were military machines, designed for one purpose.

One of them was strafing the inside of the walls, but the other was firing more deliberately on an unmoving target. Penny's eyes followed, and she spotted two figures huddled against one of the surviving walls of the main keep, Irene and Alyssa.

Light and sparks flashed around them, and her daughter had a look of furious intensity as she focused on whatever it was that protected them.

People often ascribe emotions or thoughts to such moments of stress or danger, but the truth is both simpler, and more complicated. The body acts so quickly that the conscious mind of thought and experience is left behind, merely a witness to the subliminal decisions of the heart. They analyze their actions afterward, within seconds, giving words and meanings to their doings, but the reality of such moments is immediate and without verbal description.

Penny flew across the courtyard at a speed that would have been impossible if she had consciously attempted it. Simply thinking of it would have made the coordination required unattainable, but Penny didn't think. She launched herself, a missile of flesh and blood, across the intervening space between her and the thing attacking her youngest child.

At the end she leapt, turning her body, cat-like in the air, to land feet first against the tortus's metal torso, while simultaneously driving her sword point-first into the whirling blur of its weapon. The hilt was wrenched from her grasp as the machine's weapon exploded into deadly fragments of steel and fire.

Penny was sliding downward, for there was nowhere to stand. She scrabbled for purchase, with both her living arm and the phantom arm that her body continually forgot was gone. Her right hand caught the tortus's second arm, the one bearing what she had been told was the machine's heavier weapon.

Still sliding down, she gripped the other weapon fiercely, her legs flailing beneath her. The large, box-like weapon was beginning to hum as it charged up, its torso rotating to bring it in line with Irene and Alyssa. The movement brought Penny's legs into contact with one of the thing's three legs and without thinking she wrapped her own around it.

Using her arm and legs, her slender body strained to arrest its motion, to keep the point from lining up with her daughter. Despite her awkward leverage, for a second, she achieved a stalemate. Her muscles were taut, and somewhere, deep in her chest she felt a pop, followed by searing pain. The tortus began to move again, slowly, but Penny continued to struggle.

And then the second tortus opened fire again, not at the wall this time, but at the woman struggling with its complement. Penny's world flashed red as hammer blows too fast to separate slammed into her back and legs. For a moment, her vision went black. She felt herself sliding as the tortus's main weapon lined up on its target.

The movement took her out of the other machine's line of fire, and after a second her vision returned. The arm she held onto, the weapon she was still pushing against, was already pointed at Irene and Alyssa. The humming within it had changed to a chilling whine, and she knew it was about to fire.

Screaming her rage and defiance, Penny reversed her push, pulling on the arm instead, wrenching it toward the other tortus. A heavy 'clack' sounded from the weapon, and the other machine exploded, the force of the blast slamming her back into the tortus she was wrestling with.

Penny fought to hang on. It wasn't over. The enemy machine still had its main—and most devastating—weapon left, the one she was still gripping. But her body began to fail, her hand growing weak. Tears of frustration ran from her eyes as she tried desperately to hold on.

Then she was falling. More pain blinded her as she struck the ground, insulting bones that were already broken. When she looked up once more, she saw one of the tortus's legs descending. It had taken the simplest course. It would use its multi-ton weight to crush her.

She tried to roll, but her body was no longer responding.

And then the tortus rocked backward as a stone the size of a mule slammed into it. The machine staggered, trying to maintain its balance, but the stone returned, smashing into it once more. It fell.

Twisting her neck to the side, Penny could see Irene standing closer now. Alyssa leaned against the slender girl, her arm draped across Irene's shoulder. But Irene didn't seem to notice the other woman's weight. She stood ramrod straight, her eyes blazing as she continued to batter the remaining tortus with the giant stone. Behind the two women, the side of the keep was shuddering as thousands of stone blocks surrendered to gravity without Irene's power to support them any longer.

But Irene no longer cared. Her only focus was the metal colossus in front of her. She kept battering it until the stone she was using shattered, and then she pulled more from the rubble behind her. These were smaller blocks, so she whipped them at it like an angry flock of birds.

They were too small to do significant damage, but Irene did not relent, and when the tortus began trying to regain its footing, she pulled some of the ground away, causing it to sink. It was helpless now, its last weapon ruined, while its body was hopelessly mired in the torn earth.

Irene wasn't done, however. Releasing the stones, she tried fire, and when that failed to produce results, she began slamming the downed tortus with blows of pure force, hammering it until its outer shell began to bend and deform under her assault.

Penny could hear her daughter's voice, hoarse from screaming, but she could make out the words. "Don't you dare touch her!"

Penny's world faded, and soon all she knew was a throbbing pain, accompanied by the sounds of Irene's fury as she pounded the tortus. When silence arrived, she thought perhaps she had passed out, but then she felt soft hands on her.

"Mom! Wake up! Please!"

CHAPTER 36

By the time Castle Cameron came into view, the dawn was over and it was well and truly morning, and I was feeling mostly human once more. The sky was clear, so my first sight of it was from more than ten miles away, too far to see much.

At five miles, I could tell something had happened, and I used a neat trick I had learned years back—compressing the air in front of me into a lens to magnify my view. Part of the castle's outer wall was down, the keep was half demolished, and there was smoke rising from several farms nearby.

Washbrook itself appeared intact.

A glint of sunlight on metal alerted me to the fact that there was something in the wide field that surrounded the castle. Focusing, I spotted the unmistakable form of a tortus, much like the ones I had seen near Halam, in Dunbar.

But those had been badly damaged, rendered inoperative by the efforts of Gram and Moira. This one was fully functional. As I watched, I saw its upper portion turn and one of its appendages came up. It was aiming—at me.

My initial thought was that it was ludicrous. I was still roughly five miles distant and flying at a good clip. It couldn't possibly hit me. But then again, Gary had been very emphatic when we had questioned him about these things and their weapons. *What did he call it?* I replayed the conversation in my head until the term emerged, *a railgun.* Gary had said they fired projectiles at many times the speed of sound, and that they were deadly accurate.

I changed direction, heading for the ground, and very nearly lost control of my flight. Sudden changes weren't easy when flying at significant speed, but I managed to regain control of myself. I felt something tear through the air above me, moving too fast even for my magesight to register it. A loud crack echoed in my ears, announcing its passing a split second after the fact.

Reducing my speed even further, I continued toward the ground, adding what I hoped was an unpredictable series of lateral movements. I needed to get out of its line of sight before it turned me into a soggy mess of ruined flesh and bloody rain falling toward the earth. The next few seconds were tense, but I was below the tree line before it could fire again.

I didn't land, though. Instead I increased my speed, flying just a few feet above the ground. Normally, flying close to the ground was less effort, but not at this velocity. At this speed, I ran the risk of smashing myself into jelly with the slightest mistake. I had focused the shield around me into the shape of a spear, imbuing it with all the power I could manage, but that was just to protect myself from the flow of air. If I actually made contact with anything solid, I had no doubt it would kill me and almost certainly destroy whatever I hit.

With one hand, I reached into my belt pouch and drew out one of my iron bombs. They were simple iron spheres, enchanted and packed with as much power as they could contain without spontaneously detonating. They were one of my oldest weapons, and over the years they had been useful on numerous occasions. Because of their explosive nature, they were too dangerous to carry on my person, but the pouch I wore was actually a type of portal that connected to a chest stored in the mountains.

I was following the road now, ten feet above the surface, and the wake of my passage kicked up clouds of dust and shook the trees behind me. I had to increase my altitude as I reached the turn that would take me toward Cameron, since it was simply impossible to make such a turn at my current velocity. I soared over the trees and curved to the left, catching a glimpse of the castle and the tortus briefly before I was able to complete the turn and drop back down to follow the lane that led homeward.

There was more than one tortus. I had spotted three as I made my turn. Reaching into my pouch, I took out two more iron spheres so I could adjust my plan. Encasing each iron bomb in its own small, arrow-like shield, I extended them outward, pushing them through my own shield. Just the force of the air would set them off if I didn't keep them protected, for I was moving faster than the speed of sound.

Then the trees were gone, and the castle loomed before me. One of the machines I had spotted was directly ahead. I kept one of my iron spheres on a direct line toward it as I adjusted my own path upward and to the right.

Almost too late, I realized the shield barrier around the castle was active. I was forced to use everything I had to make my upward turn sharper, otherwise I'd obliterate myself against it. I had only been planning to skim above the castle walls.

The first tortus disintegrated in a showy conflagration of smoke and flame as my body screamed through the air overhead, barely managing to avoid the shield barrier. The other two were firing at me with their spinning guns, but my appearance was too sudden for them to aim accurately. Taking advantage of the active shield around the castle I turned my flight into a looping turn that took me out of their line of fire, flying behind the castle and Washbrook in a long elliptical.

That gave me time to examine the damage, and I wasn't pleased. The husks of two more tortuses lay dead in the castle courtyard, but it was apparent they had exacted a terrible toll before they were destroyed. Half of the main keep had collapsed, and the castle wall to the east of the bailey was nothing but rubble. Bodies were everywhere, though I could see people working steadily to line them up in the yard.

As I made my circular pass around the castle, I reduced my speed. I couldn't afford to make a mistake and get myself killed, and I was already beginning to tire. The stress of maintaining such a powerful shield and flying at that rate took a lot of power. When I completed my loop and came back around, I was still moving fast, but it was a speed I could survive, something close to the speed of a stooping falcon.

I sent my two iron bombs ahead of me as the tortuses opened fire on me. The force of their barrage was too much for me and I was forced to land, braking as hard as I could to avoid doing their work for them. One of the iron bombs was struck in mid-air, exploding before it could reach its target, but the other made it.

Lacking the insane speed of my first attack, it didn't destroy the tortus it hit, but the explosion knocked the machine sideways and did some visible damage to its outer shell. Its companion was slightly closer to me, less than a hundred yards away, but still too far for me to do very much to it directly with my magic.

That was fine for the tortus, though. It continued to hammer me with fire from its spinning gun. *What did Gary call it? A gatling gun.* The attack was so intense it was hard to maintain my shield, and I was almost at the end of my strength.

Opening my mind slightly, I called on the earth, feeling its power surge into me, from my feet upward, and then I did something unusual—for me, at least. I used it to strengthen my body, increasing my speed and physical power. It wasn't something I liked, but my fight with Tyrion had been educational, so I had done some practicing.

Reinforcing my shield, I ran toward the tortus, chanting in Lycian. The spell I used was the same one I often used to make my hands impervious to fire when dealing with metal in the forge, but this time I included my entire body.

There are good reasons not to do that under normal circumstances. The spell essentially caused the flesh to become almost entirely non-conductive to heat, but the skin still radiated heat outward. If done to the entire body, the limbs could slowly freeze while the body's core grew increasingly hot. In short, user beware, proceed with caution.

A minute or two wouldn't kill me, though. I raced toward the tortus, altering my personal shield as I ran, until it glowed with an intense heat that, thankfully, I couldn't feel.

It stopped firing, and its torso rotated, bringing its railgun in line with me. *Shit!* I swore silently. I was still thirty yards away, and from what Moira had described, no shield I could create would be enough to save me if it fired.

I zigged to one side, but the weapon tracked me perfectly, so I flung out my power and grappled it directly, forcing it out of line with my body just before it fired. Seconds later I had reached it.

Matthew and Moira had both told me they were all but invulnerable to ordinary blasts of flame and even some focused lines of fire, but I was going to put that to the test. The shield around my body was glowing an intense white, and my footsteps had left burning patches of grass behind me.

Jumping forward, I gripped one of its massive metal legs in my hands. At the moment, I was strong enough to lift it slightly, forcing the tortus to adjust its other legs to maintain balance. But other than that, nothing happened. If the machine had been made of iron or steel it would have begun to smolder and melt beneath my touch already. *What the hell is this thing made of?*

Drawing on the earth, I pumped more heat into my shield, with the exception of the part covering my head, otherwise the glare would have made it impossible to see. Squeezing, I felt the metal under my hands begin to buckle. It collapsed, bent and useless long before I could melt through it. Shifting my stance, I pushed at the edge of the platform that supported its upper portion and tipped it over. Then I pressed myself against its underside and began to burn my way through.

What felt like an eternity passed before the metal began to sag slightly and I was able to dig my fingers in a little, gaining a grip on the smooth surface. Using my now considerable strength, I pulled at it, as though trying to tear the metal apart with brute force.

Despite the searing temperature and my strength, I failed. Mostly. Partly, I was hampered by the thing's thrashing legs, forcing me to continually wrestle with it to keep it in place. All I had accomplished was to create a small crack in its under-plate.

My first instinct was to reach into my pouch and get more of my iron bombs, to shove them through the small opening, but I stopped myself a second later. *If I touch them as I am currently, there won't be enough left of me to scrape into a slop bucket.* I felt like an idiot.

Stupid never dies, I reminded myself, *but I'm really putting that motto to the test.* My entire strategy had been stupid, using fire and heat when I had already been warned they were almost useless. Penny must have rubbed off on me over the years. I was being more stubborn than I was smart.

I had an opening, though, so I sent a slender lance of fire into it, probing its interior until smoke began to billow outward. An ominous crackle and sizzling white sparks shot out, causing me to back away. Then I ran, cursing my own idiocy. *I really am as dumb as I look.* A battering ram of air struck my back and tossed me like a leaf through the air as the tortus exploded.

I wound up lying flat on the ground, twenty yards away. Miraculously, my shield had weathered the blast and I had managed the landing without breaking any bones, at least as far as I could tell.

My shield was no longer glowing—I had given up wasting my energy on that fruitless endeavor—but it began to shudder as the other tortus, which had been circling around its fallen friend, opened fire. Since I hadn't yet anchored myself, my body began sliding across the green turf. The fight had started so well, but now I was getting annoyed.

It was time to switch tactics. I had played around enough, trying things I had been warned wouldn't work well. Matthew and Moira had both recommended lightning against these things, so I stretched out one hand toward the oncoming machine and sent forth a thundering stroke of actinic blue.

The hammering assault on my shield stopped, but the tortus looked fine. Its weapon spun down and the other one, the railgun, began rotating into position. It was twenty yards away and I didn't think it would miss.

For a second, I wished I'd had the forethought to take out my staff earlier. Using it as a rune channel would have made my lightning much more effective. Part of the reason I disliked using lightning was that it was so difficult to control. Unlike fire or pure force, it tended to branch and seek other directions than the user intended for it to take. But it was too late to try and pull my staff out now. Drawing a six-foot length of wood from a belt pouch was an awkward enterprise under normal conditions; trying to do so now would just make me a stationary target.

So I used an old trick. I drove my will into the ground, flinging a large mass of soil into the air and whipping it into a dirty brown cloud that obscured the space between and around us. Then I got to my feet and leapt into the air. The tortus fired at some point, but the confusion was enough that it failed to hit me.

I had often heard Cyhan warn Penny about jumping during combat, since it robbed the person in the air of their ability to dodge, but that wasn't a rule that really applied to me. Off the ground, I was more mobile than I was on it, and my magesight enabled me to see the tortus just as easily as I could have if the dirt cloud hadn't been in the air. Grasping the wind with my power, I guided myself down to hover directly above the tortus.

And then I proceeded to slam successive bolts of pure electric force into it. It continued to move without trouble after the first two or three, raising its railgun toward me, but by the fourth strike it started to twitch. I didn't stop until it was shaking and smoking, gradually raising my elevation in case this one decided to explode as well.

It didn't, which I couldn't help but feel was slightly anticlimactic after all the effort I had put into it. *Oh well.*

Once it had stopped moving entirely, I glided toward the castle, setting down softly just twenty feet from the shield barrier where the wall had collapsed. A line of people, mostly guardsmen, stood just inside the shield. My fight had attracted a crowd of onlookers. I scanned the crowd, looking for two faces in particular, Penny and Irene.

I saw neither, and my chest tightened. The destruction of the main keep had my gut twisted into knots. Where were they? Had they retreated to our mountain home? Were they safe? I didn't want to think about the worst case.

No, Irene must be alive at least. Someone activated the shield barrier. I spotted Carl Draper at the front of the crowd and I called to him through the shield, "Captain Draper! Tell Irene to open the shield for me."

He moved as close as he could, since the shield muffled sounds slightly. "No one can open it, my lord. We're trapped inside."

"That's ridiculous!" I protested. "Where is my wife? Where is my daughter?"

The guard captain's eyes drifted downward to stare at the ground.

CHAPTER 37

No, *no, no, no, it can't be!* I struggled to restrain myself. I wanted to pound the shield down, but powered by the God-Stone, it was impervious to anything I could do.

"Lady Irene is tending to the Countess in the barracks," said Captain Draper after a moment.

All the air left my lungs in an explosive sigh of relief. I had been afraid of the worst.

"Your wife was badly wounded in the attack, my lord. I do not think she will survive," he added.

I had an entirely different opinion on the matter, but I had to get inside first. "Why can't Irene lower the shield for me?"

"The control chamber was destroyed during the attack. She has no way to control the enchantment," explained the captain.

"Oh, I see," I said, nodding. Well, there was more than one way to skin a cat. Reaching into one of my pouches, I pulled out the cloth stencil for a teleport circle and laid it on the ground. With my aythar I burned a temporary circle into the soil and then picked up the cloth and folded it, putting it back in my pouch. With my finger, I burned a new key into the empty section of the circle and then stepped into it. Seconds later, I was inside the transfer house in the castle yard.

There was no one there, and when I stepped out, I saw that the rest of the people in the yard were working steadily. Some moved and organized bodies, while others cleared away rubble and stone from the courtyard. They were surprisingly calm.

Captain Draper reached me a moment later, as I marched toward the building that housed the barracks. "Did you organize all this?" I asked him, impressed by the degree of order they had achieved so soon after such an enormous disaster.

"In part, my lord, as is my duty," said the captain. "But I credit most of it to Lady Irene's orders. She has been a steady rock for us since the attack."

My chest swelled with pride at his words. "Give me a quick summary of what happened," I ordered.

"They attacked in the night," began the captain. "The outer wall was down, and part of the keep was destroyed within seconds. The shield barrier came on moments later, but two of those iron monsters were already inside. They cut our men to ribbons and continued the bombardment of the keep. Everyone inside would probably have died if it weren't for your daughter."

"What did she do?" I asked, stopping. We were at the door to the barracks, but I wanted to hear the rest before entering.

"According to Alyssa, she held the keep up. I don't really how your magic works, of course, but the walls were collapsing and then they just stopped. She kept it together for a good long while, until most of the people inside had managed to get out. Those things,"—he pointed at the damaged remains of the two tortuses—"were attacking her the entire time. Then, the Countess got here and went after them like a rabid wolf. She managed to injure one and destroy the other. Lady Irene beat the wounded one to death with a rock from what I'm told. I didn't see that part." Draper paused before continuing, "But your wife, she was hurt quite badly."

My throat constricted, and I had trouble choking out a response. "Thank you, Captain. Return to your duties. I will check on her." Then I opened the door and stepped inside the barracks.

The interior was well lit, with lanterns glowing. Most of the beds held wounded men, the survivors. As I had seen, the dead were out in the yard. My youngest daughter was kneeling beside one of the injured, her eyes closed as she turned her attention to things that couldn't be seen with her eyes.

She had almost certainly sensed my entry, but her focus didn't waver. I couldn't fault her dedication, though. Healing was delicate work and she had never had any training in it. Irene was still very new to her power.

Of course, I wanted to interrupt her. I was desperate to see Penny, but rather than spoil her effort, I examined the nearest wounded soldier with my magesight. He had suffered several nasty wounds, and though there was considerably more that could be done to assist him, I was proud of what I found. The skin had been sealed and while his ribs were still broken, at least one damaged blood vessel had mended. *With this many, she didn't have a lot of time to spare,* I figured.

Still, I was impressed that she had learned the trick for sealing skin so quickly. Irene had witnessed a lot of my discussions with her older siblings on the topic of wound healing, but she had never been able to see what we were doing directly, much less practice it. She had done well with little more than the information gleaned from those lectures.

Then I noticed the patient on the next bed over, Alyssa. She was asleep, but a quick sweep of her body told me she had a broken leg and extensive bruising. "Father?" came Irene's voice from behind me.

I turned to look at her, and it tore at my heart to see her face. In less than twelve hours, my youngest's face had gone from carefree to worn and haunted. She had been shouldering a tremendous burden by herself, and now her strong veneer was beginning to crack. "I'm so sorry—," she added.

I wanted to hug her, to let her cry it out—to do what fathers are supposed to do—make everything better, but I needed her strength still. "Don't be sorry," I replied. "You did more than anyone could expect. Bear it a while longer."

Her lip quivered a second, but then it firmed up and I embraced her. She squeezed me tightly and spoke into my chest, "But Mom…"

I cut her off before the words could undo her. "Take me to her."

Penny was in Captain Draper's private room, covered by a thick wool blanket. Her armor and clothing had been removed, and my magesight found no breaks or recent cuts to her skin. I glanced ruefully at the enchanted mail that lay across the nearby chair. It had done its job—nothing had penetrated—but once again, that hadn't been sufficient. My wife lay on her belly, and when I drew the blanket back I hissed at the sight. Most of the visible skin was black or red; massive hematomas had formed beneath the skin. She looked as though someone had tied her down and beaten her with a small sledge.

Beneath the skin, things were worse. Some of the vertebrae had been shattered and the ribs near them broken. Her kidneys were beyond help and all the other soft tissues were similarly ruined. If she had been conscious, she have would been in incredible pain, assuming she could feel anything. The damage to her spine meant she was likely paralyzed. It was a miracle she was still alive.

"I didn't know what to do," said Irene softly, her voice filled with guilt. "Can you…? You can heal her, right?"

My youngest was close to dissolving into tears, and I couldn't blame her. I felt the same, but I pushed those feelings down deep. Neither of us could afford to give in to our emotions, not yet. What should I say, though? *There's nothing you could have done,* I thought. *This is beyond anything normal wizardry can heal.* If it had been anyone else, I would have just told her it was hopeless and that the best thing to do would be to ease their passing.

But this wasn't anyone else. This was Penny. This was *my* Penny. I couldn't accept that answer, and if I said those words to Irene, neither of us would be able to do the things we needed to do. "She'll be fine," I said with a confidence I didn't feel. "Give me a few hours. I can fix this. Don't worry."

"Dad, this is my fault," said Irene.

"Shhh, don't blame yourself. This is life. None of us are perfect. If you start taking the blame for every tragic thing that happens, you'll never be able to move forward. Give me some time with her. Don't let anyone in until I open the door. Do you understand?"

My daughter nodded, blinking back more tears.

"You've done well. I couldn't be prouder of you," I added. "Go back out there and keep doing what you've done so far. Show them your strength. This is the burden we bear for the people we serve. Right now, it's just you and me, so you'll have to handle everything while I help your mom. Can you do that?"

Irene stood with her head bowed, struggling to contain it all. Her shoulders shook slightly, but then she lifted her face and rubbed her cheeks. "Yes, Father." Then she left, closing the door gently behind her.

I put the bar in place once the door closed, and then I used a quick spell to lock the latch in place as well. I didn't want any interruptions. With a few more words and a bit of aythar, I put a privacy ward around the room to prevent Irene or any of my other children, should they return, from seeing what I was doing.

Moving to the bedside, I removed the blanket and then used my power to gently lift Penny's body, sliding it to one side, making enough room for me to lie beside her. As careful as I was, she still felt it, and a low moan rose from her lips. Her eyes opened, fixing on me, piercing my heart.

She tried to speak, but only managed a few hoarse grunts.

"Don't try to talk," I told her, trying to keep my face calm. I was removing my own clothes. Strictly speaking, neither of us needed to be nude, but it simplified things slightly. After a few minutes, I finished and climbed carefully into the bed next to her. With our faces only inches apart, I gazed into the warm, brown depths of her eyes. "I should have been here," I said. "But you did the impossible without me, as usual. You're an incredible woman, Penny. I hope you know how much I love you." Then I leaned forward and kissed her lips, linking our minds as we touched.

Is Irene alright?

I should have known her first thought would be for her children. The knowledge sent a feeling of warmth through me. *She's fine,* I told her. *A little scared, but she has your strength. She's taking care of things while I take care of you.*

What about the others? she asked.

They haven't returned yet, but I believe they'll be alright, I answered. I would have lied, but doing so while directly linked wasn't easy, so I stuck to the truth. *You should be more worried about yourself.*

Am I dying? Despite her courage, I could feel the faint undercurrent of fear at the thought. It wasn't a fear of oblivion, though, but rather the fear of being separated from her loved ones.

Yes, I answered. *But we can fix this. Do you trust me?*

No. I frowned mentally, but then she added, *I trust you will do whatever it takes for my sake. I don't trust that you won't hurt yourself trying.*

Well, this will be risky. This is what I talked to you about before, a way to completely heal your body. Knowing how you felt I had decided not to do it, which is why I worked so hard to make that artificial arm for you, but now this is the only way.

Then don't do it, let me go, she told me emphatically.

I can't do that.

Yes, you can. I love you, Mort, but our children depend on you. This is a selfish risk.

Sorry, I replied. *I'm selfish, I'll admit it. I can't live without you, and our children need you as much or more than they do me.*

Mordecai!

I flinched inwardly at the strength of her disapproval, but I went on. *Listen, this isn't as bad as it sounds. You'll be the one making the decisions. So I need to explain as much as I can before I hand the reins over.*

What does that mean?

Our consciousnesses will merge, and then we will become you. My awareness will vanish temporarily, since only you can restore your body this way. You'll be the one in control, but you'll have my power.

I don't know how to use it! This isn't going to work, Mort. It's foolish, she replied with rising panic in her thoughts.

Stay calm, I replied. *It's not a matter of knowledge. This isn't like wizardry. It's more instinctive. I'll explain the main points, so you'll understand what you see and what to do.*

And if I refuse?

You can't, I told her stubbornly. *Once I hand over control you can do whatever you want, but if you don't take care of things, one or both of us will die.*

This isn't fair.

It never is, I replied. *Once we merge, you'll feel as though you're falling asleep, but when you wake up you will be alone, in a bed with two bodies, yours and mine. They're both alive, for now, and you'll see something like a flame within each of them. That's called the 'aystrylin.' It's the seat of life. In a sense, it's your soul, and it has to keep burning, or else you'll die. The power you'll be using will come from mine, but you need to keep your awareness inside your own body.*

Imagine yourself as you were, I continued, *as you were before you were hurt. You'll be able to re-imagine your body, and if you're good enough, you can remember the arm you lost too. Once that's finished, you will have to think of me. Release the power and think of me. This will be the hardest part, because it will require you to think of yourself becoming me while at the same time releasing your link to my body. If you do it right, we'll both wake up.*

She was afraid, and I couldn't blame her. *And if I do it wrong?*

Then one of us won't wake up, probably me. You'll be alone with a dead body in the bed next to you. On the plus side, you'd also be a pretty badass wizard and archmage.

I don't want to do this! she protested.

I love you, I sent, and then I opened my mind, listening to the universe. The wind thrummed in the sky above, the earth thumped like a giant drum deep below, and beside me, a beautiful woman slowly died. I listened to her flesh, and I dreamed of her heart, the greatest gift I had ever received in this world. Softly—I faded away.

CHAPTER 38

Penny woke. Or perhaps she dreamed; she wasn't really sure. The world was strange and new, and much of what she saw was hard to understand. It felt as though she was floating, suspended in a cloud. Her vision extended in every direction, filling her mind with the contents of the entire room.

What held her attention, however, were the two bodies that lay below her, Mordecai's and her own. As he had said, both contained a burning spark, but the similarities ended there.

The bodies, of course, were very different. His was heavier, more muscular, and in near perfect health, while hers was on the verge of death. What disturbed her was the flames within each of them. While Mort's burned like a blaze, with searing intensity, hers was a tiny ember, about to go out.

I don't have much time, she thought. Pushing her fear aside, she got to work. With a thought, she flowed into her body, and then she set about building the mental image she desired.

When Mordecai had described it, she had thought it would be impossible, but her mental imagery was different now. She couldn't explain it in words, but her mind was able to create visions that were so finely detailed that it surprised her. *Is this what it's like for him?* she wondered. She knew from past discussions that her husband's mind worked a little differently from most. But she hadn't expected it to be like this.

Everything is so sharp, so clear. For a moment she was envious. What would it be like to live with such vivid imagery inside your head every day? *Wait, does this mean I'm me, or am I him?*

She felt like herself, but the difference in her mindscape was an obvious reminder. *This is so strange. I know I'm myself, and yet I must have been him before. She* pushed those thoughts aside. *Remember my body, the body I had—then make it real.*

The flesh blurred, flowing into its old shape. Penny marveled at how simple it had been. *So much power, and he lives with this every day. I'd probably go mad.* Then she withdrew, gazing down on their two bodies from a short distance above them.

As expected, her body seemed perfect, but the flame within was unchanged. It was dying. She had thought that might be because of the injuries, but obviously that wasn't the case. *Was this why he didn't want to do this? Was he afraid I would see how little is left?*

Somewhere, deep down, she felt the truth. Repairing her body had been nothing. It was her aystrylin that was the problem, and he hadn't known of a way to fix that. *I'm about to die anyway.* Once more she looked at his aystrylin, to compare them.

There was something wrong with his as well. It burned fiercely, but as she looked closer she found cracks, dark veins of something *other* between the filaments of living aythar. For all the power it represented, the seat of her husband's soul was sick. *Parts of it are foreign, grafted on by those strange dark roots.*

She was afraid of what it might represent. Was it a side-effect of his time as a shiggreth, or a result of his strange transformation during the fight with the Ungol? Penny had no way of knowing, but either way it didn't bode well for him. She spent some time studying it before eventually an idea came to her. *He's not going to like this, but then again, he didn't give me a choice either.*

Diving down, she filled her body again, sitting up and marveling at her perfect health. Stretching her left arm out, she examined her hand, fascinated by its perfection. She wished she could have longer to enjoy it. Penny got to her feet and picked up the blanket, wrapping it around her naked form. Then she went to the door.

With a thought, she removed the spell locking it, simultaneously dissolving the privacy ward that covered the room. Then she picked up the bar and opened it, stepping out into the barracks.

There were beds full of wounded men everywhere, but Penny had eyes for one person only, Irene. Her daughter had been bending over one of the men, but she straightened up to look at her mother immediately, her eyes growing wide.

"Mom!" exclaimed Irene, but then her expression changed to one of confusion. "Mom?"

"Come here," said Penny, and as soon as the girl was close enough she pulled her into a tight embrace. "I love you, Rennie. Always remember that."

"He really did it," mumbled Irene. "But how? And what's wrong with your aythar? It doesn't feel right. I thought you were Dad for a minute. Is this an illusion?"

Penny shook her head. "No, it's not an illusion. It's me, and yes, he did it. But there are problems. Your father is resting at the moment. Can you send for some writing materials?"

"Why?" asked Irene suspiciously.

And then Penny began to explain, holding nothing back. She needed Irene's full cooperation, otherwise things would be too difficult, and she didn't have that much time. Her youngest began crying after the first two sentences, and they were both a wretched mess of tears by the time she was done. Captain Draper appeared at some point, but neither of them paid any attention to him or the other onlookers.

Penny clung to her daughter as long as she could, but when the servant returned with what she had requested, she began to untangle herself.

"Mom, no! Please...," begged Irene, any pretense at dignity gone.

Penny's face twisted in pain, but she pushed her daughter away. "I'm sorry, sweetling. Forgive me." Returning to Captain Draper's room, she shut the door and replaced the bar and the privacy ward. Then she sat down and began to write.

It wasn't easy, and she had to use the sand to clean up not only the occasional inkblot, but spots made by her tears as well. She spent a half an hour on it before giving up. Not because she couldn't think of anything else to say, but because there was too much. She could never write it all, and she was growing tired. *My time is running out.*

Penny returned to the bed and lay down, covering herself as well as Mordecai's body with the blanket. She pressed her lips to his before withdrawing from her body. It was the most she could do. Then she focused on the tiny spark left within her chest and began to pull.

A searing pain unlike anything she could remember burned through her, but she refused to give up. In the end she thought she had succeeded, but she wasn't certain. Perhaps Mordecai would be able to tell. Penny turned her thoughts to her husband and her only regret was that she couldn't do more.

***

I woke to find Penny's cold lips against mine. Had we succeeded? With one hand I reached over to brush her hair from her face, and then I knew. She was cold, not just her lips, but everywhere. Her heart was no longer beating.

"No!" I screamed until I ran out of air, and then I gathered her lifeless body into my arms, cradling her against me. "Why? Why did you do this? If it had to be one of us, it should have been me."

I wanted to break something. No, I wanted to break everything. Rage filled me, and for a moment I fought to contain myself. In the end I did nothing but cry, sobbing like a child with a broken doll.

My life was over. Nothing had any meaning anymore. Paralyzed, I spent an hour refusing to leave the bed, holding the empty shell of the person that had been everything to me. Exhausted by my emotions, I wanted to sleep, but even that was denied to me.

Disgusted by my own helplessness, I left the bed, but after only a single step I felt myself drawn back. *How can I leave her?* I wanted to die, and if I'd had the courage I might have found a way to join her.

But Irene needed me. So did my other children. A lot of other people did too, but at that particular moment I didn't give a damn about anyone beyond my own family.

This can't be happening.

But it was. It had happened, and I was left to pick up the pieces. How would I explain this? How could they forgive me? *Can I even forgive myself?* From the corner of my eye, I spotted a sheet of parchment on the side table. I ignored it, staring back down at Penny, but it lingered in the back of my mind. It hadn't been there when I first entered the room.

Turning around, I went to the table and snatched it up, impatient to see what it was. My privacy ward was still around the room; the door was still locked and barred. No one else could have come in, so whatever it was, it must have been *her.* My eyes blurred as I began to read:

> *Mordecai,*
>
> *I am truly sorry. I hope you will forgive me, but I have done what I thought was for the best. I tried to do what you wanted, but I discovered the truth of my condition, something you probably knew but tried to ignore. Healthy body or not, I wasn't long for this world.*
>
> *I can only imagine that this secret must have tormented you. I wish you had told me, that we could have talked, but when I imagine our roles reversed I'm not sure if I would have been able to tell you. So, I'm letting you off the hook for that one. That means you owe me one, so you can't stay mad at me for this.*
>
> *I wish I could see you. Are you angry? Maybe. One way or another, I'm sure you're hurting. If it were possi-*

ble, I'd hold you and try my best to ease your pain. Since I can't, you're going to have find a way to go on. You probably don't think you can, but I know you better than you know yourself. If it can be done, you can do it. Our children are depending on you.

But please, don't just think of them. As wonderful a man as you are, I know how selfish you can be, especially when you're hurting. Don't forget about the people who depend on us. Do your best for them. Promise me you'll remain the man I fell in love with, the man who always worked hard to protect those who depend on him.

With a strangled cry, I dropped the paper, choking on the lump in my throat. "How can I do that without you?" Several minutes passed before I was able to pick the page up and begin reading again:

These have been the best years of my life. We created a wonderful family and my only regret is not being able to remain with you, and them, for a lot longer. Please apologize to Irene for me. She saw me before I left and I'm sure she's distraught. I told her what I was doing, but she may take her anger out on you. Give her time.

Matthew, Moira, and Conall, I don't know how they'll react. Tell them I love them. In the years ahead, you'll have to tell them that and more. Tell them all the things I would have. You know my heart as well as I do. I trust they'll do well. They have to. Besides, they have the best father in the world to guide them.

Don't be too hard on yourself. It's one of your worst habits. Don't beat yourself up. We have plenty of enemies still. Don't do their job for them. I'll make you regret it if you don't find some way to be happy.

There's a lot more to say, but there's no way to write it all. Don't feel bad for me. In a way, I'm the luckiest woman in the world. Most people die alone, but I'm not dying, not really. Call me selfish, but I couldn't let go of you, not completely. I like to think I'll live on, inside your heart.

One more time, from your stubborn wife: I love you.
Farewell,
Penelope

P.S. Don't forget to make sure someone lets Humphrey out for his walks. He's just starting to get better about his 'mistakes.' I don't want him to get back into bad habits.

That was just like her. The last word was a reminder to make sure I took care of the dog. I stared at the page. "Did you really think I'd forget about him?!" I was smiling through my tears, but the smile only lasted a brief time. The sadness went on.

I folded up the parchment, and after putting my clothes back on I tucked it into my pouch. Then I turned to the door. I had to go out and face the world.

CHAPTER 39

The look on Irene's face when I emerged broke my heart, not because of anything dramatic. It was the quiet resignation displayed there that tore at me, a brief flash of hope quickly replaced by hopeless acceptance when she saw me step out. She didn't ask any questions or offer condolences. Instead she pointed at the far wall. "The worst are on that side. I've done the best I could, but I don't know what more to do for them."

I nodded and headed over to check those patients. I thought Irene would follow me, but she started for the door leading out of the barracks. "Wait," I told her.

"I've been in here for hours," she replied without meeting my eyes. "I need to check on the men working outside."

"Observe me for the first few," I insisted. "As rough as it is, this is the best opportunity for you to learn, for the future."

She stared back silently for a few seconds and then gave a faint nod.

The men along the wall were in bad shape, but I found some solace by throwing myself into my work. I could feel my daughter's attention, and occasionally her aythar, as she followed along, watching me carefully as I tended to the injured.

She had already sealed their cuts and fused their broken bones, but these men needed more. Some of them had fragments of bone that needed to be removed. "The body will absorb them with time," I commented as I went, "but if there are too many it can cause strange bouts of hysteria after a day or two." For others, I drained blood and fluids that had accumulated within the body. "The reasoning is similar here. If the body has to break down all this blood, it will delay healing and can damage the kidneys."

In a few cases she had connected veins to arteries instead of with their own kind, causing problems with circulation. It was also apparent that she didn't have much of a grasp of anatomy, for she hadn't attempted to reconnect muscles and ligaments. I pointed those out and kept working. Irene took it all in without a word, and after an hour I let her leave.

When I finally left the barracks many hours later, I found a large field tent had been set up in the main courtyard. Bedrolls were laid out, and some of the men were resting, while others were laboring over cooking fires. Irene had been working steadily, excavating portions of the collapsed keep, primarily the storerooms where most of the food was kept.

We were cut off from Washbrook, since we couldn't open the shield gate that connected the town to the castle, and with most of the keep being unusable, the tent was necessary to give people shelter to sleep.

The damage to the keep had done more than ruin the control chamber, preventing us from lowering the shield barrier. It had destroyed our family apartments. That wasn't such a big loss, since we didn't actually live in them, but it had also destroyed the portal that led to our hidden mountain home.

The only way in or out of the castle was via the teleport circles in the transfer house. Washbrook had a similar problem, so it was obvious that my first priority was to reestablish control over the shield barrier.

Before I could start, Captain Draper approached me. "My lord, have you eaten yet?"

"I have no appetite," I answered woodenly.

"You must eat to—"

"How many did we lose?" I asked, cutting him off before he could lecture me.

The captain stood straighter as he answered me, "Forty-seven men and women. Twenty-eight of those were guardsmen, and nineteen were servants within the keep."

It was easy enough to tell he wasn't saying everything. "How many of those were children?"

After a pause, he replied, "Four, milord. Many more would have died if it weren't for your daughter delaying the collapse."

"I'll want a list of their names, once we're past the worst of this," I noted.

"If I may ask, milord, how are the wounded?" There was a strong undercurrent of anxiety in his question.

"Your son will recover," I said, answering the question he truly wanted to ask. "Perry's wounds were serious, but nothing that will limit him in the future. Give him a month or two and he will be back in the training yard, making fools out of his fellow soldiers again."

Captain Draper gave out a strange coughing grunt, turning his head to one side so I couldn't see his face. When he had composed himself again he spoke up, "Thank you, milord."

"Don't thank me," I said. "I'm told your son was very brave. He earned great honor for your family and I am grateful to still have him. You raised him well."

"I have another question, Your Excellency, and I apologize for the necessity." My captain of the guard hesitated.

"Spit it out, Carl," I prompted him.

"The Countess—what should I do about…"

Her body, I finished silently. *Dammit.* "Nothing. I'll handle it." I had been avoiding the thought since I had left the captain's room hours ago.

I left him there and returned to where I had left her. It wasn't fair to keep the captain's room occupied when beds were in short supply. She was still as I had left her, still and peaceful in her repose, with a blanket tucked over her as though she might simply be resting after a hard day.

With my power I levitated her body, and took her into the main barracks, trying to decide where she should go. Ordinarily I would have used one of the spare rooms in the keep for her, but that was obviously not possible. Finally I decided on the gatehouse.

Summoning a cloud to shield us from the eyes of my people, I walked her to the bailey and carried her up the stairs to one of the rooms above the gate and portcullis. Then I rearranged the blanket to cover her face and drew a set of crystalline cubes from my belt pouch. A touch of aythar and they flew apart, forming a rectangle around her floating form. Another touch and a surge of aythar activated the enchantment, encasing Penny's cold flesh in a field of golden light.

The stasis field kept her suspended there, unchanging, even after I had withdrawn my power. It would keep her, pure and uncorrupted, for as long as necessary, until my family had returned. Until we could lay her to rest.

It was some time before I was able to compose myself again, but when I had, I left to seek out what remained of the control chamber inside the ruins of the keep. There was work to be done and no one else to do it.

***

My work was undisturbed through the rest of the afternoon and late into the night. Ordinarily I would have expected a long succession of questions from Captain Draper and others, during such a crisis, but they never approached me. In the background of my mind I sensed Irene's aythar as she moved from place to place, answering the people's concerns and giving the orders that were necessary.

I finished reconstructing the control pedestal some time after midnight. Outside the courtyard had gone silent, for most of the men had gone to sleep earlier. Though it was cold, I didn't seek a blanket. Instead I voiced a spell and wrapped myself in a warm bubble of air before leaning against one of the intact walls. Alone, I stared into the darkness, wishing for sleep.

Eventually, my exhaustion, mental and physical, won out, and I descended into a deep slumber.

CHAPTER 40

I woke with the sun shining in my eyes. My spell for warmth had mostly faded, but I wasn't cold. At some point someone had tucked a bedroll between my back and the wall and covered me with a blanket. That someone was leaning against me, her head against my chest.

What would I do without you always looking out for me? I thought, forgetting for a moment that the person I was thinking of wasn't with me anymore.

My chest ached as I realized it was Irene beside me. I should have realized sooner; her hair was a lighter shade of brown and she was still considerably smaller than her mother. I fought to keep my chest from heaving; I didn't want to wake her. Irene had been working just as hard as I had and she needed her sleep.

She should be in a warm bed, not sleeping on hard stone next to me.

Careful to move slowly, I began to shift her head, trying to get up without waking her, but Irene's eyes popped open anyway. For a half a minute, we just stared at each other, and I could see the knowledge of the previous day filtering into her mind as the cloudy dreams of the night dissipated.

"I'm sorry." Those were her first words.

I squeezed her. "You don't have anything to be sorry for."

"She asked me not to be angry with you—yesterday. I know it wasn't your fault, but I couldn't do it. I couldn't face you."

"Shhh, it's fine," I said soothingly. "Neither of us was in any shape to talk. You did the most important things." After a brief pause, I added, "You spoke to her?"

"Mm hmm," said Irene, the pitch of her reply rising as she tried to keep from crying.

Neither of us could go on, so we sat silently for a short time, and then we stood up and brushed ourselves off. Words could come later, when they weren't so damned hard to say. The sun was up, and I could hear the sounds of people moving around outside. Another day of hard labor was already in progress.

I hadn't lowered the shield the night before because there hadn't been much point with everyone asleep. Plus, I had felt safer sleeping with it active. I remedied that now, testing the new links between the repaired pedestal and the enchantment. It worked, and I felt the subtle vibration of the shield barrier vanish.

With the barrier down, people began moving back and forth between the castle yard and Washbrook. The air was filled with the sounds of people talking loudly back and forth, as well as the grief-stricken cries of the families of those who had fallen. When I stepped into the courtyard, a silence fell and people began to gather around me, questions on their faces.

Irene, young as she was, stepped in front of me and opened her mouth, preparing to speak.

Trying to protect your father? I thought. She continued to surprise me. I placed a hand on her shoulder and shook my head. "You've done more than you should. Let me." Then I straightened to address the crowd. Among the faces, I could see Sir Cyhan and Chad Grayson watching me expectantly. I guessed that they had been trapped in Washbrook.

"We have been dealt a terrible wound. Many of you have lost friends and loved ones, and I know you have questions. I have some of the answers, as well as questions of my own. The monsters that attacked us are ancient and inhuman. The attack here was a response to my temerity in challenging them.

"I underestimated them, and our loved ones have paid the price for my hubris. Many died, among them my own dear wife, your countess. I cannot bring them back. Nothing I can say will fill the void in our hearts. Nothing will atone for this. The best I can offer you is my vow to bring justice to the enemy that has done this.

"I believe I have already eliminated the majority of the enemy's forces, but I have no doubt they will recover. To prevent a repeat of yesterday's tragedy, I will step up my efforts to make certain our homes, your homes, are safe. I will continue to hunt the remnants of our mutual foe.

"Beyond this I have nothing to offer you. I have made many mistakes over the years, and many have suffered for them, though this is perhaps the deepest wound yet. History has shown that I am a failure when it comes to protecting my own, but there is one thing I have never failed at.

"You will have vengeance," I finished.

A familiar voice, deep and masculine, answered from the crowd, "I like the sound of that, though I have serious doubts about your ability to make good on your words." People hurried to distance themselves from the speaker, and as the space grew I saw Tyrion standing amidst them.

He had sealed his aythar tightly, so that he appeared to be an ordinary man, but he released the block as he threw back the hood of his cloak. His presence fell like a shadow across the crowd, causing people to gasp as they subconsciously felt the weight of his aythar expand. The crowd parted as he walked toward me.

Tyrion Illeniel, the first wizard, stopped a few feet from me, a mocking sneer on his lips. "You speak of vengeance, but you're a child playing at a man's game. Why should these people trust you?"

Irene, already grief stricken and worn, reacted before I could reply. She stepped forward, and her hand flew up to slap the stranger insulting her father.

Tyrion batted her hand away and swept the back of his fist at her, but it stopped in mid swing, caught by my power.

"Touch my daughter and die," I warned him.

The air shimmered as he tested my strength, his will wrestling my own. Staring into his eyes, I felt my rage climbing, and the ground began to tremble as the earth reacted to our anger.

"You should teach your cub how to fight before she gets herself into trouble, baring her teeth at strangers," observed Tyrion, with a look of mad intensity in his eyes.

"An' you should learn when to shut yer fuckin' mouth," swore Chad behind him. The hunter stood a few feet away, his bow drawn and one of the enchanted war arrows nocked. Cyhan stood on Tyrion's other side, blade in hand, his body tense with suppressed violence.

My ancestor smiled. "I could kill both of you in the span of a heartbeat." Then he relaxed, releasing his power and ending our battle of wills.

"Try it," growled the ranger, but I held up my hand to forestall him before he could say more.

"I did not come here to fight," announced Tyrion.

"You announce your intentions poorly then," I remarked disdainfully. "The people have suffered a great hurt and our blood runs hot. Tempers are frayed. You should consider your manners if you wish to avoid a tragic *misunderstanding*."

Tyrion laughed, but there was nothing pleasant about the sound. "I could say the same to you. Learn to control your children, or there might be bloodshed when none is desired. Where are your other offspring? I am surprised your entire brood isn't here assaulting me."

The possible implications of his words made my blood run cold. *Does he know? Were they caught?* The wrong response could give them away, unless he had already caught them. "They are away, dealing with other matters," I said neutrally.

"Hopefully they are better trained than this one," mocked Tyrion, his eyes flicking toward Irene. "It would be terrible if something ill befell them."

"Is that a threat?" I asked tensely.

My ancestor's face changed, as confusion flickered across his features for a second. He had sensed the incipient violence behind my words and it surprised him. "No," he answered. "I came today to offer my help, and perhaps my advice as well, though I doubt you will heed it."

He doesn't know, I realized. If he had, he wouldn't have been surprised, and he wouldn't have made that last remark without following it with a more direct threat. "Help?" I questioned, letting my own surprise show.

Tyrion nodded. "With your enemy, the ancient enemy of the She'Har, the ones who attacked your home. You said you will exact vengeance on them. I have the means to make your wish come true."

My first impulse was to demand how he intended to do that, but as my anger cooled I realized we still had a rather large audience. "Let's talk about this elsewhere."

Tyrion arched one brow, glancing at my ruined castle. "Where do you suggest?"

"The one place left that can show you the proper hospitality," I answered. Then I turned to Cyhan. "Stay with Irene. Guard her life with your own. Until I return her word is law." Glancing at Chad, I added, "Come with me. You can help me introduce our guest to the best that the Muddy Pig has to offer."

Chad answered with a wicked grin. "Gladly. Finally, ye've recognized my true talents."

My ancestor frowned. "Muddy Pig?"

***

Fifteen minutes later, we were comfortably ensconced in the warm interior of Washbrook's finest (and indeed only) tavern. We sat at an old table in the corner of the main room, Chad's favorite spot, not that it mattered; the tavern was empty. Everyone who might have considered drinking at this time of day was occupied with the aftermath of the attack on Castle Cameron.

None of the staff would have been present either, since they were likewise busy, but Chad had sent a runner for one of the hostesses to come and assist us. The waitress in question was now leaning over the table, delivering a set of three small glasses.

She had dark hair, bound up in a practical braid, and I couldn't help but notice that she angled her body in such a way that Chad had a better view of her figure than the rest of us. That wasn't what concerned me, though. "What's this?" I asked, indicating the glasses.

"McDaniel's finest whiskey," replied the waitress, Danae, with a mischievous wink that also seemed directed mainly at the huntsman.

"Whiskey?" said Tyrion, the word unfamiliar to him.

They hadn't had distilled spirits in his time, I remembered, but Chad spoke first. "It's a man's drink. I figured you'd like it."

It certainly wasn't to my liking. The stuff was a guaranteed way to ruin the 'morrow. I usually stuck to beer or wine. Besides, Penny usually frowned on me drinking spirits. My throat grew tight as I realized that wasn't something I needed to worry about any longer.

Chad saved me from needing to comment, raising his glass. "Cheers," he said, waiting for us to lift our own before downing the fiery liquid in a slow swallow, relishing the taste.

Tyrion followed his example, and I was gratified to see my ancestor struggle to keep from choking as the amber fluid burned his throat. I managed mine with more grace, and the burn helped me get my thoughts back to the present. "So, what did you have in mind?" I asked.

Danae was back and filling our glasses again before he could reply. I covered mine with one hand. "Beer, please."

She started to turn away, but Chad pointed at his glass and Tyrion's. "You know better'n that, darlin'. Just leave the bottle before ye fetch our worthy Count his milk."

Danae filled their glasses, casting wicked looks at the ranger as she handed him the bottle afterward. I had been in the Muddy Pig quite a few times, but I couldn't recall her ever being so obvious before, and I wondered if anything had happened between the two of them that I was unaware of. *Not my business,* I told myself.

"The She'Har were fighting this enemy for millennia before they came here," began Tyrion after draining his second glass. "As I'm sure you're aware."

I nodded.

"During that time, they developed specialized krytek for sniffing out ANSIS. Considering the current situation, I think you need them," added my ancestor.

In fact, I had thought about it. I had even planned on asking him during my last visit to his island, but after the disastrous fight over Lynaralla, I had discarded the idea. My pride had kept me from considering it again. "You aren't a father-tree anymore," I observed.

"My tree is still there," explained Tyrion. "I can merge with it whenever I choose. I will produce the krytek and find the enemy for you, if you will show me how these teleport circles of yours work."

My beer had arrived, so I took a long drink while I thought over his proposal. Since the rebirth of the She'Har, Tyrion had never shown any interest in learning anything about modern enchanting. Then again, this was only my second time talking to him in human form.

When I didn't answer right away, Tyrion smiled at my hesitation. "Worried that I have some sinister ulterior motive?"

"We aren't exactly friends," I said honestly. "And after my last visit, I wasn't sure we were even allies any longer."

"I have a vested interest in this world, just as you do. Neither of us profits from letting ANSIS have it," explained Tyrion. Danae placed two more mugs in front of him and Chad, each filled to the brim with frothy brew.

"Why do you want to learn about teleportation enchantments?" I asked.

"Aside from the fact that they are obviously useful for a wide variety of things, I'll need them if I am to report what the krytek discover to you in any reasonable timeframe," said Tyrion. He lifted the beer to his lips and swallowed. His eyes widened after a second and he took another, longer drink. "I thought you said this was beer?"

"It is," I replied.

Chad sneered at him, "Some things have improved since yer day. Good beer is a sign of an advanced society."

I studied my chief huntsman with interest, noting that his accent had almost vanished. It didn't happen often, but as always, it made me wonder about his past. How much of his rustic demeanor was real, and how much was an affectation?

"Beer tasted nothing like this in my time," observed Tyrion, eyeing his mug with new admiration.

"Ye can't get anythin' like that livin' as a tree," commented Chad dryly.

Tyrion snorted. "I might have rethought the choice back then if we had had this to drink."

Bullshit, I thought. *You had no choice. Your family rejected your twisted ideas and your daughter stuck a knife in your back.* Despite his attempts at being amiable, I had no intention of forgetting what an utter bastard my ancestor was. His eyes met mine for a moment before he turned them back to his drink. I wondered if he could guess what I was thinking. I hoped so.

"You haven't answered yet," said Tyrion. "What do you think of my offer?"

Rather than speak, I used my finger to begin drawing a glowing circle in the air. I followed that with a smaller one within it, and then I began adding the runes that went between the two. I named each as I went, until I had finished. Then I pointed out the two empty areas. "The keys go here and here. One is the key of the destination circle, the other is the key that names the circle you just created."

Chad looked disgusted. "Are ye really gonna try and teach him that here an' now? I'm gonna wind up sober again afore I've had a chance to get drunk."

"I have no desire to spend any more time in this man's presence than necessary," I said harshly. Then I proceeded to explain the formula for calculating a key to designate a new circle. I never paused or repeated myself, and when I had finished that I drew a finished key. "This is the key for the general-use circle at my castle." As soon as I was done, I let the glowing symbols fade away.

"How's he supposed to remember all that rubbish?" asked Chad.

I downed the rest of my beer and gave Tyrion an appraising stare. He had the same flawless memory I did. "He'll remember. Send word to me if you find them." Then I turned to go.

The bottle of whiskey on the table was at the forefront of my mind. Chad saw me glance at it and then gave a subtle wink. I knew what he was communicating, but I doubted he knew that I had a second reason for looking at it. I had a strong urge to take it with me. I wanted nothing more than to drink myself into oblivion.

Summoning my inner discipline, I left. I had too many things to do to surrender my wits, and I certainly didn't want to relax around my homicidal ancestor.

In the background, I heard Chad resume his customary banter. "So, Tyrion, tell me. I know the She'Har elders are trees, but are ye properly described as a hardwood or a softwood?"

CHAPTER 41

The house was cold and silent as I left the room that held the teleportation circles. It was over two thousand years old, but the walls and roof were still strong. The air was always a comfortable temperature, and despite its age, there was never a hint of dust or mold. Tyrion had laid down the foundation of the Illeniel house in Albamarl, in a time before modern history had even begun.

He had named it 'Albamarl,' the Erollith word for 'white-stone.' It was a bit of irony that the city was named after it, though I was one of the few people aware of that. Over the twenty centuries since that time, generations of Tyrion's descendants had built, rebuilt, expanded, and remodeled the place. Each and every stone that made up the walls was enchanted, providing the house with a timeless indestructibility.

I had first come to explore the dwelling in my youth, accompanied by my friends, Marcus, Rose, and Penny. Though it belonged to me, I had never lived there aside from spending a few weeks now and then when I needed to be in the capital for an extended period.

Consequently, I didn't have many memories in the place, and those I did have mainly consisted of moments with Marcus, Rose, Penny, and occasionally, Dorian. *All who are now dead, except Rose,* I thought darkly.

My purpose for coming there was twofold. One, I wanted to check on the Queen and my son, Conall. If ANSIS had assaulted Cameron Castle, there was every possibility that they had also attacked the capital. My second reason was that I needed a way to get to my mountain home so I could make sure that my mother and the others had escaped danger before the keep had collapsed.

I could have simply flown. I knew where my secret house was located, obviously, but it would have taken time to get there. By coming to Albamarl, I could use the portal in the Queen's palace to access my home directly.

Unlike every other dwelling or place that I frequented, there were no teleportation circles in my family's private residence. I had made a rule concerning that when I built the place. Teleportation circles were a security risk. Anyone who learned the key to a circle could make a circle to take them to it—assuming they were a mage, of course. For that reason the only magical methods of entry to my home were the two portals I had constructed, one leading to my castle (now destroyed), and the newer one that connected to a closet in the Queen's residence.

A portal is more secure. It can be deactivated. It's also defensible, whereas you never knew when someone might appear on a circle. That was why the teleportation circles leading to Castle Cameron were all located in the yard outside the keep, within a special building that had guards watching it around the clock.

Descending the stairs to the first floor, I couldn't help but feel a lonely emptiness sink into my bones. It wasn't something I had felt there before, but now, thinking of my absent friends, it was inescapable.

I didn't linger. And once I opened the door to the street, I was glad I hadn't. My nose immediately picked up the scent of smoke. Things hadn't been quiet in the capital. The door to my factor's office across the road was closed and barred, though with my magesight I could sense David Summerfield and his paramour, Sarah Beckins, hiding within. Farther in, I could detect more people hiding in one of the storerooms. *Her family, I'll wager.*

Crossing over, I knocked.

"Who is it?" came David's tense voice.

"It's me," I replied. "Your employer. Can you let me in?"

After several minutes of shifting and moving furniture, David finally opened the door a crack, peering out suspiciously. "Is it over?"

"I have no idea," I told him honestly. "I just arrived. Tell me what happened."

"Fire, chaos, metal monsters, terror in the night," muttered David. "I don't understand any of it. The city hasn't been safe."

"Is that why you have Sarah and her family barricaded in with you?" I asked.

David blushed. "They had nowhere safe to go."

"Relax," I told him. "I approve of your caution. Can you give me a better description of what's going on?"

He shook his head. "Sarah's father said he hasn't seen anything like it since the God-Stone War. I didn't see much myself. We locked ourselves in early on, but we heard plenty—thunder, explosions, men screaming."

I nodded and turned away.

"Where are you going?" he asked worriedly.

"I have to find the Queen," I answered. "Go ahead and put your barricade back in place. I'll send word later if the city is safe." Reinforcing my personal shield, I took hold of the wind and lifted myself into the air.

From high above, it was readily apparent that Albamarl had been through interesting times. Thin plumes of smoke rose from nine different spots, areas that on closer inspection appeared to have burned down the day before. Thankfully, there weren't any active blazes that I could find.

At the center of the city lay the royal palace, and like Castle Cameron, one of its exterior walls had been destroyed, though the damage was more centralized. In the streets I spotted several tortuses that appeared to have been battered into immobility. Worried, I flew to the main gate and approached slowly—on foot. I had no desire to create a panic by flying in unannounced.

There were several guardsmen on duty, and they bade me to wait. I hadn't expected that, but their intent became clear when Carwyn, Ariadne's dragon, appeared a few minutes later. The massive dragon sniffed at me before studying me with wary eyes. "Lower your shield," he said with a gravelly voice.

That surprised me. "You know it's me, Carwyn. You can recognize my aythar."

His voice grew deeper and more threatening. "Lower your shield or prepare to face me. No one enters without being inspected."

I did so.

A minute later he announced, "He's alright. Let him in." Then he left, returning to whatever he had been doing before my arrival.

Inside the palace I saw some signs of damage, but nothing like what had happened to Castle Cameron. Servants and soldiers moved to and fro in a frenzy of activity, reminding me of a hive of bees that had been disturbed. Most of them ignored me as I headed for the throne room.

Benchley met me at the doors. "Your Excellency, the Queen has left instructions in the event you appear. Bear with me for a moment and I will announce you."

I waited, studying the hallway while he went in. Everything appeared normal, but my eyes picked out some suspicious dark stains on the rose granite walls. Either the cleaning staff had gotten lax or someone had made a considerable mess recently.

The doors opened after only a minute and I was ushered in. Ariadne sat at the end of a long table that belonged elsewhere. The throne room was normally used only for holding court and certain ceremonial affairs. It should have held only one seat, that of the monarch.

Two men stood on either side and slightly behind her, Sir Harold, and my son, Conall. Harold was in full armor and bearing arms. His eyes roved around the room as though he expected an attack from every quarter. His new dragon sat on his shoulders, its tail curling around his neck and trailing down his chest.

My attention was on Conall, though. I had sent him to protect the Queen, but I hadn't expected him to be standing guard next to her person like this during what was obviously a meeting. He looked almost as alert as Harold, but what worried me was the fact that he leaned heavily against an oak staff. Thick linen bandages wrapped his abdomen, and I could see stains where blood had soaked through.

Since I was distracted by my son's appearance, it took me a moment to register the people who sat at the table with the Queen. Rose was on one side and Prince Leomund on the other. The two of them were both immaculately dressed. However, while Rose sat straight and attentive, the prince-consort lounged in his chair as though he were at an afternoon social. In contrast to the two of them, Duke Cantley sat in the chair beside Leomund, haggard and disheveled. Functionaries, primarily higher-level military officers, took up the rest of the chairs. They sat on Rose's side of the table, since most of them answered to her.

Everyone stared at me, as though I had grown horns, so I broke the silence first. "What happened?"

There were several sharp intakes of breath, and Prince Leomund sneered, "Have you no knee for your Queen?" Even Rose was frowning at me, though Ariadne's face remained carefully neutral.

Shit. It had been a long time since I had been to court, and I hadn't expected to face such a formal situation. I genuflected, addressing Ariadne, "Your Majesty, forgive my rudeness. Recent events have made me careless."

"You are forgiven, Count Cameron," said Ariadne graciously. "Please take a seat and attend us. We have need of your counsel."

"You are too merciful, Ariadne," said Leomund, staring at me with a look of disgust. "This cur hasn't had the grace to attend court in years, and now he marches in as though he owns the place. I am at a loss. Where were you during our recent crisis, Lord Cameron? Would you care to account for yourself?"

"Leo, you go too far," warned Ariadne.

Duke Cantley decided to speak up. "I too would like an explanation, Your Majesty. From what we have heard, Lord Cameron may be directly responsible for this assault. He should make a good accounting of himself."

I glanced at Ariadne, waiting until she nodded before I answered, "My estate has also suffered a serious attack—"

"A feeble excuse, Lord Cameron," interrupted the prince-consort. "Lady Hightower has already informed us that you were absent from the defense of your lands."

Patience had never been my strongest suit, and my grief and fatigue weren't helping my self-control. Angry, I lashed out. "And I suppose Your Highness spends every minute in the capital, guarding the crown of Lothion? Or perhaps your hunting lodge was also destroyed? Is that why you seem so out of sorts today?"

Rose's eyes were warning me to restrain myself, though she showed no other outward sign.

The prince-consort was out of his chair now, enraged. "You dare speak to me so?"

I didn't bother standing. To do so would have implied the pompous prick represented a threat. "I will show you the same courtesy and respect you have shown me, Your Highness." Then I turned to face the Queen, ignoring him. "May I continue, Your Majesty?"

Leomund's throat issued a strangled sound that probably represented outrage. He was too mad to speak. Ariadne waved at him to sit. "Enough, Leomund. This is not the time to be squabbling amongst ourselves. Take your seat and let him continue." The prince's eyes shot daggers in her direction, but he sat down.

"As I was saying, Your Majesty, Castle Cameron was also attacked, very likely at the same time as whatever happened here. From what I saw as I came here, the source of the attacks was ANSIS, the same enemy that caused so much trouble in Dunbar a few months ago," I explained.

Duke Cantley broke in, "What is this ANSIS you speak of?"

"It stands for Artificial Neural Symbiote Integrative System," I replied.

"And what is that supposed to mean?" demanded the Duke.

"Not much, to us," I said frankly. "It's an artificial life form, a self-replicating machine entity, devoid of the force that animates living creatures in our world."

The prince-consort jumped in then, "And you thought it was a good idea to attack this ANSIS without consulting your Queen first? Your insult to this entity has cost the lives of many good people!"

How did he know we attacked ANSIS? I had explicitly told Conall not to reveal that information before sending him to protect the Queen. His accusation caught me off-guard as I tried to decide how to reply.

But the prince-consort didn't plan on giving me the luxury to think. He pressed his attack. "You didn't think we would discover what you had done? You probably also think the crown will forever be dependent upon you and your vassals for magical assistance as well. If it hadn't been for Tyrion's timely warning and assistance, we might not be sitting here now to listen to you lie about it."

Tyrion? What did he have to do with this? Struggling to regain my composure, I spoke up, "It might be easier for me to understand your accusations if I knew what happened here."

"You'd like that wouldn't you, traitor? It would make it far easier to construct a believable lie, wouldn't it?" hissed the prince-consort.

At that point, I came close to using my magic to seal his mouth shut, but the Queen spoke before I lost my temper. "Leomund! Don't make me warn you again. Lord Cameron has been a loyal servant to the crown for many years…"

Then, the doors of the throne room opened and Benchley stepped in. "The Duke of the Western Isles has returned, Your Majesty, as well as Lord Gaelyn."

"Please show him in," responded Ariadne.

Duke of the Western Isles? Who was that? I knew the name and title of every nobleman in Lothion, not to mention Dunbar and Gododdin, and I had never heard of the Duchy of the Western Isles. I craned my head over one shoulder to see who would enter.

Tyrion Illeniel marched toward the table, a faint smirk on his lips when he saw my look of confusion. Beside him was Gareth Gaelyn.

The prince-consort's brazen attitude toward me was beginning to make more sense, though I still had no idea what was going on. The two new arrivals bowed deeply to the queen and then took seats at the table across from me. Tyrion watched me with a challenging gaze, while Gareth ignored my presence completely.

Ariadne turned to Rose. "Lady Hightower, would you be so kind as to summarize recent events for the Count di' Cameron?"

With a regal dignity I would never come close to possessing, Lady Rose stood and addressed the table, "As you wish, Your Majesty. In the small hours of the morning, yesterday, assassins hidden among the royal guard broke into your bedroom. The men are presumed to have been controlled by ANSIS, the entity the Count was just describing.

Their attempt on your life might have succeeded if it hadn't been for the timely intervention of Conall Illeniel and your knight, Sir Harold.

"Shortly after that attack, a still undetermined number of metal monsters invaded the city, destroying several homes and damaging the palace wall. Two of them were dealt with by your dragon, two others by Sir Egan and Sir Thomas, but the bulk of the enemy force was stopped by the Lord Illeniel, the recently appointed Duke of the Western Isles," finished Rose.

That meant Tyrion had been in the capital before he had come to visit me. "What were you doing here?" I demanded of my ancestor.

Tyrion smiled innocently. "I came to check on my house, and to offer the Queen my support. I explained my plan for discerning the whereabouts of ANSIS and swore fealty to Her Majesty. Unfortunately, I was too late to discover the hidden assassins among her guardsmen, but I am grateful I was here to render my assistance in turning back the assault on the city itself."

"Your house…" My voice tapered off as I realized he was referring to *my* house, which had originally been his.

He nodded. "I hope you don't mind, but as I am your elder by many generations, and I *did* lay the foundations, the house is rightfully mine, regardless of my new title."

"You should be proud, Lord Cameron," said Duke Cantley. "Yesterday your family provided *two* heroes in the service of Lothion, your ancestor and your son."

Leomund sneered, "It's a shame you didn't see fit to aid them, since you knew the attack was imminent."

Ariadne nodded. "We are especially grateful for your son, Sir Conall. Without him I fear my life would have been forfeit."

My eyes grew wider. *Sir Conall?*

Rose jumped in to save me from my confusion. "The Queen has conferred a knighthood on your son in recognition of his bravery."

It was too much to take in all at once. "Congratulations, Conall," I said, but as I glanced around the table I felt alone. Rose's eyes were distant, or perhaps she was trying to give me a warning. Ariadne's face was neutral; she was constrained by her role. The others, with the exception of my son and Sir Harold, seemed hostile. I couldn't stay there any longer.

Rising to my feet, I bowed and excused myself. "I beg permission to take my leave, Your Majesty. My son is needed at home for an urgent family matter." I wanted to tell her about Penny's death, but I didn't want to announce it in front of a hostile audience, especially not with Conall present. He needed to hear it somewhere private.

"You have yet to explain yourself, Cameron!" challenged the prince-consort.

"And I shall!" I barked. "But not to you, and not now."

Conall spoke up, "I'd rather remain, Father. The Queen needs me."

Thankfully, Ariadne came to my aid. "You have our permission to withdraw, Lord Cameron. Sir Conall, attend to your father. You may return later. The danger has passed for now."

I bowed to my cousin, turned, and strode quickly from the room without looking back. With my magesight I saw my son reluctantly follow, along with Lady Rose, after whispering into the Queen's ear.

Outside the throne room, Rose's composed features relaxed. "Have Matthew and Gram returned?"

"Not yet," I replied hollowly. She was worried about her son, and I couldn't blame her for that. I wanted to tell her about Penny, but my tongue seemed stuck. Conall was staring at me, frustration in his eyes, probably wondering why I had dragged him away from his moment of glory.

"Mort, I know a lot has happened, but after that attack the other night, shouldn't you be checking on them before coming here?" said Rose critically.

Frustration, rage, and sorrow warred for first place in my heart. *I wanted to make sure you and my mother were safe.* That's what I should have said, but when I opened my mouth it was my bile that spoke, "After what just happened in there, I'm thinking I should have come here sooner. The palace is turning into a nest of vipers."

Rose's face blanched, hearing the reproach in my voice. "That was unexpected, I will agree. I don't know what Tyrion is planning yet, but it's obvious that—"

"It's obvious I could use a *friend* in there," I interrupted. "Too bad there were none to be found."

Now she was angry. "I know you're not that stupid, Mordecai. You have to control your emotions, or your opponents will use them against you. I tried to warn you, but you insisted on acting like a child. Performances like the one you just put on won't win you friends. They'll alienate your allies. Do you have any idea what the Queen is dealing with right now?"

Inside, I was falling apart. Only my simmering anger kept me from breaking down, but I didn't need an argument with Rose. As far as I knew, she might be the only friend I had left. "I don't need a lecture on political strategy right now, Rose."

I turned my back on her and started walking. "I'll contact you as soon as I hear from Gram."

She was too proud to chase after me. I had been counting on that. Behind me Conall apologized to her and then hurried to catch up.

I led him through the palace, heading for the royal residence. Once we were there, the guards stationed outside started to challenge me, but when they saw Conall they relaxed. The irony wasn't lost on me. They trusted my son more than they did me. *He's the Queen's Champion,* I observed silently.

Once inside, I headed directly for the hidden portal, but I had to cross a sitting room where Elise Thornbear and my mother were having tea. They smiled when they saw Conall and me enter the room.

"We were just talking about you," said my mother. She had Humphrey in her lap, running her fingers through his soft fur while he slept. "What happened at the castle? Is everyone safe?"

Both of the older women, as well as Conall, were staring at me, and I struggled to find an answer. A shadow crossed my mother's face as I hesitated. "Is Irene alright?" she asked.

"Yes," I said finally. "She's fine. The keep was badly damaged, but Irene is well. She held things together long enough for most of the people to evacuate."

"Thank goodness for that!" said my mother. "Things have been just as exciting around here. Did Conall tell you the news? He's been made a knight." She was beaming at her grandson with visible pride. "I can't wait to tell Penelope. She'll be so proud."

I came close to losing it then, but somehow, I held it in. "Mom, listen, I'm really tired. And I still have a lot to do. I'll be back tomorrow and we'll have a long talk. Is that alright?"

She could sense that something was wrong, but Meredith withheld her questions. "Of course. You're an important man. Don't let me hold you up. You can tell me everything then."

"Thanks," I told her, and before Elise could add anything, I left.

CHAPTER 42

"**D**ad?" asked Conall as we stepped out of the portal and into the quiet of our home. "What's wrong?"

My magesight had already detected several other familiar presences in the dining room. "Let's say hello to the others, first," I told him.

Elaine, Karen, and Lynaralla sat around the table, making an impromptu meal of some cheese and old bread. Karen grinned widely at me when we entered. "Have we got some news for you!"

"You were successful then?" I asked.

She nodded, then looked at Lynaralla. "Tell him, Lynn."

"Lyralliantha agreed to give us access. What's more, she allowed us to transport most of the writings here, so we can study them at our leisure," said the young She'Har.

It was good news, but I couldn't muster the enthusiasm I had felt a few days ago. "That's wonderful," I said glumly.

Elaine's eyes narrowed. "Is something wrong?"

Rather than answer her question, I asked, "Have you been back to the castle?"

Elaine shook her head. "No, we only returned an hour ago. Karen's been busy teleporting back and forth to bring the She'Har sculptures here."

"Let me fetch Irene. Then we can talk," I told them. "Give me a few minutes." Then I headed for the kitchen and the door that led to the back garden.

"The door to the castle is the other way," observed Lynaralla.

I stopped. "The portal is damaged. I'll have to make a circle."

Karen swallowed hurriedly. "I can take you, then."

Waving at her to stay seated, I shook my head. "We'll need a circle to use for the next few days anyway. Finish your food. You deserve a rest."

Once I was outside I cleared a section of ground and used my cloth stencil to create a temporary circle before adding the necessary keys to allow me to travel to the transfer house in the castle courtyard. Rather than simply use it, though, I took the additional step of burning the symbols into the earth, making the circle somewhat more permanent. Since it was etched into the soil, it still wasn't extremely durable—a hard rain could wash it away—but it would probably last a few days at least. Exerting my will, I teleported.

The transfer house was empty, but as soon as I stepped outside, I spotted my children. Matthew, Moira, and Gram were talking with Captain Draper in the yard. They looked tired and dirty, but their stances spoke of confidence and accomplishment, so I guessed they had been successful.

Matthew gave me a rare smile. "It worked."

"By that, he means we blew them to tiny bits without destroying the world," added Gram jovially, "something everyone conveniently forgot to tell me was a possibility before we left."

My eyes found Captain Draper's and he shook his head faintly. "Where is Irene?" I asked.

"In the barracks, checking on the men," said the captain.

Meanwhile, I could feel Moira studying me. She had already picked up on the dark pall hanging over us, and then she looked at the captain. *Don't,* I sent to her silently. *Keep your mind closed. I'll explain after we are all together.*

The captain sent a runner to tell Irene we were here. Apparently, the others had shown up only minutes before me. I began constructing a new circle inside the transfer house to allow us to teleport back to our home. Matthew joined me, offering to help. "What's wrong?" he asked quietly, having seen the odd look on his sister's face.

"Wait until we get home," I promised. Irene showed up a few minutes later, and as soon as the circle was finished, we teleported back.

By the time we entered the house, Moira's face had taken on a somber look. Irene was shielding her thoughts, but her emotional pain was painfully evident. Conall and the others glanced up from the table when we entered. "Welcome back."

A multitude of 'hellos' were exchanged, but they died away quickly as everyone waited for me to speak. Then Matthew spoke, "Where's Mom?"

Conall chimed in, "I thought she was with Irene."

At the mention of her name, my youngest daughter's eyes began to well with tears.

"No!" shouted Moira, her eyes wide with shock as she stared at her sister. "That's not true! It can't be true!"

Matthew sat down, putting his face in his hands. He had already connected the dots, but Conall was still confused. "What's going on?" Conall asked. "Why is everyone upset?"

"Your mother was badly injured during the attack on Castle Cameron," I began.

Without looking up, Matthew broke in, "I told you we should wait. We should have kept more people here."

"Irene was still here," said Conall—somewhat unhelpfully, in my opinion.

Irene was already sobbing while Moira held her. "It was my fault; I should have protected her, but I couldn't!" she yelled, the guilt in her voice wrenching at my heart.

Conall looked back at me, ignoring her outburst. "How badly injured?"

I couldn't meet his eyes as I shook my head. "She didn't survive."

"Because you couldn't wait to think up a better plan," said Matthew, his words cold and hard.

Irene shoved herself away from her older sister, glaring at Matthew. "Leave him alone. None of this was his fault. Don't you think he's hurting too?"

"The truth is what it is," muttered Matthew.

My oldest son stood, pushing away from the table. "Just shut up." Then he walked away, heading toward his room.

Conall called after him, "Wait. We haven't heard what happened."

"Doesn't matter does it?" said Matthew bitterly. "We know *why* she died. The *how* of it hardly matters. She's still dead." Then he was gone. Karen rose and followed him to his room.

"Why does he have to be an asshole?" growled Moira, channeling her sadness into irritation with her brother.

Irene left crying, heading for her own room. Conall went after her. "Wait, Rennie!"

Moira remained, staring deeply into my eyes.

"You should go with them," I suggested. "They need you more than I do."

My oldest daughter hugged me, squeezing me so hard that my ribs protested. "I doubt that," she replied, but then she went after them anyway, leaving me alone with Elaine, Gram, and Lynaralla.

Elaine and Gram sat silent, their faces numb with shock, but Lynaralla was composed, her features expressionless. Or so I thought, until I noticed a solitary tear making its way down her cheek. When the She'Har girl met my eyes, she looked lost.

"Why?" whispered Lynaralla.

I dragged her to her feet and hugged her, struggling with my own tears as I answered, "I don't know."

"Does my mother know yet?" asked Gram.

I shook my head. "No."

"Why not?"

I gave him a short summary of what had happened in the palace, ending with, "I was angry, upset, and aggravated. I wound up picking a fight with your mother. After that, I just couldn't say it."

Gram sighed. "That was dumb."

Silently, I agreed. *Dumb shit. Someone has to do it. Might as well be me.* "It's hard work, but it makes the rest of you look better."

Elaine mumbled to herself, staring off into space. "I still haven't gotten over my father." Then she put her face down on the table.

***

Gram gave me a brief rundown of what happened during his mission with Moira and Matthew. While I had been walking the road to Lancaster, the three of them had flown from Cantley over the forest, seeking the Ungol village.

The first phase of their plan had gone smoothly. They had located the village, and with some help from Moira's manipulative abilities, they had managed to walk into it with very little resistance. Unfortunately, the village was indeed infested, though it was doubtful even the inhabitants were aware of their status as hosts to a machine parasite.

Matthew had used the Fool's Tesseract, but had kept the settings conservative to avoid the risk of an explosion in excess of what was desired. The result was a tremendous blast that destroyed the village but didn't entirely eliminate the machines within it. They had been forced to spend most of the next day scouting and sending out small spellbeasts to make sure they had gotten rid of ANSIS.

When he had finished, Lynaralla shared her findings from what was now the Dukedom of the Western Isles. Their infiltration had gone without a hitch, though the two-day wait while she communicated their desire to her mother had been nerve wracking for Elaine and the others.

Aside from telling Lynaralla that they were welcome to take the writings, she also warned her daughter that Tyrion might not be entirely trustworthy. I would have loved to know precisely why she thought that, but a two-day conversation with a She'Har elder was roughly the equivalent of a minute or two of normal conversation. There just hadn't been time.

Lynaralla did get the feeling we might find some clues to her mother's suspicion in the writings they had recovered. I hoped so. I could use some good news.

After they had finished, I did my best to explain what had happened at Castle Cameron, though I hadn't been present for most of it. I assumed that Moira would get the rest of the story from Irene while they were together, but I didn't have the energy to worry about it.

I was exhausted, not because of any great exertion, but simply because grief does that to a person. Shortly after that, I retired to the bedroom I shared with—the bedroom I used to share with Penny—and curled up on the bed. I wanted to sleep.

But I could smell the scent of her hair on the pillows.

"Why did you leave me?" I moaned to the empty air, but of course, there was no reply, nor would there be, ever again.

***

At some point, I slept, and when I opened my eyes again, Penny was staring down at me with sympathy. "You look terrible," she observed.

"I've had a bad couple of days," I remarked.

"You aren't the only one," she returned. "I think I got the worst of it."

"Want to compare notes?" I said with a hint of a challenge in my voice.

She laughed. "Sure."

I had a good opener already planned. "Tyrion showed up in court. The Queen made him a duke, and he's already turned some of the other nobles against me."

Penny shook her finger from side to side. "That one doesn't count, since it applies equally to both of us. Your enemies are my enemies."

"Oh, right," I said lamely. "How about this? I think the kids hate me now."

"That does sound bad," said Penny, "but I'm fairly sure they're mad at me too."

"I got in a fight with Rose."

She gave me a look of disapproval. "Oh, Mort, why would you do that?"

"She started it," I responded, feeling childish.

Leaning over, she ruffled my hair with her hand. "I'm sure she will forgive you. She always does. Sometimes I wish you were smarter, though."

Something about her touch lifted my spirits and I joked in return, "Sometimes I wish you were dumber."

She growled at that, but I distracted her before she could retaliate. "Your turn! I got in a fight with Rose, now tell me something bad that happened to you."

Penny looked thoughtful for a moment. Then she reluctantly responded, "I got in a fight with one of those giant metal monsters."

"Just one?"

"Two, as a matter of fact," she said boldly.

I grinned. "I feel badly for them."

"Your turn," said Penny, laughing.

"I got in a fight with three of them," I boasted. "They're called 'tortuses,' by the way."

My wife shook her head, causing her ponytail to bounce to either side. I loved watching the way the light reflected from it. "That doesn't count," she replied. "You won."

I sat up in bed and gave mocking half-bow. "That's true. That fight was probably the best part of the day."

"Why is that?"

"Because I won, but you…" My voice trailed off as I stared at her, remembering. I finished with a whisper, "but you died." Tears were streaming down my cheeks.

Her face became sad. "You shouldn't have remembered that." And then she began to fade away.

"No!" I grabbed for her, but there was nothing but emptiness within my arms. I had woken, and I spent the first fifteen minutes of the morning the same way I had spent the last fifteen minutes of the night before, screaming into my pillow as I sobbed hopelessly.

EPILOGUE

A week after the attacks on Castle Cameron, I found myself standing in the courtyard, in approximately the same place where my wife had fought the tortuses. With the keep still in ruins, the final service to say goodbye to my dear Penny had to be held outside, but considering the size of the crowd that waws present it was probably for the better.

Washbrook alone accounted for nearly a thousand attendees, and that was just the locals. The Queen herself was in attendance, along with a considerable number of major and minor peers of the realm. Even King Nicholas of Gododdin and the newly crowned King Gerold of Dunbar were present.

Nicholas in particular had always had a soft spot for my wife, ever since she had saved his life from an assassin's blade many years before.

It wasn't all for Penny, of course. Walter Prathion had already been laid to rest, but the memorial service included a portion for him, as well as the men and women who had died in the recent attack. But in my heart, I knew the truth: At least half the crowd wouldn't have been there if Penny weren't among the fallen.

Speeches were given, and unlike some funerals I had been to for notable figures, I knew for a fact that those who spoke were honestly grieving. I myself gave a short speech for Walter, but when it came to my wife, my throat closed and the words refused to leave my lips.

But the Queen spoke for Penny, as did King Nicholas, and King Gerold, relaying their sincere gratitude for her service to each of them. My children were too distraught to take a turn in front of the crowd, but many others did so. I watched them and listened, but I still couldn't believe it was happening. Numb to everything, I found myself a silent witness to the greatest tragedy of my life.

Until Rose Thornbear took her place to speak on her friend's behalf. As ever, she was the picture of an ideal lady, managing even to outshine the Queen despite her somber black dress. Her legendary self-control served her well, as she calmly faced the crowd. And then she spoke, "The Countess di' Cameron was my closest friend. Penelope was a second mother to my son and..."

Rose's voice stopped, and she appeared to be struggling, as though she was choking. And then her façade crumbled. Her son, Gram, led her away, crying publicly. The only other time I could remember seeing her so undone by a funeral was when Dorian had died.

Then my mother, Meredith Eldridge, stepped forward to say her goodbyes. She was old, frail, and uncomfortable in front of such a great press of people, but my mother's pride of spirit refused to allow that to stop her. The sound of her voice pierced my numb heart, and tears began to fall before she finished her first sentence.

"Penelope Illeniel was my daughter-in-law, but I could not have been prouder of her if she were my own flesh and blood," began Meredith. "I don't know much about courtly ways or great deeds. I come from common-stock, just as she did, but no one possessed a nobler spirit than did our dear Penny. Many of you knew her as the Countess di' Cameron, and some of you knew her as a warrior, but while she excelled in those roles, what I loved her for was the care she showed to both my son and my grandchildren.

"There was no finer mother, no better wife, to be found in this world. She cared for her family with a passion that knew no limits, protected them with a fierceness that couldn't be denied, and loved us with a heart that knew no bounds. I have thanked the stars for her every day since the day she chose my son to share her love with."

The rest of the day was a misery. A large dinner was held in honor of Penny and Walter, and since I had no facilities to host it, the Queen had offered up the palace for it. Once the funeral was over, the important figures were taken there via teleport circles. The worst part was that I was required to go with them. When royalty attended the funeral for your family, some acknowledgement was required, even if they didn't demand it from you themselves. I sat through a long dinner with Ariadne and the other notables, but I wanted nothing more than to run away, to hide myself somewhere where I could grieve in peace, unobserved.

Ariadne understood this, and she did her best to keep my family's participation as short and painless as possible. My children escaped after less than an hour, and I made my excuses a half an hour after that.

Consequently, I found myself walking alone down the long hall that led from the central portion of the palace to the front gate, and I was glad for the solitude. I had no idea where I was headed and didn't really care.

If I had intended to go home, I would have made my way to the Queen's portal to my house.

"Mordecai."

It was Rose. I hadn't spoken with her since that day in the throne room, not because I was angry—I had gotten over that—but simply because I was hurting too much. Gram had been the one to notify her and the Queen about Penny's death. This was our first private moment in almost a week.

I turned to her with dead eyes. "Yeah?"

My cold response earned me a faint frown, but she pushed that aside. "How are you?" she asked.

"I'm fine."

"Don't be like this, Mordecai. You were there for me when I lost Dorian. I know what you're going through—"

I put as much sincerity into my words as I could as I interrupted her, "I appreciate that, Rose. I just need time. Alone." I should have hugged her, thanked her, opened up, but I didn't have it in me. I felt dead inside. Without waiting for her to reply, I turned and started walking away.

"Mordecai!" she called, raising her voice. "We need to talk. There are other things we can't ignore."

I turned back. "Such as?"

"The Queen has requested my presence in the capital for an extended period, due to the recent attack. I won't be able to return to Cameron for a while," she informed me.

Lady Rose was more formally known as Lady Hightower. Her hereditary duty as 'The Hightower' was overseeing the royal guard and the defense of Albamarl. Given the recent attack, it made perfect sense she would need to spend time in the capital, but there was something more in her eyes as she told me that.

I simply nodded, accepting her statement.

"Given Tyrion's sudden entrance into politics, I think my presence here may be of more value to us anyway," she continued. "Things are moving, and we need to understand his motivations better."

Us? What significance such a small word held. 'Us' represented my small group of friends and family. Over the nearly thirty years I had known Rose, 'us' had changed a lot. Originally it had been me, Marcus, Penny, Dorian, and Rose. That had been us—our little faction, out to save the world. If I hadn't been deep in the throes of grief and depression, I might have admitted to myself that 'us' now included a lot more people, like the Queen, our children, even Cyhan and Chad.

But the shadow over my heart wasn't in the mood to be so magnanimous. Just then all I could see was that 'us' had been steadily shrinking. All that was left of our original 'us' was Mordecai and Rose. And Mordecai didn't want to play anymore.

"Us?" I said angrily. "There is no *us*." Rose flinched as I said it, and I knew why, but at that moment I didn't particularly care. I wanted to hurt someone. "Us is gone. It disappeared when Penny died. Marcus is dead, Dorian is gone—there is no 'us' anymore. Get over it. Move on. Your husband has been dead for over a decade now."

Rose's face had gone pale at my words, and I would have said more, would have wounded her even more deeply, but from somewhere inside a voice in my mind warned me, *That's enough, Mort! Don't you dare take your pain out on her!*

Her shock didn't last long. Rose lifted her chin and glared at me. "I realize you're grieving, Mordecai, but that doesn't give you the right to say whatever you please."

I was already beginning to feel bad for lashing out at her, but I wasn't ready to let down my guard. "You're right, as usual. Now, if you'll excuse me, I'd like to be alone."

She didn't try to stop me as I walked away this time.

***

Three days later I was sitting at the edge of the forest, just beyond the cleared fields that surrounded what was left of Castle Cameron. A stranger might have thought I was enjoying the shade, but I wasn't really enjoying much of anything anymore. There were sheep in the field, grazing, part of my agreement with the local shepherds to help keep the area around the castle clear. I watched them slowly cropping the grass without really seeing them at all.

"This is where ye been the last few days?"

It was Chad Grayson. He had been quietly approaching through the forest. If it hadn't been for my magesight, I never would have known he was there. "What do you want?"

"I been expectin' ye to show up at the Muddy Pig for the last three days to drown yer sorrows. I didn't think to look for ye out here, lustin' after sheep. It's a little soon, don't ye think?" he responded, ignoring my question.

"No one asked you to look for me."

"Now that's no way to talk to a friend," grumbled Chad. "An' here I been holdin' a seat for ye at the tavern every night. You have any idea how much work it is, gettin' drunk every night tryin' to console a fellow who ain't even there?"

I gave him a surly stare. "You know I avoid drinking too much."

Chad grinned, pulling out a bottle of McDaniel's finest. "I'm thinkin' times like this are when ye need to let yer hair down, little girl."

I looked away from him, hiding my face. It was hard to avoid a smirk when faced with the hunter's infectious enthusiasm for the bottle in his hand. "Getting drunk isn't an option for me."

"Why's that?"

"You know why. If I get too drunk, things are liable to start breaking: buildings, trees, innocent people, that sort of thing," I answered.

Chad snorted. "Ain't no buildings out here, an' them trees been givin' me the eye for years. They deserve what they get."

"There are people," I responded. "Unless I've started talking to myself again."

The hunter unstopped the bottle. "I'll grant you that one. There's people here, but no *decent* people, and fer damn sure no innocent ones."

I grunted, then accepted the bottle, trying not to choke as I took a long pull. "That's true." I passed the bottle back to him so he could join me.

We passed the bottle back and forth for a while, until the world took on fuzzy edges and my head began to swim. "What happened with Tyrion that day, in the tavern? When I left it looked like you were planning to get him blind drunk and leave him in a gutter somewhere. I didn't expect him to show up at the palace in Albamarl."

"He gave ye a hard time, eh?"

I nodded. "You could say that. So many things went wrong that day. I kind of felt like you let me down."

"Well, I'm a little embarrassed about it myself. I kept that mean bastard drinkin' until I figured he was about ready to pass out, and then he just up and walked out, sober as ye please! Never seen anythin' like it," admitted the huntsman.

Then I understood. I wouldn't have dreamed of using my abilities in such a dangerous fashion, not while drunk, but apparently Tyrion didn't mind taking risks. *He must have reset his body to a sober state when he was ready to leave.*

"Don't beat yourself up," I consoled him. "I don't think he was fighting fair."

"Fuckin' wizards," swore Chad.

Well, archmages, I silently corrected, but the distinction was academic for most people. I took another drink, and then lay down in the grass. My balance seemed better closer to the ground.

After a few minutes Chad spoke again, "I think yer kids are worried about you. A decent man would grieve by gettin' drunk so he could be hungover at home durin' the day for his family."

That line was so ridiculous I couldn't help but chuckle. "I thought we already established there were no decent men here. Besides, that's *your* way of dealing with your problems." After a second I added, "Did they send you looking for me?"

Chad sneered, "Do I look like a fuckin' nanny?"

I tried to imagine the sort of family that would think of hiring Chad Grayson to watch their children and began laughing again.

Chad laughed with me. "That's what I thought." Then he added, "I heard the Thornbears are movin' out; headin' back to the capital."

"Yeah."

"An' that's alright with you?"

"None of my business," I responded. "Lady Hightower owes fealty directly to the crown, not to me."

"Elise don't," countered the hunter, "an' Gram was knighted by…" His words trailed off as he realized what he had been about to say. "Anyway, he owes fealty to you."

"What's your point?" I growled. "You think I should hold an old woman hostage to keep Lady Rose here? Or Gram? It's not like I'm desperate for men-at-arms."

"Yer such a fool sometimes," said Chad. "Lady Rose leaves, takes her mother-in-law and son, and before long Gram will be asking to take service with the Queen. Next thing ye know and Alyssa's there with him, an' where she goes Sir Cyhan won't be far behind. How many people are ye willin' to give up?"

"I'm a count, not a prison warden."

"Don't be an idiot. From what I heard, Tyrion and Gareth Gaelyn are both spendin' a lot of time in the capital, makin' nice to the Queen, an' neither one of 'em is particularly fond of you. Hell, your own son, Conall, is the Queen's Champion now. He'll probably be movin' out too."

I sobered up enough to give him a flat stare. "We all serve the Queen, and Ariadne is my cousin. This isn't a war. We're all on the same side."

"Spoken like a true political genius, ye dumb fuckwit!" spat Chad.

From anyone else those words would have made me angry, but from Chad Grayson it was more like a warm hug. "I never claimed to be a political genius, and I don't give a damn about politics anyway, not anymore."

"What about yer family?"

I glared at him. "What does that mean?"

"Think it through. Everyone starts leavin' for the capital, meanwhile you're here, spreadin' cheer and joy wherever you go. How long before two of yer other three kids find somewhere else to be? Before you know it, it's just you and Irene sittin' around the fire together, tellin' sad stories to one another about the good ol' days," explained the hunter.

"I think you're getting a little far afield with your speculation," I commented. "And why Irene?"

"Cuz out of all of 'em she's the only one that's as fucked up as you. That an' she's feelin' guilty about her momma. She'll be the one to stay home to take care of her broken down ol' daddy, if only out of a sense of duty," said Chad.

I growled, "Watch your mouth, that's my daughter."

"First sensible thing ye've said," remarked Chad. "You almost sound like a father, but I'll be damned if what I said ain't the truth! Keep goin' like you are and someday she'll be followin' you around, wipin' the drool off yer chin. What kind of miserable life is that for a girl?"

"Then what do you suggest I do?" I was getting annoyed by the constant lecturing.

He cursed at me, "Go tell Rose not to move to the capital, ye slackwit! What did you think I was tryin' to tell you?"

"Oh," I said, somewhat stupidly. "I thought you were saying I should start getting drunk in the tavern with you every night."

Chad shrugged. "Well, that too. There's a lot of people grievin' right now. You might as well drink with 'em."

I chuckled. "You know, for all your abrasiveness, I can't help but think you're telling me all the same things my mother would say."

"Ha! Only if yer mother was a drunken wh—" He stopped suddenly when he saw the warning in my eyes. "Well, you know what I mean."

Staggering, I got to my feet and promptly tried to fall over. Chad caught me, lending me the use of his shoulder. He wasn't half as drunk as I was.

We stumbled across the pasture, mainly due to my lack of coordination, while Chad helpfully pointed out sheep, giving them ridiculous names and making suggestions about which might keep me company in the future.

I laughed and snickered along with him, and for the first time in a week and a half I felt vaguely human. Drunk, true, but human.

"Now, what are ye gonna do when we get back to the castle?" asked Chad.

"Tell Rose to stay," I recited dutifully.

"Good, an' after that?"

"Get you a dragon!" I said cheerfully.

The hunter frowned, "I don't think that's a good idea."

"Why not?" I asked blearily.

Chad patted my shoulder. "Not sure you've noticed my friend, but yer drunk."

"Whatever," I mumbled. "I'm getting you one. You need a companion."

"Like a hole in my head," returned the hunter.

"Seriously, they're better than sheep," I told him with a snort. "Trust me!"

He slipped, and we both wound up on our asses. After another laughing fit he surrendered, "Fine. I'll take a dragon. But what about after that?"

"We tell Rose not to leave."

"We already said that!" said Chad. "After Rose, an' after the dragon, what'll you do tomorrow?"

I sat there for a moment, and then my voice grew more serious. "I'll start reading the She'Har writings that Lynaralla brought back. I need to learn as much as I can if I'm going to stop ANSIS and fix whatever the She'Har did to the world thousands of years ago."

Chad grinned. "I was hopin' you'd say that."

"You knew about the She'Har writing sculptures?" Now I was genuinely confused, since I was pretty sure I hadn't told anyone about them.

"No," said the ranger. "I don't have a damn clue what yer talkin' about. I just wanted to hear you say somethin' that sounded like ye have a purpose."

"Oh, well I guess I do," I agreed.

Then he added something under his breath. It was hard to make out, but I could hear bitterness in his voice. It sounded as though he said, "Otherwise ye'll wind up like me."

I didn't know much about Chad Grayson's checkered past, but pondering the mystery brought another question to my mind. "Hey. How long have you and Danae been—so close?"

Chad growled at me, "None o' yer damn business!"

Coming in the Summer of 2018:
The Severed Realm

Stay up to date with my release by signing up for my newsletter at:
http://www.magebornbooks.com/newsletter.html

Books by Michael G. Manning:
Mageborn:
The Blacksmith's Son
The Line of Illeniel
The Archmage Unbound
The God-Stone War
The Final Redemption

Embers of Illeniel (a prequel series):
The Mountains Rise
The Silent Tempest
Betrayer's Bane

Champions of the Dawning Dragons:
Thornbear
Centyr Dominance
Demonhome

The Riven Gates:
Mordecai
The Severed Realm (coming summer 2018)
More to be announced

Standalone Novels:
Thomas